Kasey Michael is a *New York Times* bestselling author of both historical and contemporary novels. She is also the winner of a number of prestigious awards.

LORDS OF
SCANDAL

BY
KASEY MICHAELS

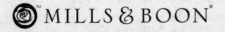

First published in Great Britain 2009
Harlequin Mills & Boon Limited,
Eton House, 18-24 Paradise Road, Richmond, Surrey TW9 1SR

LORDS OF NOTORIETY © Harlequin Books S.A. 2009

The publisher acknowledges the copyright holder of
the individual works as follows:

The Beleaguered Lord Bourne © Kathryn Seidick 1985
The Enterprising Lord Edward © Kathryn Seidick 1989

ISBN: 978 0 263 87408 2

37-0909

Harlequin Mills & Boon policy is to use papers that are natural, renewable
and recyclable products and made from wood grown in sustainable
forests. The logging and manufacturing processes conform to the legal
environmental regulations of the country of origin.

Printed and bound in Spain
by Litografia Rosés S.A., Barcelona

CONTENTS

THE BELEAGUERED
LORD BOURNE

For Joan Hohl, Rita Clay Estrada,
and remembrances of "Margarita"
...and they wonder why we write fiction...

PROLOGUE

SNAP!

The loud, discordant sound sent a flock of nesting birds, who had just moments before been chirping merrily in the branches overhead, soaring into the sky as one, calling anxiously to each other as they flapped their wings in agitation.

The girl, on the contrary, made no move to flee from the unmistakable sound of an animal trap's heavy metal jaws snapping shut, locking its unwary prey in a grip of iron. It wasn't that she hadn't felt the impulse to flee. Indeed, her heart was pounding nineteen to the dozen with fright and her muscles were quite painfully tense, silently screaming the message "Run!"

But while her spirit and flesh were willing, they could not travel anywhere as long as one decidedly heavy, extremely cumbersome animal trap had its jagged-toothed mouth stuffed full of last year's yellow sprigged muslin.

The power of speech, momentarily lost, returned just in time to give vent to the overwhelming anger that set the trapped female to trembling as the violence of that emotion rocketed through her system. "A trap in the Home Wood!" she announced incredulously to the air,

pointing out the obvious to the world at large. "Never—
never—has there been trap nor snare in the Home Wood.
Only a monster would choose to do murder to a two-
pound rabbit with a five-pound trap. It's like…it's
like…like hunting down field mice with field *cannon,*
that's what it is.'

Bending from the waist, she attempted to free her
skirts from the offending device, but to no avail. The
skirt of her gown now rent in several places (long, jagged
tears that would bring tears to the eyes of the most clever
needlewoman), she had no recourse left to her but to
drop to her knees and scrabble about in the damp under-
growth for the stake that held the trap in place.

It took a dozen mighty tugs and a good deal of digging in the soft black soil with her bare fingers to separate the metal stake at the end of the chain from its snug
home a full foot deep in the ground; a hot, sweaty business that strained her gown, dirtied her cheeks, and succeeded in enraging her to the point that the thought of
her rather bizarre appearance did not deter her for so
much as an instant as she set off hotfoot for Bourne
Manor, dragging the heavy trap, chain, and iron post
along behind her willy-nilly.

CHAPTER ONE

THE LARGE, MULTIPANED glass doors in the morning room provided a pleasant view of the rear prospect of Bourne Manor, and Lord Bourne, wineglass in hand, debated the merits of having his luncheon served on the flagstone terrace accessible through these same doors.

After only five days in his new home, Christopher Wilde, known to his intimates as Kit and now the Eighth Earl of Bourne, felt completely at ease in his new surroundings. Renfrew, the late earl's longtime majordomo, had already proved himself to be a pearl beyond price by anticipating his new master's every need, deftly guiding his lordship until he became familiar with the layout of the large manor, and presenting him with a deceptively offhand yet amazingly thorough accounting of just what responsibilities went hand in glove with his new title.

The household servants, their company numbering in Kit's estimation just slightly less than that of Wellington's largest division, all seemed to know just what they were about. The manor being a model of organization, they took pride in considering the care and comfort of their master to have priority over polishing, straightening, and the like. Unpleasant memories of broom-wielding housemaids invading his chamber while he was still abed and important papers misplaced by overzealous servants in pursuit of domestic order reinforced his high opinion of his late uncle's staff.

Leon, Kit's valet of six years' standing, had seconded his master's vote of approval, stating unequivocally that, save for the shabby state of the Home Wood—a problem already discussed, and with corrective steps having been initiated immediately as per his lordship's directive designating his trusted valet to be in full charge of the project—Bourne Manor was "as near to perfect as a body could expect to get without first croaking and sprouting wings like."

The peaceful scene spread before him now, with rich, golden sunlight lending an added brightness to the gently rolling carpet of soft greenery and the seemingly randomly placed neat groupings of several varieties of flowers, ornamental shrubs, and small trees, made it somewhat less than difficult for Kit to convince himself that he had indeed somehow stumbled into paradise.

Reluctantly Lord Bourne restrained the urge to congratulate himself yet again for having had the good fortune to recover from the wounds he sustained in battle, thereby living to enjoy this truly magnificent day (not to mention having displaced the memory of his very ordinary leave-taking of Dame England as a mere major by means of his returning to her bosom a full-fledged earl), and was about to summon Renfrew when a movement in the extreme distance caught his eye.

Stepping closer to the window, he leaned his head forward and peered intently at the vague yellow blot that was even then advancing up the slight incline with all the grace of a knick-kneed pachyderm afflicted with a bad case of annoying heat rash.

As the blot slowly gained ground, the masses of yellow separated themselves into a large expanse of some patterned material that obviously was a woman's morning gown (and sadly lacking in style, if he was any judge), and a smaller mass of wavy golden hair that surrounded the female's head like some misshapen halo and reached considerably below her shoulders, the desired effect possibly an illusion of informality that fell sadly short, appearing instead as merely unkempt.

But what's this? Kit asked himself, his attention caught by the curious sideways slant of the female's skirts and the occasional glimpse of what seemed to be a jumble of dark, heavy-looking objects attached to those same skirts. Fumbling with the latch on the glass door, Kit stepped out onto the terrace and cupped his hands around his eyes as he inspected this oddity in earnest. What he saw caused him to issue a short, pithy curse, bound down the broad stone stairs two at a time, and pelt headlong down the grassy slope only to skid to a halt before the advancing female.

"How in bloody blue blazes did you get yourself caught in an animal trap, woman? That thing could have taken your leg off. Good God, have you no common sense? Don't you even know enough to watch where you're putting your feet when walking in the woods?" Clearly Lord Bourne's questions and general tone of mingled anger and disgust could lead his listener into supposing the man believed himself to be addressing a hard-of-hearing idiot who should even now be down on her knees giving thanks to the gods on high for her lucky escape.

Just as clearly, the recipient of his lordship's recriminations believed she had somehow stepped out of the woods only to stumble headlong into Bedlam, where she was immediately accosted by one of the hospital's more violently disposed resident lunatics.

"I," she countered, once recovered from the shock of the man's uncalled-for attack, "am attached to this heinous instrument of torture and murder because some twisted, demented monster bent on destroying poor defenseless rabbits and furry little squirrels and other such *wild and dangerous beasties* has seen fit to set inhumane traps in the Home Wood. *That's* how I became caught in this contraption.

"As to my *leg,* as you have so crudely seen fit to bring that appendage into this discussion, it and its mate are cognizant of their narrow escape, which is most probably why they agreed to carry me to Bourne Manor in order that I might confront Lord Bourne with the consequences of his thoughtless act."

"*I* am Lord Bourne, madam," Kit interjected at this point, his bow a mere mockery as he relinquished neither his belligerent pose nor his menacing expression. "The traps were set in order to thin the vermin population in the Home Wood. A population that through lack of sensible containment threatens to outstrip its food supply, inflict extensive damage upon the wood itself, and cause the invasion of nearby cultivated fields where those same cute, furry innocents will proceed to steal seed and destroy growing crops. That the perimeters of the area were not posted is an oversight possibly explained by the fact that residents of Bourne Manor have been duly made aware of the traps, while trespassers can only be prepared to suffer the indignities of any uninvited guest."

"Why, you—" the young woman began hotly, then changed her tactics. "I have been accustomed to making free of the standing invitation issued me by the last

Lord Bourne to think of the Home Wood as my own, as it were, and was therefore not aware that my formerly peaceful retreat had overnight taken on the aspect of a forest teeming with snapping iron dragons. Indeed, all that is missing are the tongues of fire."

"Your apology is duly noted and accepted," Kit returned cordially, his initial anger abating at the sight of the blond, green-eyed vixen who dared debate him as an equal while mud dried into crusts on her cheeks and her gown was held captive by an "iron dragon."

The young woman's jaw dropped in astonishment. "Apology? What apology? I issued no apology! I'm here to insist you remove your traps at once. They're inhuman!"

"They're not intended for humans," Kit was forced to point out. "But I do believe Leon showed an excess of zeal in setting such formidable traps. I shall amend my order to eliminate metal traps and replace them with more humane devices that ensnare rather than chomp. The end result is the same, of course," he reminded her with a satisfied smirk. "Rabbits in the larder and the vermin population reduced to manageable proportions. It is moderation that I strive for, after all, not total annihilation."

"And my use of the Home Wood?" She hated to beg, but had to ask. "Am I to discontinue my visits?"

Kit looked down at the dirt-streaked face, appealing even through its grime as the green eyes rounded artlessly and the firm little chin, so proudly tilted while she attacked him, trembled involuntarily as she awaited his answer.

"I cannot find it in myself to deprive infants of their treats. But curtail your visits for a few days, please—just until Leon gathers up his little toys."

With nothing else left to say, the young woman made to depart the scene, but the clinging trap made the simple art of turning about a test of balance and dexterity. The sprigged muslin, already laboring under considerable stress, proved unequal to this additional insult and yet another long tear split the fabric, this time exposing a wide, knee-high expanse of white petticoat.

Tears born of frustration combined with a belated but none the less extreme sense of embarrassment made liquid pools of the girl's eyes as Lord Bourne stooped to tug at her gown in an effort to release it from the trap.

"I'll have to rip your gown even further, I'm afraid," he apologized, raising his head to smile at her consolingly. "Not," he mumbled as the abused fabric parted in two, leaving a goodly yard or more still in the possession of the half circle of grinning iron teeth, "that it's much of a loss anyway."

It is truly amazing how quickly a woman's tears can dry, leaving behind them a pair of eyes alight with a strange glitter more reminiscent of leaping flames than of sparkling water. "You owe me for this gown, Lord Bourne," she pronounced in a determined voice. "It was my very most favorite gown in the whole world!" she vowed passionately, her quest for retribution investing the lie with the ring of truth.

A healthy desire for his lunch combined with a sincere wish to be shed of his unpleasant trespasser prompted Lord Bourne to count out his astonishingly accurate estimate of the gown's cost into her outstretched palm.

And then the young woman smiled, a simple exercise of muscle that lifted the heretofore sullenly downturned corners of her mouth and reassembled the smudged contours of her face into a composition so wonderfully appealing to the eye that Kit had to blink twice before he could be assured the transformation was not due merely to a trick of the sun.

"What's your name, infant?" he heard himself ask in a soft voice, his gaze never leaving her face.

The smile wavered, slightly, then rebounded. "Jennie, my lord," she answered saucily, tilting her head and throwing him an impudent wink. "I live at the far end of the Home Wood with my father."

"No last name, Jennie?" his lordship pursued, all thought of his lunch forgotten in light of this unexpected pleasant development. The girl, he decided, might clean up to advantage, and a liaison with a comely, conveniently local wench could only serve to enhance his already comfortable existence.

She was the only child of her widowed schoolteacher father, Jennie informed him conversationally, and thus the recipient of that father's intensive tutoring—a little fillip she offered to explain her accent-free, educated speech. She had read extensively, although she had never traveled more than fifteen miles from her birthplace, and even though she led a solitary existence she was more than content with her lot in life.

As she let her voice ramble on, her words tumbling out rapidly, she ran her spread fingers through her disheveled blond curls and smoothed her damaged gown with unconsciously provocative strokes of her figure-sculpting hands.

Kit had been without a woman for nearly a month, a lengthy period of abstinence for one of his healthy appetites, and Jennie's attractions multiplied in direct proportion to the estimated total number of pleasures denied. As a gentle buzzing in his ears turned Jennie's droning voice to the sweet notes of a siren's song, Lord Bourne's better self offered no resistance when his baser self reached out and drew the girl's slight form into his strong embrace.

"Let me taste your honey, sweetings," he whispered, his eyes already shut tight as his mouth descended to claim Jennie's shock-slacked lips. Kit Wilde was ever the sort to strive for excellence in his many pursuits, and he was justly proud of his carefully learned and studiously applied expertise in the art of making love.

It was perhaps a shame that Jennie had no way of comparing Kit's technique with that of some lesser mortal's, but as a first kiss it set a standard that only a few foolhardy souls might ever presume to better.

The surprise that temporarily immobilized Jennie enabled Kit to gain a secure hold on her person, a hold that proved invulnerable to any amount of squirming and frantic wriggling on her part once surprise turned into indignation and then, as his plundering mouth touched off a series of intense miniature explosions throughout her body, into very real fear.

Oblivious to it all stood Lord Bourne, his legs slightly apart, one knee thrust boldly between her slender thighs, his hands roving freely through tangled curls and along the long curving sweep of her spine as he employed lips, teeth, and tongue to their best advantage.

Unconsciously holding her breath all the while, Jennie was slightly giddy, her vision hazy and dim around the edges by the time Kit remembered their exposed situation—placed as they were within clear view of dozens of manor windows—and put a reluctant period to an interlude that had proved intensely pleasurable, if somewhat unsettling.

For the first time Jennie looked at Kit, *really* looked at him, and she realized that the new Lord Bourne was an extremely handsome gentleman of no more than eight and twenty years, a man whose quietly elegant dress displayed to advantage his moderately tall, sleekly muscular body.

As for his face, how she could have overlooked for even an instant those intensely blue eyes or that healthy crop of thick, midnight-dark hair was beyond her comprehension. The lean, clean lines of his face were complemented by the almost too perfect chiseled square jaw that a wide, full-lipped mouth did little to soften. Taken in part, he was an impressive enough specimen; taken as a whole, the man was enough to give pause to the strongest heart.

How had she allowed her anger to blind her to the danger that exuded so visibly from every pore of Lord Bourne's body? Even worse, what nearsighted imp of insane arrogance had cozened her into believing she could dare to flirt with this obvious man of the world?

Acknowledgment of her own guilt in leading the earl to believe she was forward kept Jennie from either slapping Kit's face for his impertinence or dissolving into maidenly tears—as any well-brought-up young lady should have (any, that is, who had not yet taken refuge in a swoon).

In the short minute that had passed since the termination of their nearly one-sided embrace, neither of them spoke. They just stood there and stared at one another, each intent on their own chaotic thoughts.

Just as Kit was about to suggest renewing their acquaintance that night in some more secluded spot, visions of a cozy, candlelit supper followed by a mutually satisfying voyage of discovery upon the great barge of a bed in his private chamber, Jennie took him completely unawares by wheeling about, hiking up her tattered skirts, and racing pell-mell into the Home Wood.

"Wait!" Kit called, watching in amazement as her fleeing form was quickly enveloped by the dense growth and concealing shadows. "Jennie, you silly chit. Wait!"

No good would be served by pursuit, as the girl probably knew every tree and concealing rock and could elude him almost without effort. Besides, if he gave chase she might sacrifice prudence for speed, thus putting herself in danger of springing yet another of Leon's deadly traps.

Ah well, he decided, shrugging his wide shoulders, it wasn't as if she were about to disappear from his life forever. He had only to question the resourceful Renfrew as to the whereabouts of one blond-haired miss named Jennie and he would be halfway home. Once he located her, it shouldn't take more than a few soothing words (and perhaps a bauble or two) to coax the fair Jennie into his bed.

Secure in his estimation of both Jennie's character and the attractive lures his title and fortune must represent to someone of her modest circumstances, Kit returned to the manor, partook of a restorative luncheon, and then repaired to the library, where he penned his acceptance of one Sir Cedric Maitland's invitation to dine with him the following evening.

CHAPTER TWO

"MISS JANE, iffen ya don't stop squirmin' about like some pig caught in a gate I ain't never gonna get these tangles out, and Miss Bundy, that old cat, she'll have my head on a platter iffen you be late comin' down to table tonight. Just the thought of Miss Bundy tearin' inta me is more than I thinks I can bear."

As this whining complaint by her maid, Goldie, was reinforced by means of a restraining tug on one of those tangled locks of hair, a tug that brought tears of pain to her eyes, Miss Jane Maitland subsided obligingly onto her chair and allowed her hair to be twisted into a loose knot on the top of her head. "And woe be to anyone who doubts that the meek shall inherit the earth," Jane confided to her reflection in the mirror. "Forgive me, Goldie, my love," she said more loudly. "Far be it from me to be the cause of your catching the sharp edge of my dear companion's tongue."

"That's good," sighed Goldie, putting the last touches to her mistress's coiffure. "Seein' as how that woman's got a tongue would clip a hedge."

"Not to mention a pair of ears that can pick up the sound of your foolish jabbering at a hundred paces, more's the pity," pointed out Miss Ernestine Bundy herself, who had entered the large bedchamber unnoticed.

"Yoicks and away!" Jane chortled as Goldie hastily hiked up her skirts and propelled her ample girth toward the small door to the rear of the chamber, hell-bent on escaping the peal that Miss Bundy was otherwise bound to ring over her poor head.

"Daft woman," Miss Bundy commented, sailing into the room, her dignity in full sail. "Why any of us put up with that sad excuse for a maid, I find myself saying for what must be the thousandth time, is far beyond my limited comprehension. Really, Jane, sometimes I feel bound to point out to you that your grand gestures of charity do have the lamentable tendency of producing the most disappointing results."

"Now, Bundy," scolded Jane, rising from her seat in front of the mirror to smooth down the skirts of her robin's-egg-blue gown. "What Goldie lacks in talent she more than makes up for in heart." Twisting about to peer over her shoulder, just making sure her departing self would do credit to her arriving self, she went on idly, "Besides, the poor girl was such a sad failure in the dairy."

"And in the kitchens, and as a housemaid, and as a seamstress, and—"

"Enough, Bundy, else Papa's dinner guests will find themselves welcoming me rather than the other way round."

Ernestine Bundy, governess and now companion to Miss Maitland, had watched her charge grow from an entrancingly lovely child into an awkward, too thin adolescent until, over the course of the year following her eighteenth birthday, she had blossomed into the young woman who now descended the wide stairway ahead of her: an astonishingly beautiful creature of high intelligence, quick wit, a ready smile, and a charming way about her that could coax the very birds down out of the trees.

If she was just a teeny bit strong-willed, this was only to be expected in a doted-on only child, and surely her generous nature and propensity for seeing only the good in people would never harm her as long as her fiercely protective father and Miss Ernestine Bundy were around to cushion her from some of the more distasteful realities of life.

Openly preening over her no little involvement in the creation of the exquisite creature now politely awaiting her at the bottom of the stairway, Miss Bundy had no way of knowing that one of those "realities" was already lurking in the shadows (or, in this case, in the drawing room of Maitlands itself), ready to pounce.

LORD BOURNE had been at Maitlands only a few minutes—just long enough to be introduced to his host and dinner partner, be asked his preference as to liquid refreshment, have his antecedents inquired about, and his personal history vetted—all accomplished in the politest of ways and with a thoroughness a member of the Inquisition would envy.

Miss Abigail Latchwood, a spinster of some indeterminate years and, Kit assumed, a frequent visitor at Maitlands, was quite the noisiest person Kit had heretofore chanced to encounter, and he had encountered quite a few in his time. Obviously her presence tonight was Sir Cedric's way of assuring himself that news of his coup—being the first of his circle to host the new earl under his roof—would reach even the farthest corners of the neighborhood with all possible speed.

All in all, Kit found himself to be incredibly bored with the whole affair, and took rapid inventory of his brain, searching for a plausible excuse that would get him shed of Sir Cedric and his inquisitive guest imme-

diately after brandy and cigars. The benighted countryside around Bourne was a far cry from the frenetic activity of a Spanish battlefield, and the soldier in Kit was
not so easily mellowed that the boring duties of his new
title could yet be borne with any real grace.

If only the so-estimable Renfrew had been more
helpful in the matter of Jennie, the teacher's daughter—
that normally helpful man having disclaimed any
knowledge of either father or offspring residing in the
area. There were two Jessies in the village, and the
blacksmith had a niece named Jackie visiting this month
or more—although that damsel had hair as dark as pitch
and weighed half again as much as the smithy—but
nary hide nor hair could be found of any blond wench
named Jennie.

Ah well, thought the earl, smiling politely as Sir
Cedric described in great detail his latest triumph on the
hunting field, he'd be leaving for London within another week and Jennie's bucolic beauty would soon fade
from his memory, to be replaced by one or more of the
many comely opera dancers he intended to honor with
his favor.

Kit allowed a half smile to soften his features as he
swirled his drink and thought his private thoughts.
Boring dinner partners and a nonexistent social life
were a small price to pay for the opportunity to call
Bourne Manor his own. For a certainty it beat wallowing in the mud of Ciudad Rodrigo all to sticks—and the
rank of earl brought with it benefits no mere major
could dream to command.

While the aging Miss Latchwood preened delightedly, the proud Sir Cedric recounted his brilliant out-
maneuvering of some hapless fox, and Lord Bourne
smugly contemplated a season of wallowing in the

fleshpots of London, Miss Jane Maitland stood outside the drawing-room doors enduring her companion's last-minute adjustments to her charge's perfectly draped skirts.

"Papa will demand to know the reason for my tardiness, Bundy," Jane warned her companion, just now fussing over a loose thread daring to peek below the hem of the blue gown, "and demand an explanation for it. I shall be forced—for you know I would not be so mean as to implicate you voluntarily—to explain that my companion delayed my appearance by some fifteen minutes while she searched out nonexistent flaws in my toilette." Jane heaved her shoulders in a heavy sigh. "And then Papa will rant and bluster, and I will have recourse to tears, and you will be called for and roundly scolded for your impudence in thinking there existed even a single flaw on the person of his only daughter, and then you will be cast posthaste out into the snow—"

"It hasn't snowed in Bourne for three years," Miss Bundy was moved to point out, placing her hands on Jane's shoulders and pushing her in a circle as her shrewd eyes made one last appraisal. "You are to dine with the new Earl of Bourne, missy," she went on, heedless of Jane's sudden harsh intake of breath, "and I am under strict instructions that you are to look your very best for the gentleman. Your papa is aiming rather high, if you ask me, which *he* certainly did not, but I must admit Lord Bourne would have to look far and wide to find a countess as fair as you, my dear.' Giving one last unnecessary pat to Jane's coiffure, Miss Bundy stood back, surveyed her handiwork, and exclaimed, "There! No mere man could ask for more."

Jane wrinkled her nose in disgust. "Are you sure, Bundy? Perhaps my *price tag* is showing. Tell me, dearest Ernestine, is the marriage settlement to match my dowry, or will Papa throw in Mama's diamonds to sweeten the pot?" A slight flush lending even more lively animation to her features, Jane goaded further. "Dearest, sweetest Bundy. First you served as nanny, then governess, then companion. I had not realized your real calling was that of procuress."

Miss Bundy did not have an immediate spasm at her charge's audacity. Indeed, she did not so much as blink her pale gray eyes. All Miss Bundy, that long-suffering servant, did was to pinch Jane's cheeks to give them color, step back out of sight of the double doors to the drawing room, signal the snickering footman to step lively and announce his mistress to the company, and retire upstairs to the small brown bottle she kept concealed beneath her knitting. Life at Maitlands had long ago taught the woman the best way of dealing with either Sir Cedric or his audacious daughter was by prudent withdrawal. Jane would apologize, as she always did whenever her tongue ran away with her—not that the poor girl hadn't cause enough for anger, being paraded about for the new earl like a prize calf—and in the end Miss Bundy would allow her sensibilities to be mollified by the way of Jane's pretty pleas for forgiveness. It was a game they played, the two of them, with Jane tugging more and more at the leash of obedience every year as she grew from submissive girl to self-sufficient young woman.

Jane waited until Miss Bundy's receding back disappeared around the curve in the stairs and then, her softly rounded chin held high, she took a deep breath, sent up a quick prayer that Lord Bourne wasn't an; more of a fool than he could help, and allowed herself to ₂e announced.

The first person she saw when she entered the candle-lit chamber was Miss Latchwood. So, she thought wryly, Papa is leaving nothing to chance. If the poor earl so much as smiles in my direction that old biddy will have the entire countryside believing we have posted the banns. Nodding pleasantly to the older woman, who winked conspiratorially back at her, Jane turned her gaze in the direction of her father, just then posing at the mantelpiece under an obscure (for good reason) artist's rendering of one of Sir Cedric's epic exploits with the Mowbray men. "Good evening to you, Papa," she intoned sweetly, dropping the man a curtsy. "Please forgive my tardiness, but the time just seemed to run away with me."

Sir Cedric, seeing before him the reincarnation of his beloved deceased wife allowed himself to be charmed into forgiving Jane for keeping him from his dinner. Taking one of her small hands into one of his own huge paws, he turned her slightly so that he could introduce her to their guest of honor.

"Lord Bourne," the proud father began, "allow me to introduce my daughter—"

"You!" loudly exclaimed the earl, fairly goggling at the girl as the very air between them suddenly began to crackle.

"So much for prayers," Jane muttered disgustedly under her breath as she glared at the fashionably dressed young man with the gaping jaw.

Abigail Latchwood leaned forward in her chair, her powers of intuition telling her she had chanced to secure herself a front-row seat at what should prove to be a most interesting spectacle.

"I WOULD BE MORE THAN HAPPY to listen to your suggestions as to a solution to our problem, my lord, but I do not wish a dismal retelling of the problem itself. Do I make myself clear?"

"*You* do not wish! *I* do not wish, damn it, and since it is my feelings that concern me and I am forced to dismiss them I see no gentlemanly need to trifle over *your* paltry sensibilities."

Jane paused to mull Kit's words over a moment or two, and decided that she may have been looking at him in the wrong light entirely. Perhaps he was not the enemy. Perhaps she had been in the process of berating the only ally she had in the entire world—what with her father, Bundy, and even Goldie firmly listed among her adversaries in this matter.

"You are against this marriage plan of Papa's?" Jane asked the man now standing across from her in the herb garden, his ebony hair gleaming in the bright morning sunlight. He nodded his head in the affirmative. "Then why," she asked with a sudden return of heat, "didn't you stop Papa when he first proposed the idea last night? You don't strike me as a man who is usually at a loss for words."

Kit shook his head in astonished disbelief. "Please don't tell me you're that much of a clothhead. After your ridiculous hysterical outburst last night when we were introduced there was deuced little *I* could do to rescue the situation."

"My *outburst?*" Jane sniffed indelicately, correcting him. "I merely muttered a small involuntary verbalization prompted, my lord, by your inelegant *bellow!*"

Kit had the decency to admit to a slight lapse of his own, caused, undoubtedly, by his surprise at seeing his wild-haired Jennie parading about as the so-proper Miss Maitland. "But," he rallied quickly, "it was not I who then fell apart like soggy tissue paper in the rain and confessed to every tiny detail of our meeting at Bourne Manor—right down to that truly sickening, simpering recital of what in fact had amounted to nothing more than a simple stolen kiss. Miss Latchwood nearly swooned dead away."

"No she didn't. She wouldn't do anything so self-defeating—it might cause her to miss some juicy bit of gossip. Lord!" Jane shuddered at the memory. "I was hard-pressed not to offer her the loan of my handkerchief, she was drooling so copiously."

"So you instead offered her the notion that poor, innocent Miss Jane Maitland might just have been compromised by that nasty Lord Bourne," Kit sneered. *"Lord!"* he pressed, aping Jane's exclamation. "You may as well have gone traipsing over the countryside ringing a bell, calling: 'Kit Wilde kissed me in the Home Wood; Kit Wilde kissed me in—'"

"Don't!" Jane begged, clapping her hands over her ears. "Papa never told me the names of our guests, you see, and I didn't ask, as our dinner guests tend to be limited to Miss Latchwood, Squire Handley and his sister, or the vicar, and knowing beforehand just whom I shall be facing across the table does nothing to enliven my appetite. I only found out you were to be present a moment before I was announced. Under the circumstances I believe I did my best—"

Kit, plucked a stray thread off his sleeve as he interrupted wearily, "Your best? How very sad. Please, *Miss* Maitland, I beg you to refrain from bringing my attention to your shortcomings, as I am depressed enough as it is without—"

"When I am saying something, *Lord* Bourne," Jane cut in with some heat, "you will oblige me by restraining your lamentable tendency to interrupt!"

With his head still lowered, Kit raised his eyebrows and peered at his adversary. "Welcome back, my little tiger cat. I was wondering how long it would take for Jennie to loose her claws on me." Temper definitely became the chit, Kit mused to himself, admiring the flush on Jennie's cheeks and the way the slight breeze set the blond curls around her face to dancing as her agitated movements caused her casual topknot to come half undone.

Jane looked back at him in disgust. She had requested this meeting with him this morning in the hope that together they would be able to find a way out of the muddle they had bumbled into the night before, but it was obvious now that she might just as well have saved herself the bother of eluding Bundy and engaging in what that very proper lady would only construe as yet another "tryst."

"If you are quite done salving your wounded ego at my expense, I suggest we either put our heads together to find a way out of this ridiculous coil or else terminate our meeting so that you can return to Bourne Manor and barricade the doors against Papa's wrath."

If Sir Cedric's wrath were all that was to be faced, Kit would have been more than capable of dealing with it in short order. But no. Once Jennie (he refused to call her Jane) had been escorted to her room by the so-properly outraged Miss Bundy and Miss Latchwood had been sequestered in the morning room with a half decanter of her favorite cherry brandy, Sir Cedric had confessed to Lord Bourne that he suffered from a "disky heart," and any scandal surrounding his dear old child would as surely put him underground as would a bullet through the brain.

Kit was prompted to wonder aloud about how such a hearty-looking specimen—a man who rode to hounds with such vigor—could possibly be in ill health, a tactical error that sent Sir Cedric tottering posthaste to a nearby chair, a hand clutching at his ample bosom as he called weakly for his manservant. While Kit looked on, his face still showing his skepticism, Sir Cedric's solicitous valet administered a draught to the panting gentleman and, with the help of two sturdy footmen, had his employer hoisted aloft in his chair and carted off to his bed—a move that put quite an effective period to any hope of rational discussion.

Galloping home, sans one promised dinner, the earl had barked out orders for food and drink to an astonished Renfrew only to react in a most violent manner when the platter of succulent rabbit smothered in spring onions was placed before him, rudely tossing the rabbit, platter and all, smack against the nearest wall. Hours later, just before the quantity of port he had ingested lulled the young earl into heavy slumber, Renfrew heard his master proclaim sorrowfully: "Rabbits are the root of all that is evil in this world. If I were king there would not be one of the fuzzy-tailed monsters left on this whole bloody isle. Damned if there would."

Upon awakening the next morning Kit did not remember this particular profound statement, a punishing hangover being his only lingering souvenir of a truly forgettable evening; but Jennie's note served to bring his dilemma into sharp focus and he had rallied sufficiently to agree to the meeting now taking place in the Maitland herb garden. Not that their discussion had so far produced anything more tangible than a mutual agreement as to the total unsuitability of both parties for the roles of husband and wife.

And yet, his head still pounding as if a blacksmith had set up shop between his ears, and his ears ringing with Jennie's condemning accusations, Kit found himself coming to the reluctant conclusion that his carefree bachelor days could be numbered on the fingers of one hand. There was no retreat for a man of honor, no possible avenue of escape without bidding his good name a permanent adieu. Between them, the naively candid Jennie and her determined Papa had trussed him up all right and tight and delivered him neatly into the parson's mousetrap. All that remained now was to convince his "intended" of the futility of resisting the inevitable.

"Well?" Jennie demanded, breaking into Kit's thoughts. "Have you been struck dumb?"

"While I will admit to feeling slightly less than my usual intelligent self," Kit replied, a note of bitter self-mockery in his tone, "I am not about to oblige you by descending into imbecility, as even being forced to wed you, my dear Jennie, cannot make me forget I am a Wilde, and as such above any such cowardly dodge. Not that the idea is entirely without appeal, you understand."

"Then you are going to simply knuckle under, marry a woman you obviously detest—making the both of us totally miserable in the process—rather than make the least push at settling the matter another way?" Jennie's huge eyes were staring at him incredulously.

"What other way would you suggest?" Kit asked politely, taking Jennie's hand and placing it on his arm before guiding her in a leisurely stroll along the garden path.

Jennie's brow creased in concentration as she cudgeled her brain in a quest for some splendid burst of inspiration. Sadly, none was forthcoming, and upon reaching the gate at the bottom of the path, she admitted she hadn't a clue as to where to search for salvation.

"I'd be inclined to suggest prayer," Lord Bourne said, tongue in cheek, "but I doubt the Lord grants entreaties that have to do with transporting earls to the far side of the moon." Turning so that they faced each other fully before he uttered the fateful words, Kit then intoned solemnly, "Miss Maitland, I have admired you from the moment of our first meeting and can only hope that you have come to return my esteem at least in part. Please, Miss Maitland, do me the honor of making me the happiest man on earth by consenting to become my bride."

As a proposal of marriage it lacked nothing in composition, although condemned men must have sounded more cheerfully animated speaking their final words before mounting the scaffold. And if his mention of their first meeting was taken at face value, devoid of any intentional double meaning, Jennie supposed it was a much nicer proposal than she could have expected under the circumstances. It was not, however, the proposal she had dreamed of ever since reading her first Minerva Press romance.

If her heart beat faster, it was with the frantic flutterings of a trapped animal, and not the accelerated rhythm all romantic heroines experienced at the very sight of their beloved. If her breathing was swift and shallow, it was panic, not passion, that set her young breast to heaving rapidly up and down. And if her milky English complexion was very prettily set off by a sudden blush of dusky rose suffusing her cheeks, it should be remembered that agitation should not automatically be construed as excitement.

Jennie looked searchingly into Kit's blue eyes, searching in vain for some carefully concealed humorous glint that would assure her he had spoken in jest. She found none. He was serious, she concluded at last, deadly serious. Earls may not steal kisses from baronets' daughters, even if they thought they were merely indulging in a bit of a lark with some little nobody of no consequence. Violators, this unwritten law decreed, will forfeit either their honor or their freedom.

Lord Bourne had made his choice. He would marry her to satisfy the conventions. And to save her good name, she reminded herself nastily, she shouldn't forget that little favor—not that Bundy would ever let her.

"Well," she said at last, just when Kit was beginning to think she would turn him down flat and wildly wondering just why this particular notion should distress him as much as it did, "you aren't fat. There's that at least."

Kit smiled broadly, clasping her hands in his as something tightly coiled deep inside his chest obligingly relaxed. "I'm not bad either," he pointed out cheerfully, amused by her youthful bluntness.

Jennie returned his smile, shyly at first, and then expanding the smile into a wide grin. "Or ancient, full of prickles and complaints, and suffering with the gout."

"Or foul-smelling, or afflicted with warts, or widowed with six bawling brats for you to mother, or hard of hearing, or missing half my teeth."

"Or a dedicated gamester?"

"Not even on nodding acquaintance with the cent-per-centers, playing for sport but never too deep."

"Or overfond of spirits?"

"Moderation—moderation in all things—that's my motto!" he averred, conveniently dismissing his truly dedicated drinking of the night just past.

"Well then, a girl would be foolish beyond permission to turn her back on such an obvious catch as you, my lord, wouldn't she?" Jennie declared, her smile faltering a bit before shining as before.

At last she could see the humor lurking in Lord

Bourne's twinkling eyes. "Foolish indeed, Miss Maitland," he assured her, lightly squeezing her hands.

'Then…then I accept your kind proposal, sir, and I thank you." The fateful words spoken, Jennie allowed her smile to fade and dipped her head, no longer able to meet Kit's all-seeing gaze.

As she stood there, doing her utmost not to tremble and thus betray her nervousness, Kit slipped his crooked index finger beneath her chin and lifted her face toward his descending head. "A betrothal must be sealed with a kiss," he whispered solemnly before laying claim to Jennie's lips with the velvet warmth of his mouth.

Remembering their first kiss—the way he had captured her in his embrace and exercised his considerable aptitude in the fine art of seduction—Kit deliberately kept this kiss gentle, undemanding; a tentative exploration rather than an attempt at conquest, and Jennie responded by allowing her lips to soften, molding themselves to fit against his in a highly pleasing manner.

He did not wish to wed Jennie. He did not wish to be married at all until at least a half-dozen more years of bachelor-oriented indulgence and high living were behind him. He resented being pushed into matrimony at, figuratively at least, the point of a gun, and to a mere child just out of the nursery, no less.

Jennie Maitland was the exact opposite of the sort of female he had hoped to surround himself with in London. She was much too young, for one thing, besides being woefully inexperienced—possessing none of the brittle sophistication required to survive in the *haut ton*—and to top it all, he decided glumly, the outside world would consider him responsible for her well-being and behavior.

Kit had just completed two grueling years of volun-

teer duty in Spain, and he was sick to death of responsibility—responsibility for the men who fought and
died under him, and responsibility for the constant daily
decisions of command. His wound and his lengthy convalescence had sorely tried his patience, with only the
prospect of the gaiety promised in the coming London
Season serving to keep a rein on his impatience until he
was free to join his friends in an orgy of hell-raking and
carousing that would set the metropolis on its heels.

A wife could only be viewed as a serious impediment
to his plans. Husbands lacked the freedom of bachelors,
especially brand-new, supposedly honeymooning husbands. He would marry the chit and leave her at Bourne
Manor for the Season if he could, but his conscience
overrode him on that score. Besides, he felt sure, Sir
Cedric was not beneath another theatrical display of ill
health just to force his son-in-law's hand, and Kit didn't
think his constitution could bear another such performance. But going around London with a wife in train was
going to be like trying to run with an anchor—or should
he say "mantrap"—chained to his ankle, deuced difficult.

And yet…and yet, he thought as Jennie allowed him
to take her more fully into his arms, the child wasn't totally lacking in appeal. With proper tutoring, his tutoring, he could almost believe she'd eventually make a
more than tolerable bed partner.

Suddenly Kit's appetite for romance evaporated. Of
course Jennie was a kissable wench—that's how he had
come to be in this damnable coil in the first place! Too
much of this sort of thing and he'd not only be saddled
with an unwanted wife, but he'd find himself a papa into
the bargain.

Jennie looked up at him, puzzlement clouding her
eyes. What was wrong? Didn't he like kissing her? She

had enjoyed it quite a little bit herself, although she'd rather swallow nails than admit any such thing, but from the pained look on Kit's face he had found the entire experience distasteful. Well, she thought angrily, he had certainly taken his good sweet time making up his mind, seeing as how he had been kissing her for more than a full minute—she had counted to sixty-four, as a matter of fact, just to keep from doing something silly like throwing herself into his arms like some love-starved ninnyhammer.

"If everything is official now?" Jennie prompted, angry to hear a trace of huskiness in her voice.

"Hmm?" the earl murmured, still lost in his own depressing thoughts. "Yes, you insolent infant, everything is all right and tight," he assured her much like a parent shushing a bothersome child. "You may go inside now and wait for your luncheon and I will return at the dinner hour to speak with your father about the final arrangements—if he has recovered from his indisposition of last evening, which I am somehow convinced he has."

"Kit," Jennie called rather sharply, as Lord Bourne had already turned and begun walking toward his horse.

"What?" he questioned rudely, eager to be gone.

"You may not be fat or bald, your lordship," she trilled, spurred by a sudden need to strike back at the man who had so carelessly dismissed her, "but you neglected to mention that you possess all the charm and personality of a turnip."

Kit stood stock-still as Jennie flounced off with her head held high, obviously believing herself to have come off the victor in their little sparring match, before muttering as he stomped off toward his waiting mount: "Leading strings. I'll be the only husband in London who has a wife in leading strings. Impertinent infant!"

CHAPTER THREE

IT WAS A WET WEDDING. Goldie's never-ending stream of tears, accompanied by sighs, gulps, hiccups, and several ear-shattering recourses to her oversized red handkerchief were depressing enough without nature echoing the maid's sentiments by sending dull gray skies and a drenching downpour just as the bride was leaving for the church.

Nothing is quite so inelegant as a limp lace veil unless it is a wilted, water-spotted silk gown with a muddy hem, both of which Jennie wore as she trailed reluctantly down the short aisle with Sir Cedric hauling her toward the altar with unseemly haste.

The ceremony itself was mercifully brief, with Ernestine Bundy poker-faced as the maid of honor and Leon, Kit's valet, preening pompously in his role of groomsman.

With clumps of baby rose petals clinging damply to their bodies, the bride and groom made short work of climbing into the traveling coach that stood ready to embark on the day-long trip to London, with two other smaller, less elegant coaches holding their belongings and personal servants set to follow along behind.

After handing his bride into the coach, Kit ordered

his driver to head for Bourne Manor, deciding a change of clothes was necessary if their journey was to be accomplished in any degree of comfort.

Bride and groom allowed the short journey to pass in silence and parted from each other's company without regret to enter separate bedrooms and await the arrival of the servants bearing dry clothing.

A scant half hour later—the earl noting the new Lady Bourne's promptness with a pleasure he saw no need to convey to her—they were finally on their way, with Kit already bored with the confinement of the coach and wishing himself astride the spirited black stallion tied to the back of the coach and Jennie idly stroking a strange wooden carving she held lovingly in her gloved hands.

His own thoughts holding no real appeal, Kit reluctantly turned his attention to the girl perched so stiffly beside him, and his gaze alighted on the carving. "And do you plan to plummet me with that maltreated tree branch if my baser instincts surface and I attempt to ravish you here in this coach?"

Jennie gave the carving a considering look before turning her head to stare at her husband as if weighing her chances of success if she was forced to defend herself before slowly shaking her head and confessing, "I saw the carving as I passed by the main saloon and couldn't resist taking it with me as a remembrance of home."

"You consider Bourne Manor to be your home?" Kit questioned, raising his brows so that furrows formed on his smooth forehead.

Jennie shrugged her shoulders nonchalantly, replying, "The late earl encouraged me to think of Bourne Manor that way, and I was accustomed to being welcomed almost as a member of the family. He had no children, you know, and he was frightfully lonely when his wife died five years ago."

Noticing the way Jennie's tightly controlled features relaxed as she spoke of his uncle, Kit pressed on with his questions, not overly interested but conceding that a pleasant conversation was as good a time-passer as anything else he could think of at the moment. "But why that truly homely carving? You could have had your pick of the manor rather than settling for one of the scores of carvings—all looking very much like mis-shapen turtles with udders, by the way—that litter the place."

Jennie's shoulders straightened as she took exception to Kit's insulting remark. "I'll have you know that this carving—indeed, *all* the carvings—are very creditable renditions of Amy Belinda, your uncle's favorite model. He took great pride in his work, and I'll not sit idly by and let you malign his efforts."

"Amy Belinda?" Kit nudged.

"His pet cow," Jennie informed him matter-of-factly.

"Of course," her husband responded in a choked voice. "His pet cow." His face mirroring his astonish-ment, Kit prized the carving from Jennie's grasp and raised his quizzing glass to study Amy Belinda from various angles—none of which provided a clue as to which end depicted the cow's front end. "M'uncle carved this?" he puzzled. "Good God—he must have been lonely!"

"He was not!" Jennie protested angrily. "At least he wasn't once I introduced him to Will Plum. Poor man," she mused reflectively. "Will lost his wife about the same time as the earl, and as he was too old to work as a car-penter anymore he felt he had nothing left to live for.

"Well," she went on, heedless of her husband's incredulous expression, "any fool could see the two men needed each other, and once I put Will in the earl's way the two of them became the best of good friends. Will taught the earl woodcarving and your uncle thought it was just grand to capture his dearest Amy Belinda in all of her many moods."

"Cows have moods?" Kit interrupted, not that Jennie noticed.

"Their friendship lasted for five years, until old Will finally died, your uncle surviving him by only a month. Amy Belinda didn't last much longer, poor dear," she added thoughtfully, "but I imagine that was only to be expected."

"Definitely," the earl agreed, trying hard to contain his mirth. "I had no idea I had wed such a clever puss— matching such disparate persons as my uncle and the estimable Will Plum with such gratifying results. Is this a special talent of yours, or was old Will a fluke?"

Jennie knew Kit was teasing her, but she refused to allow it to rankle. She had always prided herself on her ability to settle people into niches she personally carved out for them, deriving satisfaction by aiding her fellow human beings.

Her maid, Goldie, was a prime example of the success of her humanitarian endeavors, and so she proceeded to inform the scoffing earl. "She was totally hopeless in the dairy, you understand, being mortally afraid of cows."

"Sad," Kit commented, clucking his tongue in commiseration.

"Poor Goldie. She felt herself to be an abject failure, and her mother, a widow and dependent on Goldie for her support, came to me and begged me to take her daughter in hand."

42   THE BELEAGUERED LORD BOURNE

"Naturally you agreed," Kit interjected cheerfully.

"But of course—how could anyone so petitioned do anything else?" Jennie countered emphatically. "We tried Goldie in the laundry, but the soap made her sneeze, and even I could find little to praise in her needlework. She was so dejected we could scarcely catch a glimpse of her grandest possession, for she smiled so seldom. She has a truly magnificent gold tooth smack in the front of her mouth, you know, which is why we call her Goldie even though her name is Bertha."

"This is a most affecting story. I can only wonder if I am strong enough to hear the rest," lamented the grinning earl, earning himself a killing glance from his new bride.

"I'll disregard your sarcastic attempt at humor, if only to prove my point," she told him crushingly.

"Oh? There's a point?" Kit exclaimed in disbelief. "How gratifying."

"Of course there is. The point is that there is a place for everyone if one but takes the time to seek it out. In Goldie's case the search was a bit longer than usual, as she soon proved incapable of serving at table without overturning the soup tureen or losing her grip on a stack of dirty plates. But I really had hopes for her as a kitchen assistant—you know, peeling vegetables and chopping things and such—until Papa's silly French chef threatened to hand in his notice if Goldie wasn't permanently removed from his sight."

"Got on the bad side of the fellow, I assume?" Kit opined, and Jennie vigorously nodded her agreement.

"I still don't see what all the fuss was about," she ended, her expression one of sublime innocence. "After all, it wasn't as if his mustache wouldn't grow back eventually. He removed the rest of it after Goldie's little accident with the knife, you see, which was just as well considering he looked rather lopsided with half of the droopy thing gone."

That did it. Kit was unable to contain his mirth any longer, and his full, masculine laugh reverberated inside the closed coach as he gave voice to his amusement.

Within seconds Jennie's delicious-sounding giggles blended with her husband's throaty chuckles as the two leaned against each other for support as they enjoyed the joke—causing the coachman to remark later to the postilion that Lord and Lady Bourne seemed to be taking to each other right quick-like, which was a good thing considering they was bracketed like it or nay.

After a quick stop for luncheon Jennie allowed herself to be talked into resting her head on her husband's broad shoulder, and the rest of the journey passed with Lord Bourne alternately gazing dolefully at the scenery passing by outside his window and doing his best to ignore the soft, warm bundle nestled so trustingly against his chest.

JENNIE FELT she had somehow been transported to another world. It wasn't as if her father's house had not been comfortable, and she had run tame at Bourne Manor for as long as she could remember, but nothing in her experience had prepared her for the opulence of the Bourne mansion—no stretch of the imagination could convince her that this massive structure was any ordinary townhouse.

Bourne Manor had been furnished with an eye for comfort rather than elegance, but the many-storied dwelling in Berkeley Square was crammed cellars to attics with furniture and accessories that intimidated her with their grandeur.

Even the walls and ceilings, festooned as they were

with intricate stucco designs and painted Cipriani nymphs, seemed to mock her as she roamed aimlessly from room to room, feeling smaller, less significant, and increasingly more insecure as she encountered Sheraton sideboards, Darly ceilings, Shearer harlequin tables, Zucchi pilasters, arches, and panels, Thomas Johnson clocks, Chippendale parlor chairs, and even an Inigo Jones chimneypiece that had been carted there from heaven only knew where.

"Love a duck, miss, ain't it grand?" Goldie gushed for the hundredth time, her eyes nearly popping out of her head as she followed in her mistress's wake, nearly cannoning into Jennie before she realized the girl had stopped dead at the entrance to the master bedchamber.

"Th-there's no need to go poking about in here," the new Countess of Bourne stammered nervously before beating a hasty retreat back down the wide hallway to her own chamber, closing the door behind her, and leaning against it as if to block out the rest of the world.

"Is that any way for a countess to enter a room, racing and romping and slamming doors behind her?" Miss Bundy, never raising her eyes from the trunk she was in the midst of unpacking, asked in her best stern-governess voice. "And what is that infernal banging?"

Jennie opened the door an inch, saw Goldie's hand raised for yet another assault on the heavy door, grabbed the maid's arm, and hastily pulled the plump form inside. "Land sakes, missy, what didya see in there ta set ya off like a cat in a fit?" the maid asked, darting a quick glance out the crack in the door as if to catch a glimpse of some horrifying creature barging down the hallway.

"I didn't see anything, Goldie," Jennie responded a lot more coolly than she thought possible. "I just suddenly remembered that we left poor Bundy alone all morning to unpack while we gadded about the place gawking like country bumpkins, that's all."

As Goldie had been more than aware that Miss Bundy had spent the morning toiling while she, in a very un-maid-like way, had done nothing more strenuous than inspect her mistress's new digs, and as Goldie had secretly delighted in this unaccustomed freedom, her only answer to this damning statement was to flash her gold tooth at Jennie and wink broadly before picking up a paisley shawl and making a great business out of folding it over her arm.

Thank goodness, thought Jennie, releasing her pent-up breath in a long sigh. They're both too busy either working or avoiding work to tax me further. I'll just have to learn to control myself better and not do anything else to arouse their suspicions. Why, if Goldie knew I'd been frightened by a mere *bed* she'd tease me to death, while Bundy would see it as ample reason for yet another blistering lecture on the punishment of "Evil"—the evil in this case having more than a little bit to do with "giving false witness" only to "reap what you have sown." Hummph! Jennie thought with a toss of her blond curls. I need another lecture like that like I need another freckle on the tip of my nose!

Snatching up a book from a nearby table, Jennie made her way past opened trunks and pieces of her personal belongings Bundy had divided into various towering piles, the purpose of which only she knew or cared to know, and took up residence in the deep, robin's-egg-blue velvet-padded windowseat that overlooked the square and the statue that depicted a much younger, trimmer Prinny on horseback—the royal frame all rigged out like some long-dead Roman emperor for reasons only Princess Amelia, who had commissioned the piece, knew.

The book spread open on her lap (she never did take notice of its title), Jennie let her thoughts drift to the preceding evening and what she knew had been the markedly less than regal London debut of the new Countess of Bourne—considering she had slept through the entire business.

The strain of the wedding had somehow temporarily overcome her wariness of the man she was henceforth to love and cherish and—she gritted her teeth as she had done when the minister bade her repeat the word—*obey*, and against her better judgment she had allowed herself to fall asleep against his shoulder, thereby missing her very first sight of London by night.

It was only when the sound of hushed but obviously angry voices intruded on her slumber that she had roused sufficiently to realize that she was no longer in the coach, but reclining, cloak and all, upon an extremely comfortable bed.

"It's indecent, that's what it is," hissed the first voice, which Jennie had readily recognized as Bundy's.

"God's teeth, woman, I was merely loosening the ties of her cloak, not taking the first step in any serious pursuit of debauchery," a second masculine voice had hissed back angrily.

"Kit!" Jennie remembered she had screamed—fortunately only in her sleep-befuddled mind and not aloud. Squeezing her eyes shut, she had tried to feign sleep once more, hoping they would all just go away and leave her alone, but the earl was too sharp not to notice the sudden tenseness in the lower limb he had just then been in the process of divesting of its footgear.

"Ah ha!" he had crowed, more than a hint of triumph

in his voice. "Methinks yon beauty awakes! Dash it all, foiled again. Just when I was about to have my evil way with the innocent, not to mention *unconscious,* damsel." This last was said with heavy sarcasm, which, as Jennie could have told him, sailed completely over the head of the hovering Ernestine Bundy.

That overwrought female, torn between her duty to her charge and a strong inclination to indulge herself in a bout of strong hysterics, had then somehow steeled herself to throw her body between Jennie's and that of her would-be ravisher and declared in a quavering voice, "Over my lifeless, bleeding body, *sirrah!*"

Even now Jennie's shoulders shook slightly as she remembered Kit's immediate descent into the ridiculous—clasping his hands to his chest and fervently denying any intention to harm so much as a single hair of the lady's gray head while backing toward the door mouthing absurd apologies that had Jennie stuffing her knuckles into her mouth so that she would not laugh out loud.

"I saved you for now, young lady," Bundy had told her charge as she helped her undress before throwing a nightgown in her general direction and stomping heatedly out of the room. "But I shan't always be here to protect you. Remember," was her parting shot, "you have made your bed, my dear—and now you must lie upon it!"

And lie upon it Jennie had done; long into the dark of the early-morning hours, tossing and turning but never finding her rest until a thin, watery sun rose above the horizon.

By the time Goldie had roused her with her morning chocolate, Jennie felt like the proverbial last bloom of summer—faded, more than a tad wilted, and increasingly unable to put on a brave face for yet another chilly day.

But being young, and therefore fairly resilient, by noon Jennie had been sufficiently restored in spirits for her to drag the willing Goldie on the tour that had ended abruptly at the sight of the massive bed in what she knew was the chamber she would soon be expected to occupy with her husband.

I can't do it! she shrieked silently, her small hands clenching into fists and thoroughly wrinkling the green sprigged muslin skirts now clutched between her fingers. Kit said I had to marry him. Papa said it was my duty. But I and I alone will say whether or not I have to share his bed. And I say *no!*

"Jane. *Jane!*" Miss Bundy repeated more loudly. "Woolgathering again, I suppose. Some habits never change. Why, I remember when you were seven and I found you daydreaming in that tree in the garden. I had to call you a dozen times before—"

"Before you startled me out of a very pleasant daydream, as I recall, and I toppled to the ground and broke my arm," Jennie ended for the lady. "Papa wasn't best pleased, you'll remember."

Miss Bundy merely sniffed, obviously still feeling she had been more victim than sinner in that particular incident.

"Well?" Jennie asked after some moments when Miss Bundy seemed to be lost in replaying old hurts.

"Well, what?"

"You called my name, Bundy, remember?" Jennie sighed, a small smile lighting her face as the familiarity of this little scene made her feel less an alien in an unfriendly land.

Miss Bundy puzzled a moment, tapping one long finger against her pointed chin, before declaring brightly, "I remember now. How very remiss of me.

Renfrew gave me a note earlier for you—which I opened, of course—"

"Of course," Jennie sighed fatalistically.

"Don't interrupt, Jane. All my many hours of instruction on deportment and still you—but never mind. The note says that the earl desires the pleasure of your company in the main saloon—that's the huge room just off the foyer, the one that houses the Jones chimneypiece, my dear—at half past three of the clock today. My goodness, it's that now! You'd best hurry, dear, but do let Goldie straighten your hair first."

"There's no time for that, Bundy. I'm late as it is," Jennie said in reply, already moving toward the door. Now that she had made up her mind about the direction she wished this marriage to take, she was all at once bursting with the necessity to share her decision with Lord Bourne—whom she graciously acknowledged to possibly have some slight interest in the business.

THE EARL OF BOURNE was pacing the main saloon, glass in hand, looking about him with what he hoped was bored disinterest. *This place is a far cry from your bachelor digs in the Albany off Piccadilly, even if Byron, Macaulay, and Gladstone shared the same address, Kit, my lad,* he mused, positioning himself with one arm propped negligently (he hoped) upon the mantelpiece.

If only he could get over the disquieting feeling that at any moment some long-lost Wilde with a better claim to the title would come bursting through the door and roust him outside and back into the real world.

Kit had never dreamed he would one day inherit his uncle's title, lands, and great wealth. In fact, the most he had hoped for—when he dared to hope at all—was for the old boy to leave him a broken pocket watch or some such useless trinket.

But fate works in strange ways; in this case by eliminating all close heirs by way of accident or unfortunate illness. And while Kit had been striving to make a name for himself as a soldier, his male relatives had all been conveniently dropping like flies in order to pave his way to the earldom.

And fate hadn't stopped at the earldom either. Dame Fate, not one to indulge any mere mortal to the point where he might tend to get cocky, had then leavened Kit's triumph a bit by saddling him with a totally unnecessary gift—a wife.

He abandoned his studied pose—his lordship reclining at his ease—to check the watch at his waist. His *late* wife, he pointed out to himself, just as there came a noise at the doorway and Jennie entered with more haste than decorum, skidding to an ignominious halt about three feet inside the double doors.

"I…um…I mean, *Bundy*…er…that is…you wanted to see…um, talk to me?" Now that's an auspicious beginning, Jennie berated herself mentally, her outward grimace bringing a pained smile to the earl's face.

Yes, infant, Kit replied silently, I do want to see you—waving goodbye as you ride out of my life. But he did not say the words. Jennie was his wife now, for good or ill, and they were just going to have to make the best of the cards Dame Fortune had so capriciously dealt them.

"Sit down, Jennie," Kit said gently, then waited impatiently as she took up her seat on a straight-backed chair positioned at the far side of the room. "Would you like me to ring Renfrew for some tea? No? Then I suggest we get right down to it."

Jennie jumped slightly—just as if he had suggested they lie down on the Aubusson carpet and proceed to make mad, passionate love—and Kit hastened to explain the reason for his summons. "We must organize this household, Jennie, as Renfrew and the skeleton staff my late uncle kept here are not sufficient to our needs if we mean to entertain during the Season."

"We mean to entertain?" Jennie asked, trying to imagine herself in the role of hostess of this great mansion and failing dismally.

"We do. Unless that presents a problem?" Bourne inquired, deliberately needling her.

"Of course it doesn't," Jennie assured him through clenched teeth, wanting nothing more than to box his lordship's ears. "I'll set about hiring extra staff as soon as possible."

"Renfrew will arrange things with a reputable agency, and you will only have to select from a group of eligible applicants." Kit saw no possible way Jennie could land in the briers with the resourceful Renfrew to guide her.

"Oh," Jennie murmured confusedly. "I had thought to place an advertisement about, as we do at home sometimes if the need arises."

Kit quickly explained the folly of ever advertising for domestic help—heaven only knowing what sort of riffraff might then show up in Berkeley Square looking for a handout. At Jennie's nod he promptly considered the matter to have been satisfactorily settled and went on to discuss a more delicate topic—one he had been secretly dreading to broach.

"Jennie," he said gently, dropping to one knee beside her chair, "after giving the matter a good deal of thought, and with due consideration of your sensibilities and the uniqueness of our situation, I have decided not to ask for my husbandly rights just yet. I believe we should first become more comfortable with each other."

"Oh, *good!*" Jennie exclaimed happily, before she could temper her response. "That is, I mean, *why? …* No! Don't answer that. I don't mean *why,* exactly. Disregard that if you will, please. What I mean to say is—thank you." As Kit's eyebrows shot up, she stumbled on hastily, "No! I didn't mean that either, did I? I'm sorry I interrupted you, my lord," she said, belatedly striving to behave like something more than completely brainless. "Please, continue. You were saying—"

"Actually, pet, I was done *saying,*" he told her, stifling his amusement at her obvious agitation. But this amusement changed rapidly to confusion as Jennie's eyes took on a hard glint and her chin lifted in determination. "Now what?" he was then foolish enough to inquire.

Jennie, who should have been feeling nothing less than tremendous relief, had suddenly decided that the man in front of her was nothing less than the greatest beast in nature. How dare he decide not to exercise his rights? How dare he tell her anything? It was *she* who would do the telling!

As Kit watched, Jennie's face did its little chameleon trick yet again and became soft and almost pleading in its woebegone expression. "Then you do not want me, my lord? I do not appeal to you—perhaps even repel you?"

Looking up at her, his heart touched by her wide, sad eyes, Kit protested passionately, "Of course I want you, infant. You appeal to me immensely. Isn't that how we found ourselves in this situation in the first place?"

Now Jennie smiled in earnest. Rising to look down on her still-kneeling husband, she informed him brightly, "That is a great pity, my lord husband. For I do not want you, which is why I was so glad you requested this meeting. I was looking forward to telling you that you may have taken my hand in marriage, but that is all you will take from me." So saying, and with her gape-mouthed husband looking on, she swept out of the room, at last looking every inch the countess.

CHAPTER FOUR

KIT ENTERED the dim main room of the Guards Club and cast his eyes about in the gloom with the alert, roving gaze of a man who has served on the Peninsula. He quickly spotted and nodded to several acquaintances, but it was not until his scrutiny was rewarded with the sight of one fellow in particular that he smiled and started across the uneven sanded floor of the converted coffeehouse.

"Ozzy, you old dog," he called out loudly as he advanced on a painfully stylish young man of fashion sprawling at his ease at a table in the corner. "I knew I could count on you to be here."

Ozzy Norwood, who had just then been profoundly contemplating a fly walking backward up the table leg and wondering that such powers would be given to a mere insect and yet denied one such as himself, was so startled at this violent intrusion upon his thoughts that his legs—which had been propped on a facing chair—slid from under him and his rump took up a closer association with the hard floor.

His mood, as he had over the years become accustomed to his own clumsiness, was not darkened by his ignominious position, and he swiftly if not gracefully regained his feet in time to be caught up in Kit's enthusiastic bear hug of a greeting.

"Kit! Kit by damn Wilde! I'd heard you cashed it in at Badajoz," Ozzy exclaimed when he could get his breath. "You're no ghost, though. My bruised ribs can attest to that, by God! Let me loose, you great hairy beast, and let me look at you. What a sight you are, man."

What Ozzy saw was his old friend and fellow officer: a little leaner, perhaps; a little tougher, most definitely; but those smiling eyes were still those of the Kit Wilde Ozzy had hero-worshiped since they were both in short coats. "You look wonderful, friend, and I mean it truly. Sit down. Where did you spring from? Last I heard you were wounded and not expected to make it. I took a ball in the shoulder in a damn silly skirmish in some benighted Spanish slum village soon after Badajoz and sold out—my heart just wasn't in it, what with you gone and all—but I couldn't get word of you anywhere. It was as if you fell off the face of the earth. Girl! Bring us a bottle of your finest! Sit *down,* I said, Kit, and stop standing there grinning like a bear. Have you nothing at all to say for yourself?"

Kit could only laugh and shake his head. "I find it gratifying in the extreme, Ozzy, that some things never change. You're still chattering nineteen to the dozen, and woe betide anyone who dares to attempt to slide a word in edgewise." Seating himself across the table from his friend, he took up the bottle the servant wench had brought and drank from it, saying, "Best order another for yourself, old man, as I've got plans for this one."

"Girl!" Ozzy bellowed, thinking Kit was out to make a night of it and more than willing to match him drink for drink. "Bring a bottle. Bring a dozen bottles! Eh?

Oh, yes, Kit, of course. And two glasses, you silly chit; what kind of heathens do you think you've got here?"

Three hours and more than a half-dozen bottles later, Kit and Ozzy were still sitting at the table, their reminiscences of the Peninsula having brought tears as well as smiles as their thoughts passed over events past and friends lost, and they were at last ready to speak about the present.

"Earl of Bourne, is it?" Ozzy repeated, clearly pleased for his old friend. "Well, if that don't beat the Dutch. And there you were hobnobbing around the muck of Spain like the rest of us, just as if you was ordinary folk. Why ain't you rubbing shoulders with the rest of the nobs at White's or Boodle's, instead of this lowlife at the bottom of St. James's?"

"Oh, cut line, Ozzy. You belong to both those clubs, and Almack's to boot, as I remember your tales of that woeful excuse for a select gathering spot for the *haut ton* and the ugly ducklings your mama forced you to bear-lead around the floor."

"Snicker all you wish, you cynic," Ozzy shot back, thinking to trump Kit's ace, "but you'll soon be hounding me to get you a voucher—need one, you know, if you're on the hangout for a wife. Stands to reason you'll be wanting to settle down now that you're a blinkin' earl."

Kit drank deep from his glass. "I'll take you up on that offer of securing a voucher, but I have to tell you, friend, I have been nothing if not thorough since last we met. Within a week of hitting these shores—having happily put those months of convalescence in Portugal behind me—I acquired a title, a large estate, a, I must say, considerable fortune, *and* a wife."

Ozzy sat up straight in his chair, knocking his half-full glass over into his lap in the process. "Ain't you the downy one! How could you get yourself tied up so fast? It's not like you was hanging out for a wife so soon— no rich young bachelor would be so dense as to forgo the joy of wading through the debutantes for at least one Season on the town. Tell you what, you were in your cups—or suffering from some lingering fever caused by your wound. I'm right, aren't I? Say I'm right, Kit, and then tell me her name. Is she pretty?"

"Put a muzzle on it, Ozzy," Kit implored, his head beginning to reflect the combined assault of drink and his friend's garrulous tongue. "Her name is Jane Maitland, and her father's land runs alongside my estate."

"Greedy bugger, ain't you?" slipped in Mr. Norwood, earning himself a hard stare from the earl, who had hoped to find more sympathy from his oldest and best friend.

"That's an insult, Ozzy, damned if it ain't," the new earl declared, slurring his words only slightly. "Damned if I won't cut you dead when next we meet. Besides, Jennie's a charming enough nitwit; I might have pursued her anyway, without her father threatening revenge if I didn't do right by her."

"You did *wrong* by her? And who's Jennie? Thought you said her name was Jane." Clearly Ozzy was perplexed. "You know, Kit, sometimes you don't make a whole lot of sense."

"I've been known to have that reputation," Kit said ruefully. "Ozzy," he continued, leaning forward across the table confidingly, "I need your word of honor that this goes no further."

"Word of a gentleman!" Ozzy swore, then hiccupped. "I'll be quiet as a tomb, I swear it." He leaned forward to put his nose smack against Kit's. "Spill your guts, my friend, Ozzy's here."

And so, as the dusk gave way to darkness, and before drunkenness turned to near insensibility, Kit told his tale to his awestruck audience.

When the story was done and Ozzy had commiserated with his friend's ill luck, the question was raised: "And what are you going to do about the chit? Can't wish her gone, can't do her in, not without the father kicking up a fuss."

"Do with her?" Kit repeated, concentrating on the mighty task of directing his hand in the general direction of the bottle before him. "I don't see that I have to do anything with her. After all, Ozzy, how much trouble can one small female be?"

FOR THE NEXT WEEK, Kit was conspicuous in Berkeley Square only by his absence—a fact Jennie duly took note of, sent up fervent thanks for, and secretly credited to her masterful handling of that single interview the day following their hasty marriage. Sure that her parting shot had put her firmly in the position of power—with the tenor and direction of their marriage to be dictated solely by her—she felt she had left the earl with no option but to cool his heels while she became "more comfortable" with their delicate situation.

And she had been immensely "comfortable" in his absence, as Kit had seemed to abandon even his half-hearted suggestion that they get to know one another better. If the truth be told, there were times Jennie almost forgot she was married at all, pretending instead that she was in town for the come-out her father had promised, then conveniently forgotten to deliver. If only Renfrew would refrain from calling her "my lady" every time she so much as passed in the hallway. And if Bundy would only cease her endless sermons on the behavior befitting a countess (and the folly of thinking one could play with fire without being burned—as if Jennie's inadvertent compromise was the act of a misbehaving child with Kit cast in the role of a highly combustible match). And if only Goldie would stop dropping into a comical knee-cracking curtsy each time Jennie looked her way—which had driven Jennie to walking about with her eyes averted in some other direction, leading to more than a few stubbed toes and bruised shins.

But her companions as well as the facts were against her. Only Kit, by his absence, gave her any respite, and at times she could almost find it in her heart to be in charity with the man. Almost, but not quite. After all, if not for his, as Bundy called them, "male urges," she'd still be at home, dreaming safe dreams about the handsome knight on a white charger who would rescue her from the fire-breathing dragon and carry her off to his castle, where they would live happily ever after.

But even though he was seldom seen, the earl's presence in Berkeley Square could not be denied. Every day after rising at the heathen hour of eleven, Kit breakfasted in his rooms, allowed himself to be dressed by Leon, who was still determined to turn a perfectly presentable Corinthian into a dashing darling of fashion, and exited the mansion, his departing form variously disappearing around the corner of the square on foot, vaulting into the seat of his new curricle and giving his horses the office to start, or bending himself into the smart town carriage that then bore him off in the regal style befitting his station—always with Jennie discreetly watching his leave-takings from behind her curtained window, happily waving him on his way. Where he went did not concern her. She was only grateful to have him gone.

Renfrew, on the other hand, had a pretty good idea of just what his lordship's travels encompassed. Struts down Bond Street on the arms of his cronies, tours through an assortment of low taverns, forays into the world of ivory turners and cardsharps at seamy private gaming hells, hours spent in the blue room at Covent Garden negotiating an opera dancer's current asking price for her oft-solid virtue, and an innocent prank or two aimed at livening the watch's dull existence would all number among the earl's activities, unless things had changed mightily since Renfrew was last in London town.

Natural high spirits and the thrill of being reunited with his boyhood friends might have explained this earnest pursuit of pleasure that nightly had Kit beating the rising sun home by less than an hour, but Renfrew knew there was another, deeper reason.

It was the dream. The dream that sent Renfrew scurrying from his warm bed on the first night of the new earl's residence at Bourne Manor, the wicked, panic-filled dreams that tore ragged moans and hoarse screams from the sleeping man's throat until Leon's soothing voice could penetrate the panic and lull the tormented earl back to sleep.

Leon either did not know or would not divulge the nature of the recurring nightmare that had the earl calling the name Denny over and over again, the memory whose nocturnal reenactment moved the man to dry sobs and broken pleas for help.

The dream seemed to have disappeared, the last nightmare occurring the night before the earl's marriage, but Renfrew knew it wasn't so. The earl was fighting the nightmare in the only way he knew—by not falling into bed until he was either too exhausted or too deep in his cups to dream at all.

The old butler, who had served the Wilde family man and boy, could only stand back and let his master battle with his private demons, knowing the outcome but not daring to overstep his place by telling his lordship he was fighting a losing battle.

Renfrew could only watch and hope, believing the gentle child he had watched grow into the giving, compassionate young woman the earl had married was the only key to the man's salvation. Yet Jennie and Kit might as well have been residing on separate continents for all they saw of each other. It was enough to make a stronger man than Renfrew despair. But not Renfrew—he only bided his time while making plans of his own.

As part of his project designed to invest Jennie with some passionate feelings for this particular Bourne domicile and her position as mistress of all it contained, Renfrew spent three full days acquainting her with every stick of furniture in every room of the mansion, impressing her with the history of this original painting and that priceless set of engraved silver plate.

His efforts were not in vain. Jennie was not impressed by the wealth spread out before her, but rather with the stories of the Bourne ancestors who had furnished the mansion with such care and love. That the responsibility for maintaining the beauty around her as well as placing this generation's personal stamp on the place by way of worthy additions of art and other accessories that would reflect their times while not detracting from what had gone before was now hers was not lost on Jennie. It surprised her, though, to realize that she was more than eager to take up the challenge.

The more mundane side of running a household, neatly catalogued in a half-dozen closely written ledgers, did not inspire the same creative urges. In fact, after pretending a studious perusal of just two of the big black leather-bound books, Jennie pleaded a headache and Renfrew kindly moved the dratted things out of her sight.

"Renfrew," Jennie proposed, once the butler had poured her a bracing cup of tea, "I'd like to strike a bargain with you. If you will consent to managing the household accounts, acting as secretary or whatever, I shall, besides offering you my eternal gratitude, undertake the hiring of the additional staff his lordship tells me we require."

Happy to see her showing such an interest, such a willingness to involve herself, no matter how indirectly, with his lordship's comfort, Renfrew agreed with alacrity. After all, he told himself airily, what could go wrong in the mere hiring of household staff?

And with that thought Renfrew proved yet again that, be he earl or butler, a male is still a male—never failing to underestimate the tremendous potential for disruption that churns just beneath the surface of those apparently fragile feminine forms men so condescendingly refer to as the weaker sex.

THERE WAS A GREAT DEAL of perverse satisfaction to be derived from flouting your husband's wishes, Jennie learned as she and Goldie climbed back into the town carriage after concluding her business with the clerk in charge of placing advertisements in the *Observer.*

She was pleased with the wording of her advertisement—certainly the clerk had seen no reason to change so much as the placement of a single comma—and she rode home secure in the belief that this more personal form of advertising would result in bringing to her door a fair number of robust, hardworking country folk who were new to London and eager for honest work they could not find due to lack of references.

That's what she wanted. Country folk. Plump, red-cheeked farm girls and strong, raw-boned farmers' sons who'd remind her of home. After all, what did she want with a passel of top-lofty London servants who were known far and wide for aping their masters while at the same time despising the very people who paid their wages?

She had done the right thing, she was sure of it. The fact that she had planned her trip to the newspaper office to coincide with Bundy's monthly retreat to her couch due to a regular-as-clockwork migraine headache proved nothing to the contrary, absolutely nothing.

As they rode along the crowded street, Jennie rechecked her list. Heading it was the need for a chef—Renfrew had informed her that Kit had specifically requested a French chef—followed by notations calling for three additional footmen, two kitchen helpers, a pair of experienced stable hands, at least two more housemaids who could double at serving table, and, perhaps even a tweeny to run errands between floors if she could find one.

It seemed ostentatious to require nearly two dozen people to care for the needs and comforts of a family consisting of two young, healthy creatures who by all rights should be capable of fending for themselves.

Of course, they weren't two *average* people, she amended mentally. After all, how many English couples live in eighteen-room houses containing a conservatory, two separate dining rooms, and a veritable barn of a ballroom? Bundy said the Bourne mansion was no more than a fit setting for an earl and his countess. Jennie wisely refrained from wondering aloud if this particular earl and countess didn't look just a tad out of place in their grand surroundings—almost like children playing at being all grown up.

Kit, she had to admit, at least looked the part, having visited his tailor before traveling to Bourne Manor so that an entire new wardrobe had been waiting for him in Berkeley Square, but she knew her own simple gowns to be sadly provincial. Which was why the Bourne carriage was just then coming to a halt outside a fashionable shop in Bond Street (this part of her trip also deliberately planned around Bundy's migraine or else Jennie knew she'd be the first countess in history to be dressed entirely in concealing white dimity gowns matched to sensible, serviceable jean boots).

Goldie was in her glory as she stood gaping and gawking throughout Jennie's lengthy session with the modiste. A young woman of definite tastes that had previously taken second place to her budget, Jennie worked her way purposefully from one end of the selling room to the other, selecting lengths of material with an eye to color and texture and never once bothering to ask a single price.

In the space of an hour Jennie had matched the materials to sketches the delighted modiste swore on her hopes of heaven were designed with just madam countess in mind. "That exquisite waist! That so entrancing swell of bosom—so innocent, so alluring! The regal carriage of a princess, the fine molded arms of a Greek goddess. The hair of an angel, the skin of a newborn babe. *Ooh la la!* That the countess would deign to honor this humble establishment with her attention. I will be the making of a poor, struggling widow in a foreign land. Once madam is seen in public the *ton* will demand a like transformation— an impossible task, to duplicate such beauty, my lady, but one must make a living." On and on went the modiste.

Two hours after entering the shop, Jennie departed, her head still buzzing with the Frenchwoman's ridiculous compliments and fervent expressions of gratitude (the latter being more readily believed if Jennie had but known the total of the bill). She changed her mind about shopping for shoes, bonnets, gloves, and other accessories, putting off that errand for another day even if it meant she must listen to Bundy's prudish criticisms of her every choice. She had a headache of her very own now, the result of the modiste's incessant chatter and a growing hunger for her lunch, which may have accounted for her almost violent reaction to seeing her husband strolling down the opposite side of the street, a soft, clinging bit of frailty hanging from each elbow.

It was ridiculous. Why should she feel this almost overpowering urge to dash across the street and plummet the two slyly simpering creatures about the head and shoulders with her reticule? And when she had done with them she would deliver a bash or five on the noggin of the stupidly grinning ignoramus who was acting less like a married man than Prinny himself!

She stood stock-still on the flagway, rooted to the spot by her anger and her inability to do more than mentally mangle the cause of her upset.

"*O-oo-o,* lookee, miss," Goldie piped up loudly at exactly the wrong moment. "There's his lordship himself, out for a breath of air. *Yoo-hoo! Your lordship!*" she trilled in a high, carrying soprano, her voice succeeding in reaching the earl above the noisy street sounds and the animated chattering of his companions.

"Oh, my *God!*" Kit breathed in exasperation as he spied Goldie and his wife—his oddly *erect* wife—on the opposite side of the street. What a coil! He couldn't abandon the two females on the crowded flagway, and he wasn't such a gapeseed as to drag them with him and introduce them to his wife of seven days. Yet to ignore his wife entirely was courting disaster. Besides, that dratted maid would probably keep bellowing like a sick calf until he acknowledged their presence. He was damned no matter what he did!

And the Lady Luck, in the form of one Oswald Norwood, came sauntering toward him, and Kit began to believe in good fairies. "Ozzy, my dearest friend," he intoned bravely, "would you be so kind as to escort these ladies to a hackney? I'm afraid I've forgotten an urgent appointment."

Ozzy was delighted, a fact Kit did not linger to learn, hurrying instead across the street, neatly dodging horses and vehicles that dared to get in his path, to stand smartly, and just a bit breathlessly, in a direct line between his wife and his too recent companions. "I did not know you had planned to visit the shops, my dear," he said with studied nonchalance.

Jennie leaned a bit to the left and peered over his shoulder at the females, who still stood where Kit had left them. "Obviously," she drawled sweetly, "else you would have asked me to join your party. Wouldn't you?"

Wretched chit! he swore silently, acting just as if we had vowed fidelity or some such rot. Which they had! he remembered with a jolt. "Party?" he improvised rapidly. "Oh, pet, you mistake the facts entirely. Those young ladies are—er—cousins of my friend Ozzy, the man with them now. I was just lending them my company while he dashed off a moment to speak with an acquaintance he hadn't seen for some time. Merely holding the fort, as it were," he ended with a limp laugh.

"Really?" Jennie's voice conveyed her disbelief. "It's a shame they had to rush off without so much as an introduction. But perhaps we can have them to dinner one evening. We know so few people in London, you know." It was amazing how calm her voice sounded, considering she was still seriously contemplating homicide.

"Yes, well, er, you shouldn't let the horses stand too much longer, Jennie," Kit said in a sudden inspiration. "Allow me to escort you home, and, er, we can take luncheon together. I've been so busy establishing my bona fides at the banks and seeking out friends from my army days that I'm guilty of neglecting you, aren't I, puss? I confess to feeling ashamed."

You could charm the pennies off a dead man's eyes, Jennie decided nastily, hating herself for feeling her outrage slowly melting under Kit's engagingly open grin. Now her anger was somehow redirecting itself, turning away from her husband and centering on her own overreaction to seeing him in the company of two, she reluctantly acknowledged, beautiful females, when she herself didn't care two sticks for the man personally. In fact, had Kit only promptly shepherded his wife into the coach he might have come out of the whole episode with nary a scratch, so angry was Jennie with herself. But Lady Luck had deserted him too soon this sunny spring day and the storm clouds were gathering, soon to rain all over his victory.

"Kit," came the voice of Ozzy Norwood as he joined his friend after sending two very disgruntled ladies on their way back to Drury Lane. "I demand you return my favor and introduce me to your beautiful companion. Two for one may not be a fair exchange, but then a simple mister cannot command the same privileges as an earl, what? By the by," he added, securing his friend's coffin with a few finishing nails, "this one makes those two warblers look like yesterday's kippers, stap me if they don't. Can't blame you for dumping them in my lap and loping off like that."

A large rock—possibly Gibraltar itself—was lodged in Lord Bourne's throat, making coherent speech impossible, although he did try a time or two, gasping and choking badly before subsiding into silence and glaring at his grinning friend.

Just as Ozzy's eyes were belatedly taking in Jennie's simple but well-cut gown and the presence of a female much resembling a lady's maid standing in front of what looked suspiciously like Bourne's town carriage— a small glimmer of light beginning to grow in his pleasantly vacant face—Jennie stepped into the breach and took charge.

Extending a small gloved hand in his direction, she said brightly, "You must be one of my husband's good friends—one of those selfish creatures who so monopolize his time in lengthy sessions reminiscing about your shared youths. But I'll forgive your interruption of our honeymoon, as I know how greatly Kit enjoys reliving his childish exploits. He must, mustn't he, as I have not seen him above a moment or two since we arrived in town."

"It's all my fault!" Ozzy sacrificed bravely. "He didn't want to be with us, you know. We fairly *begged* for his company. Don't blame him, my lady, I implore you—"

Jennie pretended to pout, throwing out her full bottom lip, thereby nearly inciting her husband to violence, then brightened visibly as she said, "I have it! You must come to dine. Just as soon as our French chef is in residence—say, a week from today? And bring your two cousins, as I do so pine for some female companionship. After all, sir, any friend of Kit's cannot help but find welcome in Berkeley Square. Isn't that so, dear?" she asked the mute earl. Was that smoke she saw coming out of her husband's ears? she thought, feeling rather full of herself.

"You're kind, ma'am," Ozzy blustered, his overtaxed intellect reeling under the barrage his *faux pas* had unleashed and powerless to maneuver out of range of attack. "Too—*too*—kind. Indeed," he said, attempting an air of worldliness, "Kit is undeserving of such a fine lady as yourself."

"Why thank you, sir," Jennie responded. "I quite agree. But then we so seldom get what we deserve, don't we?"

At last Kit found his tongue. "Oh, I don't know about that, my love," he put in, leading her toward the open door of the coach. "Some of us get *exactly* what we deserve. In fact, one of us might just get it this very night if she continues asking for it so blatantly."

"Really?" Jennie exclaimed, bravado masking the fact that her knees were beginning to experience a decided tendency to quiver. In a much lower voice heard only by her husband she added, "My papa always warned me that people who choose to live in glass houses should beware of tossing rocks. Look to yourself, my *love,* before casting any stones at *my* behavior. Retribution can be demanded on both sides."

After delivering this stunning *coup de grace,* Jennie turned, inclined her head to her husband's friend and incidental tattletale, and allowed herself to be assisted into the carriage. Blond head held high, she concentrated on her second verbal victory over her husband and determinedly resisted any thoughts concerning her ridiculous overreaction upon seeing Kit enjoying the company of any female besides his wife—who wouldn't cross the street with him if he asked her to, which, she owned sourly, he hadn't.

As the carriage drove away Kit turned to his lifelong friend, ready to do murder in broad daylight while standing in the middle of crowded Bond Street. "Now, now, Kit, old chum, it was an honest mistake," Ozzy began, hastily backing up a step. "You never told me your wife was such a looker. Anyway, wives ain't supposed to be pretty. They're supposed to have big dowries and buck teeth. And hatchet noses. And…and…and scrawny chests—"

"Keep your filthy mouth off my wife's chest!" Kit was so overcome as to bluster before realizing exactly what he was saying. "Never mind that! What in thunder did you think you were about, prancing over here like some hound in heat and cadging in a tryst with my wife as if she were some trollop we'd share between us? Are your brains entirely to let that you'd mistake a lady for one of your loose women? I ought to call you out for this, Ozzy, I swear it!"

Ozzy cast his eyes about furtively and spoke out of the side of his mouth. "Attracting a crowd, sport. What say we toddle down to White's and settle this quietly over a bottle? My treat, o' course. Call me out, you say. You wouldn't really do that, Kit, would you? Deuced unsporting of you, knowing what a fine shot you are, don't you think?"

Looking around, Kit reluctantly realized the wisdom of Ozzy's warning—while hating to credit his friend with even a small portion of brainpower at that moment—and roughly grabbing the fellow by the elbow, he surreptitiously pushed him along the flagway as if unsure Ozzy wouldn't bolt if he relaxed his hold.

It took more than one bottle before Kit could find any small bit of humor in the scene lately enacted in Bond Street, but no amount of wine or conciliating chatter on the part of Ozzy would make Kit believe Jennie could be induced to speak to him again much before the first snow of winter.

CHAPTER FIVE

FOR A MAN who had so distinguished himself in battle as to have been mentioned in dispatches more than a half-dozen times, Kit showed a remarkable lack of courage when it came to confronting his wife. Perhaps this reluctance to face her stemmed from the fact that he knew himself to be totally in the wrong—as even the slapdash marital habits of the *ton* included at least a show of fidelity, certainly during the first flush of the union.

So Jennie was left to wade her way through the long list of applicants who replied to her advertisement—their numbers making a long, snaking line that stretched from the servants' entrance into Berkeley Square itself—while the earl continued making himself scarce.

Five days after their meeting on Bond Street, Kit at last ran out of diversions and found himself, at only three in the afternoon, at loose ends. Lacking any other alternative, he directed his mount to the rear of Berkeley Square, dismounted in front of the stable doors, turned, and walked headfirst into a mountain.

"What the devil?" Bourne exploded once he had regained his breath. Looking up, quite a good way up, actually, his startled eyes took in the sight of an enormous, hairless, black head fitted with glittering black-bean eyes; a gargantuan head that sat atop the largest man Kit had even seen.

Two hands as large as hams reached out to steady him, nearly crushing his shoulders in the process, as Kit rocked slightly on his heels. The man must be all of seven feet tall, the gaping earl told himself in amazement. I can only hope he's a friendly beast.

Recovering his dignity and firmly stamping down any impulse to turn tail and make a run for it, Kit inquired softly: "What—er, I mean, *who* are you?"

"I be called Tiny," the giant rumbled from somewhere deep in his massive chest.

"Naturally," the earl quipped ruefully, his quick sense of the ridiculous coming to the rescue.

"I be the earl's new groom. Who be you, sir?"

"I be—er—I'm the earl, actually," Kit informed him, stepping out of Tiny's large shadow and back into the sunlight. "So, you're my new groom, eh, Tiny? Tell me—who hired you?" Kit held out a hand before Tiny could answer. "No, don't tell me, let me guess. Lady Bourne, right?"

"Lady Bourne, she be a queen. I be ready to die for her," Tiny growled passionately. "I be ready to kill for her. With these hands," he swore, holding out his large fists and then clenching them tight.

Kit swallowed hard and stretched his neck. "Good, Tiny. I like—um—*loyalty* in a servant. But I asked her ladyship to secure two grooms." He looked the giant up and down, still amazed by the man's size. "Or did she think she had?"

"'ullo, guv'nor," came a thin, high voice as Tiny stepped sideways to reveal the person standing behind him. "Goliath's m'name and groomin' nags m'game. Me an' Tiny 'ere 're a team, ye ken. Worked the travelin' circus till it went flat, an' yer missus took us up. Right pretty piece too," Goliath added with a wink, earning himself a menacing growl from Tiny.

"A dwarf," Kit breathed in amazement, looking down on the tiny man. "A bloody dwarf." And then, remarkably, he grinned. "Why not? Why the bloody hell not?"

"You be wantin' Tiny ta take yer horse?" the large man asked almost timidly, belatedly remembering his mistress's hint that the earl was best humored at first, until he felt more at ease with his new staff.

"That's very kind of you, Tiny," Kit thanked the man as he turned and headed toward the rear of the mansion. "Just toss him over your shoulder, why not, and carry him into his stall. I'm sure he'll give you no trouble."

Goliath let out a giggle and executed a perfect, if compact, backflip. "'e likes us, Tiny," the delighted dwarf crowed, jumping up and down on his sturdy, stubby legs. "'ome at last we is, boyo, 'ome at last!"

JENNIE PACED the drawing room in mounting apprehension. Kit's behavior had been courtesy itself since their unfortunate meeting in Bond Street, not only refraining from taking out his threatened revenge on her person, but allowing time and distance to separate them from the nastier memories of that meeting.

Since she had spent a very busy week interviewing possible servants for the mansion, Jennie's memories of that fateful meeting had been given a chance to mellow, so that now she could recall little of her former anger, concentrating instead on the ludicrous image of her infuriating urbane husband at a total loss for words. Of her other, more unsettling feelings at having spied two obvious ladies of the evening dangling from her husband's sleeves, she refused to think at all. It only confused the issue, whatever it was.

She'd been granted time, and time was what she had needed. Time to complete her new wardrobe, and time for some of her new things to be delivered, so that she could, when the time came, face him in her new finery. That was important. She needed the outward trappings of her new title about her when her husband confronted her demanding she explain about the servants she had hired.

Oh, yes, she mused knowingly, there would be quite a grand to-do then. She was not a complete fool. But she must make him understand her reasons for hiring Tizzie and Lizzie, Tiny and Goliath, Charity—the poor, dear thing—Bob, Ben, and Del, and Irvette and Blessing. Even Montague, the French chef Kit had particularly requested, would require a good deal of explaining on her part, she knew.

Now the time and space Kit had granted her began to wear on her nerves. She yearned to have him summon her, ring a peal over her head, and have done with it.

Bundy had told her he would. Even Goldie had clucked her tongue at the sight of Charity—the poor, dear thing. Renfrew, Jennie silently blessed the man, had said nothing, possibly because Del's happy "Mornin', guv'nor" as he took up his proper footman position in the foyer had robbed the majordomo of coherent speech.

Deep in her heart of hearts, Jennie knew she had grossly overstepped herself. She had been commissioned to hire the servants, of course she had been, but she had not been given *carte blanche* to employ the odd assortment of humanity she had chosen. But they had needed jobs so desperately, she consoled herself. All those other, qualified applicants, who had presented themselves, references in hand, would have no difficulty in finding positions.

But Tizzie and Lizzie, for instance, had little hope if she turned them down. Where could two overage, out-of-work Shakespearean actresses find work if even the lowest traveling troupe would not hire them? And as for Charity—the poor, dear thing—she might well expire in a filthy gutter if Jennie hadn't taken her on as tweeny. Not that Charity could climb the stairs very much in her present condition.

Surely Kit would understand. Jennie picked up a Dresden statuette of a young maiden and scowled into its placid, peaceful face. And a herd of elephants might dance on the head of a pin. Of course Kit wouldn't understand! Why should he? Hadn't the man already proved himself to be a heartless beast capable of compromising an innocent maiden, marrying her, and then deserting her in the midst of a strange city?

Jennie rapidly worked up a full head of steam, all her heart directed at her cruel husband, the heartless monster from whom she must protect her latest batch of ugly ducklings and pitiful misfits. How dare he question her judgment! Who was he to set himself up as arbiter of all that was required to make a good and loyal servant? Well, she thought, now in a high state of temper, just let him say one word against her choices. Just let him dare!

Kit's entrance into the drawing room at that precise moment was not exactly a triumph of superb timing. "Good day, m'love," he began cheerily enough. "And what are you about today?"

Jennie whirled on him in some heat. "And just what is *that* snide remark supposed to mean?" she sneered, her green eyes narrowed into wary slits. "How unhandsome of you, Kit, how very unhandsome of you!"

"I make you my compliments, ma'am," Kit drawled, executing an elegant leg in her direction. "That is quite a novel greeting. Am I, I sincerely trust, going to be given an explanation for it, or am I to be summarily executed for my sins without even so much as a hearing?"

Jennie tossed her blond curls and sniffed. "Oh, you think you're so very droll, don't you?"

She ain't exactly falling over herself to be nice to me, Kit told himself, hiding a smile. Possibly she feels attack to be the best defense. I wonder what she believes herself to be guilty of, for I doubt I have been in Berkeley Square frequently enough to have done anything too lamentable. "What is it, puss?" he prompted, lowering his rangy frame into a chair and stretching his legs before him. "Have you overspent your allowance? If so, don't fret, for if that fetching creation you are wearing is part of the reason I forgive you with all my heart. You really do clean up quite nicely, pet, if I must say so m'self."

Having successfully taken himself out of the pan and placed himself squarely in the fire, Kit subsided into silence, content to watch the sparks now emanating from his wife's eyes.

Plopping down on the settee opposite his chair, Jennie spat nastily, "Oh, do be quiet. I know very well you have just come from the stables, dressed as you are. Don't tell me you don't have something cutting to say to me about our new grooms, for it won't fadge, Kit, truly it won't. Well," she nudged, "go on—have done with it. Tell me I am the greatest fool since time began— even Bundy would not gainsay you."

Kit had the audacity to assume a crestfallen expression. "How low your opinion is of me, ma'am. I had nary a thought but to praise you on your finds. What splendid grooms Tiny and Goliath will make. Goliath can tend horsey hoofs all the day long without ever complaining of a sore back, and Tiny—why, the man is invaluable. If one of my blacks comes up lame I've simply to set Tiny between the shafts and I'll have the fastest curricle in all London, possibly all England."

"Don't you make fun of them," Jennie shot at him angrily. "Don't you dare make fun of them!"

The smile left Kit's handsome face. "I do not make fun of them, Jennie. It is you who demean them by thinking they are in need of your protection. It is you who sees them as different, not me. Oh, I admit to being momentarily startled by their rather, er, different *appearance,* but I believe I recovered in time so as to not embarrass either them or myself." He leaned back and crossed his legs at the ankle. "Actually, pet, it is you who should be apologizing to me for believing I would let some sort of prejudice against people who are a bit different influence my consideration of their talents. If they prove to be good grooms, they shall stay. If not—" his voice hardened fractionally "—no power on earth will induce me to keep them on. Do we understand each other?"

Jennie had the good grace to feel ashamed of herself, and said so—quite prettily—causing Kit's smile to return. It was then, as she was enjoying this show of friendly compatibility, that she decided to press her luck.

"Tiny and Goliath are not the only servants I have hired. You may not be so generous when you have met them."

"Again you malign me before the fact." Kit sighed theatrically. Really, this getting along with wives was not so bad after all. Jennie was proving quite easily maneuverable. She was also, as he had observed earlier, growing to be quite easy on his eyes. Marriage certainly did have its compensations. Hard as it was to believe, he was beginning to truly enjoy her company.

What a pity she was not more worldly or he might be tempted to bed her. Yet, he surprised himself by thinking, he was glad she was not worldly, had little experience of men such as himself. Disturbed by this train of thought, he swiftly turned his mind back to the subject at hand. "Tell me about the rest of our staff, pet. If I am going to live here I guess I should make myself at least tokenly acquainted with them."

Look at him, Jennie told herself irritably, sitting there looking so smug and self-satisfied—and so wretchedly handsome, she added reluctantly. Oh, he thinks he's got me right in the palm of his hand. The high and mighty Earl of Bourne, condescending to be nice to his simple, countrified wife. How dare he try to manipulate me this way! Even worse, how dare he succeed so handily!

She would have verbally taken him to task then, but she could tell, by the disgustingly satisfied smile on his face, that she might just as well save her breath to, as Goldie said, cool her porridge. Well, if he intended to be disobliging she saw no reason not to do likewise. "I see no need to give you a recital of our serving staff, seeing as how you are home so seldom and unlikely to run into other than those on duty after midnight."

So it sits like that, does it, Kit mused, raising one speaking eyebrow as he took in Jennie's flushed cheeks. The kitten has her back up yet again. "I would perceive the wisdom of your words, kitten," he told her with a maddening smile, "except for one thing. I have decided to change my ways, knowing myself to be guilty of shamelessly neglecting you. Dear me," he exclaimed, feigning astonishment as Jennie leaped to her feet and stared down at him openmouthed, "I do believe I have

said something to upset you. Is it the thought of our finally acting the part of man and wife that so discom-
modes you? Or, might I hope, do I misread your
agitation? Perhaps, be still my foolish heart, you too
wish for this closer association?"

Jennie stomped away from the settee and took up a
position nearer the doorway to the foyer. "There are
times, my lord, when you can be unbelievably crude,"
she said crushingly.

Before Jennie could make good her exit, Kit leaped
up from his chair and loped across the room to capture
her shoulders in his strong grip. He did not know what
imp of mischief had possessed him—surely he had not
entered the drawing room with any such thoughts in
mind—but suddenly he felt himself overpowered by an
undeniable need to feel Jennie's softly pouting mouth
beneath his own.

He told himself he was merely kissing her as a means
of shutting her up, but he knew he was lying. The high life
he had been living ever since he came to London had included being in the company of many beautiful women—
women who neither railed at him nor accused him of
every evil under the sun. No, the women he had spent time
with were all generous females, giving to a fault—for a
price. Yet he had not once sampled their wares, even
though his pockets were now well lined enough to set up
his own stable of fine fillies. He had flirted, he had
teased—but he had not bedded a one of them.

Jennie, her heart fluttering madly, stared up into Kit's
strangely staring face, unable to know what was going
on in his mind. If she knew that the thought of a small,
blond slip of an unwanted bride had kept her dashing
husband celibate she would not have believed it. That
was probably why, although he looked about to speak,

her husband said nothing. He only continued to stare—taking his own sweet time about it too.

As the tension in the air became nearly thick enough to slice, he acted. Abruptly dragging her soft body up against his lean, hard frame, Kit swooped like a bird of prey and claimed Jennie's unsuspecting mouth in a nearly ruthless kiss.

The flash of feeling was instant and just as intense as he remembered. Almost at once his lips softened, moving sensuously as they molded themselves to the warm contours of Jennie's. He felt the heat rising within him as he pressed his body more firmly against her yielding form, and his heart leaped at the very moment he felt the tenseness leave her and her hands begin to inch up to clasp his waist.

As for Jennie, she wasn't thinking at all. She was leagues past rational thought and had been from the moment she was first rudely captured in Kit's arms. Try as she might to tell herself it was fear that held her captive, she knew she was only deceiving herself. She wanted Kit to touch her, to kiss her. Perhaps she had subconsciously been hoping for just such a reaction when she had insulted him. This and a lot more she would sit alone in her room and dissect later. Much later. Right now she would give in to the enjoyment of the moment.

But all good things must come to an end, and this interlude was no exception. Why he looked up he did not know; perhaps a noise distracted him—although he found it hard to believe anything could have distracted him, so intense was his concentration on the logistics of transferring their activity from the doorway to the settee—but suddenly his eyes were taking in the sight of a small, mobcapped servant girl surreptitiously crossing the foyer.

"Bloody hell!" he exclaimed, releasing Jennie so abruptly she nearly fell. "That chit's *pregnant!*"

Jennie shook her head a time or two, trying hard to bring herself back to reality. "Increasingly," she corrected at last, striving for a bit of dignity. "Charity—the poor, dear thing—will be presenting us with a little bundle of joy in about a month."

"In a pig's eye she will!" the earl countered hotly. "It's not a home for fallen women I'm running here, damn it all." All thoughts of shared passion forgotten, Kit rounded on Jennie and ordered coldly, "Get rid of her. Now! Today!"

Her hands planted firmly on her hips, her head and shoulders leaning toward him for emphasis, Jennie responded, "Charity is my choice for tweeny. You said I could have one if I wished. Well, I wish. I shall pay her wages out of my own allowance if necessary, but I promised that child a home, and a home she shall have!"

Kit lifted a hand to his pounding head. "Who's the father? Do we employ him as well?"

Now Jennie was in her element. "We do not, my lord. The father is a peer of the realm, already married and father to more children than Adam. He seduced poor Charity within a month of her employment in Grosvenor Sq—"

"Spare me his name, infant," Kit cut in resignedly, "else you may yet tell me it is my duty to call the cad out to avenge the chit." Reluctantly nodding his head in surrender he sighed, "All right, Jennie. Charity, as they say, begins at home. I guess our home is as good a place as any. But for the sake of our unnamed peer, I suggest you keep Charity abovestairs until after her confinement."

"You are not going to fight me on this?" Jennie asked incredulously, finding it hard to accept this easy victory.

"I be fond of my own skin, I be," the earl quipped in imitation of Tiny's peculiar phrasing, "and I be leery of your setting your great giant after me if I refuse."

Kit's magnanimity, as well as the lingering softness she felt for him after their embrace, combined to put a smile back on Jennie's face. "Should I spare you more surprises and tell you about the rest of the staff?"

The Earl of Bourne, that so beset and beleaguered man, merely shook his head in denial. "In consideration of my sanity, pet, I believe you should refrain from such an inventory and leave me to discover them one at a time. Although I cannot imagine that anything can surprise me anymore." Turning to quit the room, he added one last thought. "Other females content themselves collecting bric-a-brac, y'know. But I guess that would be too tame a hobby for you, wouldn't it, kitten?"

He left then, taking her furious blush as his answer, and went in search of his valet and a hot tub, leaving Jennie alone in the drawing room to relive his kiss and her daring response to it.

"Tonight, my infant," he whispered under his breath as he climbed the wide stairs. "Tonight we will resume what Charity, that 'poor, dear thing' you have taken under your wing, interrupted. It is more than time I began acting the husband."

THE HEADACHE that had been the excuse Jennie offered in order to get out of dining with her husband that evening became a reality a few hours later. Pacing alone in her bedchamber (having effectively banished Bundy and Goldie with her tearful pleas to be left alone in her misery), Jennie's abused head rang with her companions' parting words that echoed over and over in her ears: "You'll have to face up to your actions sooner or later, missy."

Jennie tossed her head arrogantly as she tried to dismiss Bundy's words. "No, I don't," she denied aloud. "I can go home to Papa and never set foot in London again." Her triumphant grin faded abruptly as she realized her title-conscious father would send her back to London so fast her feet wouldn't touch the ground.

"I can take refuge in a convent," she announced to the empty room, then made a face as she realized the absurdity of such a move. "Well, what else can I do?" she asked her reflection in the full-length mirror. "I can't very well disguise myself as a man and ship out on some vessel bound for India. I get seasick on the pond at home." She leaned her forehead against the cool glass. "Maybe I'll just hide away in here until I go into a decline and Kit loses interest." She raised her head slightly to look into her own eyes. "Oh, fudge!" she exclaimed pettishly and turned away from her reflection.

Tossing her dressing gown across a chair, she crawled into bed, pulled the covers over her head, and tried to find peace in a good night's sleep.

Three hours later, still tossing and turning in her rumpled bed, Jennie heard Kit's footsteps climb the stairs and halt outside her door. She held her breath for an eternity of time before his footsteps moved on down the hallway to his own door, then tried to ignore the sound of Kit's voice as Leon helped the earl in his preparations before retiring. It wasn't until the valet could be heard closing the door behind him on his way out that Jennie felt she could relax at last, and it wasn't long until sleep overcame her.

"Denny!" a voice called urgently. "Denny, what happened? Hold on! I'm coming!" Jennie sat straight up in bed, eyes wide with fright, her heart pounding in her chest. Someone had called her name. "Denny! Oh no,

Denny!" the masculine voice cried yet again, torment in every syllable.

It wasn't her name that was being called, Jennie realized. It just sounded like it to her sleep-fuzzed mind. Her bare toes hit the floor as she involuntarily responded to the anguish in Kit's voice—for she could tell it was her husband who was calling out, probably in the throes of a nightmare—and, being Jennie, she had no other thought but to go to him and comfort him, her dressing gown left behind forgotten on the chair.

Swinging open the connecting door between their chambers, the door that had remained firmly closed all the time they had resided in Berkeley Square, she stumbled through the dim light cast by the full moon out that night and made her way to the side of the large bed. Fumbling with the familiar implements, she at last lit the candle next to Kit's bed, and her husband's face came into view—a face ravaged with some pain that twisted his features and drove his clenched fists into the mattress on either side of his body.

She reached out her hands and shook his shoulders. "Kit. Kit!" she whispered loudly. "Kit, wake up. You're having a nightmare." But Kit was too far away to hear her, his mind locked in some hellish place her voice could not reach. Again, Jennie didn't think; again, she acted. She crawled into the bed and put her arms around his thrashing body, pressing her cheek next to his, and began to croon softly, as one would to a distraught child.

"Denny!" Kit breathed, seeming to quiet a bit. "I knew I could find you. The cannon—where did they all come from? Ambush, Denny, caught napping." Kit's hands reached up and clamped themselves around Jennie's slim form. "So much blood, Denny. Ah, my side. It hurts like hell. Where's Denny? He was next to me when the ball hit. Denny?" Kit's muscles tightened, and Jennie nearly cried out in pain as his grip punished her soft flesh. *"Denny!"* Kit rasped, the pain in his voice bringing tears to her eyes. "Jesus, Lord, Denny, where are you? *For the love of God, where's the rest of you?"*

"Kit!" Jennie called loudly into his ear, giving his cheek a firm slap as she outwardly strained for control, ignoring her own fear at the sight of his wide, sightlessly staring eyes. "Wake up, my poor darling," she implored on a dry sob. "Please, Kit, wake up!"

She watched anxiously as his eyes blinked once, twice, and then seemed to focus on her face. His hands, crushing her upper arms in their superior strength, relaxed slightly. "It was just a dream, Kit. A nightmare."

Kit's chest was heaving as he struggled to regain control over himself. "Dreaming," he rasped, taking a deep, shuddering breath and letting it out slowly. "Only a dream, only a dream," he parroted, giving his head a slight shake. He reached down somewhere deep inside himself and summoned up a small smile. "And you came to wake me up and chase the bogeymen away. Thank you, kitten."

Leon and Renfrew, standing in the hallway in their nightclothes, exchanged glances and turned away, each returning to his own bed, to think his own thoughts. The valet's hand had been on the doorknob when Renfrew restrained him, shaking his head silently and cocking his head toward the door and mouthing, "Listen." They heard Jennie's voice struggling to be heard over Kit's cries, and both men waited, Leon barely resisting the urge to comfort his friend and master, and Renfrew silently praying that the near strangers on the other side of the heavy wooden door might learn more about each other before this night was over.

Never knowing the two servants had been outside the door, Jennie and Kit, their emotions heightened by the events of the past few minutes were suddenly tinglingly aware that they were alone in the near dark, lying side by side on a bed, their arms wrapped around each other. When Jennie, in her nervousness, squirmed slightly, the movement brought their bodies even closer together, a fact Kit was not backward in realizing.

"Thank you, kitten," he breathed into her hair. "I must have given you quite a fright."

"Hrummmph, umm-wumpum." Jennie's mouth, pressed firmly against his bare neck, garbled her words, and Kit responded by chuckling deep in his throat. "What was that?" he asked, moving his head away only marginally in order to look into her face.

"I said, 'You're welcome,'" Jennie repeated, flushing hotly under his intense gaze. Pushing against his shoulders with her hands she tried to rise, mumbling rather incoherently about returning to her own chamber.

"But what if I should have another nightmare?" Kit questioned, using his own hands to push her back down against him. Then, all traces of humor leaving his voice, he asked her softly, "What was I dreaming about, kitten? I never remember much, although I'm fairly certain it's the same dream over and over again. Leon wakes me, my throat raw with screaming, my body drenched in sweat, but I can't remember anything but this—this feeling of terror."

He looked so lost, so vulnerable. Jennie could no more leave him than she could turn away a starving child. Allowing herself to be gathered against his chest, she whispered, "You called for someone named Denny. At first, when you woke me, I thought you were calling my name." As soon as she began speaking Kit had grown rigid under her, and she knew he was upset. "Who is…was…Denny? Was he a friend?"

"Lord Denton Lowell. The closest friend, the only friend any one man could ever need or want," Kit told her in a low voice. "He, er, he died on the Peninsula."

Jennie remembered Kit's ramblings about Denny, and a tear formed in the corner of her left eye and splashed onto her husband's silk-clad chest. "You said something about your side. You were injured in battle, weren't you?"

The earl's right hand unconsciously rubbed up and down Jennie's bare arm as he returned into his memories. "We were caught unawares. We were to leave for home in less than a week and thought we had seen the last of battle. I don't know where the enemy came from; we had thought we were in a safe place behind the lines. I took a piece of exploding shell in my side, and Denny…and Denny…"

Jennie touched her fingers to his lips. "Shhh. Don't talk about it. Don't think about it."

Kit covered her hand with his own and placed a slow kiss on her palm before laying her hand on his chest. "I have to talk about it. I never have—not to anyone. Maybe if I tell someone, these damned dreams will stop and you and Leon can get some sleep," he quipped, vainly trying to inject some humor into the tense atmosphere.

"I must have been knocked unconscious for a while," he pursued doggedly after a short pause when he seemed to retreat inside himself, talking as if he were reciting a lesson by rote. "When I woke up, the first thing I noticed was the pain in my side. And then the blood—there was blood all over me. Everywhere men and horses were screaming, and smoke stung my eyes. I looked around for Denny, but I couldn't find him. I crawled on my hands and knees in the dirt, looking for him, calling for him…"

"Oh, Kit, please stop—"

"No!" he nearly shouted, staring at the ceiling. "I have to say it. I dragged myself over to where Denny's mount lay, a bloody hole in his belly, and that's when I saw him. When…when they found me I was still trying to put Denny back together." He turned toward Jennie, his eyes burning fiercely as he tried to explain. "I tried, kitten, I really tried. But… but the pieces…the pieces didn't fit."

Jennie could stand no more. "Stop it! Please, Kit, stop it!" she pleaded, sobbing as she hid her face in his neck while one bunched fist beat ineffectually against his chest. Kit grabbed at her hand and tried to calm her, suddenly cast into the role of comforter, but his words had taken the innocent child named Jennie and rudely catapulted her into the real world, where sometimes the handsome knights did not prevail.

He rose up, pushing Jennie onto her back and catching her flailing arms above her head. "Jennie…kitten… hush, sweetheart. I'm sorry," he crooned as her hurt whimpers slowly subsided.

Did he know that her tears were for him? For him, and for Denny, and for all the soldiers who were still dying in that awful, awful war? "No, Kit," she whispered huskily, "don't be sorry. I didn't mean to cry. It's just that it's all so awful…so cruel—"

He looked down into her tear-bright eyes and confused, defeated expression, and his heart swelled with fierce, unfamiliar feelings for this caring, compassionate girl who cried for him. "Jennie…kitten…I…*oh, God,*" he groaned passionately as his mouth came down over hers.

CHAPTER SIX

NOTHING COULD BE this comfortable, this delightfully warm and soft. Jennie couldn't suppress a small sigh as she snuggled more deeply into the cocoon of creature comfort provided by Kit's embrace—although her sleep-befogged mind had yet to identify it as such. She was too intent on indulging herself in a few more moments of blissful sensuality, allowing the demands of her pleasure-seeking body to keep her mind uninformed as to its actual source. But nothing, not even such innocent bliss, can last forever, and at long last, Jennie began to surface from her slumber.

Stretching out one small hand, she encountered a smooth expanse of warm flesh that she instantly recognized as Kit's bare left shoulder. His entire body stiffened and her huge green eyes opened wide as the events of the previous night came rushing into her consciousness willy-nilly. "Oh, Lord!" she whispered almost under her breath. "What have I done?"

Slowly, praying all the while, she tilted her head back until she could see her husband's face. Her prayers were answered—he was still sound asleep. If her luck only held until she managed to disentangle herself from his slack hold, she could escape to her own chamber, hide her traitorous body beneath her covers, and try to pretend nothing had happened. Please, she silently entreated any kind spirits who might have been listening, just let me get away from here without waking him.

Slowly, and with incredible stealth, she backed her body toward the side of the large bed and angled one foot toward the floor, which was maddeningly far away. Ducking her head, she slipped Kit's right arm into position across his own chest and allowed her arms to trail behind her as her other foot hit the floor and she slid her body over the edge of the mattress. Another inch or two and she would be completely free of the bed. She held her breath as she slid closer and closer to the floor, releasing it in a long sigh only as her knees made contact with the rug. She'd made it! Now all she had to do was find her nightgown, wherever the dratted thing was, and steal across the room to the adjoining door. She gave a slight shiver—it was rather cold on the floor—and adjusted her plan. She could send Goldie to retrieve the nightgown later, even if it meant she'd have to listen to the maid's sly jokes. She could not dare remaining in Kit's chamber much longer, or else Leon might arrive to wake his master only to catch a glimpse of one hastily departing naked countess. Weighing her options in the twinkling of an eye, she chose Goldie as the lesser of two evils.

Jennie swiveled on the balls of her feet and prepared to creep across the wide expanse of carpeting that lay between her and safety, and had in fact begun to take a small step when her head was enveloped in a cloud of sheer white silk. Her nightgown! Where had that come from?

"Good morning, wife," came a calm male voice. "Going somewhere? Surely you'll wish your nightgown?"

Jennie looked over her shoulder and upward to see

Kit's leering face looking down at her from the edge of the mattress. That he was actually there looking down at her was bad enough, but to know that she could see him almost as clear as day *through* the nightgown still covering her head was enough to send her into an immediate attack of hysterics.

"Close your eyes, you lecher!" she yelped in a most unloverlike way. While Kit obligingly hid his eyes (though not his wide smile) behind his hand, Jennie struggled with the cursed nightgown, nearly ripping it as she fought her way through its folds to find the neck and arm openings hidden there.

"All right, you beast, you may open your eyes now," she said as she laid her hand on the doorknob in anticipation of showing him nothing more than her rapidly departing skirts.

"Hey, kitten, wait a moment!" Kit called after her as she disappeared on the other side of the closed door. "You haven't even given me my morning kiss. And after last night, too," he ended on an exaggerated sigh of longing.

Jennie's head reappeared through the partially opened door just long enough for her to say a highly colorful, definitely improper word and disappear again, leaving Kit to howl in delight at her display of temper.

Once safe in her own room and under the covers just as she had planned, Jennie bit down hard on the soft cushion of her thumb as she struggled with the memories that now crowded into her mind. Had she really allowed him to…encouraged him to…aided him in his desire to—oh, Lord above, she *had!* How could she ever hold her head up in his presence after her shameless behavior?

But it had seemed so right, felt so right at the time.

She had been listening to his nightmare, comforting him. When had everything changed? How had she reverted from the comforter to the comforted, and when did the comforting turn into something deeper, something infinitely stronger than the mere wish to give each other ease? Somehow, without her knowledge, compassion had become passion, and that passion had led to…

Well, her common sense intruded, never mind now just where it had led. She poked her head out from under the covers to check the time on the mantel clock, planning to calculate how soon Goldie would be barging in with her morning chocolate, and came nose to nose with a smirking Lord Bourne.

"Up for air, are you?" he questioned cheekily before vaulting casually onto the mattress to lie at his ease on his side, one hand propping up his head as he gazed up at Jennie just as if he weren't the most obnoxious, insufferable beast in creation. "You dashed off before I could claim a kiss from my dear bride. *Tsk, tsk,* how naughty you are, puss," he said with a sad shake of his dark head. Reaching up, he snaked a hand around the back of her head, pulling her down to within an inch of his smiling mouth. "Pucker up now, sweetings, and give your husband his due."

"I'll give you a punch in the chops," Jennie retorted, wrenching her head from his grasp.

Kit allowed his head to plop down onto the pillow. "Oh, woe is me," he mourned in mock dejection, "the chit spurns me. And after all we were to each other. I believe I am cut to the quick."

How dare he! Jennie thought, incensed. He has taken what had been a beautiful—although, perhaps, in the clear light of hindsight, unfortunate—interlude and turned it into an object of fun. Does he spare my blushes, even a little? He does not. Has he so much as the slightest consideration of my finer feelings? He has not. Does he show the least bit of shame for having taken such elaborate liberties with my person? Far from it. So what does he do? He crashes in here and tries to make a May game out of me, that's what he does! Her fury getting the better of her, Jennie grabbed hold of her pillow and swung it square at Kit's head.

"Hey, what's all that about?" the laughing earl protested, grabbing the fluffy pillow and throwing it to the floor, where his prone body, having been the recipient of Jennie's none too gentle shove, soon joined it.

"Get out of my chamber!" she ordered, hanging over the edge of the bed, the better to shout at him—a tactical mistake that soon had her body joining his on the rug. "At the risk of understatement, Lord Bourne," she intoned crushingly, once she had caught the breath her ignominious fall had knocked out of her, "I *loathe* you!"

It had taken him a while—quite a good while, actually—but at last Kit realized that Jennie wasn't just putting up a token show of anger. She really meant it—she hated the sight of him. How strange, thought the intelligent, but still rather young Earl of Bourne—so perhaps his confusion was excusable. How very strange. My recollections of last night are far from unpleasant. Surely she couldn't be finding fault with my performance. After all, I know she has no way of comparing me to another, and even in the heat of the moment I can tell the difference between a cry of distress and a cry of passion. And that was passion last night, sure as check, he assured himself in self-defense.

Perhaps if Kit had been older, had a few more years of exposure to the gentler sex under his belt, he would have realized that Jennie was too shy, too inexperienced, to find any pleasure in verbally rehashing the events of the previous evening. An older man might have handled the "morning after" with a good deal more finesse than had Kit. But Kit was not older or more experienced. And he had bungled his role of loving husband—bungled it badly—and now he would have to pay the piper.

Or would he? As he fought to control Jennie's flailing limbs without injuring her, Kit slowly began to get angry. What was the chit carrying on about, anyway? he reasoned with typical male logic. It wasn't as if *he* had entered *her* chamber in the middle of the night dressed in next to nothing and hopped into *her* bed was it? No! And was it he who had cradled her in his arms and shed sweet tears for her? Again, no! And if he reacted in the same way any red-blooded male animal would react when put into the same circumstances, he'd be damned if he'd spend the rest of his life wearing sackcloth and ashes like some dreadful sinner. If there was blame to be placed in this whole business, then let it rest on the head that deserved it—Jennie's!

"Here now!" he exclaimed, grabbing Jennie by the shoulders and pressing her back against the carpet. "Fun's fun and all that, kitten, but me thinks thou dost protest too much. After all, it was you who seduced me, y'know."

"*Me! Seduce you!*" Jennie screeched in disbelief, her body shocked into rigidity. "Well, if that isn't above all things stupid. You ruin me, and then you have the gall— the absolute gall—to blame me for my own ruination?"

"Ruination, is it?" Kit retorted acidly. "That's a bit strong, don't you think, Jennie? After all, we are married. Besides," he ended, softening a little as his ego surfaced, "it wasn't all that bad, was it?"

"*Oh!*" Jennie exploded, rising to her feet to brush her

tangled gold locks out of her eyes. "The conceit of the man!" Dramatically pointing toward the door, she pronounced regally, "Get out, my lord, or I shall tell you just how *bad* things could really become if I put my mind to it, sirrah!"

Kit took in Jennie's thunderous expression, mentally complimenting the accuracy of his memory when it was applied to his recollections of the sweet curves hardly concealed by her thin nightgown, and slowly got to his feet. "All right, puss, I'll leave. But try as you might, my dear, last night did happen, and it happened because you came into my chamber, not through any fault of my own."

"I only entered your chamber because of your nightmare," Jennie protested weakly, hating to see any logic in Kit's statement.

"Perhaps. And, if I have not mentioned it before, I do now thank you, kitten," he said, sobering for a moment. "But you stayed to comfort me after I awoke, didn't you?" he pointed out, driving his point home with a vengeance. "How dare you stand there and tell me I'm a cad just because I took what was offered me!"

"Well," Jennie returned, determined to brazen it out, "how dare you be angry with *me* for having the *audacity* to be angry with *you!*"

That piece of feminine reasoning was beyond Kit, and he belatedly saw the wisdom in returning to his own chamber before things became so muddled that Jennie ran home to her father in a pet. He had enough on his plate without that! Left alone, Jennie might eventually see their unplanned lovemaking in a more charitable light, and him along with it. Not that he would pine away to nothingness if she never shared his bed again, but damn it all anyway, he had rather enjoyed her company, even if she hadn't been the bride of his choice.

Left alone once more, Jennie launched her body onto the bed and indulged herself in a cleansing bout of tears which settled absolutely nothing, but at least kept Goldie and Bundy from asking too many questions.

HIS MASTER WAS in a fine temper this morning, Leon mused placidly as he deftly caught the spoiled cravat that went winging past his shoulder and handed his lordship a fresh one. That it had something to do with the young countess Leon was certain, but since Renfrew, that old stickler for propriety, had pulled him away from the door last night, Leon was left to ponder whether or not the rumpled state of the bed had anything to do with it. It was unusual for his old major to keep anything from him, Leon having served as his batman in Spain, but the servant instinctively knew that he was not soon to become privy to this latest secret.

His toilette having suffered sadly for his haste, Kit left his valet to straighten the mess his dressing room had become and slammed out of his chamber, intent on quitting the mansion without breakfast and heading for the nearest club that saw nothing wrong with a purely liquid breakfast. Grabbing the stair rail, Kit swung himself onto the stairs and pelted toward the foyer, only to be stopped in his tracks by a reedy cockney voice exclaiming: "Coo, Del, wouldya clap yer glims on the fine gentry mort! Puss like a thundercloud 'e's got. 'ang me fer a bachelor's sprig iffen it ain't the arl 'imself."

The object of this speech inclined his head and took in the sight of three banty-legged creatures dressed in Wilde livery standing at some semblance of attention near the wide front door. He knew what they were supposed to be, they were supposed to be footmen, but they looked for all the world to be escapees from Newgate—

low toby men who made their living by picking pockets and breaking into people's houses. Another example of my wife's discerning judgment of character, he decided angrily. *But these three cutpurses make Goliath and Tiny look like the cream of the crop!* Forcing his feet to carry him closer, he stopped on the bottom step and introduced himself.

"See, Del, Oi told ya it were 'im," the first footman said to the man standing closest to him before turning to his employer. "Morning', guv'nor," he chirped, tugging at his nonexistent forelock with one grubby hand. "Oi be Bob, m'self, an' this 'ere be Del an' 'is little brother, Ben. We's yer new footmen, like."

It had been a rough morning so far for the earl and he was not in any mood for this. What he was in the mood for was yelling, which he proceeded to do. "The bloody hell you are! You'll damn well be out of my house before I get home," he railed at them as Bob hastened to open the front door. "And *without* the family silver, or I'll bloody well turn you over to the constable!" he added, sticking his head back in the door before taking himself off down the steps and bounding up behind his pair of blacks and giving them the office to start.

"D'ya really think 'e'll set the bus-napper on us?" Del asked Bob in a quavering voice.

"He most assuredly will *not!*" replied a feminine voice, and the three small men turned to see Miss Ernestine Bundy descending the staircase, twin flags of color lighting her otherwise sallow face. "Not that I approve of you—er—*gentlemen* for one moment, you understand. If it were up to me I'd have you all out of here before your feet even knew they were moving. But it was Miss Jane—I mean, Lady Bourne—who had the hiring of you, and it is she and only she who can have the firing of you. It is only fitting—as his lordship, being away in the wilds of Spain for these past years, must surely have forgotten. Such a breach of etiquette," she sighed, shaking her head at the earl's indiscretion. "Lord knows I'll have my hands full trying to keep this household within the bounds of courtesy and propriety."

"Whew, boys, there's a 'ell of a goer, iffen ever Oi clapped my peepers on a finer piece!" Bob pronounced, awestruck, as he watched Miss Bundy's departing back disappearing into the morning room. "Kinda puts me in mind of mine aunt."

"Yer not sayin' that rum blowen is anythin' like that bawd in Tothill who calls herself an abbess—'er wit that covey of barber chairs and bats she calls 'er girls?"

Ben cuffed Del's ear in reprimand—for how dare he call Miss Bundy a whore? Miss Bundy was a fine lady, that's what she was; and if she were an abbess, he'd bet his eye and Betty Martin she'd have a better stable than one filled with bawds common enough to be called bats or barber chairs! To the uneducated, like Renfrew, who was listening to this interchange with great interest from the other side of the drawing-room door, a barber chair was a whore so common she allowed a whole parish to sit in her to be trimmed, and a bat—why, that unfortunate creature was no more than an ugly whore who could only get a customer after dark, when no one could see her face. In consideration, it might be seen as a good thing that Renfrew's education was lacking in this area, for not even Miss Bundy would prevail if Renfrew got on his high horse and decided Ben, Del, and Bob must go.

Del, holding his injured ear and sniveling into his sleeve, apologized to Ben, obviously the leader of the small gang, and peace once more reigned in the foyer. The three then took up positions on the long bench and rubbed their hands in eager anticipation of the vails the Bourne guests would offer them when they visited, and the revenge they would wreak on any so silly as to try to slip them a bum copper.

KIT WAS CHIRPING MERRY by noon. By three he was half seas over, and by five of the clock he was quite in his altitudes, which was how Ozzy Norwood found him when he sauntered into the club.

"Kit, old fellow, how goes it?" Mr. Norwood inquired, genially, sitting himself down in the chair next to his friend. "Dashed early in the day to be so deep in your cups, isn't it? What's to do? Surely it can't be your lovely wife who has you diving into the bottom of a bottle—and more than one, by the looks of it. What's forward? Bad news from the Peninsula?"

Kit looked up at his friend from beneath his furrowed eyebrows. "Ozzy," he remarked, spearing the man with his eyes, "you've known me almost all my life. Can you recall any great sin, any terrible crime, I may have committed in that time that I should be so cruelly persecuted now?"

"Persecuted, Kit?" Ozzy repeated, clearly at sea. "Nonsense, man. You're an earl, you're neck deep in money and estates, and your wife is the prettiest thing I've seen in three Seasons. You're *blessed,* man, not persecuted."

"She hired a black giant named Tiny and a dwarf who calls himself Goliath to man my stables. I've got three lowlife felons guarding my front door and a pregnant tweeny sniffling and sniveling her way up and down the hallways, and heaven only knows what other surprises await me in the remainder of the staff. And if that's not bad enough, I now have a wife who seduces me and then says it's *my fault!* What do you call that, Ozzy, rolling in the lap of happiness and pure bliss?"

While Kit's first comments did no more than extract a small, bemused smile from his friend, his last statement had Ozzy eagerly pulling his chair closer, his tongue nearly hanging out as he silently urged his friend to continue his monologue.

Lord Bourne leaned back in his chair, cradling his glass between his fingers. "Ah, I have got your attention, have I, Ozzy? Were I not so well and truly corned, I should die before admitting it, but Jennie has me as you see me, totally beyond thought of my own dignity. I shouldn't be telling you this," he went on, leaning confidingly in his friend's direction, "but I find myself in quite a quandary. It seems I had a bit of a nightmare last night—something I won't go into now—and my dear virgin bride, overhearing my calls of terror, came into my chamber to comfort me. Came into my bed, actually," he added as a sort of afterthought. "Anyway," he pressed on, pulling a face as he tried to concentrate his mind on what he was saying, "I woke up to the sight of my half-naked wife with her arms around me. Well, one thing led to another, so to speak, and suddenly we…er, never mind."

"Are you quite sure?" Ozzy inquired shakily, trying not to sound as eager as he felt. "Really, old man, I'm more than willing to listen to whatever you have to say. Go ahead, Kit, it's me, your old schoolboy chum—pour your heart out!"

Kit was drunk, but he wasn't totally beyond rational thought. Smiling a secret smile, he said shrewdly, "Use your imagination, Ozzy, if you cannot rely on your own experience. Perhaps you may have read a book—I do believe I once recall your saying you have read a book—that will explain the interlude that followed."

"Spoilsport," Ozzy commented gloomily, pushing out his full lower lip in a disappointed pout.

Kit laughed, although his humor did not last long. "Down, Ozzy, you're making a spectacle of yourself, salivating like that. I don't know why I am talking about this with you anyway, seeing as how you're not married and are unacquainted with the vagaries of the female mind."

"I am not. I have three sisters, you know," Ozzy pointed out mulishly. "You're the one lacking in experience—I've years of trying to cope with females."

"And have you learned anything?" Kit was so desperate as to ask.

Ozzy nodded his head vigorously. "I learned not to try to understand 'em. They're kind of like good whiskey—you don't try to analyze how it came to be, you just enjoy it."

"Yes, well, that may work well enough for you, but then you're not sitting here getting pie-eyed trying to figure out how you came to be the guilty party just because you made love to your own wife—and mighty good lovemaking it was, if memory serves. Well, I'll tell you this," Kit said earnestly, his liquid libations making him a little bit pot-valiant, "it'll be a cold day in hell before I'll let that silly chit dictate to me! I am master in my own house, and I'll not have some wet-behind-the-ears child cast me in the role of villain. In fact," he said, rising rather unsteadily from his chair, "I think I'll go home now and tell her so. And I'll jolly well toss her three footmen onto the flagway, just for good measure!"

"Good evening, gentlemen," came a silky voice from behind Kit. "Ozzy, mind if I join you? It seems my friends are late."

Ozzy got to his feet and extended his hand to the modishly attired gentleman who had spoken. "Dean, how good to see you. Where have you been? It's been an age."

Kit subsided into his chair, somewhat awestruck by the sight of the man Ozzy introduced as Dean Ives, a tallish, thin young sprig of fashion whose top-of-the-trees appearance would have made Leon weep with ecstasy. Mentally comparing the dashing Mr. Ives with the rather short, chubby Mr. Norwood, Kit could find little that would make anyone believe these two had a single thing in common. Yet, Kit noticed as the two fell into conversation, it seemed as if they were almost bosom chums—or had been until Kit returned to town and began monopolizing so much of Ozzy's time.

Why this friendship should bother Kit he had no idea, except for the rather selfish one that had him realizing that he had always quite enjoyed the near hero worship with which he had always been treated by Ozzy. Perhaps that is why he regarded Dean Ives in a rather cynical light, listening to the man's conversation for no more than a few minutes before deciding him to be an overly ambitious, vainglory sort of fellow, and a moody chap into the bargain. I'll bet he used to tie cats to trees and light their tails, he thought nastily, curling his lip. He couldn't suppose anyone more totally opposite to the mild-mannered, foot-in-mouth Ozzy if he tried.

It may have been this uneasiness, or this selfishness, that changed Kit's mind and had him accompanying Ozzy and Dean on a round of drinking and gambling rather than returning home to have it out with his wife. Kit didn't know.

He did know, even as tipsy as he was, that it was definitely the lesser of two evils.

CHAPTER SEVEN

TWO DAYS HAD PASSED since "it," as Jennie tended to think of the incident, had happened—two days during which she had spent her time variously devising ways to avoid her husband and wishing he would present himself so they could have it out once and for all.

At eleven of the clock on the morning of the second day, Renfrew entered the drawing room and presented his mistress with a heavily embossed card "Miss Lucille Gladwin to see you, my lady," he said, making her perusal of the calling card an unnecessary exercise. "Shall I tell her you are not at home?"

"Lucille Gladwin?" Jennie pondered aloud, tapping the edge of the card against her teeth. "Lucy Gladwin!" she exclaimed at last, her memory having been sufficiently nudged so that she recalled a distant cousin named Lucy—a rather rough-and-tumble tomboy, if her recollections were correct. "Oh, dear, can it really be she? Send her in at once, Renfrew. She's m'cousin, you know, and I shouldn't like to think we've kept her waiting."

Jennie rose and moved toward the door, her hands held out in front of her, and Lucy hastened into her cousin's embrace. "Thank goodness, Jane," the bubbly brunette vision in stylish pink-and-green sprigged muslin exclaimed. "For a moment there I thought you had forgotten me, not that you'd ever be so shabby as to forget the cousin who nearly drowned you in the lake. But, I tell you sincerely, it gave me quite a turn to be standing out there in the foyer with those footmen of yours. I had the uneasy feeling they were toting up the price of every stitch on me and planning their resale in Petticoat Lane."

"Not really, Lucy," Jennie laughed, leading her cousin to the settee, "but I would advise you to give them generous vails on the way out if you ever plan to set foot in Berkeley Square again."

"Jane, dear, I can't believe it! Look at you, you're all grown up!" Lucy exclaimed, bouncing up and down on the settee like a child who'd just been offered a treat. "I'm prodigiously sorry I haven't been to see you sooner, but Papa had banished me to the hinterlands for some folly or other I committed—I disremember right now which one it was—and I only just saw the wedding announcement in the *Gazette* when I returned to town and caught up on my reading of the back editions. One must always strive to stay *au courant* with the gossip, you know. So tell me, however did you snare an earl? I'm hanging out for one myself, you understand, and making a dashed mishmash of it so far, so you see my interest is truly self-serving."

Jennie made a face. "Actually, it was quite easy, Lucy. I just got caught in an animal trap, impulsively impersonated a village lass, was then punished for my sins by means of the earl's haphazard attempt at seduction, and *ta-da*—I'm a countess! It was really prodigiously simple."

"He *compromised* you!" Lucy chortled happily, clapping her hands in glee. "Oh, how delightfully romantic.

And now, of course, the two of you are madly in love and about to live happily ever after. Jane, you always were the lucky one."

"And you were always twice the dreamer I was," Jennie returned, forcing a laugh.

Lucy was not so overcome with her visions of true love not to notice the unhappiness in her cousin's eyes. "Jennie," she inquired concernedly, using her childhood pet name for her younger relative, "I know Christopher Wilde has something of a reputation as a womanizer, but I have it on the best authority that he has not so much as a single dasher in keeping since his return from the war. Oh, dear," she went on, seeing Jennie's frozen expression, "I fear I have shocked you."

"Not really, Lucy," Jennie assured her. "Association with Kit has taken me a long way from the schoolgirl miss you remember. I am a woman now, a wife—more's the pity."

Lucy sensed a juicy story somewhere and leaned forward, intent on prying every single detail out of her cousin, which was not a difficult thing to do considering Jennie's unhappiness and her natural reluctance to confide in Miss Bundy.

Within a very few minutes Lucy, wearing a sympathetic expression worthy of the most compassionate father confessor, had the whole of it, and her indignation knew no bounds. "That cad," she pronounced severely. "That unmitigated cad! Well, I can see I have arrived on the scene none too soon. How dare Kit—I shall call the monster Kit, since you do—incarcerate you in this great mausoleum whilst he gads about town like some carefree bachelor out on a spree? And then to *use* you like some sort of unpaid mistress—why, it is the outside of enough, I vow it is. Shabby, absolutely shabby!"

Jennie, although embarrassed at having bared her innermost secrets to Lucy, cousin or not, was intrigued. Here, she thought, was a true woman of the world—a woman who had three London Seasons beneath her belt. Surely Lucy would know just what to do, just how she should go on. If she were to put herself in Lucy's hands—as her cousin had already so kindly suggested— Kit would never know what hit him!

"'ere ya go, dearie, tea an' cakes, jus' like that old buzzard Renfrew said fer us ta bring ya. Sit up now, dearies, and 'ave at it." Lucy raised her head at this interruption and her mouth dropped open in amazement at the sight of two mirror-image dyed-blond women of indeterminate years, their faces made up like the lowest of painted harridans and their full figures tightly contained in the uniforms of parlor maids. They looked, she thought dizzily, like characters from one of Sheridan's lesser plays—a farce, no doubt.

Jennie looked up at the newcomers, smiled kindly at their appearance in the uniforms she had ordered made for them, and bade them put their burden on the table. "Thank you, Tizzie. You too, Lizzie, although I must remind you once again, it is not necessary for you to follow along in Tizzie's footsteps constantly. You must learn to operate independently of your sister sooner or later. Not that I'm reprimanding you," she added hastily as Lizzie seemed about to burst into tears.

The maids dropped elegant curtsies worthy of a matched set of duchesses and departed, watched all the way by the greatly intrigued Lucy, who felt she had somehow been catapulted onto the stage at Drury Lane. "I give up, Cousin," she said when at last she could find her voice, "Who or what were they? If I had been drinking, which I must point out is something I never do since that sad incident at Vauxhall last year, I would vow I was seeing double."

Jennie laughed, Lucy's bewildered expression banishing the last of her doldrums. "Those were my new housemaids. I have hired quite a bit of staff since my arrival in London. Tizzie and Lizzie are 'resting'—as actresses say when they are out of work. Of course, since they have been resting for the past eighteen months or more, I do believe they should revise that and say merely that they have chosen to retire. Not that they had not tried to find employment on the stage; but there is little call for identical twins nowadays—especially female twins 'on the windy side of forty,' as Tizzie explains it. The poor dears were desperate, you know. I had no other option but to employ them. After all, only a heartless creature could cast two such helpless lambs out into the street."

Lucy dissolved in giggles as her memory was jogged by Jennie's story. "Oh, Jennie, how this takes me back! Do you recall the summer you were ten and I was sent— much against my wishes, you know, since I was all of fourteen—to bear you company while our fathers went gadding off somewhere in the wilds to hunt some poor defenseless animals? I'll never forget Simpkins, the groom you employed in your papa's absence. He was wanted for murder or something, wasn't he?"

"He was not!" Jennie protested vehemently. "Well," she temporized, "I guess he was, at least a little bit, wasn't he? But it was all a misunderstanding, you know. Anyone of any sense could see Simpkins wouldn't harm a fly. And I was proved correct in the end, if you'll recall, and Simpkins was exonerated from all charges. He's still on the estate, you know," she added complacently, "although Papa refused to keep him on as groom after he fed Papa's favorite stallion half his pork pie one afternoon when he was too fatigued to fork out a new load of hay. Simpkins is now in sole charge of Papa's guns and fowling pieces—it seems he has an uncanny knack for firearms."

"I wonder why," Lucy pondered, tongue in cheek.

Wiping her hand daintily on a napkin after disposing of two of the sugar cakes served on the tray, Jennie changed the subject and began pumping Lucy on the various social doings currently on the agenda in town, and her cousin was soon prattling nineteen to the dozen about the many routs, balls, and parties the two of them could attend just as soon as she put it about that the new Countess of Bourne was ready to enter Society. "Lady Sefton's card party is tonight, and my invitation extends to include a second person. It will be prodigiously boring, but Sefton is such good *ton,* you know. What say we launch you this very evening? After all, if you wait for that disagreeable husband of yours to take you about, all your new gowns will be sadly out of date."

Talk of gowns soon led the two women upstairs for a critical perusal of the countess's new wardrobe. Goldie, sitting in a corner where she was repairing a rent in one of Jennie's underslips with large stitches and unmatched thread, was quietly amazed at the thoroughness with which Miss Gladwin inspected and disposed of first one outfit and then another, at last deciding on a demure yet stylish white silk frock decorated with blue stitching at the neckline and hem.

Goldie was then called front and center and given detailed instructions on the proper way of dressing her mistress's hair—casually upswept in the Grecian manner, with only a few seemingly haphazardly cascading curls dangling at her nape, a charge which left Goldie speechless, as it was the only style she knew. The maid curtsied and fled the room, part of her unbelieving of her good luck, and the rest of her shaking with the fear that one day Miss Gladwin would demand another hair-style entirely.

Miss Bundy, entering from the hallway just as Goldie sped by, head down and muttering something that sounded much like "woe is me," took in the situation at a glance and heaved her shoulders in a heartfelt sigh. "Miss Gladwin, I see it *is* you," she pronounced in much the same tones as one who had just discovered roaches in her larder.

"Ernie! By all that's wonderful, don't tell me you are still above ground. I thought surely Jennie's shenanigans would have put you to bed with a shovel long since." Lucy crossed the room to envelop the stiff person of Miss Bundy in a warm embrace. "Now, now, Ernie," Lucy scolded, stepping back a pace, "don't tell me you still haven't forgiven me for putting that toad in your bed?"

There were times, as Jennie could attest, when Miss Bundy could be the best of all good fellows—although those times were admittedly few and far between—and then again, there were times when the dear lady could be a gargantuan pain in the posterior. Clearly, Jennie could see from the faint rush of scarlet running up the back of her companion's scrawny neck, this was to be one of her less fun-loving days. "Did you have some-thing particular in mind, Bundy, or is this purely a so-cial visit?" Jennie asked as casually as she could, knowing full well Bundy was not above tossing Lucy out on her ear and saying it was on orders from her papa.

"This note just arrived from Boodle's, as you can see by the wax imprint. I would imagine it is from the earl," Miss Bundy informed her, handing the note over un-opened—and therefore quite reluctantly.

Jennie ripped open the missive with little regard for the elaborate seal and read the note with ever-increasing fury. "The nerve of the man," she said feelingly as she crumpled the missive into a ball and tossed it in the general direction of the fireplace. "He has *ordered* me to reserve two extra places at table tonight for his friends—he who hasn't shared a dinner table with me since our marriage." A martial light came into her eyes as she began pacing back and forth in high dudgeon. "For two pins I'd serve swamp grass on stale toast!" she said wickedly. "That would set him down a peg or two!"

"Pooh," Lucy said breezily. "That's letting the bounder off entirely too easily. Here now," she pronounced firmly, taking in Jennie's woebegone expression, "don't you go turning into a watering pot on me. If it's revenge you want—and I clearly believe you have every right to demand it—I believe I have a sure idea for throwing a bit of a rub in his lordship's way."

Every family had its black sheep, Ernestine Bundy knew, but why the Gladwin girl couldn't have had the good sense to be living in the wild outbacks of Australia or some such place she never would understand. The minute Renfrew had told her the identity of Jennie's visitor, Miss Bundy had felt apprehension flow into her body and become a crushing sensation in her breast. And within minutes of encountering the horrid child the woman's worst imaginings were well on the way to becoming fact. "Now see here, Miss Lucy," she began heatedly, only to be cut off by a languid wave of that young schemer's slim white hand.

"Now, Ernie, don't fly up into the boughs," Lucy warned with a chuckle. "You cannot have lived under the same roof with the newlyweds without sensing something is amiss between them. Jennie cannot allow this situation to go on if she is ever to establish herself as mistress of this household. Now," she said, pacing back and forth as she thought and spoke at the same time, "as I understand it, Kit's impolite order has been issued with no thought to any plans his wife may have made. I see no reason for the master of the house to be denied a dinner at home with his cronies; m'father raised me too well to deny any man on that head. *However,* I likewise see no reason for Jennie to forgo her own plans just because of some last-minute whim of her unthinking husband. Lord Bourne shall have his dinner, sure enough, but Jennie shall also have her night out at Lady Sefton's," she ended triumphantly. "Who said a girl can't have her cake and eat it too!"

"Lady...Lady *Sefton?*" Miss Bundy stammered, clearly much impressed. Who would have thought Lucy Gladwin could wrangle such a coveted invitation? Of course, Miss Bundy couldn't deny her baby the chance to move in such exalted circles. Knowing defeat when she tasted it, the companion retired from the field, leaving the two girls to plan and giggle their way through the afternoon.

THE EARL OF BOURNE was dressed all in blue, his velvet coat a light robin's-egg shade that contrasted nicely with his darkest midnight-blue inexpressibles; the whole set off by a snowy white lace-trimmed cravat tied in the latest style, and onyx jewelry of elegant, understated design. Admiring himself in the mirror in his dressing room, he did not need (though secretly enjoyed) Leon's flowery praise, believing himself amply armored for the task at hand—bowling over his recalcitrant wife with both his charm and his good looks.

Kit saw this night's tame entertainment as a foretaste

of things to come; a sort of gentle easing into society that would stand Jennie in good stead for the months of grueling social engagements that loomed ahead of them. Ozzy, he knew, was the perfect dinner companion for this, their first entertainment, as the man was as much renowned for his good *ton* as he was notorious for his mediocre intelligence. The only fly in the ointment was in the person of Dean Ives, a man Kit, even after two days' close acquaintance, just could not seem to like. But the fellow was a prime example of a tulip of fashion, one of those sarcastic, cynical sorts that breeze through the *ton* like scraps of yesterday's newspaper blown in the wind, and Jennie must learn to deal with his type sooner or later.

One last check of his toilette completed, Kit bounded down the steps to see if his wife had preceded him to the drawing room. It wouldn't do for her to be either overdressed or underdressed. He could only hope Miss Bundy could be relied upon to guide her in such matters. But when he entered the room he realized he had beaten her downstairs, and he was forced to content himself with sipping from a glass of wine while he waited for her entrance, which was not long in coming.

She looked wonderful! Kit straightened himself from his lounging position against the mantelpiece and crossed the room hurriedly to place a kiss on the back of her white-kid-encased hand. "You are ravishing tonight, kitten," he drawled smoothly, inwardly delighted when his words brought a warm blush to her cheeks. "You do me proud."

It was now or never, Jennie thought, gently disengaging her hand, which he was still fondling in the most disturbing manner. "Thank you, my lord, for your kind words," she replied in a small voice before moving to stand near the wine decanter in hopes he would take the hint and offer her a drink. Clearing her throat, which suddenly felt strangely dry, she launched into speech before her courage deserted her entirely. "What a shame I shall not be here for dinner, as Montague has planned a veritable feast. Please do try to eat all of it," she added swiftly, her tender heart forcing her to warn him of the French chef's abhorrence of seeing plates returned to his kitchen half-full.

Kit did not hear her warning, for he was too intent on the first part of her speech. "What do you mean, you will not be here?" he growled, grabbing her rather fiercely by the elbow. "Did you not receive my note? And where the deuce would you be going anyway? I was not aware you knew a soul in town."

Jennie looked rather pointedly at Kit's restraining fingers before gazing directly into his deep blue eyes (eyes so compelling her resolve nearly melted then and there) and coolly asking him to remove his hand from her person. "I have an invitation to Lady Sefton's card party this evening," she told him with some asperity. "My cousin Lucy Gladwin was kind enough to allow me to share her invitation. You see, husband, I am not destined to molder away in Berkeley Square just because you refuse to do your duty and introduce me to society. I am not entirely without resources of my own."

"Lucy Gladwin!" Kit exploded angrily. "That female disaster? God give me patience!"

Jennie stood up very straight, her chin reaching for the ceiling. "How dare you, sirrah! Lucy is not a disaster but a very dear, sweet person. I will not stand here and allow you to insult her. Have the goodness, sir, to step aside."

"In a pig's eye, I will!" Kit shot back, standing his

ground, planting his fists firmly on his hips for good measure. "I am your husband, madam, and I have every right to dictate where you shall go and with whom. Lady Sefton may be unimpeachable, but Lucy Gladwin is next door to a hoyden and no person for you to be seen with either formally or informally. God, madam, I wouldn't be caught dead within twenty feet of that incorrigible minx."

"Then I suggest you retire to your chamber, my lord, for she shall be arriving here at any moment. And if you make a scene, Kit," she warned direly, "I shall lie down on this carpet and throw a tantrum that will have your high and mighty guests dining out on their story of the Earl of Bourne and his mad wife for a month or more. Do I make myself clear, sir?"

"You dare to flout me?" Kit bellowed, clearly losing control of the situation. What imp of perversion had ever made him believe that Jennie was a reasonable, fairly biddable chit? The harridan now staring him down bore all the soft vulnerability of a charging Prussian, and he was at a loss as to how to deal with her.

Luckily, or unluckily, depending on whether or not Renfrew (who was standing outside the door) really desired to know how the argument would have turned out, the sound of the knocker interrupted the sparring pair and they swiftly took up positions at opposite ends of the room to await whatever guest was first to come through the doors.

"Look who we met outside, Kit, old fellow," Ozzy said in greeting as he entered the room, a smiling Lucy Gladwin hanging from his arm and Dean Ives bringing up the rear. "I haven't seen Lucy since that day she raced her curricle against Lord Beazley's in the park. Was that before or after your escapade in the reflecting pool, Lucy? I disremember, seeing as how you're always running some sort of rig."

"Now, Ozzy," Lucy admonished her grinning admirer as she caught sight of Lord Bourne's darkened features, "you mustn't embarrass me by bringing up past indiscretions. Since my sojourn in the country I am a veritable pattern card of respectability. I have to be, else I forfeit my allowance for the next decade, or so says my poor oppressed papa. I beat old Beazley all hollow, by the way," she added with a wink.

Jennie chanced a quick look at her husband and cringed inwardly at the thought he may have been just a teensy bit correct in his assessment of Lucy's behavior. Not that she was about to change her plans at this late date, especially now that he had stated his opposition so adamantly. "Lucy, dearest," she trilled brightly, welcoming her cousin, "you are just in time. If we tarry, Renfrew will be late in calling the gentlemen to dine— a sin of such magnitude I shudder to think how Montague will react. Gentlemen," she went on, curtsying sweetly in the newcomers' direction, "I do not believe we have been formally introduced."

Mr. Norwood, endlessly grateful that Lady Bourne was willing to overlook their first, rather lamentable meeting, hastened to introduce Mr. Ives and himself, as Kit showed every indication of having been stuffed and permanently mounted in front of the mantelpiece. Jennie liked Ozzy even better on this second acquaintance, but there was something about the knowing look in Mr. Ives's handsome face that reminded her of a weasel stalking a mouse. He was, she thought idly, just a little too smooth, a little too handsome for her liking; not like Kit, who had just enough of the raw youth about him to make him seem human.

After the introductions, and knowing full well that Kit wouldn't dare a scene in front of his friends, Jennie made short work out of bustling Lucy out of the house, pausing only to warn the gentlemen to be sure and eat all their peas.

CHAPTER EIGHT

LUCY'S PARTING ASSURANCE, tossed over her shoulder as Jennie half dragged her through the foyer, that her maiden Aunt Rachel—just then resting in the Gladwin coach outside—was to serve as their "respectable" chaperon for the evening did little to placate Lord Bourne's raging temper. If left to his own devices, in fact, one could only cringe in fearful anticipation of just what form his anger would take. But he was not given the option of being left alone as he, his weary brain reminded him, had dinner guests. Dinner guests, moreover, whose wide grins showed just a little bit too much enjoyment in their host's predicament.

"Gentlemen," he said with a social smile that failed to hide his chagrin, "I am being a poor host. Allow me to get you each a drink before Renfrew calls us to dinner." So saying, Kit went to the side table and poured three generous drinks, downing his own in one gulp before serving his guests. Get 'em drunk, he thought sagely. Get 'em drunk and they'll never remember in the morning whether a hostess sat at the bottom of the table or not.

When Renfrew summoned the small party to the dining table, Kit pulled the man aside for a moment and whispered his wish that his guests' glasses be topped up whenever they so much as took a sip of wine, and Renfrew, having served the Wildes for more years than the present earl had had hot dinners, did not so much as raise an eyebrow at the request.

For the next two hours and more the men feasted on some of the finest victuals served this side of Prinny's table, washing down each course with the best wines to be found in the Bourne cellars. Mr. Ives commented more than once on both the quality and the quantity of both, adding rather tackily his own estimate of the price of each exotic foodstuff and vintage. Indeed, Ozzy was so amused by his friend's assessing remarks that he dared to tease Dean by asking him if he intended to upend the dinner plate and check to see the crest of the manufacturer, a remark that drew a killing look from Mr. Ives and a raised eyebrow from his host.

Although the food, all prepared in the best French style, was everything that Kit could have asked for, the choice of five desserts seemed, to him, to perhaps be overdoing things just a tad. His dinner partners, stuffed chock full of buttered lobster, duckling, a variety of vegetables served in creamy sauces, and other delicacies, were likewise hard-pressed to do more than token justice to the impressive array of pastries and cakes that were meant to close their meal. A few bits of cheese and some cracked walnuts were desultorily picked over, but the groaning tray of sweets was returned to the kitchen virtually untouched as the men lit cheroots and leaned back in their chairs to watch Renfrew serve them with generously filled goblets of finest port.

The evening, Kit congratulated himself silently, seemed to be a success, even without Jennie's presence. He'd show the chit just how little she meant to him either way. He admitted that no matter how odd her choice in footmen and maids seemed to be, she had really outdone herself in filling his request for a good French chef. If he hadn't felt so out of charity with her he might have even believed he could be brought to compliment her on her choice. But no, he thought, savoring his small revenge, let her wonder whether or not he was pleased. Keep her dangling, that's the ticket, he decided. If she really wanted to please me she would be sitting opposite me right this very minute instead of gallivanting about town with that inane Gladwin chit.

Drat Jennie anyway! he thought, setting down his goblet with more violence than he had intended, causing his companions to look at him oddly. He had planned this evening as a sort of peace offering—a small introduction to society that, if she conducted herself correctly, would serve as a forerunner to other, larger engagements where he would magnanimously serve as her tutor as she dipped her toes into the stream of high society. She was his wife—certainly there was no way out of the marriage after the events of the other evening—and if she enjoyed herself in London it might make her come around a bit in her feelings for her new husband. Oh, the plan made sense, all right—at least to a man it did—but he had not counted on her finding her own way into society. Instead of being pleased at his efforts on her behalf she had deliberately flouted him, just as if he hadn't had her best interests at heart.

It is amazing how a man can rationalize away his own desires and have them appear as altruistic sacrifices, but then men have since time immemorial assumed they knew what was best for their women and then acted on those assumptions without ever once asking those same women whether or not they wished such a sacrifice.

Kit, being no worse or better than any of his fellow male ancestors, was now reacting in a typically male way—if Jennie didn't appreciate what he had done for her, he decided firmly, then he'd be damned for a dolt before he ever did anything nice for her again!

While Kit variously plotted revenge and entertained thoughts of sweetly forgiving Jennie as his fingers made casual inroads on the fastenings of the fetching gown she had worn that evening, Ozzy and Dean, feeling more than a little well to go, idly discussed the possibility of the three of them adjourning to one of the discreet houses on the fringes of Mayfair that specialized in the comforts of lonely men. Ozzy was just about to suggest the White House as one possible destination when there came a loud commotion at the doorway that led back to the kitchen.

"What in blazes?" Kit said irritably, turning in his seat to see what was going on, only to be startled into silence at the sight of the very large, burly man dressed in the all-white uniform of a chef who was at that very moment advancing upon his lordship waving a very menacing-looking meat cleaver. Bob, Ben, and Del, looking about as effectual as minnows trying to swim upstream against a tidal wave, hung from the wild chef's arms and were carried along, their feet nearly a foot above the floor.

"Sacrebleu!" the irate Montague bellowed in his deep, highly accented voice. "Show to me the *canaille* who dare fling Montague's tarts back in his face! A work of art, tossed aside like *entrailles, bagatelles!* Montague, he shall skewer the *coquin,* of a surety he will!"

"Quick, guv'nor," Ben yelled as Montague turned to shake Del off his arm as a giant flicks away a flea, "Make a break for it. Oi've got 'im."

Renfrew slipped from the room, unnoticed in the melee, as Kit, his army training coming to the fore, rose from his chair and delivered a punishing blow directly into Montague's ample midsection, which slowed him down a bit but did not stop him. Ozzy, never much in the way of anything athletic, did his little bit by tossing his goblet full of port at the chef—thinking to cool the man a bit—and then retired from the fray, sliding his pudgy frame under the Sheraton buffet table and his head behind the brass spittoon. Dean Ives, sitting farthest from the scene of the action, merely continued to sip delicately from his goblet and await further developments—which, fortunately for Kit, were not long in coming.

With a crash that set the china and crystal to shaking, the baize door swung back against the wall as Tiny advanced into the room with all the grace of a benevolent gorilla. *"Arrrrgh!"* he growled as his huge, beefy fists encircled Montague's neck and lifted the irate chef a full two feet off the floor, Ben and Bob falling to the carpet like autumn leaves caught in a breeze. Kit dropped his fists and stared, as did everyone else in the room, and it is possible the Frenchman would have choked if Goliath, entering the room in his rapid, skipping gait, hadn't grabbed onto Tiny's pants and climbed up the giant to whisper something in his ear.

Tiny looked at Goliath, who nodded once before sliding back down the mountain to the floor, and Montague, his face a truly lovely shade of purple, was allowed to live to cook another day. Bowing in his lordship's direction, Tiny shrugged his great shoulders shyly, smiled his sweet, stupid grin, and allowed Goliath to lead him from the room like a tame puppy. His anger effectively choked out of him, Montague—who had lost more than one job due to his lamentable temper—lapsed completely into French as he tried simultaneously to apologize to his master and hide the deadly cleaver behind his back.

"Now, now, m'lord," Renfrew soothed placatingly as Kit showed every intention of finishing the job Tiny had started, "there was no harm done. Lady Bourne had warned me about Montague's temperament, but somehow I had forgotten about it and allowed the plate of desserts to go back to the kitchen without first emptying it. Montague is a wonderful chef, sir, it's just that he gets a little touchy about his, er, creations. The rest of the staff humors him by hiding any leftovers out of sight—indeed, we have the best-fed staff in all London town, if I do say so myself, but you know how it is, every once in a while there's bound to be a little slipup. It's just a good job," the man ended earnestly, "that I remembered about Tiny in time."

"Yes, Kit," Ozzy put in as he crawled out from under the buffet. "Your lady *did* warn us to be sure to eat all our peas. Seems the fault lies with us—being as how we were put on notice. Now, now, old fellow," Ozzy went on as Kit showed some lingering signs of impending explosion, "think again of that lobster. Would you be so daft as to give that up just because the man has a bit of a temper? I call that very poor sporting of you, Kit, in truth I do."

In the end, Montague was allowed to return to his kitchen—where Ben, Bob, and Del had already effectively removed any remaining bits of evidence by filling their bellies with the riot-causing sweets—and the gentlemen, one still silently fuming, one obviously amused, and one curiously silent, adjourned to the drawing room, where, after a few minutes of rather anticlimatic conversation about such tame doings as the war and other mundane events, the party broke up at the ungodly early hour of eleven.

As Ozzy stepped out the door into the steps he ventured a parting shot at his friend. "Kit," he said, his lips trembling with suppressed mirth, "I'll say one thing for you—you sure know how to give a fellow a good time. Really, perhaps you ought to give a thought or two to charging admission to your little shows."

"I don't know about that," Kit responded, somehow summoning up a smile. "After all, Ozzy, it's m'wife's menagerie, not mine. You'll have to ask her."

"Oh, her ladyship's a prime right one. I have no fears on that head," Ozzy returned jovially. "Keep this up, Kit, and the Bourne mansion will become *the* place to see and be seen and your lady the premier hostess in the entire *ton!* Give her my regards," Mr. Norwood ended, skipping lightly down the steps to the flagway and saluting his friend before turning to enter his waiting carriage.

"I'll be sure to do that," the earl called after him, his smile becoming a little strained around the edges. Once the carriage had driven off, the smile, which had been frozen on his face like a Gunther ice, melted slowly and reformed itself into a fierce grimace. "Give her my regards, the looby says," he told the night sky before slamming the heavy front door with a satisfying swipe of his hand. "Of course I will, Ozzy, old fellow—and *then* I'll murder her!"

IT WAS JUST STRIKING TWO when Jennie came tiptoeing carefully up the stairs to her chamber, her head swimming just slightly from the wine she had imbibed in an effort to overcome the nervousness brought on by her first foray into society. Not that Lucy hadn't been by her side the whole evening, doling out gossip about some of their company while waving gaily to any number of acquaintances who called to her most familiarly as they made their way to tables already set up for tame-stakes gambling.

The card party hadn't been nearly as much fun as Jennie had thought—and certainly not as pleasurable as it should have been, considering she had chanced Kit's wrath in order to attend it. But then *ton* parties, according to Lucy, were for the most part dull as ditchwater. Jennie rather doubted this was true, or else why would Kit attend so many of them? But, she had thought as two of Lady Sefton's footmen carried a happily passed-out earl from the cardroom, perhaps men found amusement more easily come by than women.

No matter what, Jennie was now home again, and she could not help but wonder how Kit's evening had gone. Entering her chamber, her evening slippers dangling from one hand, she was just beginning to make out the shape of her furniture in the near darkness when a movement in the shadows caught her attention.

"Good evening, wife," came Kit's voice, oddly strained. "Much as I hate to upset you, I am afraid I have to tell you that your attempt at assassination failed. Your husband, ma'am, is still very much alive."

"I—I don't understand," Jennie stammered nervously, misliking the strange glitter in her husband's eyes.

Kit advanced on her, his smile making her stockinged toes curl defensively into the carpeting. "Really?" he purred, sliding a hand around Jennie's throat to finger the curls at her nape. "Allow me to refresh your memory. Do the words 'eat all your peas' ring any bells for you, ma'am?"

Jennie's stomach dropped to her knees, and she made a face that looked as if she had just bitten into a rather bitter pickle. "Montague," she breathed softly. "I knew I should have remained at home. Drat Lucy and her fine speeches about putting you in your place."

"Please, kitten," the earl said silkily, his fingers tightening just slightly, "have the decency not to include Miss Gladwin in this particular escapade. She may have been the instigator of your little mutiny tonight, but I know for a fact that it was not she who had the hiring of that maniacal Frenchman. Oh no. Montague bears all the marks of your handiwork." Exerting a bit more pressure, Kit directed Jennie's footsteps toward the bed and pushed her rump down onto it. "Do you have any idea how disconcerting it is to look up from your own dinner table to see death looking you in the eyes? It may serve to put me off my feed for a month. Well?" he asked, staring down into her fear-widened eyes, "Have you nothing to say for yourself?"

It was quiet in the room for some moments while Jennie searched wildly for something to say. At last, her wits deserting her entirely, she gave voice to the only thing that her brain could muster: "Do you not care for green peas, then, my lord?"

Kit dropped into a nearby chair and let his forehead rest on his hands. "God give me patience," he groaned, shaking his weary head. He looked up at Jennie, saw her tear-bright green eyes, and instantly felt as if he had been cruelly mistreating a lost kitten. She was such a baby—such an innocent, trusting baby. She shouldn't yet be allowed out on her own, not with her penchant for picking up strays and bringing them back with her. Unable to vent his spleen by taking vengeance on his wife's nubile body, Kit reached out his hand for the nearest object—which happened to be a rather fine crystal vase—and flung it full force into the cold fireplace.

It landed with a satisfying crash, which went a long way toward easing the constriction in the earl's chest, at least for the few moments it took for Goldie and Miss Bundy to burst upon the scene in their nightclothes, anxious to see what was amiss.

Miss Bundy's eyes took in the scene in a glance, and, as she had been informed by Renfrew of the events earlier in the evening, she had no doubt as to what was now taking place. His lordship was merely making a critical statement concerning Jennie's choice of chef.

But Goldie was another matter. In her simple brain the thought formed that her mistress was in dire danger of imminent death—or worse. Racing to Jennie's side, she flung her ample arms wide and pronounced dramatically, "You'll not get ta her lessen it's over me own dead body!"

Miss Bundy, sadly aware that she was standing before his lordship dressed only in her nightgown, but also realizing her intervention was needed, pushed herself into disgusted speech. "Goldie," she said condemningly, "there are times your ignorance would disgrace a Hottentot. His lordship is not here to do murder; it's just that the vase slipped from his hand as he was making a point in a discussion he was having with Lady Bourne. Now drop the pose of martyr you have struck and remove your scantily clad body from the room posthaste."

Goldie looked down at her coarse white cotton gown and rapidly pulled in her outflung arms to wrap them protectively around her upper body. "'Pon my soul!" she exclaimed, mortified.

"Upon yours, maybe," Miss Bundy was pushed to say unkindly, "but thank goodness, not upon mine. Now scoot!"

"You want me to leave?" Goldie asked, clearly still of half a mind to stay and protect her mistress.

"What would you suggest as an alternative?" Miss Bundy asked acidly.

From his place in the corner, Lord Bourne was heard to mumble under his breath: "We gather here to lend prayers…"

This irreverent aside was too much for Jennie, who laid herself back on her bed and began to howl with relieved laughter. Kit might be an easily lit match, but luckily, he was one whose temper burned brightly for only a moment before common sense and his wonderful love of the ridiculous effectively snuffed the flame.

Within moments of Jennie's delighted chuckling, Miss Bundy had successfully herded the confused Goldie, still vainly trying to cover her "private parts" with her hands (now placed strategically behind her as she scuttled toward the door), and Lord Bourne rose from his seat to lock the door behind them.

"Now, kitten," he began softly once the key was safely in his breast pocket, "perhaps we can discuss your punishment?"

IT WAS NEARING DAWN when the earl returned to his own chamber, a man much changed from either the angry one who had waited countless hours for the return of his delinquent wife or the amused one who had waggled his eyebrows in mock menace as he approached his wife's bed, intent only on making her feel a bit of the discomfort he had felt earlier. Now it was a thoughtful earl who paced his chamber, his hands clasped tightly behind his back.

How had things gotten so out of hand? When had teasing turned to something infinitely more intense, and vague thoughts of revenge receded to be replaced by a desire to feel his wife's warm form beneath him as he burned kisses over every inch of her soft body?

Memories of the past hours crowded into his brain, and he could close his eyes and relive every moment, almost as if he had been hovering above the bed looking down at the passionate pair clinging to each other among a tangle of sheets and blankets. Jennie's soft cries, begun in fear but swiftly turning to whimpers of mingled delight and anticipation, echoed disturbingly loud in his ears, and he sank into a chair as his mind recalled the sound of his own voice, soothing, cajoling, reassuring—and, in the end, begging, pleading for blessed release. Never, he told himself passionately, never before in his life had he felt such intensity, such a deep need to possess, to enfold, to cherish. And more—much more.

He could now recapture, with almost physical pain, the rapture he'd felt as Jennie's young head bent to run light kisses the length of the wicked scar on his side. What had he felt when she had caressed him so unselfishly? Could that strange constriction in his throat have been the first stirrings of love? "Nonsense!" he nearly shouted into the early-morning haze. "Utter nonsense! By God, I don't even *like* the balmy chit. Playing at love, just as she plays at lady of the manor. Bloody hell, the idiot picks her companions with all the discretion and judgment of a child allowed to choose her own menu—never thinking about a thing but what tastes good, and giving not a single thought to what's good for her."

That little speech gave the earl pause. It was one thing to rationalize away Jennie's predilection for eccentrics who tugged at her gentle heart, but it was another to classify himself as one of her pet projects. Could it be the affection she had showered on him so freely just a short time ago had stemmed from some warped idea of hers that he was in need of her protection and direction, like Tiny, or Del, or even the volatile Montague? Did she see him as some sort of misfit, or had her tender heart been wrung by his tale of Denny and the wound he had sustained? That would explain her gentle, ministering attitude, though, he thought hopefully, it certainly would not explain her passion.

Perhaps the little dreamer had decided that he was a romantic hero and she believed herself in love with him. Wouldn't that be a kick in the head! First he was saddled with the girl as an unwanted bride, and now he was in danger of suffering through her first encounter with puppy love. It was more than any one man could be expected to bear.

Kit crossed to the connecting door and peeked in on his sleeping wife, all curled up in a little ball in the middle of the huge bed and looking for all the world like a sleep-warmed child. His heart did a strange sort of flip-flop in his breast and he was hard-pressed not to crawl back beneath the sheets and cradle her golden head on his bare chest. He resisted the impulse, knowing full well he was getting in much too deep for a man whose very last wish in life was to be saddled with an adoring wife.

Returning to his own room once more, he lit a cheroot and went to look out his window onto the square below. She was getting to him, this child bride of his, and he'd be damned if he'd allow her to make further inroads into his self-sufficiency.

Then why, he asked himself on a deep sigh, did his arms feel so damned empty without her?

JENNIE HELD HER BREATH until the door closed, with Kit safely returned once more to his own chamber. He had stood looking down at her for so long she was sure she would give herself away. But just as she felt sure she would have to open her eyes, he had at last turned away. She didn't know why she didn't want him to know she was awake, she only knew she couldn't face him until she had time to think over what had happened between them and come to some sort of conclusion as to just what it all meant.

Had that really been her, Jennie Maitland Wilde, who had behaved with such wild, even wicked, abandon in the wee hours of the night? Could it have been the same Jennie Maitland Wilde who now lay here, shivering in a tight fetal position, striving vainly to pretend to herself that nothing earthshaking had happened? But she could not deny the facts, any more than she could deny the lingering lassitude that had her twisting slowly between the sheets so that her suddenly sensitive skin could relive in part the wonderful, cherished feeling of being held so tightly in Kit's embrace.

She *was* a wanton—there was no other explanation for it. But how could she help herself, when Kit was so very handsome, and so very *experienced!* That was it! He had seduced her *again!* No, her honest self denied as she punched her pillows and tried once more to find the sanctuary of sleep. He did not seduce me. It was…it was more of a joint seduction, with both parties equally at fault.

All right, she told herself rationally. It was one thing to allow oneself to be made love to, but it was quite another to *initiate* a second round of lovemaking. And that mad impulse to kiss away the pain of his scar—why, Bundy would die of mortification if ever I told her I had been so forward.

"So why should you be telling Bundy?" she said aloud, sitting up sharply in the bed. "You are a married lady now, not some schoolgirl who must give an accounting of her every move. Although," she went on, a ghost of a smile lighting her worried features, "it might be interesting to see Bundy's reaction to a full recitation of last night's events. For once the roles of tutor and student would be reversed, I believe." This little bit of silliness lightened Jennie's somber mood for a moment, but nothing could keep her mind overlong from her newest dilemma. It had been one thing for Jennie to disregard a single "tumble," as Goldie would term it, but it was quite another to sweep the abandoned lovemaking just past under the rug and pretend it had not happened.

Besides, she wasn't really sure she wanted to forget. She really believed she might just be doing the unfashionable—falling in love with her own husband. Then another, sobering thought intervened. Obviously Kit did not feel the same, else why would he steal out of her chamber before dawn like some thief? Couldn't he face her in the morning after the things he had whispered into her ear during the night? This put a whole new complexion on the matter, Jennie knew, worrying her bottom lip with her teeth. Now she was more confused than ever, and she mentally tried to hold back the dawn so that she would not have to face her husband over the breakfast table and try to think of something to say other than "Ah, yes, Kit. That—please do *that!*"

MONTAGUE OUTDID HIMSELF with the breakfast buffet, the menu offering more varieties of meats and side dishes than the best hotel in London. And, to show his newfound mellow temperament, he did not throw more than three platters against the wall when every offering but the toast was sent back to the kitchen untouched.

Poor Montague. How was he to know that the Bourne morning room, visited separately by the earl and countess in a series of strategic advances and retreats that would have done credit to the wiliest generals, was the last—the very last—place either of the parties would envision as a setting fit to encourage an appetite?

The earl, first down that morning, had done nothing more than order Renfrew to bring him a glass of brown ale before, looking about him like a culprit waiting for the law to clap him on the shoulder, he slipped from the house; and the countess, who had tiptoed to and from the morning-room door three times before deciding it was safe to enter, had done no more than nibble at a crust of toast before, even bearing in mind the great stress her actions were placing on Montague, she too ignobly retired from the field.

As this strange dance of advance and retreat, this playing of stay-least-in-sight, was to go on for over a week, it was no wonder that Bob, Ben and Del were soon applying to Charity—the poor, dear thing—to let out their uniforms at the waist. After all, as Bob said repeatedly as he downed yet another light French pastry, *somebody* had to keep the balmy froggie from murdering them all in their beds!

CHAPTER NINE

"THIS BUILDING is relatively new, you know," Lucy told Jennie as the other girl sat in the Gladwin private box and stared about her openmouthed. "Covent Garden burned down in 1808, I believe it was, and all this had to be rebuilt."

"It's beautiful…simply beautiful!" Jennie told her cousin in awestruck tones. "It must have cost a fortune."

Lucy laughed, partly at Jennie's naive gawking and partly at her naive observation. "Indeed it did, cousin. So much so, in fact that the owners tried to raise the prices to pay for it. Did you never hear of the O.P. riots?"

"O.P. riots?" Jennie repeated questioningly. "No, I can't say as I have. Were they very bad?"

"That, dear coz, depends on whether you were one of the owners or one of the paying public. For the owners, I daresay it was a disaster. As for the public, I do believe it was a bit of a lark. The gentlemen in the pits as well as those in the galleries spent night after night throwing oranges at the stage, rattling rattles, blowing horns, shouting and stamping their feet—even singing songs specially written for the occasion. All to get a roll-back to the *Old Prices*. It really did dampen the actors' enthusiasm for appearing on stage."

"Oh my," Jennie observed, feeling much in sympathy with the poor actors. "Do you really think that was fair?"

"Fair or not, it must have been great fun. I only wish I had been 'out' in time to participate. Why, I can remember Papa going off to the theater wearing his special O.P. hat on his head and his custom-made O.P. medal on his breast. The ladies, as I recall, had fans, handkerchiefs, oh, all sorts of things, embroidered with the letters *O.P.*, and there was barely a building in all London that did not have those initials scribbled on its walls. Papa said it was the best of good fun—what with the whole of the audience spending every night at the theater, dancing, singing, and jumping back and forth on the benches. The prices," Lucy ended happily, "were quite naturally rolled back. After all, no one can stand for long against the might of a combined assault of good, honest Englishmen."

"Oh, Lucy, you should have been born a man," Jennie said, taking in the brightness of her cousin's expression.

But the smile slowly faded from Lucy's face as she caught sight of a couple in a box across the way, "Not really, coz," she said solemnly. "Don't make it too obvious, but take a look across the way at the box three to the left of the Royal Enclosure." Jennie made a fuss of adjusting her fan and peered in the direction Lucy had indicated. "Do you see the fierce-looking old dragon in purple with those absolutely nauseating violet plumes sticking out of her head?" Jennie nodded. "All right," Lucy continued, her voice oddly breathless. "Now look at the man sitting in front of her and to her right. That is Lord Thorpe, the man I am going to marry. *Now* you can see why I am glad not to have been born a boy. Isn't he the most handsome man you've ever seen?"

Jennie trained her eyes on the gentleman in question

and could not help but agree that he was a fine-looking specimen of mankind, although she herself had a preference for dark-haired men such as Kit. Besides, Lord Thorpe had the look of the snob about him, just in the way he was casting his eyes about him now in barely concealed boredom. "Who is that girl sitting next to him?" she asked Lucy, thinking that the young female dressed in demure, rather color-robbing white must be the reason for Lord Thorpe's rather painted expression.

"That's Lady Cynthia, Lord Thorpe's fiancée," Lucy told her cousin, a rather waspish note entering her usually lilting voice.

"Fiancée!" Jennie choked, whirling to look at her cousin in astonishment. "Doesn't that rather depress your ambitions? I mean, it isn't as if the man is free."

"It does lend a bit of challenge to the thing, doesn't it?" commented Lucy irrepressibly. "I merely told you I was going to marry the man. I never said it was going to be easy."

Jennie was about to question Lucy further, perhaps even intending to try to drum some sort of sense into the widget's head, when a movement in the previously empty box a quarter of the way around the level theirs was situated on effectively robbed her of coherent speech. "Well," she snapped, when her voice at last returned to her, "if that isn't the most odious thing I could ever have imagined!"

Lucy looked at her strangely. "I don't think it's quite that bad, Jennie," she told her cousin sourly. "After all, did I rake you over the coals when you told me about your Kit? I thought you'd stand my ally in this, cousin, really I did."

"Oh, no, Lucy!" Jennie interrupted hastily. "I was not condemning *you,* truly I wasn't. It's just that I just caught sight of Kit entering that box down there. No! Don't look now for pity's sake, I think he might have seen us. He's got Mr. Ives and Mr. Norwood with him."

"Don't you wish to see those gentlemen?" inquired Lucy, still not seeing anything too out of the ordinary in the whole affair. "I quite like Ozzy myself, though I can't say I'm terribly fond of Mr. Ives. Why not leave Aunt Rachel here and trot on down to visit with them before the first act?"

Jennie spoke through clenched teeth. "Because they have three of those opera dancers you said he didn't have in keeping with them, that's why! Oh! The nerve of the man! Just because I have been avoiding him he thinks he can parade about town with some...some *lightskirts*. Didn't he know I'd be here tonight? How could he do this to me, Lucy? Has the man no sense of decency?"

"He might have, Jennie," replied Lucy realistically, "although I cannot actually speak for the man, not having ever been that closely acquainted with him; although his being an officer predisposes anyone to assume he is also a gentleman, doesn't it? As to *how* he dared to do the thing, I believe the answer might just lie in the fact that you haven't spoken a single word to the man in a week and he had no idea you would be attending the theater tonight with me. Now really, dear, keep your voice down or you'll wake Aunt Rachel, a development I'd much rather avoid, as the woman has this infuriating habit of asking entirely the right questions. Now, now," Lucy pressed, seeing Jennie's woebegone expression, "don't go into a taking. After all, it isn't the end of the world."

"Don't worry about me, Lucy," Jennie returned, rallying. "I shan't weep millstones over that beast. Oh,

I admit to having been a trifle cast down momentarily, but I have no plans other than to stay here and enjoy the play. And I'll be dashed if I'll sit and stew just because my husband chooses to display his lack of good taste in public."

Jennie's splendid recovery earned her Lucy's deep admiration, and that recovery lasted all the way to the end of the second act of *The Clandestine Marriage*—a story concerning the marriage of a rich, vulgar cit to a bored lord of the realm who openly hated the cit. The cit, it evolved, couldn't have cared less, just as long as her marriage meant she could go to court.

Was that how Kit saw her? Jennie questioned in her agitation. Did he think she saw him as a stepping-stone for him alternately to use her and then discard her, only to parade about in public with loose women to show his disdain? Well, the countess of Bourne thought, I do believe Lord Bourne is sadly out if he thinks he can depress my pretensions to "society" that easily. But before I can hold my head up in that society I must rid him of the idea that he can continue on with his ladybirds so publicly.

"Lucy," Jennie purred sweetly to her cousin as the curtain fell, "I have just had the most happy notion. I believe I shall make use of this timely intermission to pay a visit upon my husband in his box." Rising from her seat, Jennie stepped carefully around the slumbering Aunt Rachel and looked back at her cousin. "Are you coming, Lucy?"

"You must be joking!" Lucy chuckled, a broad smile lighting her features. "I wouldn't miss this for the world! I vow it will be famous, absolutely famous!"

KIT WAS NOT A HAPPY MAN, and he hadn't been one for a long time—ever since the morning he had stood gazing out over Berkeley Square trying vainly to figure out how a nice fellow like himself had ever gotten into such a mess as this. So complete and permanent had been his rapid descent into the doldrums that Ozzy, always out to do his possible when it came to his friends, had decided to take desperate measures. To Ozzy, desperate measures meant Mademoiselle Yvette de La Fontaine, Drury Lane's latest answer to the Englishman's love of "finest French pastry." Too fatigued to enter into an argument with his well-meaning friend, Kit agreed to accompany Ozzy and Dean to Covent Garden, La Fontaine and two of her friends from the chorus making up the remainder of the small theater party.

The actress, dressed to within an inch of outright ridiculousness, and smelling to high heaven of some heavy French scent, seemed to think she had reached the very pinnacle of success in being seen on the arm of the wealthy, handsome Earl of Bourne and planned to make the most of the evening. Hanging daintily from his lordship's arm ever since the Bourne carriage had picked them up from their temporary quarters in Clerkenwell, La Fontaine had worn a dreamy smile brought on by visions of the jewels and furs the earl would shower on her once he had established her in a discreet love nest somewhere on the near fringes of Mayfair. So intense was her absorption in her dream that she did not notice that the earl was paying next to no attention to her.

While Kit sat mute in his seat, variously wishing it were Jennie who sat by his side and wondering if it might still be possible to rejoin his regiment and die a heroic death in action, Ozzy, feeling very full of gallantry and good spirits at his coup in getting Kit into company once again, took an inventory of the occupants of the nearby boxes. The house was full tonight, he noticed idly, with all the world and his wife out to see the play and be seen. There's a good-looking yeller-haired wench, he remarked idly to himself before, suddenly sitting up very straight in his chair, he exclaimed: "Good God, man! Kit, look over there a moment. It's your wife—and looking fine as ninepence, if I do say so myself."

Kit's ennui disappeared instantly, and he leaned forward just in time to see his wife turning back toward Lucy Gladwin—too late to see the look in her eyes, but definitely in time to see the stiffness of her spine and the bright flush of color running up her neck. "This'll set the cat among the pigeons," he muttered under his breath before saying more loudly and with every intention of lacing his speech with a languid drawl, "So it appears, Ozzy. What of it? Lucy's aunt is with them, so they're adequately chaperoned. Do sit back, man, else you'll fall into the pit and Celeste there will have to endure the play without your services as interpreter."

Ozzy, never known for his quick wit, was still sufficiently up to snuff to know having your wife and your latest flirt under the same roof—even a roof so large as that of Covent Garden—was not exactly a sought-after experience. While marveling at Kit's show of unconcern, Ozzy was much more impressed with Jennie's behavior, as he was sure she had seen them by now. "Like that girl excessively, you know," he approved aloud, turning in his seat to look Kit square in the eyes. "And you know what, friend? I don't think I'd like it above half if you were to hurt her. Game as a pebble, your wife, and it kind of damps one to think she might be made uncomfortable because of your shabby behavior."

"You're becoming damned moral, Ozzy," remarked

Kit sarcastically, "considering it was your idea I accompany you here tonight."

Dean Ives, so far a quiet bystander in this exchange, decided it was time to change the subject. It wouldn't suit his purposes to have the earl and Ozzy at daggers drawn. Leaning across the back of his own companion—rudely pushing her drooping ostrich feather headdress out of the way without so much as an excuse me—he endeavored to engage the men in a conversation. "You missed a most invigorating spectacle this morning, gentlemen. A few friends and myself went to Holburn to view a badger being drawn in a menagerie there. I must say, those places employ the most extraordinary-looking people. I wonder, Kit, these servants of your lady wife's—do you think any of them came from there? I know you have a giant and a dwarf. Do they do tricks, d'you think? I say, perhaps they juggle?"

"How would you like to juggle your front teeth?" Kit inquired pleasantly enough, effectively putting an end to the discussion, and it was difficult to tell just who of the party was most grateful when the curtain rose on the first act.

When the curtain fell again Kit chanced a quick peek in the direction of the Gladwin box, just in time to see his wife departing through the door at the rear. Where the deuce could she be going? he thought angrily. And unaccompanied as well. But no, there goes Lucy, trailing behind her like some grinning idiot off to see the fair. What maggot can Jennie have taken into her head now?

Kit did not have long to wait for his answer, if he had only been paying attention, as there soon came a knocking on the door of the Norwood box. When Ozzy, having detached himself from his clinging feminine companion with some difficulty, at last opened the door, it was to see Lady Bourne waiting without, Lucy Gladwin standing behind her, smiling and waggling her gloved finger at him. "Well, Mr. Norwood, have you been somehow transformed into marble?" Jennie asked, tilting her head inquiringly.

"Lady Bourne!" Ozzy squeaked, his voice climbing octaves he thought he had left behind at the age of thirteen. "Do you really think...I mean, that is to say...oh, ma'am, are you really *sure*..."

Jennie put the man out of his misery. "My husband, Mr. Norwood. Is he not within?"

Ozzy could only nod, his voice now having completely deserted him.

If Jennie had been in better spirits she might have felt her tender heart moved by Mr. Norwood's plight. But she was feeling sorely tried at the moment, and her charity was all directed toward herself. Her features hardening slightly, she looked the uncomfortable man straight in his anguished blue eyes and pushed pointedly: "Then perhaps you will have the goodness to step aside and allow us to enter."

Kit had been deep in his own thoughts and was therefore guilty of paying little attention to what had been going on at the door, but when he saw his wife guiding her skirts through the narrow opening he immediately knew what it was like for a drowning man to see his entire life flashing past his eyes in an instant.

"We have the guests!" La Fontaine lisped delightedly, being none too intuitive and not feeling the sudden chill that had descended on the box. "Will none of you fine gentlemen make us the—how you say—introductions?"

Refusing to give Jennie the satisfaction of seeing how much she had discomfited him, Kit rose and bowed to the newcomers. "How remiss of me. Of course you must be introduced. Ladies, this charming woman is my wife." He then went on with the more formal, detailed introductions, steadfastly refusing to look directly into Jennie's eyes to see the hurt he was sure was lurking there.

That Jennie was hurting was not an exaggeration. But if Kit believed that Jennie was about to let him or anyone else know it was killing her, absolutely killing her, to see her husband sitting so comfortably next to that obvious lady of the evening, they were sadly out. "You are French, Mademoiselle de La Fontaine?" she said brightly once the introductions were complete. "How marvelous. It has been an age since I've had anyone to practice my rather lamentable schoolgirl French on—do you mind?" Not waiting for an answer, she launched into a cheerful monologue touching lightly on the weather, the play they were seeing that evening, and the oppressive crush of people in the lobby clamoring for lemonade during the intermission, all conducted in flawless French.

Looking faintly dazed by this flurry of words, La Fontaine—who had been born and raised within spitting distance of Piccadilly—frowned intently, tilted her head to one side in deep thought, and then replied brightly, *"Oui!"*

Jennie clapped her hands in seeming delight. "Quite right, mademoiselle!" she trilled. Then leaning down more closely to the seated woman, Jennie delivered the *coup de grace.* "Mademoiselle," she said almost gently, *"savez-vous que vous aver le nez d'un cochon?"*

Ozzy, who had been taking a restorative sip from the silver flask he carried with him in case of emergencies, started violently, felt a bit of the fiery fluid slide down his throat improperly, and could not resist a fit of coughing that had people from several of the nearby boxes looking to see just who was dying.

It did not help Ozzy's sensibilities overmuch either when La Fontaine, totally uncomprehending that Lady Bourne had just remarked that the actress had the nose of a pig, only smiled vacantly and said, *"Merci, madame,"* before sitting back complacently to push at the curls in her elaborate coiffure.

"Minx," Kit whispered in his wife's ear as he decided the farce had gone on long enough and it was more than time someone with some sense took charge of the situation. Placing his hand firmly beneath her gloved elbow, he steered her neatly out of the box and into a corner of the nearly deserted hallway. "What were you trying to do, kitten, give poor Ozzy in there apoplexy? And you," he went on, turning to skewer Lucy with his accusing eyes. "I believe I have you to blame for most of this. Without your lamentable influence my wife would not have taken such a maggot into her head as to make a spectacle of herself by being seen in public with one of the muslin company."

"Why ever not, Kit?" Jennie cut in acidly. "It doesn't seem to bother you unduly, and you certainly have more consequence than either of us." Jennie would have said more, much more, but she belatedly realized that the vein in the side of Kit's neck was throbbing in agitation and she wisely subsided into mutinous silence.

By the time Kit escorted his wife and her cousin to their own box the intermission had been over for some minutes and they could return to their seats without being seen; but this was only after they reluctantly informed his lordship of their plans for the rest of the evening and promised not to blot their copybooks any further unless Lucy wished her father to hear of this night's work.

Once back in his own seat, the sullen La Fontaine, having unfortunately discovered just what Lady Bourne had said to her (thanks to Dean Ives, who had been only too happy to enlighten her), demanded to be taken home "toot-sweet," which suited Kit perfectly. But before he could make good his escape, Kit had to endure a few good-natured jibes from Ozzy. "I told you your wife was a rare right one, old fellow. Lead you a pretty dance, she will, and I can't think of a fellow more deserving of it, I swear I can't. Tell me, for I must admit to a great deal of curiosity—what are you going to do now? Murderers hang, you know."

Kit's remaining store of humor—not a great amount—evaporated at the sight of Ozzy and Dean wearing such broad grins at his expense. "What happens now is that I escort Mademoiselle de La Fontaine back to her lodgings and then go on to meet my wife at the after-theater party she and Miss Gladwin plan to attend. As to what you two do, why, you may go to the devil for all I care, seeing as how it was your idea to come here tonight in the first place. If you recall, all I was looking for was some company at billiards at the Royal Saloon."

Looking down at the men with a fierceness that would give a charging rhinoceros pause, he said coldly, "I need not remind you that anything that happened here tonight will go no further. My wife is still so unknown in town that no one was probably aware she was even in this box tonight. As for Miss Gladwin, nothing she does surprises anyone, and I doubt the gossips will even bother to prattle about this latest ruckus of hers. Gentlemen, do I have your word?"

"Need you ask?" Ozzy responded, trying his best to look insulted. "Don't worry your head about us. Just go and do the pretty with your wife, old fellow. We'll take care of things here."

"Indeed yes," Dean Ives seconded. "It was ever so amusing an interlude, but you may rest assured, my dear fellow, that my memory is most adaptable. Anything for a friend, you know," he added ingratiatingly, thinking to himself that his lordship might put on a fine show of disliking his wife but deep down there was a good chance the man was besotted with the chit. Not that he could blame him overmuch, for the girl was a tempting enough morsel, but Mr. Ives knew better than to allow his heart to rule his head. So he kept these thoughts to himself, knowing they would not be taken kindly if he offered them as advice, and filed them away in case he should ever have use of them. One never knew what could be helpful to a man who lived by his wits, as did Mr. Ives.

THE TON PARTY already in progress in the luxurious townhouse located in Portman Square was, in its hostess's estimation, a roaring success, sure to be talked about as one of the grandest crushes of the Season. Of course the Season was young yet, actually only in its infancy, but Lady Kenwood knew she had set a high standard that would have her dearest friends gnashing their teeth when it came time to plan their own tame entertainments.

Jennie and Lucy, having arrived long after the receiving line had been dismantled, found it easy to blend in with the crowd standing about the fringes of the over-heated ballroom where a sprightly country dance was in progress. This was Jennie's first real exposure to society, her experiences with local dances at home not able to hold a candle to this exhibition of rich surroundings and impeccably dressed guests. Indeed, if it hadn't been for the knowledge that Kit was soon to join them she might have been able to abandon herself to the enjoyment of the scene. As it was, she felt like a prisoner about to be led to the block, and her furrowed brow and rather fierce expression kept the gentlemen, more than a few of whom had decided there was a real beauty in their midst, at a distance.

It was left to Lucy to procure for them glasses of champagne, which she did with little difficulty, as she seemed to be on a friendly, first-name basis with nearly every gentleman in the room. It was likewise left to Lucy to keep up a flow of meaningless chatter, as Jennie had sunk immediately into the doldrums the moment she was sure Kit was out of sight. Unfortunately, when she did at last find her voice, it was to point out that Lord Thorpe and his two female companions had entered the room.

"Now watch this," Lucy whispered in her ear. "Lord Thorpe will deposit the chaperon with the other wallflowers lining the perimeters like vultures, dutifully dance this next set with Lady Cynthia, fetch her a glass of champagne before herding her back to her keeper, and then take off for parts unknown. Honestly, I can't fathom how the man expects to spend the rest of his life with that plain pudding—he can barely stand to do the civil with her now, and they are only betrothed, not bracketed. For an intelligent man, sometimes he seems as thick as a post. So what if Lady Cynthia is good *ton*? I'd wager my hope of heaven good *ton* never kept anyone warm at night!"

"Lucy," Jennie scolded, trying vainly to hide a smile, "you are incorrigible. Anyone who didn't know you would think you were horribly fast. Besides, it isn't like you to be so catty."

"Oh, really," shot back Lucy with a sly look. "And

who was it, Miss Prunes and Prisms, who walked bare-faced into a theater box containing her errant husband and three high flyers 'nice' ladies like yourself are sup-posed to pretend do not even exist? Besides," she ended rationally, "I am not merely being catty or mean. I am merely trying to save Lord Thorpe from himself."

"And *for* yourself?" opined Jennie, just as Lord Thorpe, following Lucy's earlier predictions to the let-ter, deposited Lady Cynthia with her chaperon and saun-tered off in the direction of a collection of gentlemen who were standing deep in discussion in a corner of the room. "There goes Lord Thorpe, Lucy," she pointed out, "just as you said he would. It seems you have been making quite a project out of the man, if you know his habits so well."

"Project?" her cousin parroted. "My dear child," she chirped, giving her dark curls a toss, "I intend to make his lordship my life's work. Oh, dear," she ended, tak-ing in Jennie's startled expression, "I fear I shock you yet again."

Although her cousin's honesty was a bit unsettling, Jennie, being the sensitive person she was, could hear the hurt that hid behind Lucy's flippant speech. "No, you widget," she soothed softly, "I am not shocked. I am, however, apprehensive. Lord Thorpe is an engaged man. It would distress me greatly to see you disap-pointed, which just may be the case this time around. Getting your own way in matters of the heart is not as simple as boxing Cousin George's ears to make him stop pinching you every time your back was turned."

"I know that, silly," Lucy agreed easily enough. "But then again I don't want Lord Thorpe to *stop* bothering me—heavens, I'd settle for making him aware of my ex-istence for a start. Then," she said innocently, "we shall just let nature take its course. Now, Jennie," she soothed, leading her cousin to a nearby chair, "you just sit here and wait for your gallant husband to drop off his actress and join you. I'll just toddle over there and see if I can't get Lord Thorpe's attention. Oh! There's Kit now—remember, coz, to keep your chin up. It wasn't you who was peacocking about with another man. Don't let him bully you!" And before the flustered Jennie could grab Lucy's hand—hoping her cousin's presence would keep Kit from giving her a bear-garden jaw in public—the girl was off, determined to take advantage of this opportunity of catching his lordship on his own.

Jennie watched Lucy until the girl disappeared in the crowd and then reluctantly turned to see if Kit had spied her out. Her stomach dropped to her toes as she saw he was even then advancing purposefully toward her haven in the corner, his handsome face looking quite unusually grim. Well, she thought, stiffening her spine, my conscience is easy. Let him try to berate me, just let him try, and I'll give him a piece of my mind. Who does he think he is, anyway—my keeper? No, her uneasy conscience reminded her, he thinks he's your husband—a thought that seriously undermined her resolution to give as good as she got in the coming exchange of insults and recriminations. Being a wife, she decided, letting out her breath on a sigh, certainly had its disadvantages.

Kit could see the conflicting emotions chasing themselves across Jennie's face as he approached her through the crush of people racing onto the dance floor to take up positions for the deliciously intoxicating first waltz of the evening. Much as he still felt the lingering chagrin of having been made to deal with an enraged Piccadilly harpy's disgusting imitation of a French fit, he could not sustain his anger when he thought again of Jennie's masterful set-down of that same actress. Whether she was purring like a kitten in his arms or spitting like a lioness protecting her territory, which is how he liked to think of her attack on La Fontaine, Kit found that he was hard-pressed to find a single thing about Jennie that did not appeal.

Coming up beside her, deliberately approaching her from behind, he whispered into her ear reassuringly: "If you promise to sheathe your claws, madam, I'm willing to convince myself that this is our first meeting of the evening."

Whatever Jennie had been expecting, it hadn't been this. Whirling to face his, to her mind, stupidly grinning face, she spat, "Oh, aren't you just! How very *condescending* of you, my lord, considering it is your own guilt you are willing to overlook. How very much-minded of you indeed! It must be that it is so intellectually elevating to be with a woman who speaks French. *Oh la la, monsieur,*" she lisped mincingly, "you are, how you say, such a *pompous ass!*"

Kit accepted her biting condemnation without a blink, knowing he deserved all that and more from her. As for the impropriety of her appearing in his theater box earlier, he was already convinced she had suffered enough for that particular indiscretion and was not about to set her off again by bringing up the subject. Deciding that this particular battle did not matter so much as did the question of just who eventually won the war that had so far described their marriage, he merely bowed, saying, "Your trick, ma'am, I fancy," and then totally destroyed her composure by placing a hot kiss on the bit of skin that peeped from beneath the looped buttonhole of her kid glove at the inside of her wrist.

Jennie knew Kit was pitching it rather high, overacting his part in their little farce more than just a tad, but she was entirely too female to do more than stand back and enjoy his attentions while they lasted. Unfortunately, since her husband's intentions lay more with getting his wife alone in his bedchamber, he did not waste much more time in cheerful flirtation, but went straight to the problem that was foremost on his mind. Where was that incorrigible nuisance Lucy Gladwin, he asked his dreamy-eyed wife—who was still holding her wrist protectively with her other hand—so that they could corral her and her Aunt Rachel and hustle them out of here?

The earl's question brought Jennie rudely crashing back to reality. She had been so apprehensive of Kit's arrival, so sure he was to ring a peal over her head for her unforgivable behavior at Covent Garden, that the thought that their uncomfortable coolness to each other this past week had dissipated like fog evaporates beneath the warmth of the sun had effectively blocked her mind to Lucy's problems.

"Oh, dear," Jennie faltered, casting her nervous gaze quickly about the room. "I don't know where she is anymore. She was over there, trying to get Lord Thorpe to notice her, though I can't for the life of me see why, toplofty snob that he is, and engaged too into the bargain. But I can't see her anymore. Do you suppose she's off in some chamber or other crying her eyes out with disappointment?"

Kit snorted indelicately. "I'd find it easier to imagine that it is Lord Thorpe who is hiding himself away behind a potted palm, his knees knocking in dread lest Lucy spy him out and make a cake of herself for his benefit. Blister it, Jennie," he said feelingly, "that girl has more brass than my Aunt Martha's favorite candlesticks!"

"She's in love, Kit," Jennie put in placatingly. "Or at least she thinks she is. I only hope she isn't about to suffer a sad disappointment of the heart."

"She ought to suffer a stinging pain in her hindquarters, administered by that harum-scarum father of hers who should have taught her better," Kit said authoritatively. "Thorpe is one damned officious so-and-so, although I grant he's known as a true Corinthian, at home on turf or table. Actually, I imagine he'd be tolerable, if he didn't have such a fine opinion of himself. Not that I have ever had much to do with him—his set is older, you know. But from all I've observed of the fellow, rank, fortune, and lineage are all that concern the chap. Even his marriage, I've heard, was arranged more for its blending of blue blood than anything else. Why, Lucy has about as much chance of snagging Thorpe as she does of turning her flea-witted father into the Dean of Cambridge. Don't frown, kitten, it's not as if you don't know I'm right."

Of course Kit was right, not that it hurt Jennie any the less to hear it. But she had no time to tell him this, as she could at last see the diminutive Lucy off in the distance, engaged in conversation with not only Lord Thorpe but Lady Cynthia as well. Jennie tugged on Kit's sleeve and nodded her head in the small group's direction, and Kit turned just in time to see Thorpe's brutal dismissal of Jennie's cousin, executed with an insulting sneer, followed by the pointed turning of both his and Lady Cynthia's backs.

"That rotten bastard!" Kit was startled into saying, suddenly feeling quite protective of Lucy, who was even then blushing hotly at Thorpe's cold dismissal. "Come on, kitten, it's time we effect a rescue," he said from between clenched teeth. "I only hope I meet that bounder at Jackson's. How I'd love to get him in the ring and give him a sound drubbing!"

The Earl and Countess of Bourne, still largely unrecognizable to most of the company, made their exit from Lady Kenwood's triumph in considerable haste, cognizant of Miss Lucy Gladwin's trembling lower lip that warned of an imminent explosion—whether into tears or into a *faux pas* of immense magnitude, they were not about to linger to ascertain. Dragging Aunt Rachel in their train, they descended the broad staircase, and Kit signaled for his carriage and that of the Gladwins to be called for immediately.

While the aunt was bustled into her carriage alone, Lucy was led to the Bourne carriage, where Jennie plunged into a blistering condemnation of Lord Thorpe, Lady Cynthia, and the *ton* at large as she looked into Lucy's woebegone little face and saw the first crystal tears making their way down the girl's cheeks. "Don't you let those horrid people depress you, Lucy," she pleaded, holding the other girl's hands while Kit sat back in a corner, feeling about as useless as a wart on the end of Prinny's nose. "You're miles too good for either of them, you know."

It was disconcerting to see the normally bubbly, irrepressible Lucy Gladwin sunk to such depths of despair, and neither Kit nor Jennie could be brought to point out that she had brought her disgrace on herself. But, although down, Lucy was far from out, and so she said once her initial burst of tears had spent itself. "That Lady Cynthia and her missish airs don't depress me for a second, you know," she told her companions with some heat. "She is only digging her own grave by acting like some *grande dame*. It can only be a matter of time before Lord Thorpe realizes what a dull stick she is. It is just that I hadn't expected *him* to behave so cruelly. Why, he actually had the meanness to imply that we were never properly introduced and then turned his head away, cutting me dead."

"Arrogant jackass," Kit put in conversationally, earning himself a jab in the ribs from his wife.

"Oh no, Kit," Lucy protested, still intent on protecting the man. "He cannot help that he was raised to believe he is the greatest thing since the invention of fire! There is a wonderful man beneath that air of superiority—I just know it."

"Of course there is," Jennie agreed unconvincingly, secretly believing the only thing that could ever force any common sense into his lordship's handsome blond head would be a heavy, blunt object.

"Of course," Kit echoed, a small bit of humor entering his voice. "The question remains, though, ladies, why anyone could possibly care enough about the fellow to take the time to dig for it."

The carriage pulled to a halt behind the Gladwin equipage, and Lucy was forced to keep her rebuttal for another day. Once she was gone, Kit slid an arm around Jennie's shoulders and pulled her more closely against his lean frame. "Now, isn't this cozy?" he asked, breathing into her curls as the carriage moved off toward Berkeley Square.

CHAPTER TEN

IT WAS A MIRACLE the two of them were even speaking to each other. Heaven only knew Jennie had a full budget of woes, thanks to Kit; and his life had not exactly been a bed of thornless roses since her advent into it. But they were both young, both strongly attracted to each other, and, at this comfortably romantic time of night, disposed to putting their squabbles aside for the moment and simply enjoying the fact that, for the moment at least, they seemed to be in harmony with each other. Youth had many drawbacks, but the ability to adapt readily to most any situation certainly couldn't be termed one of them.

So it was a conspiratorially merry pair that ascended the stairway of the Bourne mansion shoes in hand, alternately giggling and shushing each other as they made their way to the master bedchamber, Kit pushing up the tip of his aristocratic nose and oinking under his breath and Jennie giggling behind her hand as she pleaded halfheartedly for him to stop being such a goose.

It was only once they were in Kit's chamber, the door safely closed behind them, that Jennie began to feel the first tremors of uncertainty. She had been here before, as if she could forget, and even now, even with her feelings running so deliciously high, she was not quite sure that she should be here again. Each time they had been together it had ended badly. So why was she taking yet a third chance at heartache?

Kit could sense Jennie's sudden reluctance, even as he was mentally stripping her of her lovely evening gown and planning his strategy meant toward getting her into his bed with as little fuss as possible. "What's amiss, kitten?" he asked, trying for normalcy. "If you're worried about undoing that long line of buttons marching up your back, never fear. I am more than willing to act the lady's maid for the evening. Don't be shy, kitten," he coaxed, smiling as he walked toward her. "I promise to close my eyes if that's what's bothering you. I am nothing, you see, if not discreet."

Taking refuge in anger, Jennie sniffed and retorted, "Discreet, is it, Kit? Oh, aren't you just? That's pitching it rather high for a man who was just this evening cavorting about in public with that horrid actress. If you had an ounce of decency you'd be down on your knees begging forgiveness for your indiscretion, and not standing there grinning like a bear and trying to get me into your bed!"

Jennie's plain speaking effectively doused Kit's ardor, and conversely ignited his temper. "You picked a plaguey queer time to be splitting hairs over which of us was indiscreet, madam. *I* did no more than any man, single or bracketed, has ever done. It was *you*, my dear, who set a precedent tonight by making a public scene the likes of which would put Caro Lamb's worst folly in the light of a schoolgirl prank." Considering the fact that Caro Lamb had been said to have once danced naked on a dining-room table in front of a roomful of titled gentlemen, that *was* really pitching it rather high, and Kit knew it the minute his words were out. But, he could see, the damage was already done. Jennie's lower lip began to tremble, and it looked as if she was about to break into tears.

But Jennie did not cry, although she was sorely tried not to burst into tears at Kit's unfair insult. It took her a moment or two to get herself together, but in the end she tilted up her chin and decided to state her position once and for all and then walk out of the room, head held high, never to darken his lordship's door again. "It appears, husband, you see me in the light of a resident freak. After my behavior tonight, for which I shall *not* apologize, I may just agree with you. However, I will not take this blame alone. Did it never occur to you that I was left to fend for myself in London, having never been offered any assistance from you? And what is a great deal more to the point," she went on, clearly extremely incensed, "I believe I have managed extremely well on my own, having assembled a staff and found someone of good standing who agreed to shepherd me about London whilst my erstwhile husband was off behaving like a mongrel dog who had slipped his leash. So don't you tyrannize over me, Kit Wilde!"

Jennie in a heat was a treat to Kit's eyes, and he almost made the fatal error of saying so. Instead, common sense intervened and he struck a pose of husbandly penitence. "It *was* my fault that we had such an unfortunate incident tonight. I only went with Ozzy because he'd been badgering me to accompany him. If I had only known that you planned to attend the theater tonight…"

"You would have volunteered to drag me along like a good husband?" Jennie finished for him, crossing her arms over her chest and allowing her slipper-clad toe to tap out a lively tattoo on the floor.

Kit had been a soldier long enough to know when defeat was inevitable. So realizing, he opted for a dignified surrender in the hope he would be allowed to keep his sword, as the saying went, and retain at least a semblance of honor. "I've neglected you terribly, haven't I, kitten," he soothed, gathering her into his loose embrace and stroking her back as a child strokes a favorite pet.

"You've been horrid," Jennie mumbled into his chest, not seeing any reason to dress the thing up in fine linen.

"That's my kitten," Kit said, a laugh rumbling deep in his chest, "not drawing in her claws until she's sure she's drawn blood. All right, sweetings, I've been horrid. But am I completely beyond forgiveness? Even if I solemnly promise to mend my ways? After all, I haven't been so bad, have I? I haven't cut up nasty about Montague once since he took that cleaver to me. And didn't I only cuff Del's ear for copping my gold watch the other day, when I could just as easily have tossed him out on his dishonest rump?"

"He said he was only keeping his hand in, so to speak," Jennie protested feebly, "so as not to get rusty."

Kit knew Jennie was weakening, and he immediately took advantage of the situation, slowly maneuvering them toward the wide bed as his hands made short work of the line of covered buttons that represented his last barrier to her capitulation. "Of course he was, kitten," he concurred easily, nuzzling her ear with his warm, talented lips. He had her on the coverlet now, and by the way her soft arms were encircling his neck, he was certain that this evening would have a more than satisfactory conclusion. Nothing, he mused self-satisfyingly, was so bad that a little lovemaking couldn't make it right.

There came a sudden knock at the door, followed by the sound of a low-pitched argument going on in the hallway. Kit muttered a violent oath and rolled over onto his back, searching his memory once again for some sin he had committed that he was being tortured this way. Recognizing Miss Bundy's voice, he called out, "Bundy! What in thunder are you about out there? Can't a man have a little peace in his own bed?" The inadvertent double-entendre caused him to chuckle a moment before his temper regained the upper hand. "Damn it, woman, speak up! You were loud enough before."

Being no more pleased by the interruption than her husband, Jennie was still quicker than he to realize that Bundy would not disturb them unless something very important was happening. Struggling back into her gown, which gaped badly now that its buttons were all undone, she scrambled off the bed and opened the door. "This had better be good," she gritted between clenched teeth, surprising herself by realizing she was feeling more than a little deprived at being interrupted.

"Oh laws," Goldie whined from her position slightly to the rear of Miss Bundy. "I knowed it was wrong ta bother his lordship when he was frolickin', and so I told Miss Busybody here."

Miss Bundy, who did not look lightly upon being termed a busybody, was quick to put an end to the maid's lamentations. "Goldie," she said with a hard edge to her voice, "you haven't the wit of a flea. And it's not as if there were anything else to do, what with the tweeny bawling like a sick calf and calling for Miss Jane."

Jennie deciphered enough of this interchange to realize that Charity, that poor dear thing, was the reason for this late-night intrusion. "What's wrong with Charity?" she questioned the agitated Miss Bundy, drawing the woman inside and closing the door on the teary-eyed Goldie. "Did she have a bad dream?"

Miss Bundy's exacerbated nerves did not need this naive assumption to push them beyond the point of no return. Having had Jennie in her charge since the girl was in soggy drawers, Miss Bundy now addressed the grown woman as if she were still a child. "Is she having a bad dream? If that isn't foolish beyond permission—as if I wouldn't know how to deal with such a thing without banging down his lordship's door in the middle of the night. No, she is not having a bad dream. The chit *is* a bad dream, and now she's about to do just what I warned you she would do when you took her in. She's about to, er…" And here Miss Bundy's resolve deserted her, seeing as how the earl, wrapped now in his maroon dressing gown, was standing there staring at her as if she were the oddest creature in the world.

"What's wrong?" Jennie persisted, clearly perplexed. "What could Charity have done that's so upset the household? After all, she's only a baby."

Kit rubbed his nose and chuckled softly, shaking his head. "She certainly is, kitten," he concurred easily. "And it appears the baby is about to have a baby. Am I correct, Miss Bundy?"

The older woman, now looking as if she were about to have a spasm any moment, only nodded her head. "I know absolutely nothing about such things," she whined, wringing her hands.

"Yes," Kit smiled, taking the woman's arm and leading her out of the room, "I was reasonably certain that you didn't. Never fear, Miss Bundy, all shall be well. You just go wake Renfrew and tell him what's going on, and then you go back to bed. You look as if you need to rest a bit. Renfrew will take it from here."

Closing the door firmly on Miss Bundy's back, Kit turned to face his wife, his mind now firmly locked on the subject at hand—getting her back into his bed and taking up where they had left off when they were so rudely interrupted. But at the sight of Jennie, sitting on the edge of the bed and putting on her satin slippers, his brow furrowed and he was forced to ask her just what she was about.

"I'm going to Charity, of course," she answered civilly. "She needs me, I know she does, because she made me promise to stay with her when her time came. She's so dreadfully young, you know."

"And you're so very old?" Kit questioned, pushing her back down on the bed by the simple expedient of placing his hands firmly on her shoulders. "Renfrew will call in a doctor," he reasoned patiently. "I arranged the whole thing with him when I first saw Charity's condition. The doctor is probably on his way already. Besides, you're much too young to be witness to such a thing."

"Oh, stuff!" Jennie protested, removing his hands and rising once more to her feet. "If ever I heard a faint heart, it is you, Kit Wilde. I've seen kittens and puppies born a hundred times. There can be little difference between the species."

Kit smiled evilly. "I don't know about that, sweetings. If Charity has a litter, though, I'll be the first to admit to your reasoning." His handsome face hardened when he realized that Jennie was serious; she had every intention of being a witness to the birth. Grabbing her elbow as she made her way purposefully to the door, he acknowledged her loyalty but at the same time insisted she listen to reason. She had no place in any room where a birth was about to take place. A *conception,* he mused to himself without so much as one single pang for his selfishness, was quite another matter!

Looking down at Kit's hand, her expression telling him that she was not best pleased to see his fingers still clutching her person, Jennie told him coldly, "You can either detach that hand, my lord, or grace us with your presence in Charity's room. These affecting demonstrations meant to impress on me the delicacy of my station do nothing but highlight your own self-interest. Now," she ended regally, "I suggest you either unhand me or prepare to witness the birth yourself, because *I am going to sit with Charity!*"

Kit was tempted, sorely tempted, to take up Jennie's challenge, but in the end his eyes slid away from her penetrating stare and his hand slipped from her arm. Jennie marched from the room with the look of someone going off on a mission of destiny, and Kit, desperately wishing there were someone about he could lay violent hands on and so rid himself of this nasty urge to crush something, stomped off downstairs to the drawing room and proceeded to get roaringly, messily drunk.

JENNIE WAS SPENDING the morning at home, having been kept up most of the night attending the birth of Charity's son, George, named after the Prince Regent, and not his natural father—a man Jennie had commented was anything but natural. Renfrew had been a brick through the whole thing, calmly ordering everyone about and then, once the hubbub was over and the doctor gone, taking charge of having the softly snoring earl carried to his bedchamber, very much the worse for the prodigious amount of brandy he had consumed.

Having given Renfrew the morning off, telling him he deserved a lie-down in his quarters, and finding that

Bob, Ben and Del had deserted their posts in favor of the kitchen where Montague was busily whipping up some strawberry tarts, Jennie was forced to answer the knocker herself, which is the only reason she was now sitting across the tea table from the smiling Dean Ives. At their first meeting she had thought the man handsome, but closer inspection revealed the man's rather mean-looking, close-set, ice-blue eyes, and his looks fell off rather sadly once her own eyes concentrated on the man's single bad feature. Perhaps she was just tired, she thought charitably; after all, it wasn't as if the man had ever done anything to put her off.

"I'm sorry Lord Bourne is not up and about yet this morning," she apologized sweetly, pouring tea, and then making a great show of yawning behind her hand, "but we had a bit of a to-do here last night and the whole household is at sixes and sevens this morning." If she thought Mr. Ives would take the hint and cut his visit short she soon saw that she had sadly mistaken her man, for he merely nodded his understanding and then sat back comfortably, looking as if he had every intention of taking up permanent residence on the red satin Sheraton chair.

"Yes," he said, looking at her quite oddly out of the corners of his eyes, "I can imagine it was not the most tranquil of evenings once you and Bourne got around to discussing that little contretemps at Covent Garden. But not to worry," he consoled her, waving his hand negligently as Jennie stiffened in her seat. "I for one will not let it be bruited about town. Besides, it was probably Miss Gladwin, that bold piece, who put you up to it in the first place."

"You are above yourself, sir!" Jennie shot back, clearly intending to order the man from her house, but she was not able to finish what she had intended to be a thundering scold by Ben (his mouth circled with white flour and bits of sugar), who entered the room and announced that Miss Gladwin, that "right rum blowen," was without.

And so it was that Jennie had to content herself with giving Mr. Ives a look that would blister paint before rising to greet her cousin, whose woebegone face served to drive anything but concern for the other girl out of her mind. "Lucy, pet," she commiserated, drawing the girl down beside her on the settee, "you're looking burnt to the socket. It was I who was up all night, not you."

While Jennie and Lucy held hands and whispered under their breath, totally ignoring the man who should have had enough sense to excuse himself from this intimate family gathering, Dean took the time to observe the pair and adjust his ideas accordingly. He had thought Jennie to be an easy touch, but she had shown him that she could be a cool hand when one of her own was attacked. Indeed, if that hellcat Gladwin chit hadn't shown up so conveniently he knew he'd be out on his ear by now, no doubt with a sound admonition never to darken the Wilde door again. Since that possibility did not at all suit his plans for staying close as sticking plaster to the young, wealthy earl and his beautiful wife, he immediately set about the task of making amends for his verbal *faux pas*.

He tried flattery first, thinking to work his way back into the countess's good books by waxing almost poetic over the beauty of Miss Gladwin's bonnet; but when Lucy merely wrinkled her nose and said, "What, this old thing? Are you losing your eyesight, Mr. Ives?" he knew that Lucy at least was too smart to let fine words cut any wheedle with her, and he once more retired from the field but, unfortunately for the ladies, not from the premises.

Jennie had the softest heart in creation, but she became a tiger in the defense of her friends, and therefore she felt not a single qualm as she persisted in whispering to Lucy, pointedly excluding Mr. Ives from the conversation. Wilde has the devil's own luck, that neglected gentleman was left to think, filling his ice-blue eyes with the sight of an animated Jennie describing the wonder of Charity's new son. From his observation last night at the theater, Mr. Ives felt that his lordship had deep feelings for his bride, no matter how sadly he neglected her, and he wondered if that affection could be turned to his own advantage.

As this new train of thought interested him to the exclusion of milking whatever he could from a ridiculous conversation consisting mostly of exclamations about the tininess of infant fingernails and the softness of infant skin, Mr. Ives stood, bowed gracefully from the waist, and took his leave, an action that caused Jennie to mutter feelingly, "One can only hope he plans a prolonged sojourn to the Antipodes."

But the ladies were not to be left alone for long, as Del, bits of sticky strawberry hanging from his livery, soon arrived to announce that Mr. Norwood, "that catercousin to the guv'nor, is 'angin' about in the 'all, and iffen the pantler don't get 'is arse ata anchor in the 'all soon there'll be no tellin' who all will soon be 'ammerin' down the door." His dire warning delivered, Del rubbed a finger along the front of his jacket, and turned to depart, leaving Ozzy to ask what in the world was a pantler, and did her ladyship know she had thieves for footmen?

"Thieves, Mr. Norwood?" Jennie repeated coldly, clearly taking exception to his bald statement.

Ozzy was nothing if not direct. "Thieves, my lady,"

he insisted, grabbing Del just as he was about to make his getaway. "I passed Mr. Ives in the hallway and could not help but notice that your footman here picked the man's pocket just as he was going out the door. By the by, what was Mr. Ives doing here, anyway? He seemed like a man who had a lot on his mind—barely took the time to say hello, and him that's known me anytime these last three years."

"Mr. Ives was making a thorough pest of himself," supplied Jennie tersely, "which is a trait of his you must be aware of if you have indeed known him several years. What's more to the point at the moment, however, is what horrid thing he must have done to poor Del here to have the man revert to his former bad habits."

Del knew a champion when he saw one, and he made short work of pleading for his mistress's sympathy. "That queer cove never gived me no blunt fer 'oldin' 'is lily shadow or famlin' cheats, missus," Del whined piteously. "A man o' three outs, that's wot 'e be, so Oi jist sorta dipped me fambles inta 'is pocket-like, seein' as 'ow Oi be a dab at it, an seeing' as 'ow ya said we wuz ta get tipped by all those 'igh an' mighty folk what's come 'ere. Don't send me ta Newman's Tea Garden, missus, like some Anabaptist."

"'ere now," Ben admonished Del sharply, giving the smaller man a quick clip on the top of his head as the acknowledged leader of their small gang entered the room, having overheard the commotion from his station in the hallway. "Shut yer clapperjaw, ya fool, it don't do ta patter flash 'round the missus." Having satisfactorily dealt with his underling, Ben turned to Jennie. "Wot's 'e done, missus? We be birds of a feather, y'ken, but never there be no arch rogue or dimber damber among us. Wot's 'is be mine, missus, so iffen Del's gone an' got 'is bumfiddle in a sling, mine be there wit it."

"No pattering flash, you say?" Mr. Norwood put in, striving hard not to laugh out loud at both Del and Ben's cant language and the ladies' shocked reaction to it. Mr. Norwood could only surmise what their reactions would be if they understood even half of what the two footmen were saying, what with references to Newgate, Anabaptists, and a part of the human anatomy that females were allowed to sit upon but were otherwise admonished not to admit existed at all.

But Jennie was too overset to pay more than token attendance to anything that had been said. Her primary concern was that Del had done what he had promised never to do—practice his pickpocketing talents on one of their guests. Never mind that Mr. Ives was not a valued friend of the family, and keeping the fact that he had cheated Del out of his earned tip to one side, Jennie knew that Kit would not allow such doings under his roof. Del would be tossed out into the street, and Bob and Ben with him, unless she could keep this little fracas from ever reaching her husband's ears.

Really, she thought uncharitably, all this fuss over the unpleasant Mr. Ives. It seemed incredibly silly to cut up stiff over what Del had seen as his right—taking the tip Mr. Ives had neglected to give him. "What did you get from Mr. Ives's pocket, Del?" she asked kindly, trying to marshal her wits about her before Kit, who had the most maddening habit of showing up just when he wasn't wanted, came on the scene.

"Not much blunt," Del answered, chagrined, showing off a few coppers that hardly seemed worth the risk of being caught in the act of putting his hand in a gentleman's pocket. "The cove must be laid up in lavender, missus, 'cause 'e sure ain't got deep pockets. All Oi got fer m'troubles in these coppers an' a tin tatler that don't even tick. An' this," he ended, passing over a slip of paper with some scribbling written on it, "Weren't 'ardly worth it."

Lucy, who had been considerably lifted from her doldrums by the footmen's shenanigans, came over and took possession of the scrap of paper. "It's an address near Holborn, and not a very nice one if I recollect my geography correctly," she said, squinting slightly as she tried to read the paper, which was quite smudged. "Whatever would Mr. Ives be doing with something like this in his pocket?"

"Nothing about Mr. Ives would surprise me," said a voice from the doorway as Lord Bourne, looking sadly out of sorts, sauntered into the drawing room. Ben, showing why he was the leader of his small band, quickly nudged Del, and the two hastily took their exit, fervently hoping that their mistress would find some way of explaining the scrap of paper without involving them.

The footmen were in luck, for Kit was too full of his own thoughts to spend overlong dwelling on insignificant matters. "I learned something about your Mr. Ives last night, from La Fontaine, as a matter of fact. I make free with her name, ladies," he said, bowing to Jennie and Lucy, who were trying hard to blend into the background, "because you and the lady in question have, thanks to my wife's odd sense of what is correct, already been introduced. Anyway," he pursued, turning back to Mr. Norwood, "it would seem your Mr. Ives is heavily dipped on his expectations. La Fontaine tells me he is nearly fully occupied nowadays in outrunning the duns. I thought I'd mention it, Ozzy, before he applies to you for a loan."

"That's mighty decent of you, Kit," Ozzy said, grimacing, "but I fear you are too late. He's into me for a monkey already."

"Whatever did Mr. Ives want with a monkey?"

Any remaining tension dissipated with Jennie's naive question. "Silly," Lucy laughed, hugging her cousin to her. "A monkey is sporting language for a sum of money—quite a considerable amount," she added with a quick look toward the blushing Mr. Norwood.

"Yes," that man concurred. "It would appear your man was right, my lady. Mr. Ives is indeed a man of three outs."

Kit, not quite understanding what was going on, translated. "A man of three outs is one who is without money, wit or manners. Did Mr. Ives insult you, kitten?" he asked, more than ready to take umbrage. "I could do with a good punch-up."

Jennie assured her husband that she had not been insulted, merely bored to blinders by Mr. Ives's interminable visit earlier in the morning. "Really, it was excessively odd of him."

"Odd?" Lucy teased. "Perhaps you have acquired a beau. Oh dear, cousin, I do hope you will not allow your head to be turned by Mr. Ives's attentions." Lucy would have said more, but the earl's fierce scowl stifled the words in her throat.

"Lucy," that aggrieved gentleman said, "you're bidding fair to become a thorn in my side."

"Oh, Kit," Jennie protested quickly, "how very bad of you."

"Here, here," seconded Mr. Norwood. "That was very insulting, old fellow. Damned if I won't cut you dead when next we meet."

Jennie may have wanted Kit's attention diverted in

some way, but to have her friends glaring at her husband as if he were the second most evil thing in the world did not suit her plans. "Montague has conjured up a fresh batch of his marvelous strawberry tarts, my lord," she sighed longingly, slipping her hand through her husband's arm. "Do you think you could ring for some? I have this overwhelming craving for one that I don't believe I can deny for much longer."

"A craving?" her cousin asked breathlessly. "Never say, Jennie, that you're increasing. How utterly famous!"

If Jennie's try at diverting her husband fell a bit short of the mark, Lucy's enthusiastic exclamation certainly did not. Turning toward his wife as if she had suddenly sprouted a second head, he asked incredulously, "Are you, kitten? You never said anything."

"No, I most certainly am not!" denied his bride fiercely. "And I think it is beyond anything stupid how everybody is pressing me so. Only this morning my papa wrote asking much the same question. Really, if everyone is so set on having a baby around they'll just have to make do with Charity's infant." She then placed herself in front of her husband and mourned. "And you didn't even ask if it's a boy or a girl."

Relief, mixed with another emotion that seemed strangely like disappointment, spread through Kit, and he put his fingers beneath Jennie's chin and said gravely, "Forgive me, kitten. I stand before you agog with curiosity. Exactly what did Charity have—a little housemaid or a little underfootman?"

"Go ahead, Kit, mock me," she said imperturbably, "but I think it was famous, holding little George as he lay wrapped in his blanket. And he shan' be a footman for some London slavedriver either. I an already making plans to have Charity and her son sent to Bourne

Manor as soon as may be. George is going to grow up in the country where there is plenty of fresh air and…and milk, and things like that." As this last was delivered in tones that warned that any contradiction of her plans would be looked upon as a personal insult, Kit only bowed his approval of the scheme and turned to ask Ozzy if he wished to stay and share luncheon with the rest of the family, adding that he naturally included Lucy in those plans. Mr. Norwood, mentally canceling his earlier intention of visiting his tailor to talk about an extra inch of buckram padding in the shoulders of his new puce jacket, agreed with some alacrity, smiling sweetly at Lucy and thereby giving Jennie to believe she sniffed a romance in the air. The subject of Mr. Ives, his financial state, and, fortunately for Del, the note that had been found in his pocket was dropped in lieu of talk of a more general nature, and harmony seemed once more to reign in Berkeley Square.

CHAPTER ELEVEN

KIT SURPRISED JENNIE by staying closer than sticking plaster all the rest of the day, declining Mr. Norwood's kind offer of allowing the earl to join him for settling day at Tatt's, Bourne saying that since Ozzy owned so much blunt thanks to his poor choice in racing nags, he would rather not be witness to watching a grown man blubber.

As for Lucy, that intrepid creature had only stopped by to tell her cousin that she had wangled an invitation to a picnic in Richmond Park that, rumor said, Lord Thorpe and Lady Cynthia were sure to attend. She wished she could have acquired an invitation for Jennie, but, she owned ruefully, it had been difficult enough to blackmail her friend Lady Standorf for the single one she had managed. Her aunt, that intrepid soul, was to chaperon her, Lucy told them, her eyes twinkling with mischief, so it would be easy as pie to slip away from her and somehow strike up a conversation with the love of her life. The wink Lucy gave Jennie on her way out the door gave Kit to murmur, "If I were more of a betting man I'd lay a few pounds on that vixen. If she ever gets the bit between her teeth, Thorpe doesn't stand a chance of holding out against her. I'd pity him if he weren't such a damned toplofty bastard, if you'll pardon my blunt speech, kitten. It's just that I've somehow developed a small fondness for your cousin—odd, madcap creature that she is."

"Papa says it runs in the family—coming from my mother's side, you understand," Jennie told him with a smile. "Bundy says Mama was also considered an eccentric in her younger days. Something to do with her penchant for saving her fellow man from the evils of gin."

"It figures," replied Kit laconically, his lips twisting in a one-sided smile. "Thank goodness you didn't inherit her Methodist ways."

And so it turned out, with their friends otherwise occupied and with neither of the Wildes much inclined toward walking out that day, that they somehow found themselves enjoying each other's company for a leisurely luncheon, a restful afternoon sitting about in the conservatory, and for the entirety of one of Montague's superb dinners. It was only after he joined her in the drawing room that Kit began to feel restless and, remembering an invitation to a friend's evening party, he put forth the suggestion that he and his wife make their formal debut as a couple. "M'friends begin to tease me that all this talk of my being bracketed is nothing but a bag of moonshine. It's time I get some of my own back by showing off my pretty wife!"

After a full day of friendly camaraderie, this plan for the evening suited Jennie right down to the ground, and she readily accepted his invitation before he changed his mind. Calling for Renfrew to have Tizzie please fetch down her cloak, Jennie ran to the large mirror in the room and did a quick inventory of her face and hair, tucking a single errant golden ringlet back where it belonged. Her gown, she knew from Goldie's glowing praise and Bundy's tsk-tsking concerning the low cut of the bodice when she had first put it on, was good enough to grace any hostess's ballroom. Besides, hadn't Kit already commented on how well the emerald-green silk complimented her eyes?

Tizzie and Lizzie burst into the drawing room, the former carrying Jennie's velvet-lined cloak and the latter toting a small reticule that was sewn in the same silk as her mistress's gown. After wrapping the cloak lovingly about Jennie's shoulders, Tizzie stepped back a pace and struck a dramatic pose. "'When you do dance,'" she quoted in awful tones, "'I wish you a wave o' the sea, that you might ever do nothing but that.'" Her recitation done, Tizzie swept her audience a dramatic curtsy while Lizzie, the reticule hastily stuffed under her arm, applauded lustily, verbally adding a "Bravo!" or two when her enthusiasm momentarily outran her shyness.

"That was truly splendid!" Jennie told the aging actress sincerely as Tizzie rose creakily to her feet. "I vow I am impressed."

"That was Shakespeare, kitten," Kit whispered into her ear as he led her toward the door, "and I vow I am about to be sick. Let's away before she starts on Hamlet's soliloquy, as that would unman me entirely!"

DANCING WAS ALL right, Kit owned silently, if one didn't mind prancing about like a trained puppydog for all the world to see. *All we need is to wear ruffles about our necks and carry a red ball in our mouths*—he thought of himself and his fellow males who had just lately been forced to caper about the ballroom in a mad country romp—*and we would resemble a canine performing troupe.* Thank the Lord that Jennie cared as little for such tomfoolery as he did and had readily acceded to his wish to see what was about in some of the other rooms. A good sport, that's what his kitten was, he sighed happily.

"I will be your banker," Kit told his wife now as he held out a chair for her and urged her to take a seat at the round gaming table that was one of a half dozen or more that filled the small, elegant salon just outside their hosts's elegant ballroom.

"Oh," Jennie replied, looking up at him as he prepared to take the adjoining seat, "we are to play for money? All Papa used to allow was matchsticks, and even then he beat me dreadfully."

"You've played faro before?"

"No-o-o-o," she admitted slowly. "Just a little whist. Does that mean I can't play?" she ended a little sorrowfully, preparing to rise to her feet and surrender her chair to another.

But Kit assured her that although faro was not usually considered a game for females, private parties sometimes included a small-stakes table such as this one. It didn't hold a patch on Devonshire House, but then nothing much did. While the rest of the company waited patiently, Kit explained the rather simple rules for this game that had accounted for the ruin of more good men than every woman since Eve, and then thoughtfully sent a servant to procure some liquid refreshment while he divided the betting chips evenly between them.

Some call it beginner's luck. Others, those on the losing end, term it as the devil's own luck. But no matter what name her fellow players chose to put to it, Jennie's luck that evening had Kit heartily wishing he could carry off dressing her in breeches, and slipping her in the door at either Brook's or the Great-Go. A small crowd began to gather around as Jennie won draw after draw, making a shambles of the precept that in faro the odds always remain clearly in favor of the dealer. In a town so known for its love of gambling that Walpole had once remarked that he could not garner a teaspoonful of news in the whole city except what was trumps, word of Jennie's ongoing *coup* traveled quickly, and soon a multitude crowded into the small room, Dean Ives standing inconspicuously among the awed audience.

When at last Jennie tired of her easy victory, saying simply that she found faro to be tedious and boring, Kit stared down the remaining players who felt it a mite unfair to have the woman leave the table a winner and the two walked through the gaping crowd just as a waltz was being struck up by the indifferent orchestra.

"Oh, a waltz," Jennie sighed longingly. "Truly, this is the *only* dance that makes a whit of sense, without all that prancing up and down and separating from your partner for minutes at a time. How can anyone be expected to hold a civil conversation with a person who is forever tippytoeing off into the distance?"

His pockets bulging with Jennie's winnings and his chest near to bursting with pride at her triumph at the gaming table, Kit executed a creditable leg to his lady, saying, "May I have the pleasure of this dance, ma'am, if you are not otherwise engaged?"

If the violinists were not of the first stare, and the conductor more than a little inattentive to the tempo, these lapses were lost on the young couple now gliding around the floor with eyes only for each other. So obvious was their enchantment that several romantically inclined dowagers were pressed to comment on it, while more than a few disgruntled bucks were heard to say they too could fall head over ears for a chit who had just very nearly broken the bank at faro.

Dean Ives, holding up a wall in the shadows near the dance floor, took the bucks' jealous gibes a step or two further. The Countess of Bourne was lovely enough before winning so handily tonight. Now that appeal had doubled—not only for Kit, but for Mr. Ives as well. He smiled as he watched the earl wrap his bride carefully in her cloak before shepherding her out the door, thoughtfully tapping one long finger against his smiling mouth. Ah yes, the little blond countess was becoming more valuable with each passing day.

THE MOONLIGHT coming through the window cast elongated shadows across the two figures who lay tangled amid the bedclothes on the wide mattress of the master chamber. The soft female sigh of contentment followed by a low, satisfied male chuckle were the only sounds to be heard, the rest of the house having all gone to sleep hours earlier. The night belonged to the couple snuggling close together under the satin coverlet, and they were making the most of it, with no intention of wasting a single moment.

"Listen!" Kit whispered, his soft breath tickling his wife's ear.

Reveling in the warm afterglow of their lovemaking, Jennie arched her throat so as to ease his access and questioned softly, "To what? I don't hear anything."

"Precisely, my love," Kit chuckled, raising himself on one elbow and playfully tickling Jennie's cheek with one of her golden curls. "No interfering Bundys, no birthing tweenies—just sweet, blessed silence. Even Lord Clive has consented to leave us alone. Perhaps people are at last giving the new Earl of Bourne some of the respect his lofty station entitles him to."

Jennie sat up straight in the bed, her movement toppling Kit from his position and landing him flat on his back. Clutching the covers to her breast, Jennie asked, "Lord Clive? I've never heard of the man. Who is he? Why would he bother us?"

"I knew it was too good to last," Kit muttered ruefully, running his fingers through his dark hair. "Me and my big mouth. You'd think I would have learned better than to speak my mind around you, my adorable busybody." Kit lifted himself up to plant a kiss on his wife's nose, robbing his words of any sting, but not diminishing her curiosity by so much as a single hair.

"Who is Lord Clive?" she persisted, holding the bedclothes tightly about her as, once her passion had been satisfied, her modesty in front of her new husband came bounding back full force.

"Right," the earl said, adjusting his pillow behind him and lying back against the headboard. "First things first. First Lord Clive, and then—" he smiled wickedly, waggling his eyebrows at her "—the seduction. Ah, kitten, you blush so delightfully."

Lord Clive, Kit told his wife while helping her plump up her pillow next to his, or, to be more precise, Robert Clive, Baron Clive of Plassey, was the man England recognized to be the founder of the empire of British India. After distinguishing himself in battle against the French, he had eventually been made governor and commander in chief of Bengal. But when ill health had forced him to retire and return to England, his enemies had accused him of using his offices in India to line his own pockets. Parliament had impeached him, and although he had eventually been acquitted, his illness, added to his feelings of disgrace (and a rather sad addiction to opium), took their toll, and the baron had committed suicide in his home at number forty-five, Berkeley Square.

"And now his ghost is said to haunt the garden in the center of the square," Kit ended, pleased at the way his little tale had served to bring Jennie back into his arms, where she shivered deliciously at the thought of a ghost wandering about among the plane trees and flowering shrubs that filled the center garden.

"Is he an angry ghost?" she questioned, her green eyes wide.

Kit placed a kiss on her curls. "No, kitten—not that I know of, anyway. I would imagine he is a sorrowful ghost; wandering about wringing his hands—trying to reclaim his lost honor."

"How terribly sad!" said Jennie sorrowfully. "Someone should do something about it. Try to vindicate him, or something."

Seeing the light in his wife's eyes, Kit knew he had to distract her, head her off as it were, before she could build up a full head of steam, or else there was no knowing what maggoty idea she would take into her head as she set about wiping the smut off Lord Clive's escutcheon. It wasn't as if he didn't pity the man, but heaven knew he had enough to deal with riding herd on Jennie's *living* projects, without trying to compete with a dead one.

"Well, puss," was all he said, sighing dramatically, "it *is* common knowledge that people will do very strange things for money. You should know, seeing as how you rode roughshod over your gambling partners tonight in order to gather in a tidy little fortune for yourself."

He had her attention now. "What fortune?" she asked, startled into sitting up again, this time without bothering to drape the covers about her bare upper body. "You said we were playing for tame stakes. And I only used one color chip—they were such a lovely shade of blue, you know."

"Those lovely blue chips were worth more than any other chip on the table, kitten."

Her eyes narrowed into slits. "How much were they worth, Kit?" she asked, a bit of steel creeping into her voice.

"Twenty pounds apiece," he answered her lightly, crossing his hands over his face as he pretended to duck out of the way of her soon to be swinging fists.

But Jennie sat stock-still, mentally remembering how she had blithely thrown one blue chip after another, betting recklessly and then laughing in delight as the pile of pretty blue chips in front of her grew into a multitude. "How much did I win, my lord?" she asked, shutting her eyes tightly against his answer.

"Er...I...er...w-e-l-l-l...er..." Kit strangled, reluctant to say the words. But when Jennie held up her small clenched hand to within an inch of his nose and repeated her question he blurted out rather loudly, "Five thousand pounds."

"Five thousand pounds!" Jennie squeaked unbelievingly.

"Give or take a pound," Kit said and shrugged, trying hard not to show his amusement at her bewildered expression.

Jennie fell back heavily against her pillow, muttering over and over, "Five thousand pounds. Oh my Lord, *five thousand pounds!* Whatever will I do with such a vast sum?"

Rolling onto his side, the better to slip an arm around her slim waist, Kit crooned, "You could always use it to hire a ship to send all your little lost lambs across the sea."

His words snapped her out of her small spasm. "Of course!" she exclaimed, sitting up once more as Kit examined his now-empty right arm and muttered something unmentionable under his breath. Him and his big, flapping mouth. Never talk to a woman when she's between the sheets, old son, he berated himself, else you'll end up being jolted around like a jack-in-the-box without a moment of pleasure to show for the jostling. Maneuvering himself upright again he began kneading Jennie's shoulders as he dropped nibbling kisses along the length of her neck, trying to bring her attention back to a more romantic topic.

"The money was gained from gambling," Jennie told him as his lips traveled to her left shoulder before blazing a trail down her spine. "Therefore, it should be used for good—to benefit mankind in some way. Don't you see it, Kit?" she asked, twisting in his grasp in order to face him. "Our servants are all well to grass, living as they do under our protection. But there are so many, many more living in squalor all over London. This money should be for them!"

Nuzzling Jennie's back provided sufficient stirring of Lord Bourne's hot, young blood to have him agreeing to house every London derelict under his roof. "Of course, kitten," he agreed, pulling her closer so that his lips could find the soft curve of her breast. "Anything you say, my love," he sighed, moving his head so that his searching mouth could narrow in on its delicious target. "Anything," he promised hoarsely, before the need for any more words was forgotten entirely and quiet ruled the night once more.

THE EARL AND COUNTESS of Bourne woke the next morning at nine to refuse Goldie's offer of morning chocolate, and then spent the next hour satisfying quite another appetite before Kit remembered an appointment with his man of business and left Jennie to snuggle down beneath the sheets and go back to sleep. And so it was almost noon when the countess strolled into the drawing room and stood staring at a particularly unlovely vase with a look of utter rapture.

She went into luncheon when Renfrew requested it of her, but after watching her play with the food on her plate for several minutes Ben deftly snatched it from in front of her before it became entirely inedible. It was one thing, he told his fellow footmen, to eat up all the leftovers, but he'd be switched if he'd stand by idly and watch Montague's creations be turned into a whopping great mess of gray something or other by some lovestruck ninny who couldn't be trusted to know a wax bean from a wax candle.

Still comfortably serene within her cocoon of happiness—for Kit had just that morning told her he actually believed he had fallen in love with her—Jennie wasn't even slightly put out when Ben entered the drawing room to inform her that Mr. Ives, that "queer fish," was asking to see her. "Send him in, Ben," she said serenely, "and Ben, try not to judge others so harshly. We are all God's children, remember. Show a little charity, hmmm?"

"Yes, ma'am," Ben returned sagely. "But iffen ya don't mind, Oi'll be keepin' m'blubber shut 'n' m'charity ta m'self. That's a cove would take yer eyeteeth, iffen ya catch m'drift, ma'am."

Mr. Ives spent the first five minutes of his call in the usual mundane chatter about the weather and how well his hostess was looking in her new jonquil morning gown—which served to remind Jennie of her former opinion of the man as being a crushing bore. Oh well, she thought, resigning herself to at least another quarter hour of insipid talk, perhaps the poor man is lonely and in need of company.

Dean could see by the glazed expressionlessness of Jennie's eyes that he was losing her, and he decided to move directly to the point of his visit. "I was witness to your great run of luck last evening, my lady. After deciding to call today and congratulate you on your success I wondered if I'd find you at home or if you were already out dashing about the town spending your winnings."

If he had wanted her undivided attention he had succeeded. Sitting up very straight in her chair, Jennie informed him coldly, "I think that is excessively bad of you, my good sir. While my time spent at table last night was, I freely admit, the greatest good fun, I am not the least bit pleased to be saddled with all this ill-gotten booty. After all, it is not as if I have the slightest need for it."

The victim of this impassioned attack merely sat back comfortably in his own chair and smiled. "I thought as much, ma'am, but I wanted to be sure I wouldn't be putting my foot in it to speak my mind on the subject." Seeing the spark of interest in her eyes, he wondered silently just how much of a bag of moonshine she could be made to swallow. "It would sadden you to know, Jennie—may I call you Jennie, seeing as how I feel I know you so well?—that there are an astounding number of homeless children in London, living a hand-to-mouth existence that would bring tears to the eyes of the strongest man. I most abominate speaking of such things to a lady, but I feel in my heart that you are sympathetic to the plight of these poor innocents." He had her now, he congratulated himself happily, for the moment contenting himself by heaving a sorrowful sigh and allowing a mask of sorrow to settle over his handsome features.

"Indeed, yes, Mr. Ives!" Jennie agreed eagerly. "As a matter of fact, Lord Bourne and I have already decided that giving my winnings to charity would be a praiseworthy resolution to the problem. But tell me, how is it you are interested? It pains me to say this, but I had not thought of you in such a light…. Oh, forgive me," she begged earnestly at his stricken look, "that was very, very wicked of me."

He waved her apology away. "No, no, Jennie, you have every right to question me. I know I resemble any other gentleman of the *ton* racketing about town, seemingly without a single worthwhile thought to my name. But, I tell you honestly, I can no longer keep up the charade. I have run through my patrimony trying to help homeless orphans, and am even now deep in debt due to my softheartedness, but it would never do to let my friends know of my plight. It is only now, speaking here with you, dear lady, that I feel free to open my soul about my secret activities."

"I never would have thought…never mind," Jennie amended hastily. "Mr. Ives—Dean—it would be my greatest pleasure to contribute to your worthy cause. I won over five thousand pounds, you know, and that should go a long way toward easing the plight of those pitiful little creatures. I do intend to set aside five hundred pounds that I have decided to invest for my tweeny and her young son."

Mr. Ives manfully hid his distress at this news and plunged full force into his description of the house he had set up to care for thirty orphans he had personally taken under his wing. By the time he finished, Jennie was more than agreeable to driving out with him immediately to see the little angels for herself. Kit had put forth his low opinion of Mr. Ives, she knew, but that was before the man had shown her this other side of himself. Once Kit knew the truth he would see why she was so eager to go with the man now, her winnings tucked safely in her reticule. Her tender heart felt dreadful about misjudging the man, and, in typical Jennie fashion, she overreacted by giving him her complete trust.

Within moments they were on their way in Mr. Ives's hired carriage, Jennie asking questions as quickly as they popped into her head—wanting to know the names and ages of the children she was about to meet, and if the women who ran the orphanage were careful about the regular use of soap and the absolute necessity for vegetables in a growing child's diet. She would have gone on, but as the scenery outside the carriage grew increasingly depressing and squalid she stopped talking and only stared, compassion wringing at her tender heartstrings.

CHAPTER TWELVE

"GOOD AFTERNOON, BOB," Lucy chirped happily, stepping inside as the footman opened the wide door of the mansion in Berkeley Square. "Is my cousin not ready yet? Do tell her to hurry, for, as my aunt made sure to remind me as I alit from the carriage, it would not do to let my papa's horses stand about in the breeze."

"Her ladyship ain't 'ere," Bob informed her, still engaged in a silent struggle to relieve Miss Gladwin of the glove she held tightly in her left hand "'ere now, give over, miss. Oi'll be givin' 'em back when yer off, promise. Ben'll 'ave m'bum fer a 'itchin' post iffen 'e sees Oi ain't doin' right by ya. It's yer famble cheats wot Oi'm apposed to lift, an' liftin' 'em's jist wot Oi'm affixin' ta do."

Lucy accepted Bob's explanation, hastily stripping off her left glove and handing the pair to him, asking worriedly, "What do you mean, Lady Bourne isn't here? We made arrangements to drive out together this afternoon in the Promenade. I have it on the best authority that Lord Thorpe will—never mind that. Where did she say she was going? When did she leave?" By now Lucy was sitting on the settee in the drawing room, her papa's prime bits of blood forgotten, and Bob, clutching the coveted famble cheats to his bosom, was staring down at her, his head awhirl with trying to remember all her questions. Dealing with the quality, he reminded himself for the hundredth time, was no lark in the park.

"Oi ken answer ya that, missy," Ben offered, sauntering into the room as if he belonged there. "'er ladyship lopped off inna bankrupt cart wot that queer nabs Ives called up fer. Not wot Oi didn't caution 'er not ta go prancin' 'round town with the cove, ya, mind. Gone since just past noon, they be, an' nary 'ide nor 'air of 'er since. Missus is a saint, missy, but there be times Oi doesn't wonder wot iffen she ain't awful ta let in 'er upper rooms, no offense meant, y'know."

Wrinkling her brow as she tried to puzzle out Ben's words, Lucy at last said, "She went out for a drive with Mr. Ives at noon in a—what was that you called it?"

"Bankrupt cart, missy," Ben repeated kindly. "Mr. Ives went an' 'ired 'imself one of them one-'orse chaises the cits keep fer Sundays so as ta put on 'oity-toity airs fer the neighbors."

Lucy nodded her head in understanding. "All right," she said, considering the evidence. "Lady Bourne decided to ride out with Mr. Ives, heaven only knows why, as I for one certainly do not. But they should have returned here long ago. Perhaps an accident?" she suggested, looking up at Ben for guidance.

"Or worse," returned the footman, recalling the tingling feeling he got at the back of his neck every time Mr. Ives present. "Goldie tol' me as 'ow she fetched missus 'er winnin's afore she lopped off. Oi been askin' m'self wot a body wit five thousand pounds in 'er boung would be doin' ridin' inna bankrupt cart. Seems havey-cavey ta me, miss."

"I should say so!" exclaimed Miss Gladwin, rising

to her feet and beginning to pace the carpet. "Now, Ben," she said severely, whirling to face the diminutive footman, "I want you to tell me everything—about the money, Mr. Ives, the whole of it. And in the very best English you can muster, please, Ben, as I think Lady Bourne may be in some kind of trouble. I'm counting on you, Ben; don't fail me!"

More than a quarter hour of valuable time was spent in listening to and then deciphering Ben's tale of what had gone on during Dean Ives's visit that morning, what with the agitated servant interrupting himself over and over to give Lucy a few pithy (and none too kind) interpretations of his own regarding Mr. Ives's character, disposition, and probable parents, as well as a few other breaks in his monologue during which time he roundly berated himself for not noshing that slimy cove on his noggin and putting an end to it before the missus could go off with him in the first place. But at last Lucy understood, and she immediately sent her papa's carriage, with Renfrew riding inside, off on a round of the clubs in an effort to find Kit.

Renfrew ran his master to ground at Watier's, and the earl, with Mr. Norwood in tow acting as interested observer, made short work of driving back to Berkeley Square. "Is she back yet?" an agitated Kit asked anxiously as he bounded into the drawing room, his eyes searching for Jennie. Although the trip from Watier's was not a long one, Kit had already been through several kinds of hell imagining what could have happened to his darling wife.

"She is not," intoned a gravely solemn Miss Bundy, who, in company with Lucy and her Aunt Rachel, had been making great inroads on picturing Jennie in all manner of dire predicaments. "How dare that child tease me to death like this? I vow I feel like an afflicted parent, destined to spend the remainder of my days watching my head turn gray because of the viper I have nurtured at my bosom." Only Miss Bundy's sorrowful tone and very obvious distress kept Kit from telling the woman to stifle herself before he did her an injury.

Flying into a rage would, he knew, serve no real purpose—although it was hard to deny an almost overwhelming desire to kick something—and Kit purposefully downed a bracing two fingers of whiskey before asking Lucy to tell him everything she knew. Once the girl had delivered her small store of hard information—embellished more than a little bit by way of her fertile imagination—the earl knew they could have a real problem on their hands.

"Ozzy," he asked, "can you think of any reason for Ives to be calling on m'wife? I'd be inclined to think he asked her for a loan, but even Ives seems too intelligent to try such a ridiculous stunt."

Mr. Norwood could see that Kit was as sore as a boil and trying not to explode, and he could only hope that Kit wouldn't soon recall just who had first introduced Ives to the Wildes and take out his anger on him. "What? *Me?*" Ozzy exclaimed incredulously. "Why would I know anything? You know me, Kit, old fellow; dense as a house, that's me. I haven't a clue what maggot Ives has taken into his head. It's you that's got a brain sharp as needles. You figure it out!"

"You're a real brick, Ozzy," Kit gritted sarcastically as Lucy crossed her arms across her breast and rolled her eyes. "All right," he went on, taking a deep breath and squaring his shoulders, "I will figure it out. But," he warned, his fierce expression freezing Mr. Norwood where he stood, "once I *have* got it figured out I will expect your wholehearted cooperation in whatever steps have to be taken from there. Surely, old fellow," he drawled, "you are not so dull as to misunderstand what I am saying."

Ozzy swallowed hard and waved his hand as if to say get on with it. While the ladies sat watching from the sidelines, Kit took his turn pacing the carpet, telling everyone that he was sure Ives had fed Jennie some line of drivel that convinced her she must use her winnings to save some poor unfortunate chimney sweep or some such faradiddle. Perhaps, he told his assembled audience with more hope than assurance, once he had been successful in relieving Jennie of her heavy purse he would return her to Berkeley Square. After all, he pointed out logically, Ives couldn't kidnap Jennie, for goodness' sake—else he'd have to flee the country. "And God knows five thousand pounds isn't worth that," he ended, smiling a bit as he began to believe what he was saying. Jennie, sweet, gullible soul that she was, would be out her winnings, but she would have learned a valuable lesson about putting her trust in people who did not deserve it.

"Four thousand, five hundred pounds," Miss Bundy corrected helpfully. "Jennie quite naturally reserved five hundred pounds for Charity and little George."

"Naturally." Kit grinned, his spirits lifting momentarily. "But unless I sadly mistake my man, Ives will be paying his tailor and a half-dozen other creditors with the remainder of the proceeds. What I don't understand is why it is taking so long to relieve my wife of her winnings. It certainly didn't take Ives long to persuade her to ride out with him, if what Ben told Lucy is correct. No," he said, shaking his head, "there's something more to this, and I'd give my best bays to know exactly what it is."

The earl's bays were a real prize, and Ozzy saw his chance to have himself riding up behind them in his own curricle. "Ives has been running tame in this house before with you not home, right?" he asked in sudden inspiration. "Could it be your filly has bolted with him? After all, old fellow, you said yourself that she was an easy mark."

It took the combined efforts of Del, Bob, and Ben to keep the enraged Kit from bashing his good friend into a pulp, so great was the man's exception to the suggestion that his wife had run off with another man. "Now, now, guv'nor," Ben soothed as he dangled three feet off the floor, with his arms and legs wrapped around his lordship's waist and neck. "Anyone ken see wot the cove's dicked in the nob. Ya ain't gonna let no croaker with the wit o'three 'ave ya dancin' at Beilby's Ball?"

"What did he say?" Lucy asked Renfrew, who had by necessity become quite conversant in the footmen's mode of cant. "Ben has referred to Mr. Norwood as being crazy in the head, miss," he whispered under his breath as Kit peeled off his protectors and shook out his sleeves. "And then Ben suggested that his lordship shouldn't allow any foreteller of bad news who had only the combined wit of two fools and a madman to nudge him into doing murder and then being hanged. Beilby was a famous hangman, I believe."

"Oh," Lucy said, nodding her understanding. "Thank you, Renfrew. Jennie said I could always look to you to know the answer to anything, and she was correct. Perhaps you have a solution to our current problem you might share with us."

"Well, miss, now that you mention it," Renfrew confessed shyly, "I have been thinking it might be a good idea to call in the Bow Street Runners and see what they think."

"China Street Pigs!" the three footmen shouted as one. "What d'ya want wit' them red breasts?" Clearly the Bourne servants had no high opinion of the gentlemen of Bow Street.

"The Runners would appear to be either extremely incompetent," observed Lucy's Aunt Rachel prosaically, "or quite the reverse, considering the reaction these servants have had to the butler's suggestion." As Lucy had told Jennie, her aunt might not be talkative, but when she said something it usually made perfect sense.

Kit's grudging acceptance of his hasty apology having eased Ozzy's fears that his lifelong friend was about to do him bodily harm, the man felt no qualms about opening his mouth yet again. "Bow Street would only assign one or two men," he said contemptuously. "If your lady is adrift in London with Ives it will take a small army to ferret her out."

Kit looked about the room, noticing the collection of bodies gathered around both doorways in an effort to hear what was going on, and then counted the heads of those already in the room. "A small army, hmmm?" He smiled, spreading his arms wide. "And what would you call this gathering, Ozzy? Look around you. What do you see?"

"I see a giant, a dwarf, a madman holding a cleaver, two Drury Lane madams, and a trio of bandy-legged escapees from Newgate. And all of us, of course," he ended hastily when Lucy made a point of clearing her throat to call attention to herself.

"Oh, how famous," Lucy shouted, catching Kit's drift in an instant. "We *are* a small army!"

Kit bowed her his congratulations. "My servants, you will understand, abound in all the first-rate virtues—pocket-picking, petty thievery, head-bashing, et cetera. Although my wife would argue the point, I am sure, I believe it is time I set my servants to a job for which they are uniquely qualified. Gentlemen, ladies," he inquired silkily, turning to the assembled servants, "what say you? Can you find Lady Bourne for me?"

Ben smiled, revealing his sparse teeth. "Quicker than the cat ken lick 'er ear, guv'nor!" he replied promptly. "Jist let me an' the rest 'ave a little council o' war, so ta speak, an' we'll be off."

"Report back to me here as soon as you learn something," Kit called after the small group as they headed for the kitchen to hold a conference. "Lady Bourne may return on her own, you know. But if she doesn't, I reserve the right of rescuing her for myself. You just find her for me. Mr. Ives," he said grimly, "is mine." At Tiny's groan of disappointment Kit smiled at the giant and added cheerfully enough, "Never fret, old son. If you're very good, I just may let you have him once I'm through with him," a promise which resulted in a round of cheers from all the misfits whose devotion to the angel who had rescued them from poverty knew no bounds.

"What about me?" Ozzy asked, looking rather crestfallen at the thought of being left out of all the fun.

"You run around to Ives's rooms and see if you can pick up any clues from his manservant. Lucy and the rest of us will wait here in case Jennie comes home or…"

"Or what?" Lucy asked worriedly, coming over to Kit and laying a hand on his arm.

"Or until a message arrives telling us that Jennie is being held for ransom." Lucy gasped, and Kit wheeled on his heels, striding toward the library where he kept his pistols. He had gone through hell and more on the Peninsula, he thought ruefully as he lifted his pistols down from the shelf, but never before could he remember his hands shaking so terribly at the thought of a coming battle.

IT WAS COMING ON TO DARK when Ozzy reentered the mansion in Berkeley Square, a note held in his outstretched hand. "Here it is, Kit," he shouted, tossing the paper to his friend before dropping heavily into a nearby chair. "I had the devil's own time getting Ives's landlord to let me in, but once I had crossed his palm with a little bit of the ready he became quite obliging. Ives has cut and run, that's for sure, as the whole place was stripped bare, and I found this note on his dressing table. I imagine he left it there knowing we'd be searching his place before long." Ozzy shook his head sorrowfully, obviously blaming himself for the whole affair. "I never knew what he was like, Kit, I swear it, or else I'd never have let him within sight of your Jennie."

But Kit wasn't listening. After reading the note he rolled it into a ball and angrily tossed it into the fireplace. "He doesn't tell us anything we hadn't already figured out once Jennie hadn't returned home for dinner. He's got her, sure as check, but the kitten's gambling winnings are no more than a down payment on the sum he's asking for now. What he doesn't say is how I'm to get the ransom to him—or when the exchange is to be made. That paper's as worthless as Ives himself."

Lucy could understand Kit's chagrin, for she felt just as helpless. She had been cudgeling her brain for the last hour and more without coming up with a single answer. But now the faint glimmering of an idea shed some light on the matter, and she jumped to her feet, crying. "What about the address Del lifted from Ives's pocket the other day? I remember it as being somewhere in

Holborn. Perhaps it is a clue. Renfrew!" she called unnecessarily, for the butler was already making free of his
mistress's writing desk, searching for a slip of paper.

"Ah, thank you," Lucy said, relieving the butler of his
prize and handing the note over to the bewildered earl,
who had not been informed of Del's little lapse into his
former line of work. "We found this in Ives's pocket,
Kit. See, it's the address of a house on Cow Cross Street.
Surely this is a clue, for why else would the man have
need of such an address if he did not mean to hide our
Jennie away there while he waited for you to pay the
ransom?"

Kit looked at the paper, hope leaping in his chest. "It
may just be the address of some accomplice he has
hired to serve him," he pointed out, trying not to become
too excited. "A man can rent killers in Holborn at two
a penny, you know."

"Jack Ketch's Warren, guv'nor," Ben corrected as he
walked into the room. "That's the 'andle wot we gives
ta Holborn. That's where the missus be, all right, but
'ow'd ya ken it afore Oi told ya?"

The small army was back together once more, and
Kit readily allowed Ben to take charge for the moment,
everyone listening intently while the thief-turned-foot-
man painted a highly colorful picture of just what they
were likely to find at number fourteen, Cow Cross
Street. All the houses there were divided top to bottom
into apartments, most of them having two or more doors
to the outside, making them highly desirable homes for
thieves and other cutthroats. The house Ives had chosen
for stowing Lady Bourne in until his demands were met
was one of the largest, housing a gin shop on the ground
floor, a gaming hall on the first, and a half dozen or more
apartments converted for use by low prostitutes. The rest

of the apartments, Ben informed them, were used as dens for thieves and low toby men in the area. "'Tisn't a pretty place, guv'nor," Del added unnecessarily.

By the time Ben was finished, Goldie was lost to the small army, having been commissioned by the earl to take charge of Miss Bundy, another casualty, who had broken into loud sobs and been asked to vacate the room before her hysteria became contagious. That left Tizzie and Lizzie, Renfrew, the three footmen, Tiny and Goliath, Montague, Kit, Ozzy, Lucy, and Aunt Rachel. A mixed bag of rescuers, but the best the earl could come up with on such short notice.

Now they needed a plan. Ben took up his position beside Bob and Del as Kit stepped to center stage and took command. After a few pointed questions to each of his small assault force, during which he learned of their various specialties and individual talents, he set about utilizing each one of them to the fullest of their potential. The result was a plan that owed equally to ingenuity and good luck. It may not have done justice to Lord Wellesley's genius, but it was all they had. And, for Jennie's sake, they would make the best of it.

"AND TO THINK all this is happening because of a silly rabbit trap." Jennie shook her head as she commented ruefully on the bizarre chain of events that seemingly innocuous episode had set into motion.

"What's that?" Dean Ives, who had been consulting with his three cohorts, turned to ask, wondering if the girl had been unhinged by her abduction and taken to babbling to herself.

"Nothing that would interest you, Mr. Ives," she told him cuttingly, "as you don't stand to gain a groat by it. You know, of course, that this whole thing is no more than a great piece of nonsense. It would be famous if Kit refuses to pay you your blood money. Perhaps you should have thought of that before you began this little game. After all, Kit might not care a fig about me and refuse your demands. Oh yes indeed, Mr. Ives," she ended smugly, "I believe you just may have made a muff of it after all."

Ives came to stand in front of her, smiling down at his captive in amusement. "Oh no, my lady, I fear you are wrong there. I've seen your husband's face as he looks at you. He cares about you right enough, and I'll be willing to bet he'll pay me every penny I've asked for to have you back. I'm only sorry you have to be inconvenienced this way," he apologized, motioning toward the bonds that held her.

"No, you're not," Jennie contradicted.

"No," Ives laughed, "I'm not. I just thought it would be the gentlemanly thing to say."

Jennie would have given anything she had to be able to slap that silly grin from her captor's face; but her hands were tied securely behind her and she had to content herself with sticking out her tongue at Ives's back as he turned back to his companions. How could she have been so incredibly stupid, so trustingly naive, as to believe that farradiddle about Ives sponsoring an orphanage? Anyone could see the man hadn't a charitable bone in his entire body. Oh, Kit would roast her good for this one once he got her out of this terrible coil. That her husband would rescue her she had not the slightest doubt, only wishing that he would hurry because her surroundings, shabby, smelly, and dirty as they were, had begun to prey on her nerves. Imagine the many innocent children who were forced to live in such squalor, she thought worriedly. Surely such conditions could not be allowed to continue.

If Kit had known just where his wife's thoughts were heading, he would have made even greater haste in rescuing her.

IT WAS FULL DARK when Kit's small army descended on Cow Cross Street, their raggedy, unkempt appearances making no stir among the street's inhabitants. At a signal from their leader they dispersed, going off in small groups of two and three, while Kit himself melted into the shadows directly across from the front door of number fourteen, pulling Ozzy behind him.

"It's a good thing you convinced Miss Gladwin and her aunt that they'd serve no purpose coming here," Ozzy whispered. "Can't say as I'd like them to see what's going on over there." Kit looked to the open door of the gin shop to see two sadder examples of their fellow men as they staggered out into the gutter, a bare-chested female of indeterminate years pressed between them, sharing her wares equally with the men as they grappled drunkenly at her body.

"It's also a good thing Lord Thorpe's too high a stickler to have a reputation for taking Blue Ruin with his fellows in such places, or else we'd never have been shed of her so easily," Kit commented dryly. "But with Renfrew promising to keep them in Berkeley Square by brute force if necessary, I don't believe we'll have to worry about Miss Gladwin showing up to add her little bit to the rescue."

"She's game as a pebble, ain't she?" Ozzy remarked admiringly.

Kit pulled a face. "She is that, Ozzy, but I'll take my Jennie any day. They may both be full of heart, but m'wife's decidedly more restful. I don't know that I could stand Lucy's determined streak over the long haul.

I tell you, Ozzy, it will take a strong man to keep that chit on the leash. Jennie may rule me, sport, but at least she allows me the illusion of being in charge. Take this mess with Ives, for instance. If it were Lucy hidden away in that building I'd be worried senseless wondering what scheme she was hatching in her head to free herself. Jennie, the sweet love, will remain calm, knowing it is my place to effect the rescue. It warms a man, truly it does, to know the love of his life invests him with so much trust."

Ozzy merely sniffed, thinking his friend looked more than a little smug, but he was not envious of Kit's good fortune, merely thankful he himself was heartfree and able to enjoy his women without having to feel responsible for them.

A movement from across the garbage-strewn street caught their attention, and Tizzie and Lizzie, a drooping Montague supported between them, came into sight. The former actresses were dressed to the teeth in matching costumes they had worn when portraying ladies-in-waiting some twenty years earlier, and their painted faces and outrageous plumed coiffures fairly screeched that these were two practitioners of the world's oldest profession.

Montague was a sight to inspire awe in his audience, which, thanks to the dramatic caterwauling of Tizzie and Lizzie, was growing by leaps and bounds. When Tizzie had produced the costume, Kit had known at once that it would come in handy, being, as the actress described it, "a suit o' clothes for a ghostie, picked up fer a song at a sale on Drury Lane." It consisted of a bloody shirt, a doublet curiously pinked, and a coat with three great eyelet holes upon the breast. A bottle of "genuine-looking human blood" was included in the sale, and Tizzie had made liberal use of the fluid, copiously dousing Montague's head and chest with the gory confection.

"Oh, good sirs, 'elp us please!" Tizzie cried as Montague moaned and lapsed into incoherent French. "We wuz set upon by footpads," the actress informed her audience, "and they 'ave done murder to Misyoor Montague. 'elp us, do, ta get 'im inside."

"'elp us, 'elp us," Lizzie parroted, allowing her low neckline to droop just a bit more under the strain of lugging the ample Montague toward the gin-shop door, and the sight of her buxom figure prompted three slightly built beggars to break from the crowd and offer their assistance to the ladies.

"'ere now," said one of the beggars, a man covered head to foot in hideous running sores meant to illicit pity from passersby who would then drop pennies in his cup, "Oi'll 'elp ya, girlie."

"Hard to believe those sores aren't real," Kit commented, watching Ben take charge of the situation, Bob and Del assisting him as all five moved inside the gin shop and commandeered center stage by means of Montague's bloody appearance and the women's loud lamentations of woe and impending disaster.

"'e's dyin', 'e's dyin'," Tizzie screeched, ripping at her hair as Montague groaned and allowed his tongue to loll obscenely from the corner of his bloody mouth.

"Not 'ere, 'e ain't!" the tapster contradicted angrily. "Get 'im the bloody 'ell outa m'shop afore Oi finish the job wot the other coves started. 'ave 'im do 'is ruddy bleedin' somewheres else."

"Lizzie," Tizzie shouted loudly as the tapster moved to make good his threat, "show 'em the beans. Iffen they sees the lour mebbee summun will 'elp us fetch pur

Misyoor Montague a autem bawler—'tis too late fer naught else but the eternity box for 'im anyways."

At Tizzie's reassuring wink, Lizzie reached deep inside her bodice and pulled out a leather drawstring bag heavy with gold. The crowd of raggedy beggars and narrow-eyed cutthroats concentrated their attention on the bag Lizzie held aloft, and it took no more than a second for one of their number to make a grab for it—the man with the open running sores, to be exact.

Instant pandemonium broke loose in the gin shop on the ground floor of number fourteen as the leather pouch came undone and a shower of gold guineas rained down among the crowd, who dropped to their knees to scrabble in the filth after the bouncing, rolling coins.

"Now!" Kit hissed to Ozzy, breaking from the shadows as Del stood in the doorway and waved the all-clear. As Tizzie and Lizzie, their part in the scheme completed, were led out of the shop by Bob, who had been commissioned with the job of returning the ladies safely to Berkeley Square, Kit and Ozzy slid into the gin shop undetected, squeezed past the mass of humanity pummeling each other on the floor, and passed through the door Ben had promised them led to a stairway to the upper floors. When Kit took one last look back into the shop it was to see Montague, his gunshot-rent, bloody shirt easy to spot in the fray, happily knocking heads together as if it were the greatest of good fun. "Come to me, little cabbage," Kit heard the chef croon, stalking the tapster who had refused a dying man sanctuary, and the earl only wished he could stay and watch more of the melee.

The sounds of the fight reached the ears of Tiny and Goliath, who had been standing at the rear of number fourteen waiting for precisely that signal to begin their part of the rescue. "Up we go," Goliath chortled as Tiny boosted his small friend up to the windowsill far above them. Goliath disappeared for a moment, only to reappear at the back door into the alley, which he had opened from the inside. "In ya get, Tiny," he whispered from the darkness. "Hoist me up now, friend—we's ta track up the dancers afore that Ives cove can trig it outta 'ere. We'll teach 'm ta snaggle our missus!"

IVES HAD BEEN BUSY composing an inspired note to Lord Bourne detailing instructions on the delivery of the ransom when the commotion from the ground floor reached the apartment on the fourth floor. Sending one of his fellows downstairs to check on the noise, Ives was not best pleased to see his captive smiling at him, obviously certain that her rescue was at hand.

"I warned you, Mr. Ives," Jennie said pleasantly. "You will soon be prodigiously sorry you have gone up against my husband. He's been mentioned in dispatches, you know, for his bravery in battle. I do believe you are about to see all your nasty plans fall to pieces. Perhaps he will go easy on you if you release me now. Else—" she shrugged diffidently "—I vow I will not be held accountable for the consequences. Lord Bourne has a fearsome temper when he's been crossed."

Ives did not like the effect Jennie's calm assurance had on his two remaining hirelings. Damn the woman anyway, he thought fiercely. She's supposed to be crying and swooning, not sitting there grinning like a child who's just been handed a birthday treat. Didn't the chit know anything? So far the only fear she'd shown at all was to worry that everyone else would be worrying about her. It just wasn't natural, Ives reflected, giving the countess a nasty look, and besides, it took all the fun out of the thing. If he was going to have to gather up the ransom and flee the country the least she could do was act as if he intimidated her a little bit.

When his cohort came back to say that it was a big to-do about nothing, only some fistfight among the customers of the gin shop, Ives felt it was his turn for a little gloating. "So much for your awe-inspiring soldier husband, madam. There'll be no rescue, only a gentlemanly exchange—his money for your life. No one knows you're here, you know, and even if they did it wouldn't do them any good. I can just see it now—the high and mighty Earl of Bourne sauntering down Cow Cross Street, sticking out like a sore thumb. He'd have his throat slit in a minute for his trouble." The man's features turned hard as he attempted to wipe the smile from Jennie's face once and for all. "Now shut up, or your husband is going to be paying good money for a lifeless corpse."

But it was Jennie who got in the last word. "I doubt it, Mr. Ives. Kit wouldn't pay a bent penny for you— dead or alive!"

THE STEEP, NARROW STAIRS led up into the darkness, twisting and turning as they rose past three floors of apartments that Ben told his master were rented out by the month, the day and, at times, the hour, for any number of reasons—none of them very savory. By the time the small party reached the fourth floor, Ozzy was holding a scented handkerchief to his nose to smother the combined smell of cooked cabbage, old sweat, and human waste. The tilted floor creaked slightly as they tiptoed across it, heading for the nearest door. Kit put his ear to it, listening for some sound, and then stepped a few paces back, clearly intending to break down the barrier with his shoulder, but Ben stopped him just before he could fling his body against the wood. "'ere now, guv'nor, iffen ya wants ta dub the jigger, 'ow 'bout usin' the locksmith's daughter?" the former pickpocket asked quietly, dangling a large set of keys in front of Kit's eyes invitingly.

"Ben's a right fine dimber damber man, ain't 'e, guv'nor?" Del whispered, obviously proud of Ben's talent in relieving the tapster of his keys. "It's proud Oi am wot knows 'im."

While Ozzy stuffed his handkerchief into his mouth to stifle his mirth, Kit bowed his head to Ben and took possession of the keys. Silent as a band of mice tiptoeing over cotton wadding, Kit turned lock after lock along the long hallway, trial and error showing him that a single brass key fit all the doors. All but two of the rooms were empty, with a snoring drunk and a couple lost in each other and unaware of any intrusion being the sole inhabitants of the other rooms.

But when they reached the second-to-the-last door near the end of the hall, Kit motioned that he could hear voices on the other side of the wooden barrier. Pocketing the set of keys, Kit chose to crash through the door by running against it full tilt with his shoulder, a move that caught the four men inside the room unawares and served to set loose a rousing cheer from the female tied up in the corner. Unfortunately, this move also caused Kit to cannon out of control all the way to the far wall, and while Ozzy quickly nabbed one of Ives's hirelings and Ben and Del succeeded in tackling and sitting on the second, the third man and Ives scrambled out the doorway untouched.

Dropping a quick kiss on the end of his wife's nose, Kit ran back the way he had come in time to see that

Ives and the last man had split up, the hireling heading for the back stairs (and the waiting Tiny), and Ives choosing to escape via the front stairs that led to the gin shop. "Watch Jennie!" Kit called back over his shoulder as he made a grab for the rickety stair rail and set off in pursuit of Ives, anger lending wings to his feet.

Ives had reached the ground floor and had taken two steps into the gin shop when Kit, launching himself like a pouncing tiger, caught him from the back, the two of them tumbling into the middle of the fight that was just then winding down. As Kit dragged Ives to his feet and set himself in a sparring attitude, the crowd quickly formed a circle around the two combatants, eager to see what looked to be a fine display of cross-and-jostle work.

They were not to be disappointed. Both Bourne and Ives had studied under Gentleman Jackson, and being much of the same size and weight, the men put on a much better show than any mill in recent memory. But anger lent strength to Kit's punches, and it was not long before Dean Ives lay sprawled against the bar, his legs splayed out in front of him as he lapsed into unconsciousness. While Kit stood at the ready, more than willing to go a few more rounds, Ben entered the room and, looking about happily, spied a nearby slop jar, the contents of which he dumped over Ives's head, supposedly to revive him.

The ring of onlookers, still cheering over the spectacle, parted then, and Goliath came bounding into the room, doing handsprings as he made a path for the giant Tiny, who was carrying the third hireling under his arm like a sack of grain. "I be done wit 'im now," Tiny told the earl, dropping the unconscious man at Kit's feet. "D'ya be wantin' 'im dead, master? 'e's jist sleepin' fer now, but I be 'appy ta fix that iffen ya jist give Tiny the word."

Sight of the huge black man had the customers of the gin shop at number fourteen thinking wistfully of their homes and beds, and the crowd thinned rapidly, leaving the tapster quite alone to face the strangers in his midst. "Makes me no never mind," that man piped up helpfully to answer Tiny's question. "Jist git 'em outta 'ere, an' Jack Gooden'll keep mum about it."

"I'll just bet you will," Kit opined thinly, his level stare effectively wiping the smile from the tapster's face. "Why don't you be a good fellow and play least in sight for a bit, hmmm?" Kit suggested smoothly, and the man, wiping his broad hands nervously on his leather apron, backed hurriedly toward the open door to the street.

"Take care of things here," Kit ordered Ben, turning toward the stairs once more, looking every inch the earl even dressed as he was in Renfrew's shabby gardening clothes, intent on returning to his kidnapped bride and thus missing Tiny's actions as, following Ben's orders, the giant picked up Ives with one hand and hung the man on a hook by the collar of his stylish jacket.

Kit ran up the stairs two at a time, dabbing a trickle of blood from the cut on his cheek lest Jennie fly into the boughs demanding he see a doctor. Bursting into the room down the hall from the fourth landing, a bit breathless from both the fight with Ives and his long climb, his eyes searched out Jennie, who was rubbing her wrists where her bonds had so recently been. *"Kitten!"* he shouted, breaking into a wide grin as the sound of his voice had her blond head jerking upward, her beautiful face alight with joy.

"Kit!" she exclaimed, hopping to her feet and pitchforking herself into his widespread arms. "I *knew* you would come for me."

Raining kisses over her face and neck, Kit at last gave in to the fear that he had felt at thinking he had lost her—lost his darling kitten—and as Jennie's arms closed tightly around his neck he growled fiercely, "Oh, my love. My dearest, dearest love. I'll never let you out of my sight again! I adore you, my little kitten."

Ozzy clamped his hands down over Del's ears and turned the footman toward the door. "Come with me, my good man. You're too young to see this. Besides, it does me a bad turn to see one of my own kind drooling and slobbering like some lovesick calf." So saying, Ozzy Norwood shepherded his charge and their two captives out of sight of the loving couple and in the direction of the gin shop and more manly pursuits—like trussing up the baddies and hauling them off to the roundhouse before going somewhere private and getting themselves roaring drunk.

IT WASN'T UNTIL MUCH LATER, shed of their well-wishers, bathed, fed, and snuggled up together in the large bed in the master chamber in Berkeley Square, that Jennie brought up a subject that had been teasing at her mind. "Kit, darling," she crooned, lazily marching her fingers up his bare chest, "about Mr. Ives's helpers. They were not a very nice sort, you understand, but there was this one young one…"

"Oh?" Kit urged, his intuition telling him he had better gather his wits about him before she spoke again.

"Yes," she went on thoughtfully. "They gagged me, you know, until I promised not to scream. The young one—I think his name was Hughie—he used my own handkerchief when I protested about the dirty rag they were planning to use. He was so young, Kit," she went on, shifting slightly to look up into her husband's eyes imploringly. "Not a hardened criminal, surely. So I was thinking…"

The Earl of Bourne, feeling a comforting warmth growing deep in his chest, merely smiled and sighed, "Go on, kitten. I'm listening."

EPILOGUE

SIR CEDRIC MAITLAND was in his glory, dandlying his grandson Christopher on his knee while his proud parents looked on fondly. "Do you like that, Christopher?" the man asked the toothless, smiling infant. "One day soon I'll take you riding to hounds with me."

"What?" Kit asked, feigning shock. "With your disky heart?"

"What disky heart?" his father-in-law blustered before ducking his head sheepishly. "Oh, that. I was only funning with you, son, didn't you know?"

"I knew," Kit answered softly, lifting his wife's hand to his lips.

Sir Cedric relaxed and decided to take credit for his daughter's happy marriage. "You'd have gotten around to marrying my baby girl sooner or later. I just helped things along a bit."

Jennie laughed at her papa's silliness and went back to the mail sitting in her lap. Spying her cousin Lucy's childish scrawl, she opened the letter and steeled herself to decipher the crossed lines dotted with inky blotches and crossed-out words. "Oh dear," she sighed at last, putting the letter down.

"What's your cousin up to this time?" Kit asked, taking in his wife's frown. "Don't tell me she's still chasing poor old Thorpe all over creation."

"It's ten times worse than that, darling. It seems Lord Thorpe has somehow been turned out of society in disgrace and Lucy, that dear, sweet girl, has sworn to clear his good name."

Kit cocked his head to one side. "That's our Lucy—never say die."

"Well, I think she's wonderfully brave!" Jennie declared, rising to pick up Christopher and kiss him before handing the child over to the loving care of Tizzie and Lizzie. "Time for your nap, sweetness," she crooned, nuzzling the infant's chubby neck, "and time for our luncheon."

As they adjourned to the dining room arm in arm behind Sir Cedric, Kit kissed Jennie's temple and soothed, "Don't fret, kitten. If I know Lucy, and I'm afraid I do, London is about to be set on its collective heels!"

"Yes, love." Jennie smiled back happily. "And Lord Thorpe—I wonder how he'll fare, once Lucy gets the bit between her teeth."

Kit chuckled at the thought. "I can't say for sure, but I'll wager my best hunter the toplofty Lord Thorpe will never know what hit him!"

"Poor man," Jennie giggled, her green eyes dancing. "What I wouldn't give to be there when his lordship realizes Lucy intends to become a dragon in his defense."

"I'm afraid you'll have to miss the fun, pet, as Christopher and I have need of you here. Most especially me. Didn't you say you were going to show me your secret place in the Home Wood this afternoon?" he said, waggling his eyebrows at her conspiratorially. "The place nobody else can find where you like to lie on the soft grass and gaze up at the sky through the overhanging trees?"

"Why, Christopher Wilde," Jennie simpered suggestively, leaning into his shoulder as he pulled out her chair. "Whatever do you have in mind?"

"Dessert, my dear," he whispered in her ear, sending a delicious tingle up her spine. "Just a little dessert."

"What a lovely idea," Jennie breathed softly, blushing like a young maiden as her papa discreetly coughed into his napkin, pretending he hadn't heard a single word of the lovers' exchange.

Supremely satisfied with himself and the world at large, he then leaned back comfortably in his chair, silently hoping that Montague had prepared his favorite strawberry tarts for dessert. To each generation its own idea of pleasure, Sir Cedric heartily believed, and at *his* age, downing three strawberry tarts—his and Jennie's and Kit's—in one sitting was all the adventure he could stand. With any luck at all, he then told himself complacently, making yet another wish as out of the corners of his eyes he watched Kit and his daughter gazing into each other's eyes like moonstruck calves, young Christopher is not destined to be my only grandchild.

Happily, as it turned out, Sir Cedric was not to be disappointed on either account.

THE ENTERPRISING LORD EDWARD

To congenial Eddie Charles and his lovely wife,
Kay – otherwise known as my parents –
on the occasion of their wedding anniversary.
I love ya, guys.

PROLOGUE

"YES, YES. I BELIEVE I like this new way you've found with my cravat. Very well, Burton, I think I'll do now, thank you. It's time for me to sally forth once again into the fray. She still hates me, you know. It's most lowering for a man like me, who's so used to females falling at his feet. And don't frown—I know I'm being immodest. It's part of my boyish charm. You don't suppose there's some way to go about this?"

Burton looked up at the author of these self-serving statements as that man's upper body was reflected down to him in the dressing-stand mirror. As usual, his master was the epitome of sartorial perfection, although his servant would be the last ever to tell him that. "There's always incarceration, I imagine, my lord, if you've the stomach for it."

Lord Edward Laurence allowed his fine broad shoulders to slump forward dejectedly, momentarily destroying the fine line of his new evening coat. "You're always so subtle, Burton. Papa should never have set you loose in his library, you little demon. 'Incarceration.' Oh, yes, indeed, that alternative would send my poor sire to spinning in his grave for sure. No, I've no real alternative, do I? But you could at least offer me some compassion, you know. I'm too young to be purposely contemplating coming to such a sad end, even if she is so superior a female."

"Yes, my lord," Burton answered quietly, unimpressed by this show of despair, for he knew it to be only that, and his master was more than ready to meet his fate. "If you've done with admiring yourself, shall I fetch your evening cloak?"

"You may, confound you. It isn't seemly, Burton, to appear always in so much of a rush. I'm sure Reggie can be left to his own devices for a few more weeks without all of Lyndhurst Hall coming to grief. Do you suppose I should let Monty have the writing of my epitaph? Something like 'Here lies Lord Edward; gone the way of Matrimony'?"

"Your father, rest his long-suffering soul, would be most proud of you, my lord," the servant said bolsteringly, clambering onto a nearby handy chair so that he could slip the burgundy satin evening cloak around his lordship's shoulders, adding, "although I doubt he'd have gone so far as to endorse your methods of ensuring the line."

Lord Edward grinned into the mirror, gifting his servant with a reflected wink. "We both agree I must marry, little general, and soon, but I don't recall promising not to have myself a little fun along the way. Besides, the female I'm considering can't see me for dust, something she has brought home to me quite forcefully every time we meet. Dear me, do you suppose that's why I've chosen her? Perhaps I am insincere; perhaps I have not totally reconciled myself to my fate."

Burton sniffed derisively as he replaced the chair in a corner of the dressing room and tugged his waistcoat lower over his protruding stomach. "I still believe a more straight-forward method to be best, as we are pressed for time."

Shaking his head in the negative, a movement that sent a single lock of dark blond hair tumbling back down onto his forehead, its favorite resting place, Lord Edward replied mischievously, "Too tame by half, Burton, old man, and too damned boring as well. Although I imagine I could fling a sack over her head and spirit her off to Gretna and have done with this intrigue. Be happy I'm only planning to make her aware of me for a start. Besides, I must still get her down to Lyndhurst to make sure she and Reggie will be compatible, before I actually allow myself to be led to the altar. Who knows, it may turn out that she is the wrong solution altogether. I couldn't be happy with her, no matter how well we might suit, if she couldn't be happy with Reggie."

"She's suitable," the little servant said, getting some small measure of his own back as he followed his master out onto the landing and down the stairs. "After all, she doesn't like you, does she?"

CHAPTER ONE

"GAD, NED, BUT I LOVE A FARCE!"

Lord Edward leaned back in the seat in his private box and drawled, "But, my dear Monty, much as I hate to see you cast down, I do believe the author's intent was quite serious."

Lord Henry Montgomery was immediately crestfallen, lowering his almost nonexistent chin onto his cravat and thrusting out his thin lower lip. "If you're correct, Ned, it means that I have vastly overestimated the man. I believe him to be *deliberately* awful."

"You must be shattered," Lord Edward observed mildly, his lips twitching as he delighted in his friend's chagrin. "However, the little warbler is rather nice, if a bit chicken-breasted. Or am I wrong, and you aren't harboring plans in her direction?"

"I am not!" Lord Henry, flushing, protested at once, before adding more softly, "Besides, Del's already stolen a march on me, blast him for a clumsy, overgrown Romeo. He's meeting her for a late supper, unless he's been telling tales, which wouldn't surprise me."

"Leaving the two of us to brave the Duchess of Chilworth's party alone." Lord Edward sighed deeply, as if resigning himself to the inevitable boredom of the evening, then added more hopefully, "One can only hope Lady Georgiana will still be free for a waltz. My heart is already pitter-pattering at the thought."

Lord Henry snorted derisively. "Hah! Your heart never pitter-pattered in your entire life. It beats most slowly and regularly all the time you are breaking female hearts throughout Mayfair—or at least it did the last time you were in town. So far this Season you have been almost dull. Time was you'd have given Del a real run for his money with that songbird. I gather it is Lady Georgiana's turn to crumple at your feet now that you're confining yourself to eligible young ladies. At least she'll do it gracefully—she's a remarkable dancer."

Leisurely rising from his seat, as the play had at last ground down to its uninspired conclusion, Lord Edward stood back to allow his friend to pass in front of him and out into the crowded corridor. "How you malign me, Monty, all because I have committed the grave sin of— at long last—growing up. Yes, you have found me out. It's true—I am on the lookout for a wife."

"Surely you jest!"

"Strange, is it not? Perhaps it has something to do with my advanced age. But only think about it a moment, Monty. I'll soon be celebrating my thirty-second, you know. With my dear brother Reginald already knocking at the door of fifty, and showing no signs of taking himself a wife, I really must consider setting up my own nursery. It is no more than my duty."

"You actually want me to think about Naughty Ned becoming serious about a female," Lord Henry mused, pursing his lips. "The mind reels. But surely not Lady Georgiana? That's taking sacrifice a step too far, if you ask me. But never say I didn't stand by you. Shall you be wishing for me to compose an ode to her vacant green eyes—not that she'll understand more than every third word of it."

They slowly made their way through the crush leading down the staircase to the street, the taller Lord Edward thoughtfully guiding his friend by the elbow as he spied out his carriage waiting a little way down the street. "Poetry is always nice," was all he said, remembering his earlier jest to Burton. "You don't approve of Lady Georgiana, Monty?"

"As a pretty ornament to be worn on your sleeve, perhaps, Ned. But as mother to these children you seem to be wanting? Hardly. She's totally lacking in wit. I read her my poem *Love's Splinter Smote My Eye*—you remember it, I'm sure, as you said it was one of your favorites—and all she had to say for herself when I was done was to blink those outrageous eyes at me and ask if I'd seen a physician about having the thing removed. I nearly wept, I tell you."

Lord Edward hid his amusement in a discreet cough, gave his driver directions to bear them to the duchess's residence in Portman Square, and then followed his friend into the carriage. "She may be deeper than you think, Monty," he pointed out helpfully, "and meant her words as a literary criticism. Had you thought of that?"

"Of course she did," Lord Henry responded waspishly. "Forgive me for doubting her. Lady Georgiana is deep. She's as deep as the Dead Sea. Now explain to me, if you can, her comment that Byron was being rather mean to have called his friend Boatswain a *dog* in the inscription on the fellow's own tombstone."

Now Lord Edward threw back his head and roared in utter delight. "She didn't! Did you explain to the poor dear that Boatswain *was,* after all, a Newfoundland?"

Lord Henry was laughing now too, for, he reasoned,

if Lady Georgiana had insulted the great Byron as well, he was in good company. "I did," he said, barely able to control his voice for his mirth. "She said—and I swear, Ned, she did it with a straight face—she said it didn't matter one whit to her if the unfortunate fellow *was* a foreigner, Byron showed a sad lack of manners."

When he had recovered from his fit of hilarity, wiping his streaming eyes with the crisp white handkerchief he had pulled from his coat pocket, Lord Edward said, "Now I know she must have been hoaxing you. *Nobody* could be that obtuse. I will have to make a special point of standing up with her at least three times tonight."

Lord Henry sat stiffly in the far corner of the carriage, his beaky, pointed nose stuck high in the air, bracing himself against the inevitable jostling caused by the poor condition of London's streets and Lord Edward's driver's utter disregard for his passengers. "Old Horry will be *aux anges* when she hears it, I'm sure," he said archly, "—if she can remember your name."

CHAPTER TWO

"OLD HORRY"—known more formally as Hortense, Her Grace, the dowager Duchess of Chilworth—decided that she had spent sufficient time in playing the gracious hostess.

She had been standing at the head of the long curving stairs of the mansion for what must have been hours, greeting everyone and his wife, having her hand hurtfully wrung by beefy, overzealous fists, being poked in the eye by deadly ostrich plumes as paper powdered and scented cheeks were pressed against her own, being called upon to remember titles, and faces, and—worse yet—the names and dispositions of various faceless offspring that meant less than nothing to her but seemed of the utmost importance to the proud parents who mentioned them—all while standing on that hard marble floor in quite the most uncomfortable slippers it had ever been her misfortune to wear.

"They are rather lovely, though," she mused aloud, at last quitting her post and moving toward a chair she knew to be particularly kind to weary bones. "All silvery, and with the sweetest bows."

"I beg your pardon, Aunt Hortense?"

"Oh, it's you…um…"

"Emily, Aunt Hortense, your sister's eldest," Emily Howland supplied, trying not to sigh.

"M'sister's child? Which one would that be, dear?"

"Minerva, Aunt Hortense," Emily clarified. "She's the one with the large teeth," she added carefully, thus avoiding the next sure-to-be-asked question.

Emily had been in Portman Square for just above a month, the poor relation sent to companion her cousin Georgiana during the latter miss's come-out. But each time she approached her aunt she had to introduce herself as if for the first time. The woman was sweet, but she was becoming just a bit wearing. Surely nobody could be this vague—although her mother had warned her it was so.

"Just tell her about my teeth," Emily's mother had told her as she kissed her daughter good-bye in Surrey. "I once bit her arm badly when we were younger, and it seems to have left an indelible impression. Perhaps you might try it yourself, my dear, if all else fails."

"Of course…Emily. I knew that," the duchess said now, smiling up into her niece's face, for the girl was unusually tall. "You don't have her teeth, thank goodness, do you? What a horrid brat Minerva was, and it *was* my kitten, after all. But why are you standing here, child? Shouldn't you be with Georgy?"

"Georgiana's dancing, Aunt, and has been since the very first. She's had no end of partners, although I've been careful not to allow her more than two dances with any one gentleman, just as you told me. I thought I might offer you some refreshments."

Her grace lowered herself carefully into the chair, feeling more fragile this evening than usual. "How sweet. How thoughtful. How very…um…er…"

"…considerate. Yes, of course, Aunt," Emily hastened to supply a suitable word when the duchess began to falter. "There's some lovely punch in the other room, if you'd care for a drink."

"Punch, Miss Howland? Nonsense! Only nectar of the gods will do for the dearest Duchess of Chilworth. Monty, be a good sport and fetch some for her grace at once!"

Emily's back stiffened angrily at the familiar-sounding voice and she turned to confront Lord Edward Laurence, disapproval evident in her set expression. The man was fast becoming the major bane of her existence. "You," she said flatly, refusing to lift her head so that she could look into his mocking eyes.

"C'est moi," Lord Edward agreed happily enough, only slightly inclining his head to acknowledge her rude greeting. "And how fares our resident dragon this evening? Have you found other employment as a serving wench, or has Lady Georgiana at last managed to slip her leash? I had begun to fear the two of you were joined at the hip."

"Sirrah!"

"Now what?" he asked, frowning down at her bowed chestnut head. "Oh, I've been indelicate, haven't I? It's a failing of mine. Allow me to rephrase that. You were joined at the *hand*. There, never let it be said I was ignorant of your sensibilities."

"No, let's not," Emily muttered darkly, turning to leave. "I prefer to believe you merely ignorant in general."

Lord Henry stepped quickly into the breach, having just paid his respects to the dowager, who had made it patently clear she didn't know him from Adam, although she professed delight at seeing him again. "Allow me to accompany you, Miss Howland. I took your advice of the other day, you know, and procured a copy of that book at Hatchard's. Tell me, did you catch the particular irony the author demonstrated in chapter two when he described the…"

Lord Edward watched the pair drift away into the crowd, Lord Henry's balding head nodding up and down agitatedly as he hung on Emily Howland's every word while she answered his rapid-fire questions. How does Monty succeed so easily with the woman, when he always fails? Perhaps he shouldn't take such joy in baiting her. Later, Lord Edward promised Miss Howland silently; I will see to you later.

Turning back to his hostess, he carefully introduced himself—as always, being sure to mention that his late father was the very man who had once been brought to fight a duel for love of her more than two score years ago—and stood back to enjoy her usually incomprehensible, yet always delicious, conversation.

The dowager didn't disappoint him. "Archy's boy, of course. Dear Archy. Dead, ain't he? I could have married him, you know, but he was blond, wasn't he? I can't seem to tell blonds apart, except for dearest Georgiana, of course, as I've lived with her all of her life, and she's such a beautiful child. Girls must be easier. But the men are different somehow. They all look…um…er…"

"Alike?" Lord Edward supplied, wondering yet again how anyone, even Old Horry, could have forgotten his departed Papa's protuberant strawberry-red nose.

"…alike, yes, thank you," the dowager continued happily. "It wouldn't do, would it, to be constantly forgetting what your own husband looked like. And only consider our unborn sons! Imagine how hurt they would have been if their own mama hadn't known them! Why, it might have destroyed them utterly, or at least served to *twist* them in some terrible way, if you take my meaning. You're blond, aren't you? Tell me, my dear, have you ever encountered the problem?" The dowager frowned up at him, clearly distressed for him.

"Not recently, your grace, no," he assured her, patting her hand. "Though I could consider wearing a tag with my name penned on it pinned to my jacket, I suppose."

The duchess sighed. "Oh, heavens, yes. If only everyone were so considerate. I cannot begin to tell you the trouble it would save." Then, smiling at him, she bobbed her head up and down in satisfaction. "It's good you haven't had the problem, my dear, for you seem to be such a nice boy."

Lord Edward, who was no longer a "boy," and who definitely had never before been described as being "nice," tilted his head to one side and gifted his hostess with an angelic smile. "Thank you, madam, I'm sure. Not that I don't sympathize with your difficulty concerning us blonds, of course. It must be quite taxing on your nerves."

"Oh, dear me, yes," she went on earnestly, deciding that this boy was just the sort of fellow her daughter should encourage. "You can imagine what it was like for me in the old days when everybody wore those terrible, itchy…um…er…"

"Wigs?"

"…wigs, yes. A person would walk into a ballroom chock-full of nothing but flour-coated heads and black beauty patches. Of course it was impossible to *know* anyone—unless they had oddly colored eyebrows. The red ones were the most outstanding, as I remember. I think that's how I came to say yes to dearest…um…er… Oh, dear, how terrible! I seem to forget…"

"Charles, ma'am?" Lord Edward prompted hopefully, believing the duchess to be speaking of her husband, who had been dead these fifteen years, definitely too long for her grace to have kept his name in the fore-front of her mind.

"Charles? Yes, Charles—that's it! Thank you. It wasn't until I read about our engagement in the *Times* that I realized dearest Charles was a duke. I just knew that he was the lovely young man with the red eye-brows and the black star stuck to his left cheek, al-though I never told him, of course. He might have gotten upset."

That did it. Lord Edward choked out something about hurrying Lord Henry along with the refreshments and escaped before his sense of humor caused him to fall into public disgrace. He had planned to ingratiate himself with the duchess, who was an integral player in his plan, but it was more than obvious that buttering up Old Horry was naught but an exercise in futility. The duchess wouldn't remember him above a minute, no matter how well she thought she liked him now.

But instead of seeking out his friend, he turned his attention to ferreting out the location of Lady Georgiana among the throng of gracefully gliding dancers, easily spotting her gleaming blond head near the fringes of the polished floor, furiously fanning herself as some young fool all but drooled on her satin-clad feet.

As he had imparted to Lord Henry earlier, Lord Edward thought Lady Georgiana to be one of the most beautiful females he had ever seen, and he stopped for a moment to observe her, for he was an admirer of beautiful things. Lady Georgiana was so small, so daintily formed, so ex-quisitely feminine. She was, in fact, the epitome of English beauty, with soft blond curls, dimpled ivory skin, delicate roses in her cheeks, and wide emerald eyes—eyes that were quite clear and untroubled by any real intelligence.

However, with his mind and heart already otherwise engaged, all this beauty made no lasting impression on Lord Edward, though he did find it difficult to bring himself to believe Lady Georgiana was quite as cotton-headed as his friend Monty swore she was.

As he stood watching the young woman brandishing her fan to the detriment of her aspiring swain's shirt ruffles, he found himself idly thinking that it was unusual for Lord Henry to complain about this lack of brain-power, for intelligence was not usually all that high on any of Monty's or any of his friends' lists of prerequisites in choosing a mate.

After all—he knew these friends would figure—if their children had Lady Georgiana's looks and her husband's brains, those children could consider themselves well-provided-for. That it probably would not occur to the majority of these men that their offspring could conceivably have their looks and Lady Georgiana's brains—or, actually, her lack of brains—reflected only, Lord Edward believed, on their upbringing as Englishmen, and not on any real lack of common sense on their part. They were men, weren't they, and as men they had control of their own destinies. Besides, these gentlemen would doubtless argue, Lady Georgiana was Old Horry's daughter, proving once and for all that daughters resemble their mothers, and their unborn sons would be quite safe.

He might have thought the same as his friends had his life been different, Lord Edward realized, straightening his shoulders and thanking his lucky stars that Reggie had forced him to rethink his priorities, else he might never have looked deeply enough to discover his true love. Now he had only to play out his scheme meant to return him to Lyndhurst as soon as possible, his intelligent, levelheaded, yet he was sure, lovable prospective wife on his arm—a mission in which the adorable widgeon Lady Georgiana played a major role, whether she knew it or nay.

Smiling his most ingratiating smile, Lord Edward started forward once more, bowing and nodding his way through the throng that crowded the fringes of the dance floor, intending to whirl Lady Georgiana about the floor before he and Monty took themselves off to Lady Chilworth's game room for a space, a place less likely to contain a half-hundred marauding mamas on the hunt for fresh husband meat to toss to their man-hungry offspring.

He would then return to the ballroom later in the evening for a second dance with the beautiful young blond, preferably a waltz, just to stir up the pot a bit. After all, there was no reason to rush his fences, especially since the object of all these enterprising machinations was, regrettably, not in sight at the moment anyway.

"Lady Georgiana," he said, at last coming up behind her—and startling her so that she whirled about, narrowly missing taking a slice out of his nose with her fan as he bowed his greeting. "May I say that you are looking even more beautiful this evening than you did yesterday in the park? You must tell me your secret."

Lady Georgiana blinked her wide green eyes twice and said, a small frown appearing on her forehead, "Secret? Have you been speaking with Emily? It was only a very unexceptional bonnet, I vow, and didn't cost above forty pounds. Surely dearest Emily hasn't gone and blabbed it about to everyone?"

"Bonnet? I'm afraid I don't really understand," Lord Edward replied, tongue-in-cheek, wishing Lord Henry could hear her answer.

She playfully slapped his hand with her furled fan, making him wince as the ivory sticks made contact with his knuckles. "Oh, pooh, now you've tricked me into admitting I overspent my allowance, haven't you, Lord Edward? I thought you were remarking on the bonnet I wore yesterday on our ride. You were complimenting me, weren't you? How stupid of me not to understand."

"Now I must apologize, Lady Georgiana," Lord Edward broke in, noticing, out of the corner of his eye, that his quarry had reentered the ballroom, "as it was heartless of me to tease you. But perhaps we might take a refreshing stroll on the balcony, so that I can more fully explain my compliment." Miss Howland would be upon them at any moment to take custody of her charge, he was sure, and the relative privacy of the balcony was his choice for their next confrontation.

"Oh, that would be above all things delightful," Lady Georgiana gushed obligingly, slipping her hand through his bent arm. "It is quite warm in here, isn't it?"

The short journey to the balcony was accomplished without incident, although Lord Edward did take note of several menacing glances thrown at him by Lady Georgiana's thwarted admirers (as well as quickly spying out Miss Howland, who was in the process of rushing with controlled haste toward him and Lady Georgiana by way of the perimeter of the large ballroom, so as not to attract undue attention to the fact that her charge had somehow succeeded in slipping her leash), and they walked the length of the stone balcony before he helped her to a bench that was angled in the corner near the wall, barely into the shadows.

As he lowered his long, lean frame beside her, he said, "So, Lady Georgiana, how does it feel to be such a heartbreaker? You had them all at your feet in there, you know."

He watched as she nervously twisted her kid-encased hands together in her lap. "Oh, so you see it too!" she exclaimed, distressed. "I had hoped it wasn't so obvious. I don't know what to do. They're all so nice. Mama says they're all positively *dying* for love of me. I feel so terrible—it's such a *responsibility!*" She turned on the seat to look up into his eyes, her own drenched with quick tears. "You don't think it will really come to that, do you? I mean, it's not as if I could possibly marry them *all*, is it?"

In another woman, these words would sound like bragging, almost like a wild American Indian who had garnered a dozen bloody scalps for his collection and was showing them off, but Lord Edward knew she was genuinely distressed by her own popularity. "I doubt you could marry above one of them, actually. I think your mother meant it merely as a figure of speech, Lady Georgiana," he said, smiling kindly.

The moment the words were out of his mouth, he knew he had erred. Drawing herself up primly, Lady Georgiana told him, "Mama doesn't speak vulgarly, sir. Figures, indeed!"

"That's not what I meant. When I said that, it was only as a figure of... Oh, never mind, Lady Georgiana," he said, giving it up as being beyond her. Conversation wasn't the reason he had brought her out here, and if he was right, it was just about time for Miss Howland's entrance. "Just kiss me, please, else I shall die of love for you."

Her rosebud mouth dropping open, Lady Georgiana found herself caught between worry over Lord Edward's possible demise and the knowledge that, if she were to kiss *all* the young gentlemen who spoke so—and a distressingly large number of them did—she would soon be considered "fast."

His head moving closer to hers, Lord Edward cajoled softly, "Please, dear Lady Georgiana. You know you are too kind to deny me."

Swallowing down hard on her misgivings, Lady Georgiana lifted her face to his.

CHAPTER THREE

"JUST PRECISELY WHAT do you think you're about?"

This question, spoken in a rather loud, rather piercing tone, served to effectively halt the seated pair just as their lips were less than a whisper apart. Lord Edward remained where he was, his eyes closed tight against the sight of Lady Georgiana's companion, undoubtedly standing less than a foot in front of them, her hands stuck on her hips, a disapproving frown on her face. He was sure she was bound to be most wonderful in her righteous fury, even without looking at her. She was also, as he had predicted, exactly in the nick of time. He sent her his silent congratulations.

Lady Georgiana, however, did not possess Lord Edward's sangfroid. She quickly jerked up her head, her chin colliding with her swain's aristocratic nose with a resounding *twack* that brought a satisfied smile to Emily Howland's face, then hopped to her feet, hastily trying to wrap her Norwich shawl about her shoulders—and ended by entangling Lord Edward's handsome head (still leaning forward, still with eyes closed) in a mummy case of silken fringe.

"Oh, Emily, you startled me," Lady Georgiana said poutingly as Lord Edward fought to disengage himself from the trailing shawl, sputtering as one of the tassels found its way into his mouth.

"I'm so sorry, Georgiana," Emily said, patting her cousin's arm reassuringly. "Your mama has been asking after you, dear. Why don't you run along now and see what she wants."

"If she can remember," Lord Edward grumbled half under his breath—realizing he was not sure if he meant the duchess or her daughter—although, unfortunately, he was in the act of rising to his feet and did not notice the sparkle of amusement that flitted across Emily Howland's features before they hastily reassembled themselves in a disapproving frown.

"But, should I really leave you alone out here on the balcony with Lord Edward, Emily?" Lady Georgiana asked in some concern, seemingly oblivious of the ridiculousness of her question, considering the fact that she had just been very much isolated in this *same* spot with this *same* man. "You shouldn't be alone with him, you know, as you're unmarried and not properly chaperoned."

"Then you do at least understand the concept, Georgiana? How wonderful—how totally gratifying," Emily commented dryly, earning herself a confused look from her cousin. "But you needn't worry your pretty head about me, pet. I assure you, Lord Edward has no designs on my person."

Raising her hands to her mouth, Lady Georgiana giggled. "Oh, Emily, as if Lord Edward knew anything at all about designing ladies' gowns. You're so silly. Promise me you won't stay out here long. Bye-bye."

Emily watched until Lady Georgiana disappeared into the ballroom, then turned back to face Lord Edward, who was, in her opinion, the most foolish man in nature, considering the fact that he had chosen to remain behind on the balcony to take the sharp side of her tongue, when he could just as easily have escaped along with her cousin. "Lord Edward," Emily said by way of prologue, "I believe I have been placed in the uncomfortable role of proctor."

"Uncomfortable, Miss Howland?" Lord Edward repeated, his tone clearly implying he believed otherwise. "I would have said you look quite at home like this— on the verge of a scathing lecture."

"How amusing, my lord," Emily drawled, clearly more than halfway convinced that someone, somehow, should do this abominable creature an injury for his audaciousness. "Surely you realize that what you have done is totally reprehensible?"

"I don't know how that could be, Miss Howland, as you interrupted me before I could *do* anything," he informed her matter-of-factly, running a hand through his hair to be sure the passage of the shawl over it hadn't reworked its style from casual to careless. "Besides, it was totally innocent, and only in the nature of an experiment."

"Indeed." The single word held within it a world of meaning—and contempt. "How utterly heartless of me to interrupt, and just as you were about to make a breakthrough in your research, I'm sure. Can you ever find it in your heart to forgive me?"

"There's no need for sarcasm, Miss Howland," Lord Edward told her, straightening his jacket. "Kindly just proceed in tearing a strip off my hide and have done with it, please. I have to hurry away if I hope to debauch my usual three innocents before dawn."

"Please, my lord, bragging is so tedious. Are your intentions concerning my cousin honorable?"

The question, uttered so calmly, took him by surprise. He stopped the inventory of his attire to look at her, half-expecting to see that he was now being held at pistol point, but she was standing there quite calmly, awaiting his answer. Pluck to the backbone, that was his Miss Howland, and Lord Edward's opinion of her mettle went up another notch.

Emily was a tall woman—an important factor, considering his own above-average height—yet she always seemed somehow to accomplish a way of looking shorter, almost dumpy. Her heavy reddish-brown hair was done in the same mass of intricate, upswept curls as her cousin's, with none of the blond's resultant charm. Her skin appeared sallow, almost yellow, against the gray of her high-necked gown, and her strangely slanted brown eyes and winglike brows followed the same line as her high, prominent cheekbones, giving her face an exotic, almost foreign look. No, it wouldn't have surprised him if she had been holding a pistol.

Yet, with his discerning eye, Lord Edward knew that Emily Howland was basically a fine-looking woman, and had known it from his first sight of her a month earlier. Her hair was all wrong, of course, while her clothing was nothing short of atrocious, and her choice of colors...well, that he considered to be downright criminal. But this was all secondary and easily mended.

The dumpiness concerned him slightly more, although he was sure she probably only overate to compensate for her miserable position in life. After all, being a poor relation was no picnic in the park, and bear-leading the childlike Lady Georgiana while trying to make heads or tails of the dowager duchess had to take its toll somewhere. No, Lord Edward wasn't overly concerned with Emily's present looks. Not when she possessed such a fine mind, such a level head, and, most important, such a boundless affection and patience for her brainless relatives.

Perhaps if he were to tell her the truth, come smack out into the open with his real intentions, she would... But no, not yet. She wouldn't believe he really loved her, for one thing, and she might believe he only wanted to use her, for another. He'd have to bide his time until he could somehow manage to get the dowager to come to Lyndhurst Hall for a house party at the conclusion of the Season. After all, much as he was sure Emily was the one he wanted, there was still Reggie to consider. He had to see Emily and Reggie together, and then...well, everything would just quite naturally fall into place, without his ever having to tell her that he—

"My goodness, my lord, have you somehow mislaid your agile tongue?" Emily asked, interrupting his rambling thoughts. "I should think my question direct enough. What *are* your intentions?"

"Excuse me, Miss Howland, if your rudeness took me aback for a moment. My intentions, ma'am, as you were so impolite as to ask, are to quit this balcony and this ridiculous conversation as soon as may be. Now, if you don't mind—"

"But I *do* mind, Lord Edward," Emily said, stepping in front of him to block his path. "I don't like you, sir, as I'm sure you already know. I don't like you one bit, and my opinion of you is even lower now that I realize you are fully aware of the extreme innocence of my cousin Georgiana. She is naught but a babe, no matter if she is nearly eighteen. Do you think I didn't hear that drivel you were pouring into her ears? Dying for love, indeed. As if you could possibly love such an infant! She is years away from marriage. Please, credit me with at least that much intelligence. If you *were* to marry her, you'd strangle her within the week."

"I imagine this lecture has a point," Lord Edward

drawled, adjusting his shirt cuff so that he had something else to think of than his sudden overwhelming
need to kiss her.

"The point, Lord Edward, as you so crudely put it,
is that I want you to stay away from my cousin. I just
left my aunt, and she was waxing poetic about that
'handsome blond boy somebody-or-other' who would
be perfect for her Georgy. They're numbskulls, the two
of them, but they're *my* numbskulls, and I won't have
you hurting them."

"You're so loyal, Miss Howland," Lord Edward said,
complimenting her, advancing so that she involuntarily
stepped back a pace. Prudence be damned! The woman
was driving him insane. If only she weren't acting as
Lady Georgiana's chaperone. How could a person
properly court a female who wouldn't dance, or drive out
with him, or even go down to dinner with him so that they
could get to know each other? It was about time he made
her aware of him as a man who was capable of looking
at her in a romantic light. "Perhaps I am pursuing the
wrong female entirely," he continued, taking another
step toward her, aware of a light buzzing in his ears. "Do
you mind if I conduct another small experiment?"

"What…what do you think you're doing?" Emily
squeaked, suddenly not so sure of herself, and she
looked about hastily for some means of escape. It was
no good. She had somehow succeeded in backing herself into a corner.

Lord Edward's hands grabbed Emily at the shoulders
and he hauled her up against his chest as his mouth
swooped down to cover hers. He ground his lips against
hers passionately, his wide-open green eyes staring unblinkingly into her wide-open brown ones, in order to
gauge her reaction. He slanted his mouth first one way,

then the other, without ever breaking contact, employing all of his considerable romantic skill, feeling his teeth scrape lightly against hers, his hands leaving her shoulders to crush her against him from knee to breast.

It was no use. She didn't react, didn't fight him, didn't swoon. She just stood there, locked within the circle of his arms, and *glared* at him. He released her with a rush of pent-up breath, turning away in mingled chagrin and self-disgust. "I'm sorry," he muttered angrily, and he was—sorry for having succumbed to impulse, and angry for having failed so miserably in his attempt to bend her to his will.

Emily stood ramrod straight, still trapped in her corner, magnificently dowdy in her ugly gray gown, and stared out over the darkened gardens. "You may leave me now, please," she said, her voice sounding strained but unwavering.

Lord Edward reached out a hand to touch her arm, then dropped it. "I don't know what came over me just now, Miss Howland, I really don't. I've never forced myself on anyone before. It's just…it's just…well, you see, I just wanted to…"

"Is your hearing as well as your judgment impaired, then, Lord Edward? I have asked that you leave me." Emily's hands were drawn into tight fists at her sides as she struggled to maintain her composure. She was twenty, no schoolroom miss, but if he didn't take himself off so that she could collapse on the bench and give way to the storm of weeping that was building up behind her eyes, she would never forgive him.

"If you'd just allow me to apologize—"

"Apology heard and accepted, Lord Edward," she cut in shortly. "Now, please, go!"

"I'll stay away from Lady Georgiana as well, I

promise," he offered weakly, not knowing what else to say. "You're right, you know, she is just an infant. You're prudent to guard her so closely."

Emily only nodded, unable to trust her voice.

"I am really seriously thinking of marrying, you know. I need to set up my nursery."

"Oh, really? Then I can see your reasoning in pursuing my cousin. With Georgy already installed in your town house, it would simply be a matter of tossing in a rocking horse and a set of blocks to make this nursery of yours complete. Georgy would have been deliriously happy, although you might have found that you were still lacking a wife." Emily was being sarcastic again— and at her cousin's expense, too—but she couldn't help herself. She simply couldn't believe Lord Edward would possibly consider Lady Georgiana in the role of his wife. It was ludicrous. Perhaps she *had* underestimated his intelligence.

"The knife is already firmly in, Miss Howland. There's no need to twist the blade," Lord Edward said, turning to walk away. "Actually," he added, believing he might as well be hanged for a sheep as a lamb, "I believe I must rethink my requirements for a wife. I'm definitely more intrigued with feminine wit than I had supposed I would be. Now it is up to me to find a young woman with dear Lady Georgiana's gentle heart and your keen intellect, and my search will be over."

And with that final insult, Lord Edward removed himself from the balcony, to search out Lord Henry and retire to a private gaming club where, knowing his plans had just suffered a major setback—and out of his own mouth, no less—he proceeded to get himself well and truly drunk.

CHAPTER FOUR

THE CHILWORTH DRAWING ROOM was overrun with flowers, towering arrangements filling the air with their perfume while overloading the side tables and over-shadowing the smaller, more informal clutches of posies sent by Lady Georgiana's less-plump-in-the-pocket swains, who hoped their offerings would be considered to be "romantic" rather than merely purse-pinched.

It was the same in the foyer, the morning room, the small salon, and the music room. Everywhere Emily Howland went the morning after the ball, she was confronted with overblown roses, dainty daffodils, exotic orchids, and blushing violets. In an effort to escape the riot of color and cloying scent, she slipped into Lady Georgiana's ermine-hooded cloak that she found lying forgotten in the morning room, pulled open the double glass doors that led onto the balcony, and skipped lightly down the flagstones into the garden.

"At least there are less flowers out here than inside," she commented aloud facetiously before seating herself in her private hideaway on a curved stone bench that had been placed just in front of the length of hedge that separated the garden from the tradesmen's entrance. It was early, and the dew still clung to the grass, dampening her shoes, so that she slipped out of them and tucked her feet up under her skirts, knowing she was being unlady-like, but not believing anyone cared overmuch what poor relations did anyway.

The sun went behind a cloud and it began to drizzle, which was not unusual for London in the spring—or London at any time of year, she thought, for, indeed, she was not in the most charitable of moods—but still she lingered on the bench, glorying in the peace and quiet she had been seeking. It was nearly noon, and although Emily had been up and about for several hours, having spent a short, uncomfortable night filled with unpleasant dreams, her aunt and cousin had not yet stirred beyond allowing themselves to be propped up in bed with cups of chocolate and the morning post.

At least two dozen eager gentlemen callers come to continue their impassioned wooing of Lady Georgiana had already been turned away unseen, Emily's insincere apologies obviously not soothing them in the least, and she absolutely refused to feel guilty over deserting her post and allowing the Chilworth butler to bear the brunt of any other callers' disappointment in her stead.

Yes, it would take more than some damp and drizzle to oust Emily from her hiding place.

She needed time alone, time to think, although why her thought processes should be clearer this morning than they had been during the night, she had no idea. Drat that insufferable Lord Edward anyhow! How dare he insult her the way he had? She knew she was no beauty, but she certainly didn't need his snide remarks to put a final seal of certainty on the matter. And that kiss! Why, he couldn't have been any meaner, any more insulting, if he had slapped her face.

Emily decided all over again that she didn't like Lord Edward Laurence. She didn't like him at all.

On the half-dozen or so occasions she had been forced into the man's company—acting as an uncomfortable third whenever he came to see Lady Georgiana—she had concluded that he was reckless, feckless, and totally lacking in responsibility. He treated life as if it were one huge frolic, which she acknowledged must be easy enough to do, what with no wars left to be fought, a comfortable title, and endless wealth cushioning him from the realities of everyday life, while the entire city of London was his own personal sporting ground.

Besides, he was simply too perfect, too handsome for his own good—or for hers.

For one thing, he had the most beautiful green eyes she had ever seen. Not deeply emerald, like Georgy's, but a light, tender, new-leaf green, with flecks of morning sunlight forever dancing in them—a sparkle put there, she was sure, only to infuriate her, as she wondered just what was going on inside his head.

She moved uncomfortably on the stone seat, not liking where her thoughts were taking her, but unable to stop their travels.

His hair was darkly blond, almost the exact shade of the honey her mother harvested from the bees at her home in Surrey, rather than the bright guinea yellow of Georgy's, and more than once Emily had had to fight down the impulse to brush back the one errant lock that continually slipped down onto his forehead.

And those beautiful, even white teeth; ah, he had a glorious, mischievous smile. His body was perfect, not at all dissipated, as he was a reknowned, if somewhat undisciplined sportsman, and his mode of dress was fashionable without being silly.

Her hands, carefully folded in her lap, clenched into tight fists.

He had everything.

She had nothing.

To be without, to be forever on the outside looking in, was one thing; to have the insufferable Lord Edward going to such lengths to bring her shortcomings to her attention—as he had done with such devastating effect last night—was unspeakable.

Lord, how she loathed him.

And now he was actually setting himself at her silly, lovable cousin Georgy.

Oh, he may have tried to fob her off—tried to worm his way out of his scandalous behavior toward a young woman of quality by saying he had erred in believing her cousin would make him a good wife—but Emily found it hard to swallow that particular story.

After all, they *did* make a beautiful couple, almost dazzling in their combined beauty, and when it came to a female as beautiful as Lady Georgiana, her one short-coming—a total lack of brainpower—was simple to overlook. Even if her cousin weren't the most perfect collection of skin, bone, and hair to appear in London in three decades, her wealth and title were ample inducement for any suitor.

If only Lady Georgiana weren't the youngest of five daughters. Then her grace would hold out for someone of higher rank than Lord Edward Laurence, a younger son, to take her baby off her hands. But the dowager was growing weary of the social round, and eager to settle Georgy and get back to her comfortable country estate, where she already knew everyone's name (except those of her many grandchildren, but the dowager didn't believe anyone under the age of fifty counted for much in the scheme of things anyway).

Hadn't her aunt said only last night that she believed Lord Edward to be a vastly suitable catch? Emily shook her head and sighed. She was only deluding herself if she believed her grace would ever see through the man as she did. It was all but settled; dear birdwitted Georgy and the insufferable Lord Edward would probably be affianced before the week was out.

"Unless…unless someone can somehow discover a way to get through to Aunt Hortense and convince her that Georgy and Lord Edward definitely would not suit."

The moment Emily voiced the thought aloud, she realized that she was that "someone." It made perfect sense. She was close to both Lady Georgiana and the dowager duchess; she was a trusted family member; she had—thanks to her dear optimistic mother, who thought serving as companion to Georgy would land Emily a husband of her own—made herself invaluable to both the Chilworth ladies ever since they had moved to Portman Square for the Season.

She was the obvious, the only choice. But how was she to discredit Lord Edward to her aunt and cousin? Whatever Lord Edward was, whatever he did, he was accepted by the *ton,* even idolized by it.

It wouldn't be enough to drop a few veiled hints in her aunt's ear about the man's title of Naughty Ned, for such things were looked on most kindly by the older generation, who could only relive their more rakish juvenile exploits vicariously through such nonsense. And as much as Emily wished it were possible, she couldn't say that the man was actually dishonest in any way, or some such thing.

No, she'd have to think of something else, something so terrible, so completely damning, that Aunt Hortense, aghast, would have him banned from the house forevermore, an action that would go a long way to making Emily's life easier, for his presence seemed to fill her head with the oddest, almost embarrassing pictures. Emily sat and sat, as the drizzle turned the borrowed cloak sodden and heavy with moisture. She thought and thought, her slanted brown eyes narrowed into thin slits as she concentrated on her scheme.

At last, just as a cold drop of water slid off the fur to land on the tip of her nose, a small smile came onto Emily's face, and she tilted her head slightly to one side, considering the germ of an idea.

An absolutely wonderful…awful…sneaky…*glorious* idea.

"Yes-s-s," she hissed from between clenched teeth. "It could work; it just could work. What does it matter what happens to my reputation? After all, I am only a poor relation, an unpaid companion. Once Georgy is safely settled, I'll be packed back off to Surrey where I will then apply myself to being a comforting prop to my widowed mother in her declining years—to nurse my as-yet-unborn nephews and nieces through the croup, and sundry other such wild exploits indulged in by aging, on-the-shelf spinsters. It could even lend some cachet to my supposed tormented past for me to giggle over as I tend my cats. I'm sure I'll have cats," she added for no particular reason other than the fact that she liked to be clear about things, "as they're much less trouble than temperamental lapdogs."

Her decision made, Emily rose to return to the house. "Besides," she added, just to convince herself of the rightness of her plan, "it's not as if the story would go any further than Aunt Hortense's boudoir.

Yes, if it comes to that, if I find I am left with no other choice, I'll do it. Anything—anything!—to thwart that nefarious Ned!"

CHAPTER FIVE

MEANWHILE, THE GENTLEMAN Emily Howland considered to be the villain of the piece, one Lord Edward Mortimer Sinclair Laurence, was propped inelegantly in a dreadfully uncomfortable wooden armchair in the small dining room of his town house in Half Moon Street, nursing his tender head with a strong cup of coffee and wondering just what it was that he had done the previous evening that had made it mandatory he have visited upon him this morning all the terrible demons too much drink could conjure up to persecute a person.

His tongue silently complained that his mouth was a quite inhospitable residence, as it seemed to have shrunk overnight and could no longer adequately house its life-long resident, while his tongue itself was far from a matter of joy to him, being curiously fur-covered and desert dry.

His brainbox, that part of him that seemed to rise three feet above his eyebrows (and twice as wide), had been somehow rendered a near-blank, telling him only that he hurt abominably and that he must have been a bad boy—a very, very bad boy indeed.

He sipped at his coffee, nearly bending in half over the tabletop so that his weary arms shouldn't have to heft the cup, promising himself that if he lived—and at the moment, he felt this possibility to be in some serious doubt—he would never, never, *never* touch another drop of whatever it was he had poured down his throat the night before.

"If only I could remember what it was," he murmured quietly, wincing as his words echoed inside his ears like hammer blows on an anvil.

With his eyes squeezed tightly closed—the darkness behind his lids serving as a canvas upon which his headache painted a colorful fireworks display to put Prinny's elaborate peace celebrations to the blush—his mind's eye slowly conjured up the horrific vision of two widely open, curiously slanted brown eyes.

These eyes, obviously condemning, definitely scornful, looked deep inside him, straight through to his guilty soul. And although they were eyes, and certainly not to be thought able to speak, these particular eyes began a curious chant, taunting over and over: "Coward, coward, coward."

"Oh, Lord," he groaned, finally remembering. "Emily. Good grief, what have I done?"

"Shot the cat about a half-dozen times, at least according to your man, Burton. I passed him in the hall, lugging a suspicious-looking bucket and wearing his usual disapproving frown. You and Monty really must have made a night of it, Ned. You haven't been the worse for liquor in years. Is she someone I know?"

Lord Edward lifted his throbbing eyelids a fraction to look across the table to where Lord Delbert Updegrove was in the process of lowering his tall Norse-warrior frame into the facing chair and said urbanely, "Go to the devil, Del, old sport, would you?"

"Oh-ho! Struck a nerve, did I? Monty said something

about you being all arsy-varsy over The Chilworth, but I didn't believe him. I mean, Georgy's turned out to be rather beautiful—quite angelic, actually—but there's definitely no problem of overcrowding in her upper rooms, is there? Grew up smack next door to her in Sussex, you know, and I can't say as how she ever impressed me to the point I'd get myself cupshot over her. All the Chilworth females take after the mother, and we all know what a peagoose Old Horry is. Lord, the stories I could tell you!"

"Maybe I was thinking of fixing my interest with her," Lord Edward hinted to his friend, finally finding the courage to sit back in his chair. "Did you ever think of that?" Del looked disgustingly fit, from his fiery red thatch of hair to his crisp canary-yellow waistcoat and sky-blue jacket—which was as much of him that Lord Edward could or, at the moment, cared to see. He frowned, convinced his old friend looked like a mis-hued robin redbreast.

"Marry Old Horry?" Lord Delbert shook his head in disbelief. "That's where the money is, of course. But you do realize people are bound to talk."

"No, you dolt, not the dowager. Lady Georgiana." Yes, Lord Edward decided, I'm being punished. Anyone would think Miss Howland sent Del over here purposely to pummel me with his inane nonsense.

Lord Delbert poured out some steaming coffee for himself and then reached for the cream pot, promptly spilling it. "Whoops! Dashed clumsy of me, what? Well, glad to hear, it, Ned. Makes sense, seeing as how you'd want an heir. You'll get no foals from the old gal. She's past it, you know. Ah, thank you, Burton."

Burton, who had brought the extra cup into the dining room, and who was standing by, his nose appearing just above the tabletop, waiting for the accident to happen (with Lord Delbert it was not a question of whether or not there would be a mishap, but only of when it would occur), flourished a linen serviette he took from his apron pocket and promptly set about cleaning up the spill. "No trouble at all, m'lord," he assured him, deftly removing the marmalade—the preserves being so apt to stain—from his lordship's reach and personally spooning some onto a muffin for him.

Watching this little interchange, Lord Edward concluded that it wasn't necessary to clear up Lord Delbert's misconception about exactly which of the Chilworth women he had supposedly planned to wed. It came to him next to discuss the dreaded "Incident on the Balcony" with his friend, and it only served to highlight the extreme distress in which Lord Edward found himself this morning that he even considered entering into such a delicate matter with the affable but vague redhead.

"I kissed Miss Howland last night," Naughty Ned said baldly, his treacherous tongue acting with more alacrity than his sore brain.

Bits of marmalade and muffin shot into the air, lingering there for a second—like thistles caught in the spring breeze—then settled on the fine linen tablecloth, dotting its surface with colorful starlike stains as Lord Delbert, his eyes popped wide with incredulity, coughed and choked, trying to regain his breath.

Burton cursed, but only softly, as he *was,* after all, a gentleman's gentleman as well as a butler, and quickly went to work cleaning up the mess.

Not so Lord Delbert. *"You what!"* His face an unbecoming puce—and clashing badly with his hair—Lord Delbert leaned forward, bug-eyed, looking at his friend as if the fellow had somehow sprouted antlers. *"Are you out of your mind?"*

Lord Edward, knowing himself to be guilty as sin, took refuge in pettishness. "It wasn't all my fault, Del. She goaded me into it," he complained, thrusting out his bottom lip so that Burton, who had been with the Laurence family three dozen years or more, rolled his eyes and felt himself hard-pressed not to cuff the young master's ears. In the end, he settled for lifting the heavy silver teapot and then slamming it down heavily on the tabletop, three inches from his lordship's elbow, thereby warning his master not to give the whole game away.

Clapping both his hands to the sides of his head, Lord Edward let out a long, low, slowly spoken string of nastiness that did nothing to enlighten the usually indiscreet Lord Delbert as to his friend's hidden motives concerning one Miss Emily Howland, but did serve to satisfy something deep in his own soul.

When it was done, and after Burton, sniffing his disgust, had quit the room, slamming the door behind him as he went, Lord Delbert rewarded his friend by applauding softly, saying, "An inspired monologue, Ned. I really should have asked Burton to take notes, as I always seem to run out of curses beforetimes. I take it Georgy's resident she-dragon tackled you in the hedges?"

"She's not a she-dragon, Del," Lord Edward was stung into retorting. "As a matter of fact, she appeals to me most extremely. And you have it the wrong way round; I attacked *her*—out on the balcony." Then, knowing he had just made another major error in judgment, but also knowing it was too late to do anything about it, he stuffed half a muffin in his mouth and glared at his friend.

Lord Delbert sat back in his chair and inspected his friend's expression. "You really mean that, don't you, Ned? You really are attracted to Miss Howland. I can't see it, to tell you the truth, but if you say it's so, I guess it isn't up to me to question it, is it? Only one thing, Ned. If you're after the she-dra...I mean, Miss Howland aren't you going about the thing all backwards? I mean, Monty told me you were after Georgy."

"Miss Howland doesn't like me," Lord Edward replied, as if that explained everything, which it didn't, as Lord Delbert's confused frown clearly showed. "I'm using Lady Georgiana to stay in Miss Howland's company," was all Lord Edward added, thinking his plot too deep for his friend to understand.

A few weeks later, thinking back over this particular conversation, Lord Edward was to reassess his friend's capacity for deep thinking—if only to attempt to discover exactly how the affable redhead had come to leap to such a ridiculous conclusion.

CHAPTER SIX

LADY IMOGENE CARSTAIRS had prudently limited the invitations to her Venetian breakfast to include no more than three hundred and fifty of the most important of the *ton,* which of course meant that nearly twice that number of people—those others being servants, chefs, coachmen, ladies' companions, and sundry other persons of no social consequences but completely necessary to the success of the day—descended pell-mell on Richmond Park just before noon, intent on enjoying themselves with a bit of frolic in the fine spring sunshine.

Lady Georgiana particularly enjoyed informal outings of this sort, feeling so much closer in spirit to her beloved home in Sussex when out and about in the open spaces, where she could breathe clean, crisp country air and, when no one was looking, slide her feet out of her tight silk slippers and wiggle her bare toes in the cool grass.

London was wonderful—a fairyland, really—just as her dearest mama had promised, and she would have been a silly thing indeed not to adore all the attention she was receiving, but Lady Georgiana was at heart a simple country miss, more at home in familiar surroundings, where she was not forever being poked at by pushy seamstresses or being ogled by silly gentlemen who insisted upon treating her as if she were a particularly fragile crystal vase, and liable to shatter at the slightest jostle.

Emily, on the other hand, who firmly believed she had seen enough bucolic countryside in her twenty years to last her three lifetimes, was bored to flinders. Not that she didn't like the country, for she did, but town life was so much more interesting and exciting.

A person could find no end of things to do in London, what with the theater and the museums and the lending libraries and the centuries of history that confronted her at every turn. She imagined she would even like the social round, if she were to be in Lady Georgiana's position and able to enjoy all the excitement firsthand, rather than merely being allowed to observe it from a chair pushed against the wall, where she never failed to find herself jammed in between two flabby-armed, perspiring, foul-breathed dowagers.

Not that she was on the hunt for a husband. Good heavens, no! Emily was much too level-headed to even consider such a wild, improbable possibility. She was nothing like her optimistic mother, who had confided her dream that her oldest child was going to take the town by storm. *She* was a realist. She had absolutely no fortune, and certainly didn't believe herself to have been blessed with any great beauty. She knew that, as far as the marriage stakes were concerned, she was what was considered to be a dark horse.

An also-ran.

"A nag," she added aloud ruefully, reluctantly rising from her comfortable seat beneath a leafy tree to go chasing after her unwitting cousin, who was carelessly allowing Lord Hetherson entirely too much license as they strolled together near a small stream. It was one thing to allow the man to grasp her elbow as they walked along the uneven bank, Emily decided, but it was quite another matter entirely for Lady Georgiana to laugh up into his eyes as the fellow pretended to stumble while covertly slipping an arm around her waist.

After deftly removing her cousin from Lord Hetherson's clutches, *tsk-tsking* at the blushing young man over her shoulder as she walked away, Emily quickly guided Lady Georgiana back to the shade tree, lecturing her halfheartedly and feeling as if she were back home in Surrey, riding herd on one of her young siblings. Being the eldest child was not easy, but at least it had prepared her for her current position, and she quickly employed an oft-used practice—diverting the childlike Lady Georgiana from possible mischief by offering her a treat.

"You really will, Emily? Oh, that would be the best of good fun," Lady Georgiana trilled, skipping alongside her cousin, having completely forgotten poor Lord Hetherson. "I do so love daisy chains, but I have never been able to make one that looks like anything. I never seem to leave the stems long enough, and by the time I'm done my fingers are all green and the lovely flowers are all sad and drooping and I feel awful—as if I'm a *murderer* or something."

Seating herself once more on the carriage blanket that had been spread out for them by one of the army of servants that was now busily setting up more substantial seating in the middle of a large open area nearby, Emily picked up one of the flowers she had gathered earlier in order to occupy herself, then waited patiently as Lady Georgiana's attention was diverted yet again by a passing juggler Lady Imogene had thoughtfully provided to amuse her guests.

"It's really quite easy to lace the flowers together,

Georgy. Let me teach you. Georgy, please, you're no longer a child!" Emily scolded at last, as her cousin appeared about to scamper off after the performer, who, Emily noticed, had winked at the lovely young blond.

"Oh, pooh, Cousin," Lady Georgiana pouted prettily, giving the departing juggler one last wistful look. "You're no fun, Emmy. You're no fun at all. We were just having the nicest little talk."

Emily sighed, patting the place next to her. "Yes, I'm sure you were. Sit down now, dear, and we'll make your chain together, and then you can make one for me. Won't that be fun?" Honestly, she thought, keeping her smile firmly in place, I do believe it would be easier all round if I could just put the dratted child on leading strings.

The two young women busied themselves for a few minutes on slitting the stems of the flowers just so and then stringing them together, Emily's capable hands working deftly, while Lady Georgiana looked endearingly befuddled as she struggled with her recalcitrant blooms, her small pink tongue protruding from the corner of her mouth as she concentrated all her effort on the task.

It seemed a perfect time for Emily to sound out her cousin's emotions about a particular person of their acquaintance. "How do you *really* feel about Lord Edward Laurence, Georgy?" she asked after a while, keeping her voice deliberately casual. "I realized too late that I might have been interrupting him the other evening just as he was about to favor you with a proposal."

"No, you're wrong, Emmy," Lady Georgiana replied, going nearly cross-eyed as she raised two flowers to her face in order to thread one through the other. "He had already made his proposal before you came along." She giggled innocently, believing she was about to make a dashing good joke. "He had *proposed* to kiss me—and he would have, too, if you hadn't come along and discovered us."

Emily pinched the bridge of her nose between her thumb and index finger, feeling a headache coming on. Lady Georgiana might not be too bright, but she was definitely all female. "And did you *want* Lord Edward to kiss you, Georgy?" she prompted, fearing her cousin's answer.

Lady Georgiana shrugged, and one of the flowers fell to her lap, minus its stem. "Oh, drat! I told you I couldn't do this. Mama says I have six thumbs. Did you see those slippers I embroidered for her, Emmy? They're just *awful*."

"Georgy, just answer the question, please." Emily still hadn't put her plan into motion, most probably, she told herself, because she dreaded the interview with her aunt, who was bound to take forever to realize even half of what her niece was saying, confusing the issue until Emily would be forced to draw the dear dense lady a diagram; but if she found that Georgy wasn't seriously interested in Lord Edward, the entire project might be abandoned and she could save herself any amount of trouble.

"Did I want him to kiss me?" Lady Georgiana repeated, a small frown marring her smooth forehead. "I really don't know exactly, Emily. He *said* he was dying with love for me, which, you have to admit, was extremely nice of him. But then they *all* say they're in love with me, and I can't go about kissing them all, can I? I think I felt sorry for him, to tell you the truth. He was being so sweet. Yes, I felt sorry for him. There—look, Emmy, I finally got two of them to stay together!"

Oh, that's just about all things marvelous, Emily thought, despairing, even as she applauded her cousin's small success. Her cousin felt sorry for Lord Edward. For someone like Lady Georgiana, it would be a short hop from feeling sorry for a man to marrying him, just to make the poor fellow happy. She had a good, caring heart, Lady Georgiana did, but she wasn't very logical. "Do you realize, Gregory, that Lord Edward nearly compromised you out there on the balcony? I mean, your mother has explained such things to you, hasn't she?"

"Of course she has, you silly thing," Lady Georgiana averred, blushing hotly as she poked her cousin in the ribs. "That's one of the reasons I don't let *any* of them kiss me above once. I'm not so careless as my sister Henrietta, you know. Henrietta was compromised, you understand, although it's a great big secret," she whispered conspiratorially. "That's how she came to marry that awful Peregrine. Mama told me all about it—the way Perry kissed her and all. The baby's very sweet, though, so it isn't all that bad, is it?"

Obviously Lady Georgiana's education in the ways of procreation was woefully incomplete, but Emily didn't feel it to be her place to enlighten her. As a matter of fact, she thought hopefully, she might just be able to use this particular "misconception" for her own ends. "And would you want to have Lord Edward's child, Georgy?" she asked, watching her cousin's face closely, and receiving exactly the opposite reaction from the one she had hoped to engender.

"A child? I…I never actually thought about it. A child," she repeated slowly, her features going all soft and dreamy—just as Emily's features showed signs of pinching, realizing that she had made another gross tactical error. Of course Georgy would want a child—all children enjoy playing with dolls! And as if to prove the point, Lady Georgiana gushed, "Wouldn't that be sweet of Lord Edward? I just adore children, Emily. I could teach her how to sit a pony, and we could go into the village together so she could play with all the other children beside the pond, the way I used to do." She turned to Emily, her vivid green eyes dancing with childish delight. "Is that what you mean?"

Good Lord, no, that's precisely what I *don't* mean, Emily thought wretchedly, but if we were to sit here until the first frost, I would never be able to explain so you would understand. Knowing she was being a coward, Emily explained, fingers crossed, "You would have to live with Lord Edward, sweetheart. You do realize that don't you? You'd have to leave Chilworth Manor forever and ever if you were to become his wife."

Lady Georgiana's full lower lip pushed out as she digested this sad fact. "I don't ever want to leave my home—not ever! How horrid of Lord Edward to even suggest it. And I thought he liked me! Well, let me tell you, I shan't speak to that man again! Imagine that—to leave my beloved Chilworth Manor! That's horrible! Thank you so much for explaining it all to me. I told Mama I didn't think I wanted a London Season, but she insisted, you know, saying that she longed for some peace in her dotage, or something like that. Isn't it strange that she didn't tell me I'd have to leave Chilworth Manor? After all, Henrietta didn't. I shall *never* marry now."

Emily placed the completed daisy chain atop her cousin's blond curls, then gave Lady Georgiana a heartfelt kiss on the cheek. "I doubt that, my sweet, but I must admit I really am glad to hear that you aren't considering Lord Edward as a possible mate. You two really wouldn't suit, you know."

"Oh, dear. We wouldn't?"

"As a matter of fact," Emily concluded, just to add the finishing icing to the top of the cake of fibs and half-truths she had single-handedly constructed, "I understand that Lord Edward dislikes children—and that he absolutely *loathes* the country, preferring to spend all of his time in town." Carousing and making a terrible nuisance of himself, she added to herself silently.

"Oh, dear," Lady Georgiana repeated (for her vocabulary was not extensive), stiffening and grabbing on to her cousin's forearm. "There he is now, and I believe he's coming this way." To think, he was almost the father of her child! She was embarrassed beyond reason. "Oh, Emily, I don't think I can face him, really I don't. Please, do something!"

Emily carefully disengaged herself from her cousin's fierce grip, looking out over the area to see Lord Edward advancing purposefully across the grass—just as she had thought he would, just as if he had never promised to stop chasing after Lady Georgiana—Lord Delbert Updegrove and Lord Henry Montgomery flanking him on either side. Younger sons, the three of them, devoid of responsibility but all with fine old names and solid incomes to cushion them, they moved with a self-confidence that had Emily clenching her jaws until her teeth ached.

"Good afternoon, ladies," Lord Edward said in greeting, stopping just in front of the blanket and doffing his curly-brimmed beaver to bow with a courtly flourish, his companions quickly following suit. "May I say, Lady Georgiana, that you make a veritable picture sitting here, putting Dame Nature to shame with your beauty."

Well, that puts *me* firmly in my place, doesn't it? Emily thought, feeling herself beginning to wilt even as she wondered why she was upset that he was ignoring her when she should be doing celebratory handsprings that he was.

Lady Georgiana giggled, modestly holding her hand to her mouth as she rolled her eyes at the gentlemen. "Aren't you sweet! Aren't they sweet, Emmy? They're so sweet. Please, sit down."

Emily too rolled her eyes, but for quite another reason. So much for Georgy's fear of Lord Edward, she thought resignedly, carefully gathering her skirts about her to make room for Lord Delbert, whose wide, athletic frame took up a good third of the blanket.

"Georgy, you're looking fine as ninepence these days," Lord Delbert told her with the ease of long acquaintance. "I hardly know you without a smudge on your cheek from climbing trees. Lord, Monty, you wouldn't believe what a ragtag urchin Georgy used to be, following us boys around back home, nipping at our heels like a puppydog. But you've grown up real fine, honest, Georgy."

This faint praise served to happily remind Lady Georgiana that Lord Delbert—whom she had always considered to be the older brother she never had—lived almost on top of her mother's comfortable dower house on the edge of the Chilworth estate. Wasn't she a silly goose! Why hadn't she thought of Delbert before? Leaning across Emily so that she could peer intently into his lordship's rather vacant blue eyes, she questioned pointedly: "Do *you* like children, Del?"

Emily's chin dropped onto her chest in defeat, a reaction that did not go unnoticed by Lord Edward, who had covertly been watching her out of the corners of his eyes ever since he sat down. Something was going on here, of that he was sure, but he hadn't the slightest notion what it was. This lack of knowledge, of course, did not stop him from putting his own oar in before Lord Delbert, who was looking momentarily stunned, could form an answer to Lady Georgiana's question.

"Yes, Del, tell us, do," Lord Edward prodded playfully from his comfortable position, stretched out full length on his side upon the ground, his head supported by one hand as he absently twirled a daisy beneath his aristocratic nose. "You cannot imagine the sleepless nights I have spent wondering the same about you myself."

Lord Delbert, coloring to the roots of his red hair, shifted himself in embarrassment, unconsciously leaning his hand painfully against Emily's foot as he rearranged his bulk, causing her to inhale sharply and wonder if everyone from Sussex was clumsy or if she might have at last stumbled on the perfect mate for her accident-prone cousin. "Of course I like children," he protested hotly. "Doesn't everyone? What a silly question, Georgy. And here I thought you were all grown-up."

Seeing that Lady Georgiana was about to defend her question—and doubtless reveal her earlier conversation with her cousin in order to explain her reasoning—Emily stepped quickly into the breach by turning to ask Lord Henry, "Was that a new pair I saw you up behind yesterday in the park, Lord Henry? They were quite beautiful."

Lord Henry, who was known to have less knowledge about horseflesh than anyone in the world did of the composition of the moon, found himself to be inordinately pleased that Miss Howland had commented favorably on his latest purchase. "I picked them up at Tatt's just this past week, ma'am," he told her importantly as Lord Delbert snorted his poor opinion of the flashy grays. "Chose them myself, personally."

"Which explains why they can't move above a trot

without jostling you out of your seat," Lord Edward slid in, still looking at Emily. Something havey-cavey was going on—her cowhanded attempt at diversion proved it—and he quickly brought the conversation back to the point. "Do *you* like children, Lady Georgiana?"

"Yes, I do," she told him, her lovely eyes narrowed as she looked at him in patent dislike. "I absolutely adore children. But *you* don't. Emily told me."

Emily groaned aloud. Me and my big mouth! she despaired, unconsciously shredding the flowers in her lap. "Now, now, Lady Georgiana," she protested feebly, "I never really said—"

Lady Georgiana, her full bottom lip thrust out petulantly, swiftly cut her cousin off by saying, "Yes, you did so, Emmy, just before. Don't you remember? You said Lord Edward hated the country and didn't like children, not even above half. I remember it most distinctly. I'm not completely stupid, you know."

"I see," Lord Edward drawled, looking at Emily appraisingly. Yes, the love of his life was clearly up to no good. Intelligent she might be, but she certainly wasn't his match in subterfuge. "My goodness, anyone would think you were warning your dear cousin off me—as if I were totally unsuitable. Wouldn't they, Miss Howland?"

Emily decided to attack, knowing her only other option was either abject apology or ignominious retreat. She wouldn't give the dratted man that satisfaction! "They most certainly might, my lord," she averred, lifting her bowed head to glare straight into his mocking green eyes. "But, as they say, if the slipper fits—"

"Oh, ho, Ned! If the slipper fits!" Lord Henry crowed, liking the dowdy Miss Howland more and more. It wasn't that he disliked Lord Edward, whom he

had known for dog's years. Indeed, he liked him immensely. But his friend had made that nasty remark
about his grays. "Trumped your ace quite neatly, Ned,
didn't she?"

Lord Edward leaned his head back to look up at his
friend. "Enjoying yourself, Monty, are you—believing
you've found yourself an ally, someone else who shares
your low opinion of my character? Perhaps the two of
you would like to retire now to compose a couplet or
two intended to inform the rest of the world of my
shortcomings?"

"I may be wrong, Cousin, but I think Lord Edward
might be just the teeniest bit angry about something,"
Lady Georgiana whispered rather loudly into Emily's
ear, causing the latter lady to immediately long for nothing more than a convenient bottomless pit into which
she could hurl her embarrassed self.

When Emily didn't answer, Lady Georgiana leaned
across her and artlessly repeated this observation to her
childhood friend, Lord Delbert, adding innocently:
"Poor Lord Edward. But I think Emily may have mis-
judged him, don't you? It's just that she's worried I might
allow him to compromise me, you understand—Emmy
seems to know *all about* being compromised, and—"

"Georgy, you clunch!" Emily fairly screeched, causing nearby heads to turn in the direction of the small
gathering. "I mean," she continued, her voice considerably hushed, "please, Lady Georgiana, I do believe this
conversation has run its course. Why don't you and
Lord Delbert take a stroll? Perhaps you can locate the
juggler again."

Instantly diverted, Lady Georgiana hopped to her
feet, clapping her hands in delight. "Oh, Emmy, that
would be beyond everything wonderful! He said he'd

teach me how he keeps those three pretty striped balls in the air at the same time. Come, Del," she ordered, holding out her hand. "Emily says you can come too."

Lord Henry Montgomery wasn't the most swift of persons, as application to his despairing papa would reveal, but he did see that his presence beside the blanket was clearly not required. Miss Howland was too embarrassed to so much as glance in his direction, but Ned—whom Monty had always said to have the most *speaking* eyes—was being silently eloquent in his wish to see both his friends gone.

Dislodging himself from his kneeling position beneath the tree, Lord Henry muttered something to do with gaining himself a firsthand observation of the swans swimming in the small stream in order to capture their haughty beauty in a poem he was working on, and slunk his thin, lanky self off, belatedly wondering if Miss Howland would thank him for his defection.

Miss Howland was, as a matter of fact, thinking some very unlovely thoughts about the man—one of the few people she had met in London whom she had hitherto believed to be her friend—while watching him as he departed, her head tilted as she mentally sketched a bushy squirrel tail tucked between his cowardly legs. Then, no longer able to ignore Lord Edward's penetrating gaze on her, she turned her head and began a minute inspection of the woven texture of the blanket, almost as if she were considering weaving one herself.

She'd cheerfully throttle me, Lord Edward observed, noticing the way the sun filtered through the overhanging branches, to dance on Emily's hair, bringing out surprising reddish highlights. Not that I can blame her, I guess, he added consideringly, remembering his impulsive, exploratory kiss of the other evening. Even now he found it difficult to believe he had actually dared to hold this intriguing woman in his arms, press his lips to hers, feel her tautly held body against his own.

He must have been the worse for drink, he decided, trying to understand how he had allowed himself to rush his fences that way. As he had known instinctively from the first, as he had explained to a condemning Burton, Miss Emily Howland required careful handling if he was ever to convince her he was sincere in his affection for her. It was clear to him that she considered herself out of the marriage stakes, neither beautiful enough nor wealthy enough to attract a suitor of his standing. For now it was enough that he had her interest, even if she didn't spare his feelings in letting him know how much she disliked him. Once they were down at Lyndhurst Hall, once she had gotten used to Reggie, then he would tell her what was in his heart. Only then could she believe he was sincere in his affections.

When the silence between them had stretched past the point of uncomfortable and entered into the realm of the absurd, he gathered up his courage and spoke. "I must apologize most profusely for the other evening, Miss Howland," he said airly, his carefully unrepentant tone causing her head to lift proudly. "I can't for the life of me imagine what possessed me to attempt such a thing."

"Is the word 'spite' not then in your vocabulary, my lord?" Emily's shoulders were stiff and straight as she looked down at him, and she felt a small surge of satisfaction as his gaze slid away from hers. "However, now that you are apologizing in earnest—if such a lame attempt can be thus labeled—perhaps you could exert yourself yet again and secure my wholehearted forgiveness by agreeing to cease and desist your pursuit of my cousin. Contrary to what you said that night, you still appear to be very much in the chase."

"That still rankles, does it?" Lord Edward drew himself up to a sitting position, wrapping his arms about his knees. "So much so, in fact, that you have been busily filling the little dear's head with all sorts of dire warnings about me. Isn't that right, Miss Howland?"

Emily destroyed yet another innocent daisy. "Yes," she admitted through clenched teeth.

"Did you tell her I eat little children for breakfast, by any chance?" Lord Edward pushed on, clearly enjoying himself. "Lady Georgy seems convinced I detest the little dears."

"I did no such thing!" Emily was stung into admitting. "I merely pointed out to her that if she were so witless as to marry you, she could not live at Chilworth Manor or raise her children there. The rest of it…" She faltered for a second or two, then went on, "Well, the rest of it just naturally *followed* somehow, that's all."

"Indeed?"

The ramrod-stiff spine straightened yet another degree. "Yes, *indeed,* my lord, and I'm not sorry!" she declared vehemently. "I'd do it again, Lady Georgiana deserves better than you. *Anybody* does."

Lord Edward reached up his index finger and thoughtfully scratched at his lean, tanned cheek. "Even you, Miss Howland? Even you? Methinks, ma'am," he said at last, "the lady doth protest too much. Are you sure you couldn't be just the tiniest bit *jealous* of Lady Georgiana? I am said to be damned handsome, and most eligible. You could do a lot worse, you know. And, truth to tell, I do believe I could be brought to like you, in spite of yourself."

"You conceited buffoon—you utter *monster!*" Emily

gritted out the words, scrambling to her feet. "How dare you even suggest such a thing? Sir, I find you beneath contempt. Now, please leave me, or else I shall take myself off. I find I cannot be within twenty feet of you without longing to slap that silly grin from your too-handsome face."

Lord Edward, now also standing, tipped his head to one side and grinned even wider. "So, you spurn me, Miss Howland? You do realize, of course, that this means war?" he purred, sliding his hands into his pockets as if to show how little he feared physical attack.

"Meaning?" Emily asked, hating herself for needing to hear him say what she was sure he would say.

"Meaning, Miss Emily Howland, that I do believe I shall make Lady Georgiana my personal project from now on, just because it appears to bother you so. After all, I shouldn't like her to lose any sleep believing me to be the worst beast in nature, should I? I much prefer her to be madly in love with me. Old Horry is half in love with me herself—whenever I remind her exactly who I am—so I doubt I shall find much resistance on that front. I might even go so far as to make *you* fall in love with me yourself. Wouldn't that be a coup? Yes, I think I should like you to be in love with me, Miss Howland. Good day."

Emily's mouth opened and closed several times— fishlike, she thought wretchedly—as she struggled to find something damning to say in rebuttal before he bowed politely and bid her farewell, once more leaving her with nothing but her own fury for company.

CHAPTER SEVEN

FOR THE NEXT THREE WEEKS—twenty-one truly forget-table days and a like number of frustrating nights—Emily Howland fretted and seethed, powerless to thwart Lord Edward's determined assault on Lady Georgiana's heart, dreading the moment she would be called to her aunt's boudoir to be informed of her cousin's betrothal to the dastardly lord.

Nothing she said to the contrary—and Emily had tried everything from threats to downright pleading—could convince her cousin that Lord Edward was any-thing but "the sweetest man in the whole, entire world," especially (drat the man for being so underhanded any-how, and may a pestilence infest all his houses) when he was behaving just as he ought—bringing flowers, com-plimenting Lady Georgiana on her gowns, and spend-ing his every moment running tame in the mansion in Portman Square just as if he had a right to be there.

If Emily had truly believed her cousin's emotions to be seriously engaged, she would have days earlier thrown convention to the four winds and belted the smil-ing Lord Edward square in the chops (an unladylike ac-tion, but no more than he deserved), but she knew Lady Georgiana was too flighty to have really developed more than a passing interest in his lordship. She was still more than happy to accept the advances of her many other admirers, for one thing, and she still spoke of Chilworth Manor with more passion than she ever did of one Lord Edward Laurence.

The strangest thing was that Emily was fairly certain Lord Edward was also aware of Lady Georgiana's unconsciously fickle, immature nature. Not only was he aware of it, but it seemed to amuse him, which was just one more reason Emily longed to do the man an injury. He was clearly enjoying himself with this supposedly passionate pursuit, and she was becoming more and more convinced that he was doing it solely to infuriate her. But one never knew, did one? Betrothals had been accomplished on much less than Lord Edward's twisted form of courtship.

Tongues were beginning to wag, and more than once Emily had found herself on the receiving end of lectures given by condescending dowagers who questioned her chaperonage of her cousin. "Trotting a bit hard, ain't she?" one beplumed old harridan had suggested just last night, leering at Emily over the rim of her *fourth* full glass of wine—Emily, feeling mean but justified, had been counting.

But even worse than the scoldings of the old biddies were the endless hours Emily had to spend in Lord Edward's company, for, somewhat like Ruth, whither Lady Georgiana went, Emily was destined to go also.

When she could stand his teasing glances and veiled innuendos in silence no longer, she knew she had to do something so that she could be rid of him once and for all. And so, the morning after Lady Rutherford's ball—the one during which Lady Georgiana had stood up for no less than two waltzes with Lord Edward, *besides* going down to dinner with him—she acted.

Scratching timidly at the door to her aunt's bedchamber, Emily obeyed the command to enter and spied out the dowager duchess sitting propped up against the carved backboard of her immense high bed, her graying head swathed in a ludicrously oversize lace-edged nightcap that had dropped down to cover one eye.

"Oh, good morning, my dear," her grace chirped, pushing back the nightcap and peering myopically at her niece, plainly trying to place the child. Her visitor looked so drab, yet somehow exotic, like a strange, foreign flower wilting from the shock of being transplanted into English soil. "We're having some tea, I believe. Um, shall I have, um er..."

"Simmons, your grace," the middle-aged maid said, prompting her employer automatically as she entered the room and went to draw open the heavy velvet curtains, letting in the morning sun.

"Simmons—yes, of course. I knew that," the dowager duchess concluded happily. "Shall I have Simmons ring for some tea for you as well? It's quite good, you know. Really sets one up for the day, although I do believe I much prefer my chocolate. But I do believe I particularly asked for tea this morning. I wonder why?"

"To settle your stomach, ma'am," Simmons reminded her mistress, wondering yet again if she had enough money put by to move in with her sister in Liverpool for a restorative space. This latest job was beginning to wear on her nerves, even if her grace was the highest title she had ever worked for since coming to London. "I believe you told me you felt a bit queasy."

"I did? Oh, yes, I remember now. It was that horrid meal I had last night, wasn't it? Now, what was that—"

"River eel in parsley sauce, ma'am, a most unfortunate choice, I believe," Simmons said on a sigh, shaking her head at Emily, who was beginning to have second thoughts about her plan to use the duchess to thwart the romance between Lord Edward and her cousin Georgiana. "Shall I ring for another cup, miss?"

"Thank you, no, Simmons, I've already had my breakfast," Emily demurred, trying to convey her sympathy to the older woman with an understanding smile. "I just wish a few moments alone with my aunt, if you don't mind. I have something rather important to discuss with her, as I need her opinion."

Simmons returned the smile, sniffing her amusement. "Good luck to you, then, ducky," she whispered, picking up some bits of discarded finery and leaving through a small door cut into the far corner of the large, overheated room.

"You have a problem to discuss with me, er, um, my dear?" the duchess asked, wishing she could remember the dear girl's name. Emma, Ethel—it was something like that. "Please don't tell me you wish to return to your home, wherever that is. We're so close to settling Georgy. I think Archy's boy is quite near the sticking point, don't you? Such a nice young man—although he doesn't hold a patch on his father, of course. What's his name again?"

"Lord Edward Laurence, ma'am," Emily informed her aunt, sighing. Now she knew for certain that it was not just her imagination running amok. After all, if Aunt Hortense had noticed it, surely the situation was serious. Determinedly ignoring the curious pain she felt in the region of her heart when she thought of Lord Edward and Lady Georgiana bound together in matrimony, she pushed on, "I must tell you, dearest aunt, that I cannot in all good conscience say that I approve of the match."

The duchess was immediately crestfallen, having already mentally packed her baggage for a remove to Sussex and some longed-for peace and quiet. "Why?" was all she found herself able to ask, looking at her strange young niece suspiciously, feeling the child to be responsible for her sudden unhappy shift in mood.

"He's only a younger son," Emily substituted wildly, still hoping she might be spared from revealing the entire sordid story she had—if needs must—decided upon.

"Oh, pooh," the dowager sniffed, waving her right hand, already adorned with three rings, which she considered ample jewelry for the morning hours. "As if that means anything. He's plump enough in the pocket," she informed her niece, for, although she might not be the most intelligent woman in the kingdom, she certainly knew well enough to make sure she was not handing her youngest child over to some penniless fortune hunter who would be forever sticking his legs beneath *her* dinner table!

I should have known, Emily berated herself, having already been subjected to her aunt's feelings on the subject of money. Hadn't she told her—with a noticeable absence of her usual empty-headedness—that it was pointless to put down a load of blunt purchasing a wardrobe for Emily to replace the sadly inadequate one she had brought with her from Surrey, saying that nobody would notice her anyway, once Lady Georgiana was in the room? Not that she was entirely stingy, for she had suggested Emily avail herself of some of her cousin's castoffs—which would have been wonderful to see, for Lady Georgiana was a good half-foot shorter and definitely less amply endowed than her cousin.

"He's also known to be a sad runabout," Emily offered weakly as her second complaint, hoping this line of attack might fare better than the first. "They call him Naughty Ned, you know. He's been said to do the most shocking things."

But, just as Emily had feared, this information seemed to thrill the duchess, who proceeded to relate to her niece a long, rambling story of Lord Edward's late father that served to put his son's feeble attempts at mischief to the blush—the details having something to do with a secret wager, a brewer's buxom daughter, and some visiting foreign minister with a penchant for lower-class females, although her grace's rendition of the escapade ended lamely, as the woman had quite forgotten the ending.

Emily swallowed hard, not knowing that she had no recourse but to tell her aunt what had transpired on the balcony almost four weeks previously. Going over to sit down beside the dowager on the edge of the bed, she laid her head in the woman's lap and whispered in what she hoped were strangled tones: "I fear I must tell you. Lord Edward…he took…he took advantage of me…on the balcony…last month…at… at Georgy's come out ball, ma'am. I'm…I'm *so* ashamed."

The dowager automatically reached out a hand to stroke the girl's head. "He kissed you?" she asked at last, finding it hard to understand that anyone, once he had clapped eyes on her beauteous youngest daughter, could conceive of doing anything so foolish. "Are…are you *quite* sure of that, my dear?"

Emily's shoulders shook as if she were holding back her tears with some effort as she nodded furiously, biting on a small corner of the pink satin coverlet against the sudden rush of anger she felt at the patently incredulous tone of her aunt's voice. This was just one more insult to add to the budget of grievances she held against the insufferable Lord Edward. "Yes, ma'am—quite," she said. "He kissed me, and then he…he… Oh, I can't go on!" Why should she go on? It would totally destroy Emily's story if she told her aunt how Lord Edward had then gone on to insult her.

"Perhaps he was drunk. *That* would explain it," the dowager, still unable to believe she had heard aright, mused aloud, causing Emily to grind her teeth in outrage. "Oh, well, it was just a few kisses, wasn't it? The less said, the soonest mended, isn't that right?"

Emily sat up and glared angrily into her aunt's accepting face, stung to the quick. Obviously it didn't matter one way or the other if Lord Edward had dragged her into the dark and ruthlessly kissed her, just as long as—heaven forbid!—we don't *talk* about it.

"Oh, really, Aunt?" she heard herself saying through the strange hollow buzzing in her ears. "And if you were to return me to my mother—to your sweet sister, 'what's-her-name'—heavy and swollen with child, what would you do about that, *hmm?* Send along a polite note of apology, perhaps? Well, isn't that above everything wonderful? Good day to you, Aunt. I am *so* sorry to have bothered you!"

"Heavy and swollen with… *Oh, dear!* Oh, my goodness!" the dowager exclaimed in shock as she watched Emily flounce out of the room. "Maid! *Maid!* Oh, drat it all, what *is* your name? Come here at once! I need my vinaigrette!"

LADY GEORGIANA, shed of her constant companion for the evening, thanks to the very real headache Emily had contracted during her morning visit with the dowager, was enjoying herself mightily at Lady Agatha Winston's select party, flirting to her heart's content with her many suitors. She liked Lord Edward, liked him immensely, but she was glad he was absent this evening, as his presence seemed to keep all the other young gentlemen away.

Her mother, who was known to keep a loose hand on the reins at the best of times, was not paying too much attention to her daughter, being otherwise occupied, still trying to conjure up a mental picture of the handsome Lord Edward and the dowdy Emily Howland in anything even vaguely resembling a compromising position.

And so it was that Lady Georgiana, whose kind heart so easily overruled her lamentably soft head, allowed herself to be directed to a curtained alcove located on one side of the wide first-floor hall of Lady Winston's Grosvenor Square mansion.

Mr. Alastair Gresham, the young man who had succeeded in luring Lady Georgiana out of the main saloon, spent only a few moments cursorily inspecting the bust of Julius Caesar that occupied a pedestal in the alcove, explaining the sculpture's aristic and historic merits in such an obscure way that Lady Georgiana was convinced that her previous disregard for things ancient had been amply justified.

"Oh, Mr. Gresham, please don't continue, I beg you," she pleaded, pressing one small white hand to her forehead. "You said you had something of the greatest import to tell me, else I would not have accompanied you to this spot." Her pretty pink lips forming an attractive pout, she lamented, "And here I thought you were going to read me another poem. I particularly liked the one you read me last week, even if Emily did say that comparing my eyes to emeralds wasn't quite nice; as emeralds are so hard, you know, and they're stones too. Do you really think my eyes are like stone, Mr. Gresham?"

Mr. Gresham, far from being insulted—for he had

paid only a paltry sum for the poem, to a struggling scribbler he'd chanced to encounter in one of the watering holes at the bottom end of St. James's Street—concentrated instead on the full lower lip Lady Georgiana displayed so artlessly, wetting his own lips in anticipation of his next move. He might not have a feather to fly with, which was why he was well known in society as one of the greatest fortune chasers in the *ton,* but seducing the beauteous Lady Georgiana held more than monetary reward as a lure.

Noticing Mr. Gresham's concentration on her face, as well as the rather aggressive stance he had assumed—a stance that effectively placed her with her back uncomfortably pressed into one corner of the alcove, away from the curtained exit to the foyer—Lady Georgiana belatedly realized her dangerous position and looked around for some means of rescue.

"Oh, my dearest Lady Georgiana," the hopeful swain crooned, his lips dangerously close to her ear, "how long I have dreamed of being with you like this. You are never alone, what with the proprietary Miss Howland always so close by your side, trying her best to discourage me. I cannot but view this moment as a golden opportunity, a happy circumstance that allows me to press my—"

"That you, Georgy? Deuced silly place for a person to stand in, ain't it?"

"*Del!* Oh, thank heavens!" Lady Georgiana shrieked gratefully, pushing the ridiculously ardent Mr. Gresham against the nearby pedestal so firmly that the unhappy man found himself clutching the heavy marble Caesar to his chest, else the bust would have toppled to the floor. "Please, Del, take me away from here."

Lord Delbert Updegrove might not have possessed

the quickest brain in Mayfair, but he did have a fair understanding of this particular situation. Walking straight up to Mr. Gresham—not stopping until one foot was firmly planted atop one of the man's toes—he drew his fiery red brows together, glowered down menacingly upon the smaller man, and growled, "I believe I've never liked you above half, Alastair, you know that?"

Holding the bust protectively in front of him, Mr. Gresham, wincing slightly, carefully eased his foot out from beneath his lordship's shoe, apologized for having been so inconsiderate as to have put it there in the first place, and hastened away down the hall.

"Where's Miss Howland?" Lord Delbert inquired archly, leaning one muscular shoulder against the wall, so that Lady Georgiana once more found herself effectively cut off from the hall, not that she believed her friend Del posed any threat to her. "I swear, Georgy, you're always in some scrape or another. Don't you pay any heed at all to what Miss Howland tells you? Maybe she ought to keep you on a leash."

Tipping her head to one side, her bottom lip thrust out angrily as she took exception to the general impression that she needed a keeper, she said, "Emily's home with the headache, or so she says anyway. Personally, I think she's pining away with love for your friend Lord Edward. Mama thinks so too."

"Oh?" Lord Delbert, conjuring up a mental picture of Emily Howland, could hardly conceal his astonishment or his curiosity.

Lady Georgiana didn't really believe what she was saying to be the truth—even if her mama had just today been asking some rather pointed questions about Emily and his lordship, and waxing poetic about babies and such, although that meant even less to her daughter—

but she was just put out enough about being made to appear brainless beside her capable cousin to say something childishly spiteful.

"Then it's true?" Lord Delbert, who had just remembered Lord Edward's confession of a few weeks ago, shook his head, clearly concerned for both his friend and Miss Howland. "Who would have thought it? Sits it serious, then?"

Busily inspecting the hem of her new gown, which seemed to have somehow suffered some minor damage on the dance floor earlier, Lady Georgiana had to think a moment before she could reply to Lord Delbert's question. Was what true? What *was* Del talking about? Taking refuge in a show of temper, she returned smartly, "Are you calling me a fibber, Delbert?"

"My God," his lordship marveled, almost to himself. "I can't say as how I understand it, but if he did it, he did it, right? He *said* he did it, but I didn't really believe him. He was four parts drunk at the time, I'm sure, not that that's any excuse. No accounting for tastes, is there?"

"If who did what?"

"If Ned pulled Miss Howland off into the bushes, of course," Lord Updegrove returned hotly, unconsciously slipping into rather loose speech, but then he felt himself to be justified, as Lady Georgiana's confirmation had served to put him under some stress. "he said he did, but I thought it was the bottle talking. What are *you* talking about? You can't know anything about Lord Edward."

Now, everyone knows for a fact that bottles don't talk. Lady Georgiana certainly knew it, and she was beginning to feel rather smug. Obviously Lord Delbert Updegrove, for all his fine airs of being such a smarty-puss, didn't have a clear understanding of the situation, whatever the situation was. Did he think she didn't know anything? Well, maybe it was time to show Del that she did so know a thing or two about Lord Edward! Raising her softly rounded chin, she declared importantly, if not exactly prudently: "A lot you know, Delbert Updegrove. *Everyone* knows that Lord Edward simply can't abide children, Emily told me herself. She was quite upset about it, actually. So there!"

"Ned...Miss Howland...*children! Oh, my God!*"

CHAPTER EIGHT

"LORD DELBERT TOLD ME you weren't at Lady Winston's last night, Miss Howland." Lord Edward's tone was carefully neutral as he idly watched Lord Henry Montgomery and Lady Georgiana walk ahead of them down a tree-lined path in the park, sparing a moment to silently congratulate himself yet again that he had ingeniously maneuvered it so that he, rather than Monty, was walking with Emily. "I can only hope that you were not ill."

"I had the headache," Emily admitted shortly, uncomfortably aware of the curious tingle that persisted in her hand as it lay on Lord Edward's arm. She had another headache now, as a matter of fact, brought on by her cousin's offhand question over breakfast. "Can you help me, Emmy? What does it mean—to be pulled off into the bushes?" Lady Georgiana had asked, causing Emily to choke on her buttered toast.

"I have not the slightest idea, and you shouldn't say such things!" she had been stung into retorting, a response that had set her cousin to shaking her head sadly and mumbling something that sounded very much like "Del was right. You poor, dear thing."

Emily and Lord Edward continued their walk in silence for a few minutes, not knowing that, just a few yards in front of them, Lord Henry was listening intently as Lady Georgiana told him all about what she and Lord Delbert had learned about headaches and bushes and children—and some people named Henrietta and Peregrine, although he decided that they weren't worth the dozens of questions he would need to ask to gain a full understanding of their part in things.

It was enough to hear that his friend Ned had compromised poor dear Miss Howland. Why, if the ladies weren't present—and if Ned weren't such a deuced good shot—he would turn around right now and go slap his face, challenging his friend on the field of honor. Besides, he remembered gratefully, he had left his gloves behind in the carriage. One can't challenge a man correctly without first pelting him about the face with one's glove; it just wasn't done.

He'd have to contain himself, even consider talking the whole thing over with Del, not that *that* muttonhead would have a penny's worth of sense to add to the conversation; but at least it would give him some badly needed time in which to decide what his course of action should be, what a man of honor and decency—and limited courage—would do.

For the moment, seeing that he could think of nothing else to do, Lord Henry suggested that Lady Georgiana take the whole of her tale to her mother, the dowager duchess, since that lady was, so far, privy to only parts of it. After all, Miss Howland was under her roof, her protection. The old girl wasn't too bright, but she had raised five daughters; surely she would know just what had to be done.

"Do you feel, as I am beginning to do, Miss Howland, that we are being ignored?" Lord Edward asked after several minutes of uncomfortable silence had passed between them, inclining his head toward the couple in front of them, their two heads now nearly pressed together as they whispered back and forth feverishly, and too quietly to be overheard. "Perhaps it's time we made our way back to the carriage and returned you ladies to Portman Square, just in case Monty is in the process of offering for Lady Georgiana. They wouldn't suit, you know, and I'd hate to see the poor fellow shattered."

"Are you jealous, then, my lord?" Emily countered, unsurprised to find herself feeling somewhat evil. This man consistently brought out the worst in her. "Or perhaps, as you have been all but living in my cousin's pocket these past weeks without declaring yourself, you are being a dog in the manger, not wanting Lady Georgiana for yourself but not wishing for her to develop a *tendre* for anyone else."

Lord Edward stopped in the middle of the path and turned, looking down at Emily, inspecting her face feature by feature with his intoxicating light green eyes. "And what would you think if I were to throw caution to the winds and tell you that I don't care two snaps who Lady Georgiana marries, that she could run off with her dancing master for all it matters to me? What would you do, I wonder, if I were to tell you that I am only wooing your cousin in order to be with you? That I am madly, passionately in love with *you*, Miss Howland, and my only wish is to make you my bride? What would you say to that, my most infuriating Miss Howland? Will you marry me?"

Emily looked up into his eyes unblinkingly, seeing the dancing bits of sunlight that always lived there, her heart slowly crumbling into little pieces at her feet. How could he do this to her? How could he be so mean as to taunt her this way? "I'd say, Lord Edward," she told him at last, her chin held high so that it would not wobble as her emotions fought to get the upper hand, "that you are absolutely the meanest, most unfeeling person upon this entire earth. I know who I am, my lord, and what I am, and I don't need your nasty remarks to bring home to me the true nature of my position. Now, if you will kindly release my arm, I would—"

Lord Edward cut her off with an abrupt shake of his blond head. "You don't believe it, do you, not a word of it? Actually, I expected some initial resistance," he admitted, aware that he was rambling, but then, he hadn't realized he was going to declare himself until he'd actually opened his mouth and heard the words come tumbling out, "which doesn't really explain my behavior since first I met you, I am sure, so I don't know why I'm so upset. But I don't understand your continued dislike of me, truly I don't. I just didn't see any other way to gain your... Oh, never mind. Even Burton says... But that's another story, isn't it? You know, Miss Howland, I'm not all that unlikable. Hostesses don't bar their doors to me. Why can't you accept me?"

"Accept you! *Accept you!*" Emily was stung into exploding, unfortunately just as Lady Georgiana and Lord Henry turned and walked back to within earshot. "Lord Edward, I wouldn't have you if you were served up on a solid gold *platter!*"

Lord Henry, nodding his balding head sagely, whispered to his companion, "I see what you mean. She won't have him, will she? Poor fellow. You have no choice but to tell the dowager everything. Something must be done, and at once!"

"SOMETHING" WAS DONE; something that made perfect sense to Lord Henry Montgomery, Lord Delbert Updegrove, Lady Georgiana, and the dowager Duchess of Chilworth—a thought that in itself must be considered frightening.

Three days after that leisurely stroll in the park, and without bothering to share her plan with either of the principals involved, the dowager's solution to the delicate problem was served up to all of Mayfair with their morning chocolate.

Miss Emily Honoria Howland of Surrey, currently in residence with her aunt, the dowager Duchess of Chilworth, and Lord Edward Mortimer Sinclair Laurence, brother of Reginald Laurence, Marquess of Lyndhurst, were to be married the first day of June.

Burton, standing in just the wrong place as his master, his mouth full of hot coffee, read the announcement in the *Times,* spent the remainder of the morning carefully sponging the resultant rash of brown stains out of the front of his new waistcoat and wishing that his master would have the goodness to stop giggling.

The news was received quite differently in Portman Square, as Emily merely replaced the newspaper beside her breakfast plate (refolded most precisely), rose to her feet, walked slowly and purposefully up the stairs to her room, and locked herself inside, not appearing again for the remainder of the day, no matter how long and loudly anyone pounded on her door.

CHAPTER NINE

"I'LL KILL HER!"

This vehemently voiced pronouncement, accompanied as it was by Lord Edward's graphic visual demonstration of his intention—consisting as it did of holding his cupped hands out in front of his body and then viciously, and with heartfelt enjoyment, squeezing an imaginary neck—caused Lord Henry to insert a finger inside his collar and ease the cloth away from his neck as he swallowed with an audible gulp.

"I mean it, Monty. I've thought it over, and nothing else appeals to me quite so much. I'm going to kill her." That Lord Edward felt just the opposite, that he would truly love to kiss Old Horry smack on the mouth for her opportune, if misguided, assistance, he would keep to himself. After all, the way Del and Monty seemed to bruit every second word he said around town, Emily would see through his subterfuge in a second and he'd be back where he'd started—which, as he already knew, was a long, long way from getting Miss Emily Howland to Lyndhurst Hall, much less to the altar. He could only hope he was a convincing actor.

"Oh, I say, Ned, isn't that a little extreme? Nobody said you had to actually declare your undying *love* for

Miss Howland, now did they? All you have to do is marry her. Besides, Del said you were talking about setting up your nursery—just a few weeks ago, wasn't it?—although I must say neither Del nor I really believed you were serious. You certainly aren't the sort to lumber about with a mess of indecision, I'll say that for you. Oh, no, once you put your mind to do a thing, you just go right out and do it. What I can't understand is why you're so angry. It's not as if the poor dear did it on her own, after all."

Lord Henry's observations stopped Ned in mid-strangle, just when he was beginning to enjoy himself. As he had told Burton earlier, he always thought he had a flair for theatrics. How like Monty to burst his little bubble by not understanding him. "Miss Howland? You dolt! Why would I murder her? Who did what on their own? It was Old Horry that sent that notice to the press yesterday. I checked. Miss Howland is as innocent as I am in this stupidity…this…this *insanity!*"

Lord Henry reached up one pale hand to scratch at his nonexistent chin. Would it be foolhardy to point out that no *innocent* miss would be about to present his friend with a "token of her affection"—just about mid-February, if his calculations were correct?

Would it be gentlemanly, considering the fact that he did rather like Miss Howland, to even remark aloud about her compromised position? To be exact, would it be worth *his* neck to so much as hint at the reason for the forthcoming nuptials, after observing firsthand the extremely foul mood his friend Ned was wallowing in at the moment?

In the end, Lord Henry decided that self-preservation had a lot to recommend itself, and compromised. "Miss Howland must be in alt," he remarked noncommittally, wondering if Ned and the lady would appreciate a poem in their honor as a wedding gift.

"Emily Howland detests the very ground I tread on," Lord Edward pointed out, wondering yet again what her reaction had been to the announcement.

"I guess, then, that a poem is out," Lord Henry mumbled into his cravat. "But you can't murder the dowager duchess. Such things just aren't *done*."

Why had the dowager inserted the notice? That small bit of information still eluded Lord Edward. Pacing the carpet of his small sitting room with his hands clenched behind his back, he mused, as if to himself, "Maybe Old Horry just got the names mixed up; yes, she could do that. She must have meant to say that Lady Georgiana and I are to be wed; at least that would have made some twisted sort of sense. No, nobody's that forgetful, not even the dowager. She remembers m'father well enough."

"She never remembers me," Lord Henry put in helpfully, reaching into the nearby candy dish and selecting a tempting comfit. His friend didn't look very well, not very well at all. He looked a bit pale, as if he'd spent a restless night. Lord Henry shook his head in sympathy, then reached for another confection.

Lord Edward stopped his pacing and directed his green-eyed gaze to a point slightly higher and to the left of his friend's head. "The duchess knows she's done something very, very naughty, though. She wouldn't let me past her butler all day yesterday, and I tried a half-dozen times or more to see her. The plague, indeed. It's a good thing she's forgetful, for the woman can't lie worth a tinker's damn. I need to speak with Emily without any more delay. What time is it?"

Lord Henry pushed one skinny leg out straight and

levered his bony hips upward so that he could slip a hand into his tight watch pocket. "It's gone eleven," he mumbled around a mouthful of candy. "You going to try to breach the walls again today?"

Taking his hat and cape from Burton, who had appeared from the hallway just a moment earlier, as if anticipating his master's summons, Lord Edward slammed the curly-brimmed beaver down ruthlessly on his blond curls, saying, "Damn right I am, Monty. There's no telling the damage that old lady's already done. Now, stop stuffing your face and follow me."

"Me?" Lord Henry gulped, sinking back into the soft cushions as if hoping he could hide behind them. What would happen to him once his friend figured out the whole of it? "Why would you want me to…that is, I really can't see the reasoning behind my…oh, well…*actually*…I'm promised to Del for luncheon and… Oh, Ned, do I *have* to?"

"You do," Lord Edward retorted, looking curiously at his friend out of the corners of his eyes. "If I recall correctly, you and Lady Georgiana were acting most peculiar the last time all four of us were together. Not only that, but last night Del was over here lecturing me about remembering I'm a gentleman and to do the gentlemanly thing, or some such drivel. He was fairly deep in his cups, as was I, so I'm not really sure of everything he said. I just know it wasn't at all like Del. To tell the truth, Monty, I'm beginning to scent a rat. You wouldn't know more about this thing than you're letting on, would you?"

"Who—me? Don't be ridiculous!" Lord Henry wished his voice didn't sound quite so high, or so shrill. Rising jauntily to his feet, he grabbed his own cloak and hat and made to follow his friend out of the room. "Why would anyone ever think I knew anything?"

"I certainly wouldn't, my lord," Burton assured him, straight-faced, bowing to the young man most respectfully as Lord Henry, looking confused, politely thanked him.

THE DOWAGER DUCHESS of Chilworth was experiencing a most uncomfortable morning. Truth be told, she had been feeling most sadly out of curl ever since the previous day, when her niece had locked the door to the best guest chamber, refusing to see or speak to anyone.

The girl had accepted the meals brought to her by the servants—at last the dowager could comfort herself with the fact that the ridiculous child wasn't about to starve herself into a decline, it would be so bad for the babe—but the old woman couldn't help but feel partially responsible for her niece's unhappy situation.

After all, the chit wouldn't be in such a predicament if she herself had taken her responsibility more carefully, watched over her sister's child more closely, monitored her movements so that just such a scandal as this wouldn't, couldn't have occurred. But the girl seemed so mature, so responsible, so levelheaded.

"And so uninspiringly plain." The duchess sighed aloud into the bottom of her empty teacup. "Who would have thought she would be in any danger of being compromised—and by that sweet boy! How could I have known? The blame shouldn't all be mine. Minerva should have told me the girl had round heels. Isn't it just like Minerva to foist her hot-blooded offspring on me!"

"Your grace?"

"What is it, um, er…"

"Simmons, your grace," the woman clarified wearily. "I'm afraid I couldn't hear what you just said."

The dowager shook her head so that her oversize white linen nightcap slipped to one side, showing her thinning gray hair to disadvantage. "I see nothing un-usual in that. You weren't supposed to hear me, young woman. I was talking to myself!"

Simmons nodded, accepting this admission calmly. "Sorry, your grace, I should have known."

"Yes, you certainly should have!" Satisfied that al-though the rest of her world seemed to have somehow been turned upside down, the domestic situation was still firmly within her grasp, the duchess announced that she wished to rise, as she was expecting visitors. That handsome young man would be back today, she was sure, and this time she would see him. As her dear late husband the duke used to say, "There is no sense in delaying the eventful"—or something like that.

"And Miss Howland has expressed her desire to bid you a personal farewell before she departs, your grace," Simmons added neutrally, careful not to let her feelings color her voice. When it came to loyalty, Simmons knew full well upon which side her daily bread was buttered; but she also liked the sad-looking young miss, and was not averse to seeing the duchess get a little of her own back for landing the poor companion in such a bumble-bath. Miss Howland was not happy, any fool with an eye in her head could see that, and the duchess was the cause of that unhappiness. Now Simmons looked for-ward to enjoying the old woman's discomfort.

She was not disappointed. "Departs? Departs where?" The duchess, momentarily forgetting her ad-vanced years, as well as the height of her thick mattress in relationship to the shortness of her legs, scrambled crablike to the side of the bed and slid bumpily down to the floor, stopping only to catch her breath and to pull her snagged nightgown back down below her hips.

"She plans to go running to Minerva! I can't have

that, I just can't! Minerva's too mean; she'll do something awful to me, I just know it. She once bit me, you
know. Nasty girl, and such big teeth. I have to get them
safely bracketed first. You—whatever your name is,"
she screeched, pointing to Simmons, "don't just stand
there looking at me. Fetch me my clothing at once."

IT HAD BEEN AN UNHAPPY twenty-four hours for Emily
Howland, long hours during which she had alternately
wept and ranted and cursed the fact that she had ever
been born, if this was a sample of what the rest of her
adult life held in store for her.

As she hid in her room, traveling the long, lonely
road from blank shock, to horrified disbelief, to hideous embarrassment, to righteous indignation—even as
she, in the small, dark hours of the morning, reached a
minimal level of resigned acceptance—one recurring
thought had circled round and round within her aching
head: how much she loathed and abhorred one Lord
Edward Laurence.

She didn't know how he had accomplished it, and she
certainly wasn't about to attempt delving inside his
twisted brain to try to understand precisely *why* he had
done it, but she knew Lord Edward was at the bottom
of the ludicrous engagement announcement that had,
overnight, made her, Emily Howland, an unknown from
nowhere, the laughingstock of all London.

He had meanly teased her by hinting that he might
wish to marry her, even while his every action showed
her that he couldn't really be serious, and she had made
it clear to him that he left her totally unmoved. She
knew she had angered him, perhaps even injured his
silly pride, but she had never thought he could be so
spiteful as to subject her to public humiliation this way.

She knew what he was about, of course. He had inserted that notice in the papers just so that he could refute it, so that he and his lowlife friends could go round the town having a snigger at her expense.

How he would crow about her supposed one-sided love of him, her starry-eyed infatuation that must have convinced her to make her dotty aunt believe that he, Lord Edward Mortimer Sinclair Laurence—rich, handsome, and heir to the Marquess of Lyndhurst—had actually offered for such a poor, sad specimen as herself.

Oh, he had done the deed, all right, but he had miscalculated badly if he thought she was going to stay around to applaud him in his juvenile triumph. At four that morning, having slept not a wink since retiring just before midnight, Emily had hopped from her bed and commenced packing her trunk for the return home. Lord Edward would just have to do his crowing on his own, without his victim around to suffer the stares and whispers he had provoked.

Now, having bathed and dressed in her shabby brown traveling dress, Emily was on her way downstairs to bid her aunt and cousin a hasty farewell, just as Simmons, wearing a commiserating face Emily found to be most disheartening, came by to say that the dowager and Lady Georgiana were in the drawing room awaiting guests and wished her presence as soon as possible.

Emily had just reached the door to the drawing room when the knocker banged loudly and one of the footmen waiting on a bench at the side of the foyer jumped up to answer the summons. Eager to get her farewells over with before the visitors could be shown in, Emily fairly ran into the room, stopping only when she heard Lord Edward's velvet baritone behind her in the foyer.

"Lord Edward Laurence to see the dowager duchess

and Miss Emily Howland, if you please," the voice commanded, sending an indignant flush flying into Emily's pale cheeks and the blood pounding in her ears so that she didn't hear him add, with quiet good humor: "And I don't mean to be fobbed off with any more of your nonsense about plagues."

CHAPTER TEN

THE DOUBLE DOORS to the drawing room closed with a loud bang before Emily turned the key in the lock, successfully barring the young lord's entrance. Whirling around to place her back against the doors, she then surveyed the room in front of her, startled to see the dowager, usually a most energetic woman, lying on the settee, Lady Georgiana kneeling on the carpet beside her, vinaigrette at the ready.

"Oh, dear," Emily exclaimed, "I didn't realize! How could I have been so stupid, so self-centered? This is just as embarrassing for you as it is for me, isn't it, Aunt? Please forgive me."

Lady Georgiana, looking as radiantly beautiful as usual in a muslin gown of soft lime green, rose gracefully to her feet and advanced on her cousin. "Don't alarm yourself, Emmy, dearest," she said in a most motherly fashion, taking her stunned relative gently by the arm and leading her to a nearby chair. "Mama has had to deal with just this sort of thing before, and we'll come through famously now exactly as we did then, never doubt it. Only, please, don't be upset. Would you like some macaroons? Henrietta was most partial to them, as I recall."

"Henrietta?" Emily echoed hollowly. "Your sister Henrietta? What does she have to do with anything?"

"Oh, I remember now," the dowager groaned, clutching her hands to her bosom. "So it was Henrietta who did that. Henrietta and... Oh, dear, I can't seem to remember his name. Tall, isn't he? With depressing dishwater-blond hair?"

"Peregrine, Mama," Lady Georgiana provided helpfully, having arranged a light woven blanket around Emily's knees before returning to her mother's side.

Emily raised a hand to her forehead and rubbed at it gently, trying to understand. She knew Henrietta, of course. Her mother had told her about all of the Chilworth brood, seeming to delight in the fact that none of them was any too bright. Henrietta was the one who had made that unfortunate alliance with the third son of a country squire. Were her aunt and cousin suggesting that Emily's supposed betrothal was also a misalliance—with the male and female roles reversed, of course? It seemed likely—just the sort of comparison her relatives might make. But what did macaroons have to do with anything?

She voiced her question aloud: "Why macaroons?"

"I can't imagine," the dowager responded, shaking her head. "I much preferred onions in cream sauce myself. At least, I think I did. It's been so long, you know. Perhaps you could tell us just what it is you do crave, and Georgy can have Cook prepare it."

The soft rapping on the door was replaced by the heavy pounding of a stronger, more insistent fist. Clearly the footman had been pushed aside and Lord Edward had taken charge of announcing himself. If Emily had been unsure of her deduction, the sound of Lord Henry's shrill voice confirmed her fears. "Oh, here, here, Ned. That ain't seemly. You're going to knock it down if you keep hammering away like that. I don't think the ladies are receiving. Ned? Ned! Where are you going now?"

Turning her head so that she could follow the sound of Lord Edward's retreating footsteps, Emily suddenly realized his intent and bolted to her feet, running to close the door to the morning room that adjoined the drawing room and also faced onto the foyer, but she was too late. Her arms spread wide, one hand on each door, she was nearly knocked onto her back as the man she had been trying to avoid barreled into the room.

"You!"

This accusation, voiced by both of them at once, served to put an immediate period to any conversation concerning macaroons or onions in cream or anything else that might have entered the minds of the dowager and her daughter to the detriment of the major problem at hand. "Lord Edward!" Lady Georgiana gushed as Lord Henry, always polite, slid into the room behind his friend and rushed to help her rise. "Oh, Mama, look! Lord Edward's here."

Emily, who was at that moment glaring dangerously into her enemy's openly taunting green eyes, snapped back nastily, "Oh, Aunt Hortense, look! Cousin Emily's leaving." Turning smartly on her heels, she took three quick steps before a strong hand clamped down on her forearm, pulling her to an abrupt halt.

"Shame on you, Miss Howland," teased Lord Edward, although no one but Emily detected the faint hint of laughter in his voice. "Running away? Oh, yes, I saw the trunk in the foyer. I had thought you had more bottom than that, truly I did." He was glad to see her, he really was, but he couldn't help but feel angry to learn that she was preparing to flee London rather than see him again. Such an action certainly didn't bode well for a smooth-running engagement, to say nothing of the effect it had on his opinion of himself, which had been growing steadily lower ever since he'd met Miss Emily Howland.

Emily whirled about, her ample bosom heaving under the faded material of her gown. "You don't like that, do you? When you made your plans for my humiliation, you never counted on your victim fleeing the scene, did you? You wished me to remain, to feel each separate sting of the arrows you and the rest of London would launch in my direction. Well, so sorry to disappoint you, my lord. You'll just have to carry on without me. Enjoy yourself!"

Although Emily tugged mightily to free herself, Lord Edward wasn't about to let her go. "Oh, how like you, Miss Howland," he said heavily, his worst fears confirmed. She blamed him entirely. He must have been all about in his head to think the dowager's interference could be looked upon as a blessing in disguise. Very well then, he decided, if it was anger Emily Howland wanted, it was anger she was going to get. Far be it from him to disappoint a lady! "How very much in character you are. You've tried and found me guilty without so much as a hearing, haven't you? It never would occur to you that *I* am just as much a victim here as you are, would it? Well, then, go on, run away—run back to whatever damp, dreary part of England you hail from and raise dogs. See if I care. I've broad shoulders. I can ride out this scandal alone."

Emily stopped struggling and stood quite still, looking up into Lord Edward's handsome face. "Cats," she mumbled inanely. "I thought I'd raise cats. You...you

didn't insert the announcement? You knew nothing
about it either?"

Now Lord Edward did smile, though not at Emily
and not at all in a kindly manner, to her way of thinking. "How do you like that, Monty?" he asked his friend.
"Sharp as a tack is our Miss Howland, once you gain
her attention." Looking back at the woman in front of
him, he continued: "No, Miss Howland, I did *not* insert
the notice. Also, *you* did not insert the notice. Now,
whom do you suppose that leaves?"

"Mama, I think Lord Edward knows you did it,"
Lady Georgiana exclaimed with a sudden burst of insight, turning about to look at her mother. "*Mama!* Oh,
my goodness, Emily, look! I do believe my dearest
Mama has fainted!"

Lord Edward was maddeningly unconcerned, his
mind busy with his own problem. "She won't fall far;
she's already lying down."

Emily slowly shook her head back and forth, a small
sneer on her full, unpainted lips. "So gallant. And how
very like you, my lord," she commented before, with
one last sharp tug, she succeeded in freeing herself from
his grasp in order to minister to her aunt.

It took several minutes to rouse the dowager, although Lord Henry was naïve enough to point out that
the woman didn't look as if she had fainted—for didn't
her eyelids flutter just then?—but after a time she
opened her eyes slightly and murmured, "Where…
where am I?"

"In muck straight up to your knees, that's where,"
Lord Edward informed her kindly from behind the settee, "but we'll let that pass for the moment, won't we?
Please, madam, could you possibly explain what possessed you to insert a notice in the papers concerning

the supposed betrothal between Miss Howland and myself? We are both positively agog with curiosity, aren't we, Miss Howland?"

"But it's so simple. Didn't Lord Henry explain everything? Or Lord Delbert?"

Suddenly Lady Georgiana was the center of attention as all heads moved in her direction at the conclusion of his innocent question. Her mother looked at her in gratitude, as she believed she'd catch cold attempting to feign another swoon, while Emily and Lord Edward gazed at her in confusion. Lord Henry merely glared an unspoken warning, his huge Adam's apple working nervously in his throat.

Lady Georgiana liked being the centerpiece in any room, had liked it ever since she had sung her first party piece for visiting relatives the Christmas she was seven, and she preened a bit, adjusting the ruffle on her bodice, oblivious of the growing tension in the room.

"Georgy?" Emily prompted at last, sensing that Lady Georgiana, her little question posed, had no intention of elaborating.

"What? Oh, I guess he didn't did he? Not Lord Delbert either? How strange." Rolling her eyes, she took a deep breath and looked to her mother for guidance. "Is it seemly that we say anything? I mean, there are gentlemen present."

The duchess frowned, taking her daughter's words into consideration, while the remainder of the people in the room held their collective breaths, waiting to finally hear something that would make some sense of the situation. At last the dowager opened her mouth to speak, and they all leaned toward her expectantly. "Who's Lord Henry? Do I know a Lord Delbert?"

"That tears is!" Lord Edward pounded his fist against

the back of the settee in exasperation, startling the dowager into sitting up straight, hanging on to her wig for
dear life. "You did it, you know you did it, and we could
care less if Monty and Del are strangers to you or by-
blows from long-ago lovers you've forgotten over the
years. Now, damn it all, woman, we're waiting—*why
did you do it?*"

The dowager's eyes rolled up into her head as she
fainted back against the overstuffed cushions—and this
time even Lord Henry believed she had truly passed into
unconsciousness.

Lady Georgiana, taking her cue from her mama, and
knowing a naughty swear word when she heard it, even
if she didn't quite understand what a by-blow was,
promptly sagged into Lord Henry's arms, which was a
poor choice, really, for the man wasn't overly strong,
and the two of them ended up tumbling slowly into a
nearby chair, Lady Georgiana slumped on Lord Henry's
bony lap.

Only Emily, who was made of sturdier stuff, was unmoved by this outburst. "Congratulations, my lord,"
was all she said, calmly surveying the carnage about
them. "You have served to fell them all with one mighty
blow. But wait. Lord Henry is still conscious—or at
least I think so. Perhaps I'm being charitable, or merely
overly optimistic. Do you suppose you should pursue
your line of questioning with him, seeing as how he
can't escape? Shall I call for thumbscrews?"

Lord Edward, who was raised to be better than he
was being at the moment, but who didn't much care at
this point what anyone thought of him, barked, "Shut
up!" at his beloved and then walked round the settee to
confront his friend. "Well, Monty?"

Lord Henry was trapped and he knew it. Where was

Del when he needed him? He had been there sure enough when they were discussing how best to handle the problem. He was probably down at Gentleman Jackson's, pounding some poor soul to flinders in order to work up an appetite for luncheon, that's where he was, and Lord Henry wished, not for the first time, that his own strengths were less cerebral and more physical, for Ned was looking exceedingly dangerous.

"It wasn't my idea, Ned," he squeaked at last, shifting Lady Georgiana's inert body a shade to the left. "She's heavier than she looks. It's those small bones—they hide a lot."

"Monty…"

"Yes, well, I don't see what all the fuss is about," Lord Henry continued, now using Lady Georgiana as a human shield, holding her rag-doll-limp form in front of him as Lord Edward advanced across the carpet, blood in his eyes. "After all, you have to do the proper thing—right? I mean, you wouldn't want the child to be born on the wrong side of the blanket. The dowager has just made it official, considering you and Miss Howland wouldn't stop fighting with each other long enough to set a date yourselves. People can count, you know, and February is going to be here before you know it."

"Child? What child? Whose child? What in blue blazes are you talking about? Monty, have you been drinking?"

"Oh, dear," Emily murmured quietly, but not so quietly that Lord Edward didn't hear.

"'Oh, dear,' what, Miss Howland? Don't tell me this idiot is making sense to you."

Emily's mind returned to the conversation she and her aunt had had in that woman's chambers, and her own outburst that had something to do with being sent home to her mother "heavy with child." From there it was only a short skip to the questions Lady Georgiana had asked about "tumbling into the bushes" and her cousin's concern that Lord Edward didn't care for children. The macaroons, however, were what tied all these random bits of information into one huge misunderstanding and topped it off with a huge red ribbon.

Turning to face Lord Edward, Emily lifted her eyebrows hopefully, pinned a bright smile on her face, and raised her shoulders up to within an inch of her ears. "They think I'm pregnant," she chirped with what she hoped was a show of supreme enjoyment for a huge joke. "Isn't that above everything silly?"

"Pregnant? You? Who'd have the nerve?" Lord Edward threw back his head and laughed aloud, his laughter continuing for exactly three and one half seconds—Emily counted—before cutting off abruptly as his head snapped forward and he exclaimed: "Pregnant! You! Me? Oh, my Lord—me! *That's not funny!*"

"No, it isn't, is it, my lord? It is also not possible," Emily pointed out quite unnecessarily, leaning over to help her cousin, now conscious once again—but still vague as to how she had come to be curled up in Lord Henry's lap—to her feet. "Georgy, darling, do you think you are up to answering a few teeny questions?"

Lady Georgiana brightened at once. "I love questions," she gushed, then frowned. "Will I know the answers?"

"Oh, good grief," Lord Edward muttered as he stood next to his "betrothed."

"Hush," Emily ordered through clenched teeth. "After all, if you hadn't been so foolish as to go chasing after Lady Georgiana just to spite me, we wouldn't be in this mess in the first place. Now, be quiet, or else she'll swoon again."

"Ah, of course," Lord Edward said, leaning down so that his whispered words were audible only to Emily. "My fault again. I knew it would get back to me. Enlighten me, please: do you have any names picked out for the little darling you'll be presenting me with in—what was that date again—February?"

Emily calmly swiveled her head in Lord Edward's direction, lowered her chin against her shoulder, raised her slanted brown eyes to look into his face, and enunciated slowly: "Shut…up."

"You're not quarreling again, are you, Emily?" Lady Georgiana asked, looking as if she was about to cry. "Lord Henry and I heard you say in the park that you wouldn't have Lord Edward on a platter, but that's silly, isn't it, considering that you're getting married. You really shouldn't fight—it can't be good for the baby."

Having spoken her little piece, Lady Georgiana realized that although she had been standing there ever so long, nobody had as yet asked her a question. She decided to remedy this lapse. "Aren't you going to ask me any questions, Emmy? You said you were. I don't know an awful lot about babies, you understand, even if I am the youngest and all the others have just oodles of children. I saw our cat, Mindy, have kittens once, behind the barn. Will that help?"

That did it. Lord Edward, who had been moving back and forth between frustration and amusement ever since he had set foot inside the Chilworth drawing room, finally succumbed to the latter. Staggering over to the settee, he lifted the unconscious dowager's feet to one side, sat himself down, and then replaced her feet on his lap, patting the bony, stockinged ankles comfortingly. Then he laid his head back against the settee and laughed until tears streamed down his cheeks.

Emily stood alone in the middle of the room, her arms spread beseechingly, her mouth opening and closing like a landed salmon as she struggled to find her voice. Then, just as Lord Henry began leading the puzzled Lady Georgiana out of the room, the dowager roused, raised her head, looked around the room, and asked: "Would you like some onions in cream, my dear? You look a little queasy."

CHAPTER ELEVEN

"I MUST SAY, NED you're taking this whole engagement business rather well, considering." Lord Delbert's compliment delivered, and obviously relieved that his friend Lord Edward had not already demanded satisfaction from either him or Lord Henry on the field of honor—after having read Lord Henry's hysterical missive (an uncharacteristically ungrammatical communication, not that its recipient would notice such a lapse), he sank into a chair and allowed a deep sigh to escape his lips.

Lord Edward, his left arm draped negligently on the mantel, inclined his head in his friend's direction and gifted him with a rueful smile. "I hesitate to point out that it's just that sort of simplistic deduction that has created 'this engagement business,' Del," he reminded the man almost kindly. "I wouldn't wish to alarm you, old son, since you have yet to pick up on it on your own, but you have caught me in the midst of a bad moment. I have to decide precisely how I am going to handle things with Miss Howland so that she does not end up hating me. In the interim, I suggest you do yourself a large favor and button your lip so that I can think."

Lord Delbert digested this advice slowly—and badly.

"But Monty's note says the gel ain't really increasing, that we all just thought so. You do still mean to marry her, don't you? I mean, it's only proper. Is her family battening on you already? Pity. It was only a bit of frolic you were having, after all. Unless... Good God, Ned, the girl *was* willing, wasn't she? If you ask me, she should have been demmed grateful, considering she's without funds and totally ineligible, though it still puzzles me what you ever saw in the female to drag her into the bushes in the first place. Three parts cast away, were you?"

Once again, as it seemed to have become his custom in these last few days, Lord Edward became quite angry. Angry that Lord Delbert couldn't see Emily the way he did, angry that his friend thought he'd care a snap whether or not his bride came to him with her pockets well-lined, and even angrier that anyone would think his beloved was so loose as to topple backward into the bushes with a man she proposed to detest. *"You idiot!"* he exploded, concentrating first on restoring Emily's good name. "What does it take to get through to you? Nothing happ—"

"No, he was not drunk," interrupted the subject of this debate from the doorway, where she had been standing unnoticed for some moments, "although you are not, alas, the first person to put forth that question. Good day, my lords. I am truly sorry to intrude upon you like this, unannounced, but—"

"Shame on me, Miss Howland," Lord Edward broke in, already moving across the room toward her, his green eyes flashing both a threat and a warning to the embarrassed Lord Delbert, "if I appear to doubt your sincerity in this instance, but—"

"—but that strange little man, most probably your butler, for I cannot quite see him in the role of bodyguard—seemed reluctant to alarm your gentler sensibilities by admitting an unaccompanied female," Emily pushed on doggedly, her nose raised, as if testing the air.

Lord Edward stopped midway across the carpet and pulled a wry face. "Even while fighting the very lowering feeling that my function at this moment is one of being relegated to nothing more than that of a minor character in a farce, destined to speak only lines meant to serve as verbal bridges over which the leading player can then tread, triumphant, I feel I must ask: What, then, did you *do* with the so-prudish Burton, Miss Howland, as you are, after all, here?"

Emily's eyelids lowered, hiding her expression as she mumbled something that sounded very much like "the cabinet under the stairs," before she went on more loudly: "While your abrupt departure from Portman Square this noon was not entirely without its small portion of personal appeal to me, my lord, I do believe you could have had something more to the point to say about our supposed upcoming nuptials than to say 'see you in church' as you took your leave."

Lord Delbert's shocked gasp echoed softly in Lord Edward's snort of amusement.

"Therefore," Emily continued, refusing to be ruffled, "as my aunt and cousin have both retired to their rooms—doubtless to begin stitching 'little things,' for I fear they have yet to let it sink into their vague skulls that I am *not* carrying your child—I took it upon myself to run you to ground so that we may settle this problem as quickly"—she spared a moment to look daggers at Lord Delbert, who was leaning forward in his chair, utterly enthralled—"and as *quietly* as possible."

Lord Edward shook his head. "And arriving on my

doorstep unaccompanied in the middle of the day, Miss Howland—is that how you hope to silence all the wagging tongues in the *ton?* How comforting it is for me to have my reputation resting in your clever hands."

"I see no reason for you to be so obnoxious, Lord Edward," Emily sniffed, her pale cheeks showing a faint hint of color.

"Yes, of course," he responded levelly, gesturing for Emily to take a seat even as he longed to pull her ugly dark green bonnet from her head. The first thing he'd do once they were married would be to burn every stitch she owned! "I have this lamentable tendency to overreact. Please forgive me—and please excuse me for a moment while I effect poor Burton's rescue. The large storage cabinet, I believe you mumbled? I do hope you didn't squash his suit of clothes. He's very particular, you know, and I'd hate for him to take offense. After all, we may wish refreshments later."

Emily sat down primly on the edge of a small dusky blue divan and nodded to Lord Delbert, who had just gratefully subsided back into his own seat after standing at attention the moment she had entered the room. "You disapprove as well," she declared a trifle peevishly.

"Of locking old Burton under the stairs?" he deduced, furrowing his broad brow as he considered the question. "Can't say as it matters one way or the other to me, actually, although it must have been something to see. You're nearly twice his size…er, I mean… Why do you ask?"

Emily was not offended. It was true, after all: the butler was very small, most probably one of those dwarfs she had read about, and even if he was nearly as round as he was tall, she'd had no difficulty in grabbing the recalcitrant servant by the ear, as she was used to doing with her younger siblings, and depositing him inside the cabinet. "I was referring to my arriving here both unannounced and unaccompanied, my lord," she said mildly.

"Oh, yes, yes, of course," Lord Delbert said, embarrassed. "Surely it's not my place to pass judgment, Miss Howland. Is it?"

Emily tilted her head first this way, then that, considering. "I don't know, my lord. After all, such a piddling thing as it not being any of your concern certainly didn't stop you before—you or Lord Henry or my cousin. You all seem to have encountered little problem with your collective consciences while rushing to pass judgment on my supposed indiscretion with Lord Edward."

Lacking a suitable reply, and knowing the dratted female was well within her rights to take him to task—indeed, he was somewhat surprised she hadn't as yet conked him over the head with something heavy—Lord Delbert cravenly picked up two comfits from the always full candy dish and popped them into his mouth. After all, it was impolite to talk with his mouth full—and it seemed he had spoken more than enough already. Drat Georgy and her silly stories about babies—this entire mess should be laid at her door!

"Miss Howland?" Lord Edward reentered the room, his handsome face wearing an amused smile. "Burton sends both his regards and his congratulations—whether on our betrothal or your conquest over him in battle, I'm not quite sure—and wishes to know if you desire tea before you depart. He has also taken the liberty of sending one of the stable lads round to Portman Square to bring back a maid in Lady Chilworth's carriage. Good man, Burton, a real treasure, and he seems to have taken a liking to you. Something to do with 'gumption,' I believe. I was sure he would be all for sending you home in a hack—and sans the tea—but Burton is every inch the gentleman. We could learn from him, Del and I, if we chose."

"We don't choose, Ned, do we?" Lord Delbert was beginning to feel depressed.

"No, my friend," Lord Edward assured him gently, "we don't, although," he went on musingly, "we might wish to apply to Miss Howland here for some pointers in the manly art of defense. Tea?"

"I don't require any refreshments, my lord," Emily cut in, anxious to have this distasteful interview concluded as soon as possible. What an arrogant, overbearing… Oh, what was the use? Emily bristled momentarily, and then relinquished her anger. After all, having anyone believe that she—plain, unprepossessing Emily Howland— had lured Lord Edward into a romantic indiscretion was highly flattering.

To Her. Definitely to her. But not to him. Not to Lord Edward Laurence, who had beautiful females dropping into his arms like ripe plums anytime he desired. No, for him the supposition that he had seduced her, along with the engagement announcement, could only be viewed as an unremitting disaster, with no positive aspects to lend it some small humor or palatability. Lord Edward had every right to be upset. Emily sighed. "Now, if you would be so good as to sit down, my lord, perhaps we may get on with the reason for my visit?"

"Good heavens, yes," Lord Edward agreed almost jovially, for, he was surprised to realize, he was actually enjoying himself. "I am, I assure you, all ears, if you have any suggestions to make to the point."

Emily barely repressed the urge to box his ears, her recent sympathy for her supposed *fiancé* evaporating as swiftly as it had come. Of course she had a suggestion! Did he think she had slunk out of Portman Square via the tradesmen's door, walked a depressing two blocks before locating a decrepit, *smelly* hack willing to bear up a solitary female, and opened herself up to Lord Edward's certain-to-be-voiced insults (and Lord Delbert's asinine remarks, although, to be fair, she hadn't given too much thought as to whether or not Lord Edward would be entertaining—a gentleman, that is—when she arrived), without there being a good reason for the visit?

"Well, Miss Howland?" Lord Edward prompted when Emily didn't answer.

Emily frowned, then tried to concentrate once more on the problem at hand. "We must have the duchess insist all the newspapers involved immediately print retractions, of course," she pronounced firmly, sure she was correct in her assessment of the situation, and wondering yet again why his lordship had not seen the obvious.

Lord Edward, who had been expecting just such a suggestion from her, immediately burst into speech. "Oh, yes, of course! Why, do you suppose, did I not think of that? Perhaps it was too simple—or just too bloody ridiculous! My God, woman, is it your desire then to make us even more the laughingstock than we already are? How do you propose to word the thing? 'Dear Readers—*whoops!* There seems to have been a small error…'" He turned to his friend. "Del! Can you just imagine that?"

Lord Delbert obediently squeezed his eyes shut and tried to picture the article as it would doubtless appear in the nastier columns. Then he grimaced. "You'll have to rusticate at Lyndhurst Hall, of course. For about two years, I'd say," he prophesied at last, opening his eyes to look gloomily at his friend. "And we are going to travel to Scotland together, too, you and Monty and I. We'll miss you, Ned."

"Oh, dear, please stop," Emily said scornfully, slanting her gaze toward Lord Edward, who was doing his best to look like a puppy that had just been unfairly kicked, "else I fear I shall cry." She then shook her head to let him know she wasn't having any of it.

Lord Edward stood up and moved back over to stand in front of the cold fireplace. She wasn't going to let this be easy, and he would be damned for the greatest fool in nature if he would allow this golden opportunity to slip away from him. "Perhaps, Del, if you would be so kind as to tell Miss Howland how you foresee *her* future if this retraction is printed?" he urged, trusting Del to be his usual tactless self.

Lord Delbert chewed on this question for a few moments, just long enough for Emily to begin to feel distinctly uncomfortable, then pronounced importantly: "I imagine society will have a good laugh at her expense and then…er…*forget her.* That's if she goes home straight-away, naturally, although I'm sure the stories will follow her for some months, even in… Where is it you live, Miss Howland?"

"Surrey," Emily rasped huskily, thinking of her mother, her brothers and sisters—the *neighbors.*

"And if she remains here?" Lord Edward prodded, watching Emily closely and knowing his friend's words had at last struck a nerve. He hated doing this to her, longed for nothing more than to gather her in his arms and kiss the pain away, but it was the only way the rest of his plan could work in its new, hastily amended form.

"If she stays out the Season here in London," Lord Delbert pushed on, gaining confidence, as he felt he had their full attention, "it will be much, much worse. Everyone and his lady wife will think she was the one who inserted the notice, you see."

"And why is that, Del?" Lord Edward asked, once again knowing the answer.

"Well, that's easy enough, Ned. I'm surprised you didn't see it for yourself. Because any fool would know that *you* of all people would never actually offer for an utter nobody, a… Oh, I say, Ned, I'm late for an appointment. I really must dash. Good day, Miss Howland," Lord Delbert rushed on, already on his feet and moving toward the door, his normally ruddy complexion beet red with embarrassment and chagrin that Ned had trapped him into such a glaring *faux pas*. "It was so nice seeing you again; really it was."

"Lord Delbert," Emily choked out thinly, her head bowed as she pretended to examine the small garnet ring on her right hand, a gift from her mother and the best piece of jewelry she owned.

"I didn't want to do that, you know," Lord Edward said gently once they were alone, before, his heart going out to her, he blurted, "Oh, look here, Emily, can't you see that—"

"The young miss's carriage is without, my lord," Burton broke in repressively from the doorway, where he had been standing unnoticed for some minutes, hearing every word, understanding every motive—and therefore knowing that his master was about to confess all, thereby making a fine mess of everything.

"Go away, Burton," Lord Edward replied tersely, still concentrating on Emily's bent head.

"I'm a complete idiot, aren't I?" Emily said quietly after a long, uncomfortable silence, still twisting the cheap ring round and round her finger.

"*No!* It's all my—"

Burton, who had stayed in the doorway, for, after all, there was no other chaperon present now that Lord Delbert had cut and run—indeed, the servant was secretly surprised (and more than a little sorry) that the fellow had lasted as long as he had—pointedly cleared his throat and glared at his employer.

Lord Edward, who knew that particular look well enough from his younger days, sighed, and then inclined his head slightly in recognition of the unspoken command. As Burton had pointed out just this morning at breakfast, he still had to get Emily down to Lyndhurst Hall. The engagement announcement had played right into his hands, and he'd be seven kinds of a fool if he didn't take advantage of it. "Miss Howland," he said softly, pushing himself away from the mantel and going over to take her restlessly moving hands in his own. "I believe there is a way out of this thing for both of us— if you can find it in your heart to trust me."

Emily raised her head slowly, her deep brown eyes nearly black with pain. "Do I have any other choice? I'm listening, my lord."

CHAPTER TWELVE

IT HAD BEEN QUITE the most lowering experience in Emily's life. Even three hours later, and in the privacy of her comfortable room in Portman Square, her cheeks still burned with shame when she thought about it.

How could she have been so harebrained, so impetuous? Whatever had possessed her to ever consider running to Lord Edward for assistance? It was like running to a lion to be protected from a tiger. Had she really believed he held any answers for her—the man whose very perverseness had been the cause of all her problems in the first place?

Oh, yes, Emily mused, staring at herself in the ornate gilt-edged mirror hinged atop the dressing table—sparing only a moment to run a finger absently along the length of her nose and once again rue nature's decision to gift it with that slight bump just at the bridge—all the *real* blame could be laid square at his door.

She might have been willing to carry her share of the burden of guilt for the rather ticklish consequences of everyone's mistaken notions, but it was Lord Edward who had invited this avalanche of disaster to come crashing down around their ears in the first place, him with his nasty taunts and totally reprehensible actions.

She would never have said a word to the duchess—not a single, solitary word—if *he* had not all but dared her to do something to rid Georgy and herself of his unwanted attentions. He had merely been frolicking—reveling in Emily's frustration—knowing all along his pursuit of her cousin, not to mention that ridiculous so-called proposal he had dared to tease Emily with herself, had not been serious.

In the first place, Emily had at last calmed herself enough to realize that if Lord Edward had *really* developed any sort of *tendre* for Georgy, he would have gone straight to her to clear himself, so that the object of his affections would not be obliged to view him in disgust—as any man who had fathered a child and then refused to wed the woman he had compromised must be seen.

Raising her hands to take the pins from her hair, Emily hesitated a moment, leaning forward to look herself in the eye. "Now, why do you suppose that one fact—set as it is amidst a rare bellyful of absolutely horrendous facts—serves to lift your spirits, Emily Howland? Don't tell me you actually have some feeling for that odious man?"

She stared at her reflection piercingly until she was forced to divert her eyes from her candid inner self, and began ruthlessly pulling the pins from her hair. "Of course you don't! Don't be ridiculous!" she scoffed, knowing her tone wasn't quite convincing.

All the pins removed, she pushed her hands through the long, heavy mantle of hair and then shook her head vigorously, not realizing that the wild tangle of red-brown hair that now framed her face added a sultry hint of mystery to her slanted eyes while lending an unlooked-for air of wantonness to her generous lips and high cheekbones.

Rising to her feet, she opened the high front closing of her gown and let the garment drop to the floor, carefully averting her gaze from the mirror and the sight of what she considered her most embarrassing feature—her high, full bosom.

Bosoms were, she acknowledged, in vogue at the moment, but her seeming excess had been endlessly tut-tutted over by her nervous mama, who was a much less generously endowed and extremely modest female, causing Emily to believe that—as with her nose—nature had painted her with far too wide a brush.

To hide her "flaw," Emily had, since her early teens, worn her gowns long-sleeved and buttoned to the throat, favoring dark, drab colors that would call less attention to her unfortunate "gifts." The advent of the *empire* waistline, which so successfully concealed many a thick middle in others, completely hid the fact that Emily's waistline, on contrast to her breasts, was exquisitely infinitesimal.

Her hips, also generous, though not overly padded, were likewise forever shrouded in the heavy draperies she employed as camouflage, as were her long, straight legs. The resultant overall look of dowdy dumpiness that had caused Lord Edward some secret concern in fact concealed a figure that would have brought tears of joy to Botticelli's eyes.

But Emily, slipping a fresh, yet depressingly similar gown of muddy green—"the exact same shade as a moldy leaf," Lord Edward had commented *sotto voce* when first confronted with the gown—was blind to her unique, beautifully sculptured beauty, seeing only that she was "different," a fact that never showed to more personal disadvantage than when she was inevitably compared to her petite, finely featured, blond-haired cousin.

The dinner gong sounded jarringly just as she inserted the last restraining pin into the curled, upswept style that was so flattering to Lady Georgiana, while, alas making Emily look much like she had a weather-beaten bird's nest stuck to the top of her head, and she took a deep breath, pushed back her shoulders, and turned for the door, determined to somehow get through what she was sure—thanks to the *enterprising* Lord Edward and his nefarious "Plan"—was destined to be the most difficult evening of her life.

They were all waiting for her when she came downstairs: her aunt, her cousin, and that dreadful, dreadful man. "Good evening, my dearest Emily," Lord Edward greeted her loudly, immediately moving across the wide drawing-room carpet to bow over her hand and kiss her fingers with a show of passion that may have convinced her relatives of his ardor but only left Emily feeling used. "May I say that you are looking well this evening?"

"Yes, she does have a little color tonight, doesn't she?" her grace agreed in some amazement as Lady Georgiana helped her to her feet in preparation for moving into the dining room. "Once the uncomfortableness of the morning was over, I always felt much more the thing for the rest of the day—at least I think so. But it doesn't last, my dear, you'll be happy to know, the queasiness, that is. Except with my third—or was it my second? I had a terrible time, even with the onions in cream, and we missed nearly the entire Season."

"Mama, Emmy says she's *not* increasing," Lady Georgiana whispered loudly. "Don't you remember? she just always looks sort of green."

"You know," Emily said offhandedly as she vainly tried to extract her hand from Lord Edward's grasp, "if

I didn't know she was being sincere in her efforts to help me, I'd be tempted to box my dear cousin's ears."

Lord Edward hid a smile with his hand as he ushered Emily in to dinner. "At least she seems to have digested the fact that you're not carrying my child. Now, if we can only convince dear Old Horry—"

"Of course *you* can," Emily interrupted as he deliberately made a ceremony out of holding her chair. "I remember how convincingly you spoke this afternoon of accomplishing just such a daring breakthrough this evening. My only question is, if your plan works, what will you then do for an encore—flap your arms up and down and fly three times around the chandelier?"

"It might be easier," Lord Edward conceded before walking around the table to his own seat directly across from her, noting that the butler had already taken care of seating the duchess and Lady Georgiana.

As the first course was being served, her grace looked around the table, frowning. "We are such a small party, aren't we? I imagine I'll be expected to have some sort of do—with all sorts of people milling about, stuffing their faces and drinking the cellars dry. I wouldn't wish Minerva to think I wasn't doing the right thing for her dear daughter. Has a nasty disposition, Minerva—but then, she never was my favorite. What do you think, Lord…er…?"

"Call me Ned, please, ma'am," Lord Edward supplied kindly, deciding his opinion of Emily's mother wasn't really required. "After all, we're soon to be family. Isn't that right, darling?"

Raising her eyes from her plate, Emily saw that Lord Edward was smiling at her in a way that set her toes to curling inside her slippers. So, this was it—the opening salvo of his lordship's brilliant Plan. She loathed it already. "Yes, er, yes…of course!" she stammered, out-wardly smiling, inwardly seething.

"But, Emmy," Lady Georgiana broke in, obviously confused, "just last week you told me that you'd rather be dunked headfirst in pitch and hung out to dry in Piccadilly than allow yourself to be married to Lord Edward. She said it just last week, Mama, I'm sure she did. Didn't you just say that last week, Emmy?"

"Piccadilly?" Lord Edward repeated, looking at Emily in genuine amusement. "My goodness, darling, there are times you really do shock me. Now, be a good girl and tell your dear cousin the truth. After all, it was just a silly lovers' quarrel."

Step Two of the Plan, Emily acknowledged silently, wishing the dining table wasn't so wide that she couldn't deliver a sharp kick squarely on his lordship's shin. "That's right, Georgy. We had an argument, Lord…er…*Ned* and I, and I was just being mean." Turning to face her aunt, she continued just as Lord Edward had rehearsed her, and hating every moment of it: "We had already planned to announce our engage-ment before our spat—the one Georgy and Lord Henry overheard in the park. Naturally, when I saw the an-nouncement in the paper, I was angry that Ned had gone ahead and inserted it without telling me. Imagine my surprise when we found out you had already guessed our secret—and we thought we had been so clever, hid-ing our attraction to each other. Actually, dearest aunt, we have you to thank for making us realize that we really do belong together."

"Me?" the duchess questioned, momentarily forget-ting that she had been the one to insert the announce-ment in the first place. "Oh, yes—it was me, wasn't it? My goodness, sometimes I surprise myself." She blushed and waved her hand as if to diminish her own importance. "It was nothing, my dears, really. You don't have to thank me."

Lord Edward caught Emily's eye and winked his approval of her performance, so that she was tempted to stick her tongue out at him in a most childish way. "If you say so, ma'am, but I think you're being too modest. You can be sure we will always remember you as the person who brought us to this point…er…this happy conclusion. There is just…well, just this one small niggling thing…"

"Yes?" Hortense was leaning forward in her chair, eager to be of assistance. Nobody had ever asked for her help before, which seemed quite silly now, as she was proving to be so good at it.

"Yes," Lord Edward went on smoothly. "You see, Emily and I are having some problem with the June first date—the one you used in the announcement. As it is just a month away, I doubt we could possibly arrange everything to our satisfaction in so short a time, what with Emily's family being in Surrey, and my brother Reginald never coming to town, and, oh, just all sorts of knotty problems. Would it be all right with you if we postpone the wedding for a few months? Perhaps August would suit?"

"But…but…" The duchess looked from Emily to Ned and back again. "But…the *baby!*" The duchess might have been vague about other things, but when it came to indiscretions, she had a memory like an elephant.

Lady Georgiana laid down her fish fork with a resigned sigh and said, "Mama, Emmy isn't going to have a baby. Lord Edward only kissed her the once, and it wasn't in the bushes, it was only on the balcony. We were wrong, we were all wrong—Lord Henry, and Del, and you, and me—don't you remember?"

"Only one kiss? Not going to have a baby?" The duchess furrowed her brow, trying to get everything clear in her head. She didn't recall any Lord Henry—although the name Del seemed familiar—but she couldn't be expected to remember everything. "Well, then, why did I insert the notice if it wasn't to quash a scandal?"

"We wanted you to, ma'am," Lord Edward supplied quickly as he saw that Emily was about to open her mouth—undoubtedly to say something that would queer the whole Plan. "You were playing Cupid, ma'am, and may I be so bold as to say, you did a bang-up job of it. All of London is buzzing about it. It's just that the *date*—"

"Yes, yes, the date," Horry interrupted, very much in charge now that she understood the way of the thing. "Not increasing, huh? Well, doesn't that just beat the Dutch? This way we won't have a lot of old biddies sitting about counting on their fingers after you're married. A pity Henrietta wasn't so fortunate. Have you met her husband? I can't remember his name, but he's a dreadful, dreadful man. Dreadful child too, for that matter. Favors his father. No chin, none at all."

"Henrietta's baby is a girl, Mama," Lady Georgiana said punctiliously.

"A girl?" Hortense clucked her tongue. "It's even worse than I thought. Thank heaven I won't be the one to have the launching of her."

"The date, Aunt," Emily prodded, her fingers crossed in her lap. According to Lord Edward, everything depended on the date. If they could only get the duchess to postpone the wedding until after the Season, a discreetly worded notice in the newspapers sometime during the summer, telling of the termination of the engagement, would be no more than a nine-days' wonder.

Lord Edward had magnanimously allowed that Emily could be the one to cry off, once she was safely back in Surrey, and his plan to rusticate until the fall Little Season would silence the rest of the talk. It was a good plan, decidedly better than an immediate retraction, even if it did call for the two of them to pretend an engagement for the next month.

"August would be fine then, I suppose," the duchess pronounced at last, and Emily could hear Lord Edward's audible exhalation of the breath he must have been holding as he waited for her answer. "You'll write to your mother and, um, tell her that we, er…"

"Of course, Aunt. I'd be happy to!" Emily exclaimed, knowing the letter would never be written. News from London was spotty and delayed at best, and she planned to be home long before any word of her supposed engagement could reach her family's ears. "Mother will be so grateful to you, Aunt," she added for good measure.

Suddenly the duchess's watery blue eyes took on a haunted look. "Surely *I'm* not responsible for putting on the wedding. Am I?" Playing for the privilege was another kettle of fish entirely, and infinitely less palatable.

"Of course not, ma'am," Lord Edward hastened to assure her. "We'll be married from Emily's home. Right after our trip down to Lyndhurst Hall. You and Lady Georgiana will be so kind as to make up the rest of the house party, won't you? We'd love to have you. Isn't that right, darling?"

Lyndhurst Hall? House party? Emily's frown mimicked a gathering thundercloud as she tried to digest this latest piece of information. That hadn't been any part of the plan. What was he talking about? She had no intention of spending time at his brother's estate. Not only that, but one more "darling" and she was going to fling her dish of cherry pudding straight at his head, Emily thought, the idea appealing to her so much she had to force herself to lay down her spoon and clasp her hands together in her lap. "But, *dearest,* surely we can speak of this later? Poor Aunt Hortense has enough to consider at the moment," she said between clenched teeth, her cheeks beginning to ache abominably from the effort of constantly smiling.

"Anything you say, darling," Lord Edward replied, so pleased with himself for having slipped in that bit about the house party, he was oblivious of the fact that his beloved was within Ames Ace of murdering him where he sat.

Once the meal was done, the small party repaired to the main drawing room and Lord Edward surprised everyone by immediately going down on one knee in front of Emily, who had purposely sat in a chair set away from all the others. Pulling a small square box from his pocket, he opened it with a flourish, extracting a golden ring set with a huge yellow diamond. "I'd be honored if you would wear this, Emily. It's been in our family for generations."

Before she could think, before she could come to grips with the fact that this devastatingly handsome, eligible man was kneeling at her feet while her aunt and cousin looked on, she felt her left hand being lifted and the cold metal being pushed onto her finger. She looked down at her hand to see that the diamond, surrounded as it was by at least a dozen smaller stones, spanned her finger from knuckle to knuckle. "It…it's lovely," she said just as a good *fiancée* ought.

"No, it isn't," Lord Edward told her happily under his breath. "It's quite the most horrid piece of stone ever unearthed, but it's also the only thing I had in the house that wasn't made for a man. You've been doing splendidly so far, by the way. Nobody suspects a thing. Now, come here—I think I'm supposed to kiss you."

"No, I—" Emily protested feebly, but she was too late. Lord Edward pulled her to her feet and then brushed her lips softly with his own before turning away to accept the duchess's nearly incoherent congratulations, leaving his breathless *fiancée* to stand abandoned in the middle of the room, her mouth at half-mast.

He'd done it again, knocked her into horsetails, while he'd remained completely unaffected. It wasn't fair, that's what it wasn't, and Emily disliked him more at that moment than she ever had. Who did he think he was, trifling with her this way? Kissing her in front of her dotty aunt and romantic cousin just as if he had a right to? How were they ever going to make anyone believe they wished to end an engagement he seemed to be enjoying to the top of his bent?

"Darling?" Lord Edward prompted, squeezing her hand in silent warning. "Your aunt has just offered you her best wishes."

Emily obediently pasted an inane grin back on her face and allowed her relatives to kiss her cheek and gush over the beauty of her ring, all the time looking at Lord Edward out of the corners of her eyes and quietly willing him to remove that smug, satisfied expression from his face.

Just this afternoon he had been ranting and raving enough to bring down the house, proving that he'd rather be visited by the black death than be in the same room with her, and now he was pretending to be deliriously happy to be betrothed. And, poor fools that they were, they *believed* him! If he *did* suddenly take wing and fly thrice around the chandelier, Emily wouldn't even blink!

She was convinced more than ever before that this was all a big game to him, a lark, a delightful rig he was running to amuse himself. He was enjoying himself— he was actually *enjoying* himself! She could hear him now as he explained away this ridiculous engagement, telling everyone how he had wished to set up his nursery and, as he felt sorry for her and thought she'd make a conformable, undemanding wife—the sort a man could leave in the country with his heir and never miss—he had chosen plain Emily Howland to be his convenient, unassuming bride.

People wouldn't laugh at *him,* they wouldn't titter behind *his* back because he'd affianced himself with a woman of no consequence. No, they'd congratulate him for his brilliance, right up to and beyond the point the engagement was called off. Talk about having your cake and eating it too—the man bore off the palm!

Emily's slanted eyes narrowed dangerously as she concluded that, yet again, she was the victim. First the victim of her relatives' ridiculous suppositions, and now Lord Edward's victim as well. He had never really been concerned about her this afternoon when he and his friend Lord Delbert had gleefully pointed out the pitfalls of immediately retracting the duchess's announcement. Oh, no. He had only been thinking of his own reputation, his own ridiculous consequence.

From the moment she had first stepped foot in London she had been acted upon rather than acting, Emily decided, her opinion of her own worth dropping like a stone. She had been a brown wren, allowing people to think her dull and dowdy, allowing them to use her for their own devices.

It was terrible to feel this way, and it wasn't fair—it just wasn't *fair!* Emily's chin began to wobble, as her self-pity threatened to overwhelm her. She wasn't a mean person, she wasn't particularly stupid, so she didn't believe she was being punished or only receiving her just deserts. Yet she was a victim.

Lord Edward was leaning toward the duchess, trying to make heads or tails of some story she was telling him about her own wedding trip—if only she could remember if it was Spain or Italy they had visited; it had these lovely little waterways running through it, she knew— and Lady Georgiana was leaning against his arm, the two of them making a heartbreakingly beautiful picture. Emily's heart began to beat hurtfully in her chest, until she could no longer stand there and watch, isolated in the middle of their small group.

Walking over to the window, she stared out into the darkness, seeing her reflection and that of the room behind her in the glass. Slowly, one by one, the tears she had been holding back began to fall. She could drop dead right here and now and none of them would notice, she thought, sniffing, for her nose always ran when she cried. She hated being plain. She…absolutely… positively…hated it!

CHAPTER THIRTEEN

FIVE DAYS AFTER the dinner party, just as Lord Edward was sitting down to a leisurely luncheon of braised lamb chops, Burton excused himself to answer a loud knocking on the front door. Waving the butler away, Lord Edward served himself, still thinking about his latest attempt to win Emily's heart.

Simmons, her grace's personal maid, had proved most helpful in gaining him a list of Emily's measurements, and after spending the morning in Bond Street he had returned to his town house a happy, if slightly less well-heeled, man. So far, his amended plans had been swimming along quite nicely, and he was finding it increasingly difficult to believe that this confused engagement hadn't been his intention all along.

The first few gowns he had ordered would be ready in less than a sennight, in plenty of time for their removal to Sussex late the next week, and he was already anticipating Emily's sure-to-be-ecstatic reaction to his largess. Not only that, but a discreet peek at Simmons' scribblings had served to put a new spring in his step, for it would seem that his darling Emily was not pudgy, but merely the victim of a sadistic dressmaker. He knew she was going to be beautiful, had known it all along—

not that he would have loved her any the less if she had been in need of shedding a few inches.

Now, if he could only find some way of convincing his reluctant darling to have something done with her hair…

"There you are, my dearest Noddy! I found you!" came a high, thin voice from the doorway. "Stand up so I may kiss you on both cheeks, for you have made me the happiest of men!"

"Reggie?" Lord Edward threw down his fork and scrambled to his feet, to be immediately clasped in his brother's scented embrace. "I can't believe it. You haven't come into town for years."

"Yes, it is I. Merryvale must be scouring the countryside! Now, stand still, I said, so I might kiss you." Reginald Archibald Sinclair Laurence, fifth Marquess of Lyndhurst, then made good his threat, holding his younger brother slightly away from him by the shoulders before, as promised, planting smacking kisses on both his cheeks, "As I told the dearest Colonel just yesterday—or was it the day before? I'm so bad with dates—Noddy, you are the very best of brothers, an absolute prince of a good fellow! You have saved my life, Noddy, you have set me *free!*"

Lord Edward was confused as well as embarrassed. Reggie had always been so demonstrative, so theatrical. His garbled explosions of delight could be extremely unnerving. Backing away from him, and trying with all his might not to raise his hands and scrub at his cheeks, Lord Edward blustered, "Free, Reggie? I am? I did? I didn't know…er… Precisely *what* did I do, Reggie?"

The fifth Marquess of Lyndhurst lowered his tall, thin body into the chair Burton held out for him, affectionately patted the little man on the top of his bald head before pulling him up onto his lap like an adored toddler, and then magnanimously motioned for Lord Edward to sit down as well. "Why, you got yourself engaged to be wed to the dearest Miss Howland, of course. Merryvale tried to hide it from me, but I found it. I always find what he doesn't wish me to find. It's rather like a game we play. I will like her, won't I? Oh, I'm sure I will. Noddy, I can't begin to tell you how wonderful this is. Is that a new painting, Noddy? I don't think I like it."

Lord Edward looked across the room at the painting his brother was pointing to, then shook his head. "No, Reggie, it's not new. You gave it to me for Christmas three years ago, I think."

"Really? Burton should hide it in the cellars. It must have been during that time I thought I adored ducks above all else. But *dead* ducks? Odd, don't you think?"

"Reggie?" his brother prompted, trying to bring the conversation back to the reason for this visit. "How have I saved your life? You haven't been drinking ink again, have you? You know it makes you sick."

His lordship kissed Burton on both cheeks and then unceremoniously pushed him off his lap. "Ink, Noddy? Don't be silly. I never drink ink anymore; it turns my teeth most dreadfully blue, you know, and it doesn't taste anything as delicious as it looks. But only think— a week ago I was teetering on the brink of despair, just this side of putting a period to my wretched existence— yes, I was, dear boy, I must own it. Oast houses! I ask you, what do I know about oast houses? But now! Well, now I am reborn! A pox on all oast houses, and a pox on Merryvale for denying me my pink cottages! Think about it, Noddy! All the village houses, all in little pink rows. It would be delightful! But, do I care? No! Not I! You see before you a new man, a man with a purpose, a man with a glorious mission in his life. Did I kiss you, Noddy? I want to shower you with kisses!"

Lord Edward shifted uncomfortably in his chair. "Yes, Reggie, you kissed me, and I don't mind telling you that I wish you would try very hard not to do it again." Obviously Reginald was off on another one of his tangents. How had he gotten past Merryvale? "But suicide, Reggie? I thought we had settled that silly business when I visited with you at Lyndhurst Hall. You told me the Reverend Smithers had quite decided you against it."

Lord Lyndhurst nodded vigorously in the affirmative. "Yes, yes, he did, he did, but that was before I met dearest Colonel Musbank and heard of his Great Expedition. Tibet! Living among the monks! The dream of my lifetime at last come to fruition. Can you imagine my joy, my heartbreak, when I thought the good Colonel must leave me behind—that I was sentenced to a lifelong imprisonment at Lyndhurst Hall? They're all yelling for thatch now; as if a little good English drizzle would melt their silly heads!"

"The tenants are asking for new thatch for their cottage roofs?" Lord Edward hazarded, grabbing hold of Burton by the back of his collar as the butler tried to make good his escape from the room.

"Didn't I say that? I wanted them to come live with me, but Merryvale frowned so that I couldn't do it. He's no fun, Merryvale, no fun at all. Well, I cannot begin to tell you of my ravaged emotions to think that the Colonel would depart without me, but then, just at the last moment, just as I was penning you my final correspondence—it was quite a good note, if a tad lengthy, my best yet; I brought it with me so that you may read it at your leisure—the papers arrived from London and

I learned that you, dearest boy, had reached out to save me from death's eternal darkness."

Lord Edward looked over at Burton and rolled his eyes at this latest silliness. It wasn't that he discounted Reggie's talk of Tibet and suicide, but he knew well enough that these were just his brother's latest "interests" and he'd never really seriously try to put an end to himself—although he might just try to hike to Tibet with a ham sandwich in his pocket. Two years ago it had been building a balloon large enough to float to America that had occupied his brother's mind, and the year before that it had been the ink episode—with the marquess professing the liquid was good for the spleen. "I did, did I? How wonderful of me, I'm sure. Tell me, Reggie, how did I do this marvelous thing?"

"Why, by becoming engaged to be wed, of course," Lord Lyndhurst told him, unable to believe his brother could not see what was clear as crystal to him. "I've already told you that. Honestly, Noddy, I can't believe you've been attending. I've come to town for the nuptials, and then dearest Colonel Musbank and I are off to Tibet to commune with the monks. Noddy? You're looking most queer. Is everything all right? Don't tell me you're not getting married, for I couldn't bear it, I tell you—I just couldn't *bear* it. Not after the pink cottages. Burton, dearest sprout! Is there a length of strong rope in the house?"

"GOING TO TIBET, you say? What would anybody want to do that for, for pity's sake? It's not as if there's anything there, is it? I mean…*Tibet?* It's in Asia somewhere, right? And it's not even part of the Empire, is it? Good God, Ned, what are you going to do? Maybe it's time you gave it up and had dearest old Reggie fitted for his own straight waistcoat."

Lord Edward looked at his friend over the top of his glass, trying hard to focus on Lord Henry Montgomery's drink-blurred features. "He's not mad, Monty. Maybe a little confused, but no more so than your cousin Ferdie. Isn't he the one who thinks he's a tree? Besides, only the poor are mad. The rich are eccentric."

"A rosebush, a pink one, I think," Lord Henry corrected, flushing. "But Ferdie's only a second cousin, and a veritable nobody into the bargain. Your brother's the marquess, for God's sake. Think of the talk! No, there's nothing else for it—you'll have to put him away. Insane asylums are not so terrible—some of the best people are locked up in them."

Lord Edward laughed derisively. "Yes, Monty, I know. Asylums have become quite fashionable. I've heard it said that when you hear that someone has just come 'out,' you don't know if it means they've just been presented or *released*. But not Reginald—I won't even consider it. Our father made me promise him on his deathbed that I'd always watch out for Reggie—and, if needs must, prepare myself for the possibility of having to take his place someday at Lyndhurst Hall. Why else do you think I came to town considering marriage in the first place? My last trip home was a total disaster. Reggie's latest trick is to think up new ways to do himself in. Thank goodness he's so woefully inept at it. It's just a phase, and will pass, like all the others, but for the moment…"

Lord Delbert Updegrove, also present in Lord Edward's private chamber, and also feeling slightly the worse for drink, lifted his massive red head from his chest to ask, "Then what are you going to do, Ned, if you can't bring yourself to disappoint him? Reggie thinks you're going to marry Miss Howland, even though we all knew you never meant any such thing until we made such a sad hash of everything. You can't fool us, try as you like. This engagement isn't working. Miss Howland doesn't like you above half, you know, and would make your life a living hell into the bargain, not that I can blame her. But then *you'd* be the one we'd be carting off to Bedlam, and I don't think that's what your father wanted."

Pushing himself to his feet, Lord Edward began pacing up and down the small carpet in the center of the room, glass in hand. Much as he feared telling the whole truth to his friends, he knew the time had come to lay all of his cards on the table. "You're wrong there, Del," he said at last. "I have always meant to marry Miss Howland. I love her."

This bald declaration served to gain Lord Edward his friends' undivided attention and he sat back down to explain all that had transpired to bring them to this point. He told them how he had traveled to Lyndhurst Hall only to find that Reggie was retreating more and more from reality every day, and explained that he had decided then and there that it was time he found a wife and retired to the country to personally take charge of his brother. He told them of seeing Miss Howland with the dowager duchess, of how levelheaded and understanding she was when confronted with the dowager's vagaries, and how, slowly, he had found himself falling in love with her.

He explained—twice, as Del seemed to have a difficult time taking it all in—why, as Miss Howland paid absolutely no attention to him, he had purposely teased her, trying to make her aware of him, and how he had found it necessary to pay court to Lady Georgiana in order to be with Miss Howland, who refused to step outside the boundaries of a companion and allow herself to be approached as a young lady in her first Season.

He went on to confide his original plan, telling them how he had hoped to invite Lady Georgiana down to Lyndhurst Hall so that he could observe Miss Howland firsthand with his brother. "After all, I could not ask her to take on Reggie with me without first letting her know precisely what she'd be getting herself into, could I?" he pointed out when Lord Henry couldn't seem to understand what Reggie had to do with anything.

Last, he told them how, thanks to their misconception about the relationship between him and that same Miss Howland, he'd had to amend his plan, discovering that being engaged to the woman of his dreams settled the problem of convincing the dowager of the need for a house party. "The only really difficult thing," he admitted, "was making Emily believe I love this engagement as little as she does, or else she never would have agreed to my scheme. I had hoped she would see me in a better light if we could be together as a betrothed couple, and then there would be no need for any more subterfuge. But now Reggie is here and, much as I love him, I do worry that he might just prove to be too much for Emily right now."

"You could be right," Del put in consideringly. "Georgy tells me Miss Howland's been acting most peculiar for an engaged lady, moping about the house and crying into her handkerchief when she thinks no one is looking. Georgy is most upset, the dear girl, though I don't think either she or the duchess suspects the truth. There'd be the devil to pay if they did, I don't mind telling you."

"Crying? I don't like the sound of that," Monty interjected, his poet's soul touched. "Poor girl's been put

THE ENTERPRISING LORD EDWARD

upon enough as it is, and it's all your fault, Ned. It's a sad thing you love Miss Howland. After all, if you hated her, there's no telling how happy she'd be at this moment. I think you've gone too far this time, and I don't like it one bit, I tell you, that we have helped you to make Miss Howland miserable. You'll have to let her cry off from this engagement and find yourself another, more willing female. And you'll just have to tell Reggie the truth and then hide all the knives—and maybe the drapery sashes."

Lord Edward subsided into his chair once more, wondering why he had bothered to ask his two friends for their assistance. He'd just have to find some way to get Reggie back to Sussex without meeting Emily. Later, after she loved him, he would explain about his eccentric brother.

"Ned?" Monty questioned, interrupting Lord Edward's thought processes. "You're not thinking of putting an end to yourself, are you? I mean, it doesn't run in the family or anything? You never said how your father came to cock up his toes."

"No, Monty," Lord Edward assured him, shaking his head. "I was just thinking how much easier it would be if Emily Howland was like every other female and willing to marry the devil himself for money and a title. I'm even handsome into the bargain. Why, I could name a half-dozen damsels right now who'd marry me in a minute."

"And so modest with it all," Lord Henry inserted, still trying to tell himself that Emily Howland really favored him rather than his friend. She did like his poetry, and she had always listened to him with a great show of interest. Of course, lately she had been rather quiet, almost sullen, but that was to be expected. Being betrothed to Naughty Ned, even if it wasn't a true betrothal, was enough to put any female off her feed. The man was about as constant as a windstorm, much as Lord Henry liked him personally. "A pony says she won't have you."

Lord Delbert frowned. "Betting on it, Monty? Do you really think that's in good taste? I mean, Ned here has asked us for our help."

"May I come in, Noddy? I thought I heard voices. Oh, how nice, you have company. Hello boys. Do you have red slippers? I do, two pairs with little deer embroidered on them, but I seem to have left them at home."

The three friends turned in their chairs to see the Marquess of Lyndhurst standing in the doorway in his bare feet, dressing gown, and tasseled nightcap, smiling at them benevolently. The man was a mass of angles, all knees and elbows, even under the heavily quilted banyan, his drooping nightcap sliding down over one eye as he wriggled his long, skinny toes against the carpet. He was so thin, a good puff of wind would have bowled him over. Lord Edward's heart tugged painfully in his chest, for he loved his brother, mildly eccentric or totally insane.

"Come in, Reggie, come in," Lord Edward urged kindly, standing up to introduce his brother to his friends, and then offered him his own seat. "I'm sorry if we woke you. Are you feeling all right?"

"Fine, fine, just fine," the marquess said, nodding so that his nightcap was in danger of slipping entirely off his head. "I wasn't sleeping anyway. I'm too terribly, terribly excited about my trip. Did Noddy tell you that I'm heading on to Tibet, boys? It's all arranged. Is that sherry? Do so favor sherry. Dearest Colonel Musbank and I leave in less than two months, once I'm sure that Noddy here is safely married and settled in at Lyndhurst Hall. My heart is just fluttering and fluttering. I doubt I'll sleep a wink between now and then for sheer excitement. Just think, boys, *Tibet.* How you all must envy me!"

"About as much as I envy a crossing sweep on a rainy day," Del whispered just loud enough for Lord Henry to hear him.

"It's just absolutely delicious, boys," Lord Lyndhurst gushed, oblivious of their total lack of interest. "Dearest Colonel Musbank says we can live like kings for mere pennies—I once gave a penny to a little boy along the road. He was most grateful. He had red hair, like you— emperors, even, not that it matters. It's the land itself that excites me, and the customs. And the monks, the mountains, the beauty—oh, it's just too thrilling! No, I remember now, I gave him my *sandwich*—tongue, I believe—and he was a little girl. How silly of me! Do you think they eat tongue in Tibet? Hah! Tongue in Tibet—it almost rhymes, doesn't it? I cringe, I absolutely *cringe,* I tell you, when I think how close I came to ending it all. It would have advanced me on the wheel of life, the Colonel says, but just think of what I would have missed!"

"Being underground would have put a bit of a crimp in your plans, Reggie, I agree," Lord Edward said kindly, ignoring the subject of tongue sandwiches entirely, "but I wish you wouldn't dwell on such unpleasant thoughts. I've rung for Burton. Why don't you have him fix you something to help you sleep? It has been a long day."

A few minutes later, after Burton had come to lead his lordship away, Monty sighed and said, "He's a sweet-enough crazy man, your brother. You'll have to marry Miss Howland now, Ned, and have her fall in love with you later. I can't see any other way out of it."

Del rose to his feet, his glass held high. "To Ned and Miss Howland—the best of luck!"

Lord Edward watched as Monty and Del drained their glasses and then flung them into the fireplace. "Thank you, my friends. I have a feeling I'm going to need it."

CHAPTER FOURTEEN

"MISS HOWLAND! Miss Howland, please, you have to wake up straightaway! Oh, *please,* Miss Howland!"

Emily, who had found her rest very late the previous evening only after turning onto her stomach and placing her head beneath her pillow, moaned her protest at this rude awakening before slowly lifting one side of the pillow and peering out with one eye. "Simmons, is that you? It's still dark. Is something wrong? Is it the dowager? I pleaded with her not to eat that fish at Lord Harvey's. It didn't smell quite fresh."

The maid shook her head, then helped Emily to sit up in bed. "No, miss, it's not the old lady, beg your pardon. It's this…this *man.* He came knocking on the door fit to wake the dead a little while ago and now he's in the kitchens, eating bread and honey with Cook and all cozy-like. Says he's the Marquess of Lyndhurst, but let me tell you, if that's the marquess, then I'm the Queen of the May. He's a loose screw if ever I saw one. Please, miss, you have to do something!"

Emily squeezed her eyes closed and shook her head to clear it. The Marquess of Lyndhurst? That would be Reginald, Lord Edward's brother. But Lord Lyndhurst was in Sussex, not London. Lord Edward said he never traveled. Besides, when was the last time she'd heard of a marquess taking bread and honey in a strange kitchen at daybreak? Slipping her feet into her slippers, Emily allowed the maid to help her into her dressing gown. "You must be mistaken, Simmons. This sounds like some sort of prank to me. Have you sent for the constable?"

"The constable?" Simmons parroted, aghast. "But, miss, surely we can't! The man may be balmy, but he's Quality, sure as check. We can't have one of the Quality carted off to the guardhouse. Please, miss, let me help you get dressed so you can see for yourself what we should do before the dowager gets wind of it, or we'll be in it for sure. She'd most likely ask the queer fellow to stay to tea."

Emily sighed. "Oh, very well, Simmons. I'll go. But I'll go as I am, thank you anyway. I'm tired, and I have every intention of returning to bed once this prankster has been routed. Come with me." So saying, Emily tossed her hair—done up in a single long braid for the night but now rather mussed—over her shoulder, gave a sharp tug on the belt of her dressing gown, and headed for the servants' stairs, eager to put an end to such foolishness.

"And so," Emily heard a rather high, thin male voice saying as she stopped in the hallway just outside the open kitchen door, "once I had got all the feathers sewn to my sleeves—plus the three tail feathers, of course, that I had secured to the seat of my unmentionables— I leaned forward as far as possible, then stepped off the edge of the balcony that juts out over the gardens and flapped my arms up and down just as hard as I could."

"Lord love a duck, your worship, you coulda broke yer bloomin' neck doin' a fool thing like that! Wot happened then?" a female voice exclaimed excitedly—obviously the cook, Emily decided as she too waited to hear the rest of the story.

The man laughed, the sound full of wry amusement. "Broke both my ankles, that's what happened, more's the pity. Noddy was very put out about it, but I still say, if the wind had been with me I would have soared into the sky, just like a bird on the wing. But I don't do that sort of thing anymore, you understand, now that Merryvale has come to stay with me. Merryvale frowns on air flight, and prefers that I just keep pigeons. You did say this is where the fair Miss Howland is residing for the Season? As it's Tuesday, I was sure she would be receiving."

Emily struck her head around the doorway to peek at her early-morning visitor, suddenly apprehensive. The man was well-spoken, even if what he said didn't make much sense, and she was beginning to wonder if there might be some small truth in his assertion that he was the marquess. It wouldn't do to let him see her in her nightclothes, she thought, just as she realized that a marquess who found nothing extraordinary about taking his ease in the kitchens with the servants would probably not even notice her present attire. Besides, Simmons was right. Whoever this odd man was, the dowager would surely be taken with him. He had to be dealt with, and quickly, before the rest of the household roused.

"There she is, yer worship!" Cook crowed, catching sight of Emily, who had lingered too long at the door, struck as she was by the thin man's resemblance to Lord Edward. "Missy, his worship's come ta see ya. Ever so nice, 'e is, too."

"Miss Howland!" the marquess shouted, jumping to his feet and rushing across the bare wooden floor to take Emily's hands in his and pull her more fully into the room. "How good of you to grant me this audience.

Please, just stand there and let me look at you. Red slippers! How perfectly delightful! Oh, I knew I would love you. I just knew it!"

"Red is such a pretty color, isn't it? So bright, so cheerful," Emily answered kindly, her heart immediately going out to this strange man. She allowed her hands to remain in his as she stared and stared, no longer caring that she wasn't dressed for company, as it didn't seem to bother her guest in the slightest.

The man looked just like Lord Edward, except for the fact that he was at least a dozen or more years his senior, and he was much, much thinner, his obviously expensive clothing hanging on his bony frame. His eyes were just the same shade of light leaf green, although they seemed to burn with some hidden light that she considered to be almost feverish in nature. He looked ethereal, fragile, and she suddenly felt protective of him. "Your lordship," she said, smiling up into his open, innocent face. "How nice of you to call. Shall we sit down? I believe Cook has some muffins in the oven, if my nose doesn't betray me."

With the insight that was often a special gift of the gentle-minded, Lord Lyndhurst clapped his hands together happily and proclaimed: "You like me! Oh, how wonderful. I knew you would, just as I knew I would like you. Isn't this pleasant? Noddy will be so pleased to know we get along so well."

"Noddy?" Emily questioned, trying to hold back her mirth, unable to believe Lord Edward would ever consent to answer to such a childish nickname.

His lordship nodded vigorously. "Yes, Noddy. He's sleeping, you know. Such a slugabed. I tippy-toed past his door to steal a march on him with you this morning. After all, we really should talk about the wedding. Is your father anywhere about, my dear?"

Emily silently signaled for Simmons to leave the room and waited until the maid had disappeared before saying, "My father has been dead for more than six years, my lord, and my mother, brothers, and sisters reside in Surrey. I am only in London acting as companion for my cousin, Lady Georgiana, the youngest daughter of the dowager Duchess of Chilworth. But, please, there is no reason to involve yourself. Hasn't your brother explained to you that this engagement is only—"

Once again Emily's hands were captured in his lordship's as the marquess trilled, "Yes, yes, your engagement! Oh, how wonderful it was to read about Noddy's soon-to-be bride. You have saved my life, you know. I had despaired of going to Tibet with the Colonel, but now I can, and with a free heart. Noddy will be taken care of and you may both have Lyndhurst Hall with my blessings! It is just wonderful! You do like the country, don't you?"

Emily's left eyebrow arched ever so slightly as her smile began to show signs of strain around the edges. "Lord Edward hasn't spoken to you about our engagement, has he, your lordship?"

"Please, please, call me Reggie. And I shall call you Dulcinea. I have been reading Cervantes, you see, and it seems such a regal name, fitting for one such as you."

"Well, thank you, my lord. That's very kind of you. Please, tell me more about this colonel you spoke of a moment ago. You're planning a trip with him—to Tibet, you said? My, that seems so far away, almost another world."

The thin, sensitive face lit up like a fireworks display at this mention of Tibet. "All my life I have searched high and low for an adventure of this magnitude. Truly, all my past adventures are thoroughly cast into the shade with the prospect that now lies before me, ready to be snatched down like a fine ripe apple. Delicious! And now, dear Dulcinea, now that you and Noddy are to be married, I am free to go, free to fly into the face of adventure! I am reborn!"

"Master Reginald! I have run you to ground at last! Shame on you, calling on Miss Howland at this ungodly hour."

"Well, lookee 'ere!" Cook explained, turning to see who had spoken, a wooden spoon coated with hardened bacon grease pointing straight at Burton, who was standing just inside the kitchens. "It's one o' them dwarfs, ain't it? Isn't it cute, all dressed up like it was growed up?"

Burton puffed out his pudgy chest like a rooster about to crow, clearly intending to render Cook a blistering set-down, so that Emily ordered quickly: "Cook, have someone bring us breakfast in the dining room, if you please. Come along, my…that is, Reggie. We're only in the way here now that Cook is getting preparations under way for the day's meals."

Burton moved swiftly across the room on his short legs and took hold of the marquess's elbow, having decided that this interview was at an end. "I hesitate to point this out, Miss Howland," he interjected as neutrally as possible, "but you are still dressed in your nightclothes."

Emily looked down at herself and immediately slapped a hand against her mouth. "Oh, my goodness, I completely forgot! We were having such an interesting conversation, you see, and I—"

"Please, Miss Howland, I quite understand, and it's not my place to ask for an explanation," Burton said, accustomed to smoothing over waters either the marquess or Lord Edward had ruffled. "Master Reginald and I shall return to Lord Edward's town house, for Merryvale has come up from Sussex looking for his employer, much agitated, actually, that he should have missed him, and we should strive to calm him as soon as possible. Would it be all right if Lord Edward pays a call in Portman Square later this afternoon? To…well, to explain?"

"Merryvale's here? How nice. Now Noddy can tell him it's all right if I go to Tibet. She has red slippers too, Burton," Reggie informed the servant after bowing low over Emily's hand and turning to walk to the tradesmen's entrance he had entered the mansion through earlier. "I have found that only cheerful people wear red, you know. Noddy has done well for himself, don't you think?"

Cook watched them go. "There goes one who's all about in 'is upper works, if ya takes my meanin', miss. But 'e's 'armless, Oi'm thinkin', for all o' that."

"I think he's wonderful!" Emily defended the marquess, her chin held high as she clutched her dressing gown together at the bodice. "Dulcinea," she added more softly. "What a lovely name."

CHAPTER FIFTEEN

"THE MARQUESS HAS ARRIVED in town and is coming here?" The dowager duchess automatically lifted her hands to her head to assure herself that her new wig had not slipped to one side, as it was so distressingly prone to do. "How wonderful! How perfectly…um, perfectly…"

"Delightful," Emily completed dully, wishing that just once she had a pretty gown to wear.

"Yes, thank you. Delightful," her grace concluded. "Tell me, which marquess would that be, dear?"

"The Marquess of Lyndhurst, Mama," Lady Georgiana supplied as she stood in front of the largest mirror in the drawing room, also inspecting her appearance. "Lord Edward's older brother, Reginald. Del was here this morning and said he's a lovely man. He's come to discuss the wedding, I should imagine. Isn't that right, Emmy?"

Emily perched on the edge of the settee and watched her female relatives flutter about the large room like showy birds reluctant to come to roost. She was alternately looking forward to and dreading the coming interview: looking forward to it because she was human, and hearing the dowager and the marquess converse was bound to be highly entertaining, and dreading it because being obliged to hear them converse about the wedding was most likely going to be extremely uncomfortable. She could find her only solace in the fact that Lord Edward was bound to be as serious as she concerning the outcome of this afternoon's visit.

How was Lord Edward going to talk his way out of this latest fix? It was one thing to pull the wool over the dowager's eyes—almost too easy to be sporting, actually, if one were to be totally honest—but it was quite another to deliberately mislead the gentle marquess, who seemed to be counting so on this marriage. Oh, why hadn't she refused at the outset to go along with Lord Edward's foolish plan? This pretend engagement was presenting more problems than it was worth.

"Oh, look, Emmy, they're here!" Lady Georgiana exclaimed, peeking out the window that overhung the street. "Oh, my goodness, Lord Edward looks so strange, almost ill. Do you suppose he's sickening for something? Oh, there's the marquess. He's very thin for a marquess, isn't he?"

"Georgy, come away from there at once. You know it's not polite to stare," Emily chided, trying her best not to jump up and join her cousin at the window for some gawking of her own. So Lord Edward was looking ill, was he, poor fellow? Perhaps lying was not as palatable as he had thought it to be, when it involved telling all those shocking rappers only to *her* relatives.

Within a few moments they could hear the rap of the knocker and the three women hastened to seat themselves around the tea tray, doing their best to appear at their ease.

"Good afternoon, ladies," Lord Edward said when the butler had finished announcing them. "May I have the honor of presenting—"

"Oh, dear, that's right," the dowager broke in, her expression of polite greeting crumbling. "Archy's dead. I had forgotten for a moment. Who are you, then?"

The marquess, finding nothing at all unusual in this outburst, went immediately over to the dowager and presented himself, apologizing profusely for not being his father. "But then, alas, I never was, was I, Noddy?"

"That's all right," the dowager responded kindly, adding quietly, "but did you have to be blond? What's your name again?"

"Mama!" Lady Georgiana warned, afraid her mother would go off again on one of her depressing stories about blonds, and Lord Edward quickly completed the introductions, carefully avoiding Emily's sure-to-be-condemning eyes as he did so.

"My sweet Dulcinea!" Reginald exclaimed, bending down to kiss Emily firmly on both cheeks. "I'm in alt. You look even lovelier dressed, my dear. Doesn't she, Noddy?"

Maintaining his emotionless expression with difficulty as he watched the color pour into his beloved cheeks, Lord Edward quipped, "Not having had the opportunity to observe Miss Howland in *déshabillé*, Reggie, I have nothing with which to compare her appearance. Now, please sit down so that we can have this chat you are so anxious for. We can't stay long, remember? I did tell you that on our way over here."

"Not stay? But there is so much to talk about, isn't there? I mean, with the wedding and all," Lady Georgiana questioned, as Emily had not as yet asked her to be one of her maids, and she was so hoping to be included in the wedding party.

"Miss Howland's mother is in Surrey, Lady Georgiana," Lord Edward interposed reasonably, clearly hoping to postpone any talk of the nuptials until he could speak with Emily alone. "We will of course have to seek her approval before making any definite plans. After all, I have not even officially asked for Miss Howland's hand, have I?"

"Oh, but that's all taken care of," Lady Georgiana said comfortingly, waving away his protest with one hand. "Mama had me send the clipping to Aunt Minerva in Surrey straightaway, with a letter explaining everything. Mama said it was only proper, Emily, so stop frowning at me. Somebody has the measles, and your mama expects the rest to come down with them, so she warned us to keep you away, as it's not good for someone in your condition to be around illness. Didn't I tell you, Emmy? Aunt Minerva says all's not just as she hoped it would be, but Lord Edward seems to be a good man who is doing as he ought at last. And she forgave Mama completely, so everything is just fine."

"You…you told my mother?" Emily asked, her voice strangled as she looked to Lord Edward for help. "Why didn't anyone tell me about this? Just what did you and Aunt Hortense tell my mother, Georgy? Surely you didn't tell her that I was—"

"To be married in August!" Lord Edward fairly shouted, drowning out Emily's next words. "That's what they wrote, I'm sure. Isn't that right, Lady Georgiana?"

Lady Georgiana nodded firmly, then added, "That, and that Emily's increasing, of course. Oh, my goodness! Mama! We never wrote back, did we? Isn't that strange, that we forgot something so important."

Immediately panicking, Lord Edward quickly looked over to his brother, who had been sitting beside Emily, munching on a macaroon, hoping the marquess's mind was off on one of its tangents and he hadn't been attending—but it was not to be.

"Increasing? Dulcinea's going to have a *baby?*" Reginald's bright green eyes were immediately filled with tears and he turned to Emily, his delighted smile lighting the entire room. "A baby," he said, sighing and clasping his hands to his chest, accepting the news without any hint of censure. "Dulcinea, you have made me the happiest of men!"

The dowager was confused. "But I thought the other blond was the father, Emily. Why is the marquess so happy? I don't understand."

IT IS AN ACKNOWLEDGED FACT that, regardless of gender, education, or natural intelligence, persons of quality cannot be expected to function in this world with any reasonable level of competence without the support and guidance of the people belowstairs—their loyal servants.

They might wage war successfully without them, they might even annex colonies, invest their money wisely, and recklessly gamble away fortunes without them, but when it came to finding direction in their personal lives, the rudder that guided them—the firm hand that steered them in the correct direction, away from treacherous reefs and dangerous currents—was nearly always to be discovered taking his or her daily mutton in the servants' dining room.

And so it was for Emily and Lord Edward as Burton and Simmons, two champions of the high art of leading their masters around by their aristocratic noses, decided it was high time to take matters into their own capable hands. *Something,* they knew, had to be done to end this foolishness and bring Miss Howland and his lordship together once and for all, and it was clearly up to them to do it.

If it hadn't been clear from the outset that extraordinary measures were called for, the reasonableness of their arguments for interfering had been brought home to them with a vengeance by the events of that afternoon, for, by all accounts, there had been a rare to-do in her grace's drawing room that had ended with the marquess declaring that the wedding would take place within a week, and Miss Howland racing from the room vowing that she'd rather die in a gutter than marry an unfeeling monster like Lord Edward, who had dared to yell at a man as sweet as the marquess!

"Besides," Simmons had declared as Burton handed her the box containing the first of the gowns Lord Edward had ordered—thinking to surprise Emily with her new wardrobe once they were at the house party at Lyndhurst Hall—"she's rather a sweet child, Burton, and not at all stuffy. I like her. I really do like her."

"Are you sure you can get Miss Howland to agree to wear the gown? After all, it is a gift from Lord Edward. He loves her, you know, Simmons, even if she does detest him, now more than ever, and he says he won't force her to marry him, no matter how much he wants it."

"Don't you go fretting about a thing," Simmons had assured him. "I promise you, she's head over ears in love with your young master, though I'm sure I don't know why, for never have I seen such a sorry mix-up. Miss Howland will listen to reason. Besides, I've acted as her personal maid a time or two; *I've* seen her in her tub. I tell you, Burton, you let me have the dressing of her and we'll have his lordship on his knees at her feet in a trice, explaining everything."

Burton reached up his hand to wave a pudgy finger in the maid's face. "There is no need to descend to such plain talk, Simmons," he had pointed out, happy to remind her of just who was in charge of this enterprise. "I'll not have our Miss Howland made over into a common streetwalker."

"And neither will I!" Simmons had protested hotly. "Just like every other man, aren't you, Burton? You droll and ogle with the best of them, I'll wager, but just let a female talk about such things and you go all stuffy and condemning. Well, let me tell you, a wife has just as much right to display her wares as a Covent Garden opera dancer—maybe even more. After all, they're wives, and considered part of the household, just like that silver I was working on earlier when you came visiting to tell me of your plan. If we servants keep the silver shining and sparkling, why shouldn't we be putting a dab or two of polish on a fine miss like Miss Howland? Now, be back here tonight and I'll hold you up and let you peek through the door with me when Miss Howland comes downstairs."

AFTER SPENDING SEVERAL HOURS lying in bed in her darkened room, Emily found that her headache, if not her extreme embarrassment, had at last disappeared, and she called out "Enter" when she heard someone scratching on her door. "Simmons?" she questioned, seeing that her aunt's maid was carrying a large package.

"This just arrived, miss. You'll have to hurry if you want to have Mr. Roberto do your hair for the party tonight."

Emily blinked twice in the near-darkness, trying to clear her head. "Mr. Roberto? Isn't he Lady Georgiana's new hairdresser? Why would I want him to do my hair? And I'm not going to Lady Rathburn's party—I've already told everybody that. After this afternoon's debacle, I'm surprised anybody could think that I would."

Simmons nodded sympathetically, understanding Emily's feelings, but pushed on: "But this is a gift from his lordship. Burton delivered this himself, having picked it up personally this afternoon. You wouldn't want to hurt his lordship's feelings, would you, him being such a nice man and all?"

"His lordship?" Emily questioned blankly. "Oh, you must mean the marquess. Isn't that nice. Well, in that case I guess I might at least try the thing on."

Prudently keeping her lips sealed, Simmons only laid down the box and led Emily over to her dressing table. "You just sit here and I'll ring for some tea and a light snack. You'll just have to miss dinner tonight, miss. Then Mr. Roberto can do your hair for you."

"But, Simmons," Emily asked, "can't I first see the gown the marquess sent me?"

"Oh, that must be Mr. Roberto knocking on the door now!" Simmons sang out gratefully, ignoring Emily's question.

AN HOUR LATER Emily's bedroom floor was littered with snippets of reddish-brown hair and Mr. Roberto had finished abusing her head with the hot curling stick.

"We now take this like so on either side, and then wrap it—ever so softly, ever so smoothly—draping it along the side of the cheekbone on either side before lifting it, lifting it—so!—and securing it all with miss's best pins. Are you watching? This is important, so very important. The curls are always to be large, soft, cascading down the back like a magnificent waterfall—so!—with nothing, *nothing,* but smoothness about the face. It gives to the head a softness, you see, to bring out the miss's fine eyes, to lift the lips, the cheekbones, to frame the face—not to bury it."

The hairdresser stood behind Emily for a moment, admiring his creation, before pulling out the pins and running his fingers through her hair, destroying the effect. Then, standing back slightly, he bowed, indicating that Simmons was to take his place. "Practice, practice, practice. It is the key. I have cut the hair with magic in my scissors. There is much now that can be done with the hair, with my genius to guide you, to show you the way. We can make the curls caress the neck, or have the entire head severe, dramatic, full, but with no curl at all. The possibilities are endless with such hair, with such a head. No, no, *no!*" he scolded, pushing Simmons away. "Not like that—like *this!*"

The "head," strangely, wasn't in the least offended at being treated as if she were an inanimate object. She was sitting in front of her dressing table, staring wide-eyed at her reflection in the glass, an inane smile on her face.

WITHIN THE NEXT HOUR Simmons succeeded in dragging Emily away from the mirror long enough to submerge her body in the tub and then climb into her undergarments. But, with victory in sight, and the new gown in place, her mistress finally balked.

"I can't do it. I won't do it! It…it's *obscene!* That's what it is, Simmons, it's obscene." It's also rather chilly, Emily decided, raising her hands to cover the wide expanse of neckline visible above the startling *décolletage* of the thin, ivory-colored silk gown.

"You look fine as ninepence," Simmons argued, personally removing Emily's protective hands and placing them at her sides. "You promised to trust me, miss, if you'll remember. Wasn't I right about your hair? And that small bit of rouge and lip paint you finally let me use? And it's impossible to change into another gown—you're going to be late as it is. The dowager and Lady Georgiana went along without you an hour ago, and his lordship is downstairs, cooling his heels and waiting for you to join him. Now, please, Miss Emily, you don't want to disappoint his lordship, do you? You look beautiful."

Emily turned this way and that, inspecting herself in the mirror. The marquess might be the teeniest bit vague, but he certainly had wonderful taste. "I do look rather nice, don't I, Simmons? But…but the gown is cut so *low*, and Mama always said—"

"If I may be so bold, Miss Emily, your *mama* is in Surrey," Simmons pointed out rationally, knowing she was just one short step from exasperation, "and *you* are here." She and Burton had been planning for this night an entire week, and she didn't need for her mistress's case of cold feet to ruin everything now. 'You don't really want to wear one of your old gowns, do you, with your hair looking so pretty and all?"

Lifting a hand to her throat and the deep rose silk ribbon the maid had secured there, Emily looked at herself one more time, a small, satisfied smile playing about her lips. "All right, Simmons, you win. But if everybody laughs at me at Lady Rathburn's—and if Lord Edward dares to say so much as one nasty word—I vow I'll never, *never* forgive you!"

CHAPTER SIXTEEN

THE CLOCK IN THE HALL struck the hour of ten, rousing Lord Edward from his disquieting thoughts to wonder yet again what was keeping Emily. Did she think to merely frighten him with her tardiness, or had she decided to keep him cooling his heels until he gave up and went away without her? They had to talk, dammit; they had to discuss what they were to do next, how they were to coax Reggie back to Lyndhurst Hall without hurting him—and without Emily making things stickier by repeating that she didn't want to marry him. Surely she could see that!

Walking over to a side table, he poured himself another fortifying drink, remembering the look on Emily's face that afternoon as she had ordered him to *"do something"* and then taken her leave from the drawing room, and rethinking the saying that had something to do with confession being good for the soul. After all, once back in his town house, with Reggie tucked up for his nap and Merryvale standing guard outside his bedroom door, Lord Edward had been forced to endure Burton's lengthy homily on the worth of telling the truth, until he had been happy to return to Portman Square to have everything out once and for all with Emily. Then, if she didn't kill him, they could begin once more at the beginning, with all of his cards finally on the table, and he could court Emily the way she deserved.

Which he could only do if she'd come downstairs before his second thoughts had him scurrying for the door, his tail between his legs. Where the devil was she? Reginald had gone off to Lady Rathburn's with the dowager and Lady Georgiana hours ago, as had those two troublemakers Monty and Del, who seemed to be quite taken with Lord Lyndhurst. What a rare treat society was in for tonight, with the dowager calling Reggie "Archy" while flirting with him outrageously, and Reggie telling anyone who would listen all about his plans for his as-yet-unborn nephew or niece.

This final thought had the power to send him seeking refuge once more in drink, and as he realized his glass was empty, he walked back to the side table and spilled a generous amount into the glass.

"Lord Lyndhurst? Please forgive me for having kept you waiting so long."

Lord Edward froze where he stood, his glass halfway to his lips, his back to the drawing-room door. "Emily?" he asked weakly, suddenly wanting nothing more than to bolt from the room, and wondering if he would have been a white feather had he served under Wellington, taking to his heels the first time he laid eyes on a charging Frenchman. But no, he would be no coward when it came to facing death, he was sure. But facing those next few minutes with Emily—that was another question entirely.

Slowly, still holding on to the glass as if it would protect him in the event of attack, Edward turned to face his accidental *fiancée*.

"Oh, it's you," Emily breathed, suddenly self-conscious. "I…I had thought the marquess was waiting for me."

It was quiet in the room for quite some time, as Burton and Simmons, who were hiding in the hall just outside the door, their ears pressed hard to the panels, could attest, before Lord Edward at last rediscovered his voice. *"Emily?"* they could hear him question disbelievingly, his voice a hoarse whisper. "My God, Emily! I had thought, hoped…but, I can't believe… Well! Can that be you?"

Although Simmons and Burton were righteously beside themselves with glee upon hearing these astonished accents—spending the next few moments silently clapping each other on the back in a mutual display of congratulation—they would have laughed out loud if they could see his lordship's reaction to the altered appearance of the love of his life.

He was, in a word, dumbfounded. He was also many other things: confused, delighted, awestruck, even somewhat light-headed.

Mostly, his lordship was thankful. Yes, Lord Edward was profoundly *thankful*. She was wearing one of the gowns he had purchased for her. Surely this meant she had forgiven him for the debacle of that afternoon.

She was lovely. No! "Lovely" was too tame a word. She was beautiful! Gorgeous! Breathtaking! He blinked twice and swallowed down hard on the lump in his throat. Where did he start? What did he look at, consider, marvel over, first?

Her hair—that glorious crown that caressed her perfectly formed head, those soft, warm red-brown curls that clung to her slim throat?

Her eyes—those exotic, slanted, deep brown heavy-lidded eyes that sparkled and bewitched and beguiled?

Or those strong, high cheekbones…that strangely arrogant nose…that smooth, flawless skin…that wide, generous, moist pink mouth?

Then there was her body! Oh, God, yes, his lordship groaned silently, her body. Like an ungainly caterpillar that has somehow shed its shapeless cocoon and taken to the skies as an exotic butterfly, Emily's body had sloughed off the heavy, high-necked monstrosities he remembered and clothed itself in glory.

The gown itself was a marvel that defied explanation, an inspired design fashioned of soft, almost transparent ivory silk. It appeared to begin just under the center of her breasts, then fan out in every direction to drape in folds that barely captured each of her breasts into separate silken cages and molded her hips as they flowered beneath the tiniest waist he'd ever seen. As she took two small hesitant steps into the room, the material clung lovingly to her legs, giving him a clear mental picture of what they would look like without that thin covering.

His gaze returned to her breasts, almost reluctantly, for no matter what wonderful part of her he concentrated on, it could only be because he was not concentrating on another, equally appealing part of her.

He didn't understand. Where could those magnificent breasts have been hiding, even beneath the ugly gowns she had chosen to wear! It was sinful, that's what it was, he thought angrily, to cover up such lush beauty. His palms itched expectantly as he almost succumbed to the need to touch them, to softly sculpture their exquisite shape with his palms, to trace their perfection with his tingling fingertips.

Had he died? Was this heaven? Was any of this really happening? How had he, a poor mortal, gotten so lucky? There was a problem? What problem? Reggie? Reggie who?

"Lord Edward? Are you all right? You look so strange." Emily was having trouble understanding the shocked expression on his face. But, no, this was more than shock, though, thankfully, certainly less than amusement. He was completely nonplussed. Slowly, and perhaps meanly, although she *had* been sorely tried by the man in the past, Emily realized that she rather liked him this way—off his stride, caught off guard, and totally at a loss for speech. It was a decidedly delicious feeling, being in charge of a situation, being the one person who knew what was going on, and she felt the corners of her mouth lifting in a satisfied smile.

"Good Lord, Emily, I can't believe it! What's happened to you?"

So, she thought happily, he's found his voice at last. "Whatever do you mean, my lord?" she questioned carefully, taking a few more steps into the room. She had noted his expression when he had seen the way the ivory silk moved along with her body when she had walked, and saw no reason to deny him another look. She was more than happy; she was fast becoming drunk with delight. "I've had my hair cut—and your brother was kind enough to make me a gift of this gown. Are you disappointed in the result?"

"Disappointed?" The single word came out as a choked croak, and Emily had to look away quickly for fear she would break into delighted giggles. "A man would have to be out of his mind—that is, no, *no,* I'm not disappointed. A change of…a different way with your hair, you say…and a new gown…is that all?"

Emily sat down, carefully arranging her demitrain as she lowered herself onto the settee, then sat erectly, her shoulders back, knowing she was giving him an unimpeded view of her daring *décolletage*. She felt giddy, dizzy with her power to disconcert this man. "You wouldn't wish to know all my secrets, would you, Edward?" she teased, daring to call him by name, and then blushing as she realized that her words, meant to refer to Simmons' deft hand with the rouge pot, could be interpreted in more than one way.

Afraid that his answer to her artlessly asked question was already in his eyes, that his reaction had been too revealing, too obvious, Lord Edward took refuge in the contents of his glass, swallowing the wine in one long gulp before realizing that he was drinking far too much too early in the evening. Especially this particular evening, one during which his main objective should be remaining in complete control of himself.

"Emily," he inquired solicitously, manfully removing his gaze from her neckline and trying not to sob out loud over his loss, "would you care for a small glass of sherry? We need to talk before joining the others at Lady Rathburn's. As it is, heaven only knows what rumors our dear friends are circulating about us now."

Although they were unchaperoned and really should be leaving, the idea of a single sherry did seem appealing, and Emily accepted his offer, careful not to spill any of the liquid on her new gown. As she sat and sipped, and Lord Edward stood and gawked—there was really no other word for it, she knew with a thrilling flutter of her pulse—Emily at last realized that the only conversation taking place in the room was her internal dialogue with herself, and she was suddenly nervous all over again.

"I imagine when you say we should talk that you are referring to the incident of this afternoon?" she asked, looking up at him through her eyelashes as she had seen debutantes do to such effect while she had sat on the sidelines blending with the woodwork.

"I did—that is, *I do, I do*." Oh, this is good Lord Edward thought, mentally kicking himself. Suddenly he possessed all the eloquence of the village idiot. "To be precise, we need to discuss my brother."

Emily's features softened at the thought of the marquess. "I like your brother very much, Edward," she replied earnestly, once again using Lord Edward's name without his title. "He's sweet. I mean, look at this gown. He must have scoured London to find anything this beautiful on such short notice."

Lord Edward lowered his eyelids and shifted his eyes from right to left assessingly, realizing that he was actually jealous of his brother, but wondering if it would be worth his while to contradict Emily, for, after all, if he admitted to ordering the gown—to ordering a half-dozen gowns, actually—she would probably run straight back upstairs and hop into one of her depressing brown shrouds. Could he chance such a tragedy? No! "Yes!" he concurred, his decision made in favor of the new Emily. "Reggie is a prince of a fellow. Now, if we could only discuss how we're going to get that prince of a fellow safely back down to Sussex with his keeper, I'd be greatly gratified."

"His *keeper?*" Emily exclaimed in sudden anger. "What a horrid thing to say! You should be ashamed of yourself. Heaven knows *I'm* ashamed to be hearing such nonsense. Oh, don't think I didn't notice how you kept trying to shush Lord Lyndhurst this afternoon. Why, if that lovely man is in need of a keeper, then half the *ton* should be locked up."

Hearing this indignant outburst, Lord Edward sat down, dropped his chin into his hand, and grinned in delight. He had known she would like Reggie, sweet darling thing that she was, but he had had no idea he'd find himself in the position of defending himself against her affection for the eccentric nobleman. "Emily," he began carefully, "please forgive me for calling Merryvale a keeper—it was an unfortunate description, I agree. Believe me when I say that I love my brother very much. But you must admit that Reggie shouldn't be running tame through society. I mean, it would open him up to such ridicule. I'd hate to see him hurt."

"Or see yourself embarrassed by his rather outgoing manner," Emily added unhelpfully. "But I don't see what all the fuss is about. After all, his lordship told me just this morning that he's leaving shortly on an expedition to Tibet."

"You'd countenance such an expedition?" Lord Edward asked in sudden consternation. "Are you out of your mind? Reggie's never been able to cross the street alone without getting into some sort of scrape."

"He made it to London on his own, even if he did forget his slippers, which isn't the least surprising, for I'm sure he's never had to pack for himself before," Emily pointed out rationally, her chin tilted in defiance as she defended his lordship. "And if he's not exactly sharp as a tack, he's certainly at least as lucid as the dowager, and nobody's locked her away in the country."

"It isn't from lack of trying, I've heard," Lord Edward grumbled. "Why do you think you were sent along when the duchess insisted upon presenting Lady Georgiana? I doubt your mother, though I'm sure she's a wonderful person, has been totally honest with you, my dear."

Emily frowned, as Lord Edward's dart had hit home. Her mother had spent an unconscionable amount of time instructing her daughter on the care and feeding of the dowager before the stagecoach had carried Emily from Surrey. Not liking where her thoughts were taking her, Emily shot back defensively: "That has nothing to do with the matter at hand. We are discussing your brother."

"I want him home, in Sussex," Lord Edward declared, his handsome face suddenly looking almost mulish. "He's canceled his expedition to Tibet, by the way—not that I ever had any intention of allowing him to go there, any more than I allowed him to sail alone to America in a fifteen-foot sloop, which was his last brainstorm—having decided that it will be much more exciting to stay here in England, awaiting the birth of 'dearest Dulcinea's child.'"

"Oh, no!" Emily's tender heart was touched by this news. "He was so delighted this afternoon, wasn't he? I had hoped you were able to explain the mix-up once you had returned to your town house."

"Do you perchance mean 'explain' in the same way *you* have been so far unable to 'explain' the mix-up to your aunt and cousin?" Lord Edward chided, to prove his point. "As happy as I am that Reggie has given up this Tibet business so easily, I can't say that I'm thrilled to think that we're sitting here arguing while Reggie and the dowager are at Lady Rathburn's telling everyone about our forced 'nuptials' next week."

Emily could feel tears prickling behind her eyes as her hurt and frustration bubbled to the surface. How he hated having his name linked with hers. Did he have to make his dislike so obvious? After all, it was his teasing that had led to her problem in the first place. "Well, what do you propose we do about it," she challenged, "seeing that pretending this engagement was real was all your idea?"

Hearing the sob in her voice, Lord Edward hurried across the room and dropped to his knees at Emily's feet, still the anxious male, still rushing his fences, still hoping deep in his heart to have everything he wanted given to him without first owning up to his machinations, without first paying his dues for seeking to play romantic games with the one woman in the world he truly loved. Pulling his handkerchief from his pocket, he blotted a tear from her cheek, saying, "Please don't cry, Emily. I'm probably just overreacting, not having expected Reggie to show up here, but only for you to meet him at Lyndhurst Hall, and you do like him, just as I hoped you would, so it isn't all that bad, is it? I promise you, my beautiful darling, I'll find a way to put everything right, honestly. I never meant to hurt you."

It was a nice speech, if rather garbled, and Emily didn't believe it for a minute. Lord Edward had never gone out of his way to be nice to her before. On the contrary, she had often thought that he stayed awake nights trying to devise new ways to insult her, like that time he'd had the nerve to pretend to propose to her. Still, she allowed him to dab tenderly at her tears, her chin held high, her eyes deliberately avoiding his as her gaze darted around the room.

His lordship was many things, but he was not stupid. He knew Emily didn't believe him. *He* didn't believe him! To Emily's way of thinking, he had spent the past month in a one-man campaign bent on sending her screaming back home to Surrey, never to show her head in London again, only to end up betrothed to her. Their courtship had been a sham and their engagement was a travesty. Why on earth should she believe he had meant any of it? "Emily, my dear girl—" he began, not really knowing what to say, where to begin.

"No!" she protested, cutting him off. Did he think she had just come down in the last rainfall? She wasn't about to be taken in by this new, seemingly caring Lord Edward. It was this sudden change, this transformation Simmons and Mr. Roberto had worked on her that had him belatedly acting the gentleman with her. He had come to Portman Square tonight to ask for her help— again—only to find that his *fiancée* had been turned into a passably attractive person. "My beautiful darling" indeed! He probably found it more difficult to be insulting to well-dressed females than to unattractive companions.

"Emily? You must believe I'm sorry for everything," he pressed on, still kneeling at her feet. "I know I've hurt you, my dearest. As a matter of fact, I've spent these last weeks since meeting you examining my conscience."

Emily looked down at him and slowly raised one winglike eyebrow. "Only three weeks, Edward? I doubt you allowed yourself enough time to even scratch the surface. But forgive me—I interrupt. Please do continue. What did this examination reveal?"

Oh, she was angry, Edward thought, wincing. She was trying to hide it, but she was very, very angry, and her bewitching smile was definitely gone. Perhaps employing the handkerchief so intimately was pushing his show of concern too far. Perhaps he should change the subject, and concentrate again on their plans concerning Reggie.

Then, just as he was about to say something comforting to the effect that Reggie would soon forget this business about a baby, Emily stuck out the tip of her pink tongue to capture a teardrop that had slipped into the corner of her mouth, and Lord Edward was lost. "Good Lord, Emily," he said, his hands clenched around his handkerchief for fear he'd otherwise launch himself at her, "don't you know? I love you!"

"Wh-what?" Emily's fingers gripped the arms of her chair as Lord Edward, caught up in the emotion of the moment, rose to his full height in front of her. She felt his hands grasp her shoulders and she allowed herself to be brought to her feet, facing him, her eyes wide, her pulse pounding in her ears.

He looked so sincere, so passionately intense, and he was so terribly, terribly close to her. She could see the sparkles in his eyes as he looked down on her, watch his lips move as he said something to her that the loud rushing in her ears kept her from understanding. His hands were warm, caressing, as they ran along her collarbones, his body hard yet inviting as he drew her so very slowly against it.

She allowed her head to slip to one side as Edward nuzzled at the base of her throat, her eyes closing while she stole this one moment of happiness, this one perfect time that was surely not too much to ask for, considering what she knew she must do.

Now, her little voice screamed, now is the time to push him away, to tell him that he's mistaken, that he is just reacting to a little paint and silk, that the Emily Howland he has always disdained is still locked inside these new, pretty wrappings.

Just a moment more, just one single, sweet moment more, she told the little voice as Edward's lips blazed a trail across her cheek and claimed her mouth.

And in that moment—that one single, sweet moment she had begged her intelligent self to grant her—Emily forgot to resist. All her sane reasoning, all her devastatingly humbling deductions were tossed to the winds as her arms slid up Lord Edward's muscular chest and her fingers twined together in the heavy blond curls at the nape of his neck. Her mind shut down completely as her body, that body she had hidden for years, denying its needs, asserted itself.

Her breasts tingled pleasurably as they made firmer contact with Lord Edward's chest and her legs turned to jelly as she felt the pressure of his knee as it slid between hers. Clinging to him, allowing him to support her weight, Emily opened her lips on a sigh and allowed him entry. She was all fluid, all sensation. She was his, and he was hers. Hers for the taking, hers for the giving, hers for the moment, and let the devil take the hindmost. Tomorrow she would think about the rights of it, the wrongs of it. But tonight would be hers...

"Oh, Emily, you're so beautiful, so very beautiful. I love you. Tell me that you love me," Lord Edward whispered breathlessly against her ear, and the spell was broken. Emily stepped back a single pace, her eyes wide as she stared up at Lord Edward. She could feel her breathing deepen as her heart thumped hurtfully in her breast. All she had to do was smile, acknowledge his statement with just a small nod of her head, and he would sweep her into his arms again. A small voice deep inside her brain urged her to take what he was offering, to take it with both hands, for this was what she had always wanted, from the first moment she had seen his handsome face, from the first moment his lips had claimed hers in that kiss on her aunt's balcony. This was what she had dreamed about, this was what she had secretly hoped for as she gave herself over to Simmons' capable hands. These were the words she had believed could make her happy, could make her whole.

Well, she thought incredulously as she abruptly pushed herself out of his arms, I'll say one thing for you,

Emily Howland—when you're wrong, you aren't wrong by half-measures, you're really, *really* wrong!

"Emily, you come back here this…er… Darling! Where are you going? Didn't you hear me? I said I love you." Lord Edward was confused as he stared after her departing form. "Emily?" he repeated, collapsing into her empty chair in chagrin as he realized she wasn't coming back. "Women! There's no pleasing them. *Now* what did I do wrong."

Simmons and Burton, who had nearly been discovered peeking in the doorway as Emily bolted so swiftly from the room, and who had hastily retired below stairs to share a pot of tea and commiserate with each other, could have told his lordship precisely what he had done wrong—and, in Burton's case, could have done it through the use of some very colorful language. This opportunity not presenting itself, it was up to Lord Edward to find his way home alone—his worries about the harm the dowager and his brother could cause forgotten—to consume a decanter of port, and, sigh, hatch yet another plan…

CHAPTER SEVENTEEN

THE REMAINDER OF THE GOWNS Lord Edward had ordered arrived the next morning in Portman Square, bearing a card upon which the following was scribbled in a sloping, thoroughly masculine hand: "Forgive a besotted fool for trying to gild the lily. With all my Love, Ned."

The card, ripped into precisely twelve pieces, was ceremoniously deposited into Emily's empty teacup.

The gowns, save the lovely sprigged-muslin one Simmons lowered over her head before Emily joined Lady Georgiana and the dowager duchess for breakfast, and the elegant creation she planned to wear that evening to dinner, were lovingly put away in the cupboard in her room.

Emily was angry, yes, but she wasn't so foolish as to snip off her nose merely to spite her face!

She had then gone on to enjoy her day, having spent most of the morning outside in the small garden getting to know the marquess better before that sweet man departed for Sussex with Merryvale (a jolly retired schoolmaster who seemed to sincerely like the marquess), promising to order the refurbishing of the Lyndhurst nursery "as soon as may be" once he was home—employing "dozens of cute little bunnies, you know, with those soft, puffy tails, and they're good luck too, I believe," as the central theme for the wallpaper and other decorations if possible.

This piece of news also cheered Emily, no matter what her thoughts on "cute little bunnies," as she felt it only served to prove that Lord Edward was having the same amount of success explaining away her supposed pregnancy to his brother as she herself had been experiencing with the dowager.

Her afternoon was then whiled away pleasurably enough in keeping an eye on Lady Georgiana and the recently attentive Lord Delbert during a stroll in Green Park as she pretended not to notice the many admiring glances that were being thrown her own way.

It was only after dinner that Emily's mood reverted to melancholia, for the dowager announced that Lord Edward had earlier sent round a note particularly requesting Emily's presence in his box at the theater that evening. The mere mention of his lordship's name brought a flush of embarrassed color flooding into her cheeks, while her spine stiffened as she remembered the way the man had positively drooled over her just because of a slight alteration in her appearance.

Not only that, she reminded herself, but he had then proceeded to make an utter fool of her, spouting that nonsense about loving her and then taking advantage of her weakened condition to kiss her witless. Oh, no, Emily wasn't about to be his guest at the theater that night—not unless pigs suddenly sprouted wings!

Immediately pleading a headache—so that the dowager was pushed to comment that the child, who had been looking rather decent that day, seemed to be prone to sickness, and why Minerva had ever foisted such a fade-away miss on her, she'd never know, except that she was sure Minerva never liked her above half—Emily retired to her bedchamber, donned her oldest nightgown, and climbed into bed, determined not to cry herself to sleep again.

EMILY AWAKENED SLOWLY just after midnight, lit the candle at her bedside, then stretched out to her full length on the soft bed, feeling pleasantly warm and curiously contented. She had been dreaming about her meeting with Lord Edward the previous evening, and had fortunately wakened while the dream was still in its early, pleasant stages, just after her entrance into the drawing room—armed with a bit of paint, a cunning hairstyle, and a scandalously gorgeous gown of ivory silk.

And, she remembered, crossing her arms behind her head and grinning up at the ceiling, she *had* been a fabulous success—at least she had for a while. Her smile slowly faded as she remembered how the magical evening had skidded to an abrupt halt once Lord Edward had made his ridiculous declaration and taken her in his arms.

What a revelation that had been! Emily had thought her newfound beauty to be the answer to all her problems, her entry into the happy world of the physically attractive, where one danced all through the night and the world was always wonderful. Lord Edward's reaction to her changed appearance had rudely brought her awake to some of the least-looked-for results of physical beauty.

As he had taken her in his arms, Lord Edward couldn't have cared less if she'd had a brain like a leaky bucket—like that adorable widgeon cousin of hers, Lady Georgiana. Oh, no. Lord Edward had fallen in love—or at least had told Emily he had been *thinking* about falling in love—with Georgy's shell, her outside, her neartly displayed veneer. And now he was doing it again, only this time it was *her* newly attractive shell that was calling to his silly masculine emotions.

Emily's worst enemy all her life, her mirror, had always told her that she was plain. Now that same mirror was telling her that she had somehow become almost beautiful—and that mocking piece of glass was *still* her worst enemy!

The last of her happiness disappeared as a frown wrinkled her smooth forehead. And what absolutely *miserable* timing she had, to pick last night of all nights to allow Simmons to work her magic! If only Lord Edward had encountered her alone and unchaperoned in the drawing room that night, looking just as plainly dowdy as usual, and immediately taken her into his arms and declared his love for her, Emily could have believed him.

The thought brought her up short and she gave a short, rueful laugh. Believed him? How could she delude herself that way? She would have had someone immediately fetch the closest physician, feeling sure Lord Edward had come down with a delirium-inducing fever!

But, be that as it may, Emily decided she had to consider his reaction and how it was related to her altered appearance. Now that he had made it so very clear that her new good looks were attractive to him, she would never know if he wanted her for herself or for her pleasing exterior—or, she reminded herself, that he really wanted her at all.

She already knew, she admitted on a small sigh as she threw back the bedcovers and stood up in the darkened room. After all, he hadn't been staring bug-eyed at her "mind," had he? He "loved" her because Simmons had painted her lips and cheeks with rouge, outlined her eyes with kohl, and then sent her downstairs in half a gown, like some Covent Garden strumpet showing off her wares!

Poor dear Edward, she thought guiltily, and without realizing she was being most horridly immodest, she really shouldn't be too angry with him. He had really never known what hit him; he had never stood a chance against the new, improved Emily. He had been dazzled past the point of rational thought. After all, he was a man, wasn't he, and therefore easily dazzled?

As she walked over to the cupboard that held her new gowns, she knew she would have to explain his error to him—the poor darling. It wouldn't be fair to let him continue thinking he could be in love with her. But for now, for just a little while, would it be that awful if she closed her eyes to the truth and wallowed in his affection, like a pig in a trough? She could also search for a better analogy while she was at it, but she'd had hardly any sleep in two days and she refused to dwell on such things at the moment.

Yes, she decided, lifting her chin defiantly as she reached into the cupboard and extracted one of the gowns. Not only could she enjoy his affections for a while, she would be remiss if she did not. Besides, she had to think of poor Simmons. How crushed the maid would be if she thought all her hard work had gone for naught. Oh, yes, there was time and enough to set Lord Edward straight; time to point out that he had believed himself in love with another pretty face.

She refused to consider whether what she was planning to do was wrong, pushing all feelings of guilt firmly to the back of her mind as she laid the gown on the bed and reached for the buttons at her neckline.

After all, who had time for lying in bed contemplating a future without Lord Edward in it when she could be better employed trying on her new gowns…and seeing if she could also create the magic Simmons did with the paints and combs…and planning for her next meeting with Lord Edward…and deciding how she might best lure him into some secluded corner and— What was that? A noise had come from the darkened corner of the room; a sound much like a deep, contented sigh.

Emily hastily rebuttoned her nightgown and snatched up her bedside candle, wondering whether to investigate or merely make a run for it. Holding the candle higher as she swallowed down on the lump in her throat and took up the heavy silver candle snuffer, she took a single tentative step toward the corner, unwilling to summon help, only to find that a mouse was playing in the baseboards.

"Good evening, darling," came a voice from the darkness. "Going somewhere?"

"Who is…? *Edward?* Is that you? Good Lord! What…what are you doing here…here, in my bedroom?"

The rough sound of a match being struck against a boot sole was followed by an illuminating flare of flame as Lord Edward touched the fire to the end of his cigarillo and took several deep puffs. "I think that should be obvious, Emily, my dearest. I am sitting here watching you sleep. Or at least I was, but you have awakened now, haven't you? I repeat, are you contemplating going somewhere at this late hour? I had heard you had the headache. Do you think it is wise to go out into the night air in your condition?"

While Lord Edward was talking, Emily, never taking her eyes from him, put down the candle snuffer and searched a hand restlessly over the bedspread, hunting for her dressing gown, which she hastily slipped on after placing the candle on her bedside table. She gave a moment's thought to blowing out the candle, thereby plunging the entire room into darkness so that Lord Edward couldn't see her, but discarded the idea, not liking being unable to see precisely where he was. She decided instead to take refuge in haughtiness, even if she failed to understand how anyone could be effectively haughty when dressed in a worn dressing gown, her hair done up in a braid, and sporting bare feet.

"You are being facetious, sir," she pointed out coldly, her chin at an arrogant tilt, "and upon further consideration I have realized that any explanation you might offer would be totally unacceptable. Please, just leave now, and we shall say no more about this temporary aberration of yours."

Lord Edward allowed himself to look crestfallen. "Ah, but, darling, that would totally defeat the purpose of my visit," he objected, pushing at the lock of blond hair that had fallen down over his forehead.

Emily had tightened the sash of her dressing gown three times in as many minutes, flushing as she remembered that she had succeeded in opening all of the buttons on her nightgown before Lord Edward had bothered to alert her to his presence. Why, another moment or two and she would have… But, no, she couldn't dwell on that now. "And just what is the purpose of your visit?" she heard herself asking after having already told him she wasn't interested in his motives. Really, this being alone in a boudoir with a gentleman was most unnerving; she didn't see how those opera dancers managed it.

"Do you really want to know? I'm not sure I should tell you. After all, I thought you weren't interested," Lord Edward answered promptly, setting her teeth on edge.

"I lied," Emily shot back, doing her best not to pick up the candle snuffer and brain him with it. "Now, tell me, and then leave. My aunt and cousin will be home soon, if they aren't already."

Lord Edward sat back in the chair and crossed his legs at the knees. "Yes, I know. When I left them with Del and Monty they were already discussing making an early evening of it. The theater was a crushing bore—you were right to give it a miss."

"How did you get in here?" Emily asked, this random thought hitting her a bit late, but not too late for her to be curious about his method of entry. "Surely all the doors were locked?"

"The windows too," Lord Edward agreed, his arms now folded across his chest. "Dare I tell you that Burton—who is the best of good fellows, by the by—has been so brilliant as to procure a key to the dowager's front door? Prodigious resourceful, Burton is, my darling. You'll like his way with a saddle of lamb, too, once we're settled in at Lyndhurst Hall."

The beast of a man was enjoying himself to the point of becoming obnoxious. "I'm not going to Lyndhurst Hall with you, Lord Edward. I wouldn't cross the street with you! And I detest saddle of lamb!" Emily knew she was being drawn into a ridiculous, immature round of brangling with him, but she seemed powerless to stop herself short of going on: "So there!"

Lord Edward picked up his cigarillo, which he had laid in the empty candy dish on Emily's dressing table a minute earlier, noticed that it had gone out, shook his head at it, then replaced it in the dish. "I never did like the silly things, to tell the truth, but I felt the need to have something to do with my hands for a moment there when you were… But, no, I shouldn't be so frank, should I? What were you saying darling?"

Hating herself, Emily repeated through clenched teeth, "I detest saddle of lamb!"

"No matter," Lord Edward assured her, tilting his head as he smiled at her most benevolently. "Wouldn't you be more cozy sitting down, my love? You look deuced uncomfortable standing there holding yourself together. I didn't see anything, you know—or at least not much of anything. Not that I didn't try, you understand. You looked most fetching in that thin gown, with the light of a candle shining behind you. But we are engaged, so it really doesn't matter what I saw, does it?"

"We are *not* engaged!" Emily exploded, near tears. "How are we ever going to make anyone believe we don't want to marry if you persist in reminding everybody every second moment that we are betrothed?"

Rising from his seat, taking care to make no sudden moves so that Emily wouldn't run from him, Lord Edward walked slowly across the room, ending by standing three feet away from her, looking deeply into her eyes. "We are engaged, Emily. You're wearing my ring, remember?"

"I'm losing my mind," Emily remarked to no one in particular. "That's it. My grip on reality is slipping. I've been spending too much time with Aunt Hortense and Georgy, and now Lord Lyndhurst, and my mind has snapped under the strain. They'll be coming for me soon, to take me to Bedlam in a strait waistcoat, where I shall most probably spend the remainder of my miserable life explaining to everyone who will listen that I am not about to give birth to seventeen babies. I don't know why I didn't think of it before, as it explains everything. The rest of the world is just fine. This idiot standing in front of me right now, grinning like a painted doll, is totally lucid. No one is insane. *Except me!*"

"You're babbling, darling," Lord Edward pointed out needlessly as he rested his hands lightly on her shoulders. "Don't you think it's about time you stop fighting the inevitable and simply give in?"

Emily's wandering thoughts quickly returned to the matter at hand. "You mean, why don't I *marry* you? But that's ridiculous. You don't want to marry me; you never wanted to marry me. It was Georgy you were after, don't you remember? And it was Aunt Hortense who inserted that silly notice in the paper. We're only pretending to be engaged to protect ourselves from gossip. That was the way it was—I mean, the way it is—isn't it? But then your brother came…and you kissed me…and then you told me you… Oh, I don't know what I mean. I'm so tired, so confused."

Lord Edward's left hand slipped lightly across her shoulder so that his fingers could play in the braid that lay there. "I know it isn't polite to correct my own *fiancée,* but I fear I must point out that I did propose to you—*before* the dowager so much as picked up her poison pen. You turned me down flat, as I recall, saying you wouldn't have me if I were served up to you on a platter, or some such rot. I don't mind telling you, darling, I was crushed."

Emily tilted her head slightly, trying to disengage her hair from his grasp without being obvious. His closeness was doing strange things to her insides and she wished she could find some way to keep her teeth from chattering. "Now you're being completely ridiculous, sir. You never meant a word of that so-called proposal—you were only being hateful, as you always are with me. I didn't take you seriously for a moment, which you knew full well I wouldn't."

"And here I thought you were a smart puss," he chided, shaking his head.

Emily allowed exasperation to reign. "Oh, shut—"

There were several ways open to Lord Edward to prove that he had been sincere, to explain that he had wanted to marry Emily from the first, but he decided to take the most personally satisfying way, tilting up her head and claiming her mouth with his own.

He doesn't play fair, Emily screamed silently, trying her best to resist his charms. He either teases me or kisses me, and either way I... "Oh, Edward," she moaned against his lips, her arms going up to encircle his neck, knowing that if he was the winner in this latest battle she certainly wouldn't call herself the loser.

Kissing Emily was wonderful, but kisses such as the ones they were sharing could not continue indefinitely without Lord Edward completely losing control of himself, and he knew it, acknowledging their delicate situation by slowly, reluctantly ending their embrace and holding her away from him at arm's length. "Now," he said once he regained his breath, "are there any more questions, my darling Doubting Thomasina?"

Had she been given a few minutes to reflect in private and to recover from her beloved's gentle assault on her senses, Emily could have come up with a half-dozen questions, all very valid, but at the moment she could think of nothing to say except to babble: "You only think you love me because of my new gowns and the things Simmons did to my face and to my hair. Actually, Mr. Roberto did the things to my hair, to be perfectly honest, but you know what I mean. I think you should know that. I mean, it's only fair of me to tell you that, underneath it all, I'm still—"

Throwing back his head to laugh out loud, Lord

Edward pulled her against him, hugging her in delight. "Underneath it all, my darling, you are the most wonderful, exotic, intoxicating creature nature ever made. Where do you come up with such nonsense? And only imagine, I was first attracted to you because of your level head. Apply to Burton, my darling, if you have any more misgivings, please, but I refuse to enter into an argument with you over whether or not I love you."

Emily burrowed her head against the front of his coat, embarrassed down to the tips of her toes. "Then...then you weren't dazzled by my new appearance?"

"I've always thought you were the most beautiful woman in the world. You've just stopped hiding it, thank heaven," Lord Edward assured her, whispering the words into her ear so that shivers of delight skipped down her spine.

"And you always wanted to marry me?"

"I always wanted to marry you."

"From the very first?"

"From the very first. You just refused to pay attention," he chided her, gently nuzzling her cheek with his nose. Hallelujah! At last he felt he was making some headway!

Emily shook her head, tears welling up in her eyes. "I still can't believe it. I mean, you certainly weren't nice to me, were you? No, I don't believe it, much as I'd like to. You were compromised by Aunt Hortense's announcement, just as I was. I think I should go back home to Surrey tomorrow, and then, in a few months, if you're still of the same mind, you can... Oh, dear! That was the front door, wasn't it? Aunt Hortense and Georgy must be home." Pushing away from him, Emily grabbed Lord Edward by one hand and pulled him along behind to her door that led out into the corridor, laying her ear against the panel.

"Emily, you lovable, hardheaded nodcock, what are you doing?"

"I hear male voices too! Lord Henry and Lord Delbert must have come inside with them. You came in the front door, you said? How shall you ever slip past them without anyone seeing you? Oh, Edward, you clunch, you've done it again! How will we ever explain this away without Aunt Hortense demanding that we marry at once?"

Lord Edward reached out his free hand and pulled open the door as Emily gave out a quiet squeal of protest. "I haven't the faintest idea, my demented darling. What do you say we trip off downstairs right now and ask her?"

Emily felt the bare floor on her feet as she was half-dragged, half-pulled into the corridor, one hand firmly stuck in Lord Edward's, the other holding on to the doorjamb for dear life. "Are you out of your mind?" she whispered hoarsely, her slanted eyes nearly round with horror. "I'm not dressed!"

"My goodness gracious. So you aren't," Lord Edward answered jovially, giving her arm another tug.

"You release my hand at once!" she ordered, her voice low and full of indignation.

"You want me to go downstairs and ask that everyone come tripping upstairs to reconvene in your bedchamber?" he queried, grinning—to Emily's mind—like a jackanapes. "Del might not mind, but Monty… well, I think his gentle sensibilities might be slightly overturned, don't you? But if you insist—"

"You come back here at once!" Emily commanded as Lord Edward started off jauntily toward the staircase, her voice rising in volume in spite of herself.

"Emily? Is that you?"

"Georgy!" she exclaimed, skewering Lord Edward with her eyes. "Now you've done it! They'll all be up here in less than a minute. You had better hope you really love me, Lord Edward Laurence, for you'll have no choice now but to marry me!"

And Lord Edward Laurence, feeling more than tolerably pleased with himself, relaxed against the wall, his hands folded across his chest, and smiled at his exasperated beloved. "Yes," he announced quite happily, "I will, won't I? And unless I miss my guess, we'll be bracketed within the week. Imagine that, my darling Miss Emily Howland. Finally I stumbled on a plan that worked!"

EPILOGUE

LORD EDWARD RODE his new hunter across the lush green fields of Lyndhurst on his way back from the village, where he had been supervising the rethatching of three cottages. He reined in the horse atop a slight hill and pulled out his watch, checking the hour yet again, happy to find that it was almost time for luncheon and he could head back to Lyndhurst Hall, as he was sure his wife would be ready to leave within the hour. Turning his mount and urging him into a canter, he made for the carriage drive, planning to cut across its bottom edge on his way to the stables.

He was almost to the stable path when he spied two coaches barreling into the drive. Hauling on his mount's reins even as he gave out with an impassioned course, Edward remembered his careless invitation to have his friends back down to Lyndhurst Hall for a house party a few weeks after the wedding ceremony that had taken place the first day of June in the family chapel with his brother and Emily's family looking on, just as the dowager duchess had decreed.

At the time, it had seemed a reasonable idea, having Lords Henry and Delbert down to Sussex to bear him company, as he had always found the country to be most boring in the past, but now he took the time to wish his two good friends on the other side of the earth.

"Yo! Ned! Don't look so glum. We're here to save you from the doldrums!" Lord Delbert shouted from the open window as the first carriage flashed past, leaving Lord Edward to rein in his nervous mount by the side of the road as a mantle of dust settled around his shoulders.

"Yoo-hoo!" Lady Georgiana trilled, waving a white lace handkerchief out the window of the second coach as it too passed in front of him. "Isn't this jolly?"

"Oh, God, not Georgy too!" Edward groaned, pasting a false smile on his face for Lady Georgiana's benefit. "If the Dowager is inside that coach, Emily will murder me!" Digging his heels into his mount's side, he raced to the front entrance in the hope he could succeed in turning his friends back the way they had come before Emily came downstairs to discover them encamped in her house.

"Oh, isn't this just lovely, having us all together again?" Lady Georgiana exclaimed while standing in the middle of the foyer, dressed in a flattering rose-pink traveling ensemble, pulling off her long kid gloves as Lord Edward, slightly breathless, bounded through the open doorway. "Hello, there, *cousin*," she said pointedly, happy to be able to claim the dashing lord as a relative, even if it was only by marriage.

"Lady Georgiana," Lord Edward choked back at her, seeing his two friends in the process of handing their hats and capes to one of the underfootmen. "I hadn't expected you…er…" He faltered as the young woman began to pout "…so soon! Yes, that's it. I hadn't expected you *so soon*. I did, of course, expect you. Really, I did."

"You're babbling, Ned," Lord Henry pointed out as he

examined his reflection in a nearby mirror, carefully arranging the top of his hair over that one nagging bald spot. "It seems we haven't arrived here a moment too soon."

Lady Georgiana noticed that Lord Edward was still looking at all of them rather strangely, and decided an explanation might be in order. "Lord Henry was visiting at Del's—you know he lives almost on top of us, of course... Del, that is—and the two of them came over to see us last night—we had such a lovely visit, even if Peregrine did behave badly at having extra men at table, just as if he had the feeding of them, Mama says—and then Del said—or was it Lord Henry? I misremember— that we could make the drive to Lyndhurst in just above two hours, and that Lord Edward—I mean, Cousin Edward—had already invited them to share his boredom. Oh, dear, I shouldn't have said that, should I, even if Emily isn't down yet? Anyway, we decided, what with there being nothing to do at home, with dearest Mama down with the toothache again, why shouldn't we just ride on over, because my maid could serve as chaperone until I was back with Emily, who is used to being in charge of me anyway, isn't she, even if she is Lady Edward now—imagine, I used to be bear-led by the wife of the heir to this whole estate, isn't it boggling!— and then Emily could take charge of me, because she is a married lady now, and so...well...here we are! Is that adorable Burton here? He's so little, isn't he?"

"Ain't' she amazin'? She did that all with only two breaths. I tell you, Monty, I can't understand why I didn't see it before. Georgy's a most unusual female."

Lord Henry turned to look at his friend, wondering if the fellow had hit his head harder the other day than first was thought when he toppled from the dowager's dogcart. "Del, the girl's got less learning in her brain-

box than a half-dozen gape-mouthed goldfish," he informed Lord Delbert quietly, not wishing Lady
Georgiana to overhear him, for, after all, it wasn't her
fault if she was a fool, was it?

"No one has goldfish for brains, Monty," Del whispered back repressively, believing his words had properly
defended Lady Georgiana, then walked over to confront
his host. "Ned, what are we doing cooling our heels here
in your hallway? Not that it ain't nice enough, what with
that really outstanding suit of armor propped over there
in the corner and all, but we've seen it before, when we
were here for the wedding. Are you just going to keep us
standing here knee-deep in Georgy's luggage? You know,
anybody would think you didn't want us."

"Not want you?" came an amused female voice from
halfway up the wide staircase, and immediately all
heads turned in that direction. "Now, where would you
get a silly notion like that, Lord Delbert? Lord Henry,
darling Georgy, how wonderful it is to see you."

Emily floated down the remainder of the stairs, her
smoky blue muslin morning gown held carefully above
her ankles, as the other persons in the foyer were turned
for a time to marble, then swept across the tile floor to
slip her hand familiarly through her husband's arm.
"Edward, dearest, shall we show our guests into the
main saloon?"

"I...I...er..." Edward replied brilliantly, Emily's
bright smile rendering him almost speechless.

"Emmy?" Lady Georgiana squeaked, once she found
her voice, her glorious emerald eyes open very wide as
she quite pointedly stared at her cousin's magnificent
bosom. "Is that...is that *you?* You look even more beautiful now than before."

Lord Delbert, who had only moments ago believed

himself to be on the verge of tumbling into love with Lady Georgiana, nearly tripped over that young woman in his haste to reach Emily's side. "Please, Lady Edward, allow me to assist you," he pleaded, already extracting her from her husband's side to lead her toward the main saloon. "Ned shouldn't allow you to stand around like this, a female as delicate, as lovely as you. After all, you might take a draft."

That she might, Edward thought jealously as he watched his wife allow herself to be led away from him without a backward glance. Strutting around all but naked, that's what she's doing, he decided—forgetting she had worn that same gown only a week earlier and he had admired it greatly the whole time he was taking it from her in the privacy of their bedchamber—and he longed for nothing more than a large scarf which he could then stuff into the neckline of her gown.

"Gad, but she grows more lovely every day! I should have my pens, some paper. She deserves a sonnet, at the least."

"Monty?" Lord Edward prompted nastily as his friend, his face oddly pale, stood with his back against the far wall, staring after Emily's departing back. "I take it you are still impressed with my wife's new wardrobe."

"My God, Ned, I don't believe it!" Lord Henry exclaimed at last, slowly shaking his head. "She has turned into a goddess, a veritable goddess. I could see the beginnings of it in London before your marriage, but the transformation is total now. That face—so exotic! And that body—so…er… That is, how did I not know? How could I not notice—me, a poet! I'm supposed to see beyond the obvious. Ned, you lucky dog, you."

Lord Edward took his devastated friend by the elbow and led him into the main saloon, which left Lady

Georgiana to either pout by herself in the foyer or follow on her own as best she could, a very lowering experience for a young woman used to being the center of attention.

Upon entering the room, Lady Georgiana saw that both Lord Henry and her childhood friend Del were sitting on low stools at Emily's feet, looking up at her with the most sickeningly adoring looks on their faces. The young woman's full bottom lip pushed itself forward a quarter-inch just as her rounded chin began to wobble. Her beautiful emerald eyes, the ones Lord Delbert had told her reminded him of the color of Scottish streams in full spate—his lordship being quite the avid angler—filled with self-pitying tears. She didn't like this, she didn't like this at all.

She had come to bear her cousin company in her unhappiness, for she was sure that being compromised—not once, but twice—into marriage couldn't be looked upon as a happy event, no matter how well Emily had pretended to bear up under the strain. Witness her sister Henrietta, for pity's sake! But Emily wasn't the same anymore. She had done something to herself, to her hair, her face. Lady Georgiana already had seen that in London, but the change seemed ten times more noticeable now. She was almost pretty. Emily wasn't *beautiful,* Lady Georgiana comforted herself, because beautiful meant being blond—with great big round eyes and pink-and-white skin—and being *small,* and delicately made, and…

"Lady Georgiana? Wouldn't you care to sit down?"

Blinking her big round emerald eyes several times to disperse the tears that she refused to allow to spill over, Lady Georgiana tore her gaze away from her unnatural cousin and looked up into his eyes. "Thank you, Cousin

Edward," she gushed coquettishly, extending her hand so that he took it in his. "I thought everyone had forgotten me."

"What ho? We have visitors? Noddy, why didn't you have Burton come fetch me? I was in the nursery playing with the toy soldiers Father gave me when I was six. They'll need painting, Noddy, before your son can play with them. I think you chewed them in your cot, if I remember correctly. I've started with the red, you understand. I've always been partial to red. Hello, hello, everyone!"

Lord Edward turned to see his brother standing in the doorway—his clothing covered with dust so that it was obvious he had also been crawling around in the attics again, his fingertips covered with red paint. The marquess looked good for all that, having actually gained some weight since Emily had taken a hand with the menus, and with another—hopefully lifelong, once Lord Edward and Emily produced a child, or two—"project" to keep him happy. "Reggie," he said, depositing Lady Georgiana into a chair, "you remember everybody, don't you?"

"Of course I do," the marquess assured him, shaking Lord Delbert's hand, and leaving that man staring at the paint smudges that were left behind on his palm. "But, Noddy, I thought you and dearest Dulcinea were leaving this afternoon. The Lake District in the height of summer. Delightful! I once spent two months walking there—or was that two weeks? But what does that matter? You'll adore it! I don't understand. You are still leaving, aren't you?"

"Leaving?" Lord Henry cried, looking up at Emily in desolation, wondering if his plans for a series of sonnets would come to nothing without the presence of his Inspiration during the creation process. "You're going away?"

"Leaving?" Lord Delbert repeated, looking over at Lady Georgiana as if belatedly remembering her presence, wondering whether the love of his life would ever find it in her heart to forgive him for this momentary desertion. "That may be for the best."

"Leaving!" Lady Georgiana chortled, turning to Lord Edward, her green eyes alight with sudden joy, believing that she just might be able to stand it if Emily disappeared out of her life for a while—if only until she had Lord Delbert's ring firmly on her finger. "How perfectly wonderful!"

"Leaving," Lord Edward concluded, winking at his wife, knowing that she was enjoying this little scene as much as he, and wasn't really angry with him after all. "Directly after luncheon, as a matter of fact. You are invited to dine with us, of course, and once we are gone, my brother can bear you company."

Burton announced luncheon, and the marquess, struck just then with another brilliant idea, herded the three bemused guests into the dining room, talking nineteen to the dozen about the lovely painting party they would all have in the nursery—just as long as he was allowed all the soldiers with red coats!

"You invited them here, of course," Emily said sweetly as Lord Edward helped her to her feet, holding both her hands in his.

"For my sins, yes," he agreed, pulling her completely into his arms. "I was a bachelor much longer than I've been a husband, and I foolishly thought country life would still bore me to flinders. You know that's all it was, don't you, darling? I mean, you aren't going to go back to believing I really don't wish to be married to you?"

Emily lifted her head from his shoulder and smiled up into his adoring eyes. "Any misgivings I may have harbored have been well and truly disproved by these last few weeks, my love," she assured him, too happy to be embarrassed by her own boldness. "Did you notice? Lord Henry and Lord Delbert seem to think I'm pretty. Even prettier than you said I was in London that last week before our wedding. I think marriage must agree with me. Are you jealous?"

"Of course I'm not jealous," her husband denied, pressing his lips against her temple. "Now, let's go get this luncheon over with so that we may leave. I'm dying to be alone with you, wife!"

"First, give me a kiss," Emily demanded, pouting prettily. "After all, my darling husband, I have been very good, not teasing you for inviting the world here to share our honeymoon. As a matter of fact, I should be thanking you for not inviting them, and dearest Reggie, of course, along on our tour of the Lake District."

Putting a finger beneath her chin, Lord Edward raised Emily's face toward his. "I'll kiss you, minx, but first you'll have to promise me something."

"Anything," Emily breathed fervently, her gaze concentrating on his mouth.

"Promise me you'll send a maid upstairs for a shawl before we join everybody at table."

Emily's eyes twinkled as she laughed aloud, flushed with pleasure, for she was still very much enjoying her newfound attractiveness. "Ned! And you told me you weren't jealous!"

As he lowered his head to hers, Lord Edward whispered huskily, "I lied."

On sale 2nd October 2009

MY LORD'S DESIRE
by Margaret Moore

A Scandalous Vow

Lady Adelaide swore never to allow any man to claim her or
her lands. Nevertheless, when thrown into the arms of a valiant
knight, the beautiful heiress rethinks her solemn vow…

A Brazen Betrothal

To ransom his captive brother, Armand de Boisbaston has great
need of a wealthy – and willing – wife. Fate sends him the
Lady Adelaide instead. A woman claiming she wishes to avoid
the marriage bed, yet whose lips tell a different tale! Now
dangerous intrigues force them into a match as inescapable as
the burgeoning passion that grows between them…

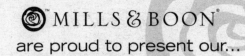

are proud to present our...

Book of the Month

Expecting Miracle Twins
by Barbara Hannay

Mattie Carey has put her dreams of finding
Mr. Right aside to be her best friend's surrogate.
Then the gorgeous Jake Devlin steps into her life...

Enjoy double the Mills & Boon® Romance
in this great value 2-in-1!

Expecting Miracle Twins by Barbara Hannay and
Claimed: Secret Son by Marion Lennox

Available 4th September 2009

Tell us what you think about
Expecting Miracle Twins
at millsandboon.co.uk/community

His innocent mistress

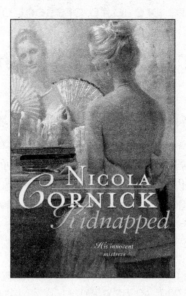

Orphaned and vulnerable, Catriona is doing
her best to resist the skilful seduction of the
scandalous heir to the Earl of Strathconan.
Then her newly discovered inheritance
places them both in terrible danger.

First kidnapped, then shipwrecked with only
this fascinating rake as company, her
adventure has just begun…

Available 18th September 2009

www.millsandboon.co.uk